PRAISE FOR

On the Bright Side

"I laughed until I cried and then laughed and cried some more."

—David Suchet

"Thoughtful, entertaining, and wise. Long may he live."

—Lisa Jewell, *Minneapolis Star Tribune*

"Humorous...A realistic and perceptive glimpse into the aging process, shaped by empathy, optimism, and vibrant wit."

—Booklist

"Highly entertaining...Wise and witty, his musings are thought-provoking and relevant to everyone regardless of age, and his delightful and charming personality will win over readers everywhere... *On The Bright Side* is the diary of an extraordinary man who lives an ordinary life. He makes an impact on almost everyone he meets, and seeks to understand the crazy world in which he resides. His clever commentary and madcap adventures will leave a long-term impression...Hendrik Groen is an unforgetta-ble and absolutely spectacular character who readers will wish they could befriend."

—*Book Reporter*

"Delightful... Groen strikes just the right note here with his wit and ironic observations... So warm, touching, and funny that you don't have to be a member of the Old But Not Dead Club to enjoy it."

—*Library Journal* (Starred Review)

"A worthy read... Darkly funny... thought-provoking, moving, and so pertinent to our times... Hendrik and some of his fellow residents form a delightfully rebellious Old But Not Dead Club, [and] the group's joie de vivre is contagious... Their friendships are likely to make you chuckle as well as move you to tears."

—*Winnipeg Free Press*

"Another amusing, enjoyable, and eye-opening read... Hendrik's bluntness is just a part of his memorable voice and the book's undeniable charm... With its dry wit and its random observations, *On the Bright Side* is alternately quirky and profound. It's more than just an entertaining read; it's sure to give you a new love and respect for octogenarians."

—*Nights and Weekends*

PRAISE FOR

The Secret Diary of Hendrik Groen

"An incredible picture of friendship...something we could all stand to emulate, no matter where we are in our lives."

—*Bookpage* Top Fiction Pick for July

"Interspersed with Groen's biting wit and comic take on aging and all it entails...A page-turning delight for adult readers of any age and locale."

—*Booklist* (Starred Review)

"Engaging and hilarious, Hendrik's diary gives a dignity and respect to the elderly often overlooked in popular culture, providing readers a look into the importance of friendship and the realities of the senior care system in modern society."

—*Publisher's Weekly*

"Poignant and true-to-life, an international bestseller."

—*Minneapolis Star Tribune*

"Amusing [and] wickedly accurate...Reading *The Secret Diary*, I was constantly put in mind of Ken Kesey's madhouse tale *One Flew Over the Cuckoo's Nest*, another comi-tragedy concerning the tyranny of institutions of the unwanted. Enjoy Groen's light touch but do not be fooled by it... *The Secret Diary* is a handbook of resistance for our time."

—*Express* (UK)

"Funny and frank—a story with a great deal of heart."

—Graeme Simsion, *New York Times* bestselling author of *The Rosie Project*

"A story about how friendship, selflessness, and dignity lie at the heart of the human experience. When I'm an old man, I want to be Hendrik Groen."

—John Boyne, internationally bestselling author of *The Boy in the Striped Pyjamas*

"Funny, tragic, and sometimes heart-rending."

—*Het Parool* (Holland)

"Hendrik Groen is king. My mother, 78, suffers from dementia. Doesn't read a newspaper or magazine anymore, only old photo albums can grab her attention for longer than 5 minutes. Hendrik made her laugh out loud, and she was reading for a good half hour."

—Ray Kluun, author of *Love Life*

"Hendrik Groen is a heart-warming hero."

—*Trouw* (Holland)

"With pungent phrasing, Groen takes down life in a retirement home. Both charming and hilarious. Four stars!"

—*Leeuwarder Courant* (Holland)

"Groen's day-to-day worries in a retirement home are just as hilarious as the diaries of Adrian Mole."

—*Zin Magazine* Debut of the Month

"Tears were streaming down my face—from laughing so hard. I couldn't stop grinning for three days."

—*Ouderenjournaal* (Holland)

"Never a dull moment with my new BFF Hendrik Groen."

—Read Shop, Hedel (bookseller)

"It reminded me of a combination between *The Hundred-Year-Old Man Who Climbed Out of the Window and Disappeared* and *One Flew Over the Cuckoo's Nest*. Wonderful! Shame it's finished already."

—Arjen Broers, Bookshop Bruna (bookseller)

"Heart-warming, funny, and poignant. It's about all aspects of life. EVERYBODY should read this."

—Bookshop Stevens (Bookseller)

By the same author

The Secret Diary of Hendrik Groen, 83¼ Years Old

On the Bright Side

The New Secret Diary of Hendrik Groen, 85 Years Old

HENDRIK GROEN

Translated by
Hester Velmans

GRAND CENTRAL PUBLISHING

NEW YORK BOSTON

This book is a work of fiction. Names, characters, places, and incidents are the product of the author's imagination or are used fictitiously. Any resemblance to actual events, locales, or persons, living or dead, is coincidental.

Grand Central Publishing
Hachette Book Group
1290 Avenue of the Americas, New York, NY 10104
grandcentralpublishing.com
twitter.com/grandcentralpub

First published in the Netherlands as *Zolang er leven is* by Meulenhoff in 2016. First English-language translation published as *As Long as There Is Life* by Michael Joseph in 2017.

First U.S. Hardcover Edition: March 2019
First U.S. Trade Paperback Edition: January 2020

Grand Central Publishing is a division of Hachette Book Group, Inc. The Grand Central Publishing name and logo is a trademark of Hachette Book Group, Inc.

PCN: 2018960525

ISBNs: 9781538746639 (hardcover), 978-1-5387-4662-2 (trade paperback), 9781538746615 (ebook)

Printed in the United States of America

LSC-C

10 9 8 7 6 5 4 3 2 1

On the Bright Side

Wednesday, December 31, 2014

According to the statistics, on this last day of the year a man of eighty-five has approximately an 80 percent chance of reaching December 31, 2015. I am going by numbers from the National Public Health Compass.

I shall do my best, but there's to be no whining if the diary I'm starting tomorrow does not make it all the way through to the end of the year. A one-in-five chance.

Thursday, January 1, 2015

Evert used to be partial to planting his New Year's firecrackers in dog poo or, even more spectacularly, horse droppings, but those were, of course, less common. He's only sorry that the bangers were much smaller back then than they are now.

"It's only that I'd risk blowing myself up, wheelchair and all, otherwise I'd love to set off a few crackers in the hall." That was his contribution to the pyrotechnics debate that's been going on for days.

In spite of a petition from the residents, our director, Mrs. Stelwagen, did nothing about getting our care home declared a firework-free zone. A short statement on the noticeboard announced she did not think it "opportune" at this time. She probably had a point, some of the residents decided, especially those who didn't know what "opportune" meant. Others thought Stelwagen didn't want to get into a spat with the local authorities.

Our Old But Not Dead Club celebrated New Year's Eve in Evert's sheltered housing flat, where cooking is allowed, an activity that's not permitted in the rooms of those of us living in the care home. With top ex-chefs Antoine and Ria in our ranks, we can't afford to pass up any gastronomic occasion.

At 11:45 we all trooped up to Graeme's room, on the top floor. We watched the fireworks from his balcony, and Evert fired off a single illicit rocket on behalf of us all, as a mutinous raspberry aimed at the management. It was very pretty.

We can't wait to see who will snitch on us.

Edward volunteered to be the scapegoat chewed out by the director, if it should come to that. He promised to make his speech even harder to understand than usual, and to present a report—in writing—at the next Old But Not Dead Club meeting.

In short: we had a blast.

I did not get to bed until 2 a.m. It's been decades since I've managed to stay up that late. Bravo Hendrik.

Friday, January 2

This past year there was a great void in my days. I had spent all of 2013 faithfully keeping a diary. That hour (or hour and a half) of daily writing had given me a sense of usefulness and value. The most salient hallmark of life in an old-age home may well be the lack of duties or responsibilities. Everything is taken care of for you. There is no need for reflection. Life goes down as easily as custard without any lumps. Open up; swallow; all gone!

There are plenty of residents who are quite satisfied with this permanent, all-inclusive holiday, but for myself and a number of my friends, the idleness of the care-home existence does nothing for our day-to-day contentment. This diary will give me a sense of purpose again. It forces me to stay alert, to put my eyes to work and my ear to the ground, and obliges me to follow the developments in our care home as well as what's happening in the rest of the world. I shall be exercising the brain cells on a daily basis to keep my thoughts fresh and organized. Brain gymnastics to keep the mind sharp. This past year I found myself thinking all too often what a shame it was that I was no longer writing things down, when, for instance, another old geezer made a spectacle of himself, the staff made a dog's dinner of something, or the director lorded it all too snootily over her underlings. I feel like throwing my hat in the ring again.

Saturday, January 3

One care home director has set a good example in the papers by telling the truth: "The standards that we, as a society, have set for the professional care of the elderly cannot be met under the present circumstances."

In other words: it can't be helped if, from time to time, a diaper doesn't get changed promptly enough, or a set of teeth goes missing, or an inmate has to be tied to the bed for a while. Unfortunate, but alas. If all the activists, all the sensation-seeking scandalmongers of the press and all thirty-two care home inspection agencies want this to change, they will have to persuade the electorate to agree to a hefty insurance rate increase. Good luck with that!

I intend to press that article personally into our director's hands.

Yes, that's a surprise, isn't it? Meek Hendrik is no more. He doesn't yet deserve to be called Brave Hendrik, but a year ago, at my dear friend Eefje's funeral, I did resolve to drop my fainthearted caution once and for all. I am more and more inclined to speak my mind, and it usually feels great when I do so. I do still need to work up my nerve, my heart in my mouth, but after some hesitation I'll jump in with both feet from the high diving board, coming up for air sputtering but triumphant. The support I receive from the other members of the Old But Not Dead Club is invaluable. Especially from Evert, who is not only my best friend but also someone who has no trouble at all speaking his mind, and he always has my back.

* * *

This year we have once again been promised a "horror winter." In spite of all previous erroneous predictions of extreme cold, this prognosis is being taken very seriously. My fellow inmates have stocked up for winter like nobody's business. The cupboards are bursting with biscuits, chocolates, soft drinks, and toilet paper. This last item is on account of the fact that we now have to provide it ourselves, due to economic cutbacks. Ever since these were instituted, we are being much more frugal about wiping ourselves, with all attendant consequences thereof. What is saved on paper is spent on extra laundry soap.

Sunday, January 4

Mrs. Stelwagen is no longer surprised when I give her a newspaper article to read or some other piece of unsolicited advice.

Stelwagen is not concerned with anything but her own self-interest: her reputation, which hinges on peace in her domain, and meek inmates. She knows I'm aware of this. She also knows that I enjoy a certain amount of support from my co-residents, which she is ill-advised to underestimate, and she does not.

The conflict between the director and the Old But Not Dead Club is careful and subtle, with the occasional small victory for one, and then the other. Open warfare would do none of us any good. The stakes are too high.

"Thank you *so* much, Mr. Groen. You have found something again that will be of use to us, no doubt?"

"Indeed. An interesting article about a colleague of yours. About standards of care and transparency about such things."

"I am all for transparency; transparency whenever at all possible. And always subject to the general good."

"The general good is a hat that fits many different heads, Mrs. Stelwagen."

"You are so right, Mr. Groen."

Such, more or less, is the tone of our exchanges. Afterward I'll usually need a few moments to calm myself down, but it's worth it. A shot of adrenaline once in a while can't hurt.

Monday, January 5

The weather was splendid yesterday afternoon, so I decided to test my ability to make it to my benches on foot. It's 430 yards to bench number one, 650 yards to bench number two, and finally another 430 yards back home. These distances are a rough estimate.

I did manage it, although with some effort. My roaming orbit has held steady for about a year, and I conclude that, in this case, holding steady is progress.

The fact is: for me, the fastest way to get somewhere is to take it slow. That way I won't fall flat on my face as I proceed from one bench to the next. The trick is to walk very calmly, yet at the same time give a sprightly impression. It's not easily done. Eschewing the Zimmer frame, I rely on a cane that once belonged to my father, which I tend to swing just a bit too high in the air. Then, catching my breath on the bench, I try to look as vivacious as possible. Vain old Hendrik. God knows what for.

The daily journal writing is already having a positive effect. I am glad I picked up the pen again, and regret having neglected it for a year.

Over the next few days I shall recap the lost year of 2014 as pertains to the happenings in our home.

Tuesday, January 6

The most important event of 2014 took place when the year was just two days old: Eefje's funeral. My darling lay there like a beautiful Snow White somewhat on in years, until the lid of the casket was closed for good.

The funeral service was solemn, with beautiful music and moving eulogies. But none of it was of much comfort to me.

The main reason I did not feel like writing for all those months is that I missed her. When I sat down at the computer, for instance, I would find myself writing her name. It has taken time for the wound to heal.

The second most important event was in November, when Grietje moved to "the other side"—the locked ward. Mr. Alzheimer arrived sooner than expected. She had begun losing her way, and then it was happening more and more frequently: both literally, attempting to find her flat on the wrong floor, and figuratively, when she suddenly had no idea what a teapot was for. She was able to laugh it off, right until the end. She was in a muddle, but cheerfully so. Never angry, never scared. The day they moved her into the dementia ward, she was seen happily trotting after the trolley carrying her belongings.

Nobody would mind having dementia if they could be like her. But when I visit Grietje I see that she is the rose among thorns.

In Hillegom, a town twenty-five miles from Amsterdam, a number of people with dementia from the nursing home Den Weeligenberg were selected to return to independent living. In sheltered housing, but still. I've had a good look around the locked ward here, but wouldn't give anyone the keys to their own room again. Unless it's to test an emergency scenario: what to do in case of a flood, a fire, or an explosion, for instance. Could it be that some of the people in Hillegom had been locked away a bit too soon?

Mrs. Quint, a professional pessimist, predicts there will be an attempt on Pope Francis's life. With half a ginger biscuit in her mouth, she was absolutely positive. "He won't make it to the end of the year, no matter how hard we pray for him," she declared, cheerfully spraying biscuit crumbs in every direction.

Evert wanted to bet her €100 that this amiable earthly representative of Jesus Christ would still be fit as a fiddle on January 1, 2016, but Quint was not quite *that* confident in her own predictions.

I must say that Francis has my warmest sympathy, if only because he rides in a white 1984 Renault 4.

I wonder what happened to that funny old Popemobile?

Wednesday, January 7

Last year was a watershed for our Old But Not Dead Club. With Eefje's passing we lost our foremost pillar of strength, and in the spring Grietje too had to stop coming along on our excursions, because she kept wanting to touch everything. That created a bit of trouble for us with the guards in the Rijksmuseum.

"I just want to know what it feels like."

"I'm afraid that's not permitted, madam."

"Oh, in that case I won't do it again, promise." Two galleries farther on, her vow was already forgotten.

But there is also good news: we have taken on two new members. On my recommendation, my friend Mr. Geert Hoogdalen joined the club in the spring. He is a man of few words and the proud owner of a mobility scooter souped up like a Ferrari. Shortly afterward Edward nominated Mrs. Van der Horst to become a member. He thought she would make up for his own aphasia, which is making his speech less and less comprehensible, as well as compensating for Geert's taciturnity. Leonie Van der Horst loves to talk, is cheerful, a bit crazy and brimming with ideas. And she likes Evert, who hardly returns the favor, which in turn makes Leonie even more inclined to stroke his bald head.

In short: two wonderful new assets for the club.

The Health Care Law has been the topic of conversation for months now. Even though we have yet to be deprived of even one cup of tea, some residents claim they are feeling the pinch of the cutbacks already.

When I asked Mrs. Slothouwer, as usual the loudest voice in the room, to give us an example of how it's affecting her, she couldn't think of anything other than, "Oh, there he goes again, Mr. Groen and his examples!"

Mrs. Slothouwer and her sister used to be a formidable team. Since her sister's sudden passing last year, the surviving Slothouwer has added her sister's portion of malice to her own.

I received some support. "Well, I, for one, agree with the Right Honorable gentleman Groen. Mrs. Slothouwer; do give us an example," Graeme said. At that point she dropped the subject.

Thursday, January 8

The news of the slaughter at the French magazine *Charlie Hebdo* has affected me deeply. It doesn't often happen that I get emotional over something in the news, but yesterday I was terribly upset all day long.

And, as if by mutual agreement, my fellow residents refrained from the usual inane commentary. Only Mr. Bakker couldn't help himself, declaring that every foreigner with a beard ought to be put behind bars.

"You mean, Sinterklaas—St. Nicholas—and Father Christmas, for instance?" asked Leonie.

"No, not them, of course not. Just the brown and black ones."

One longs to seal his mouth with duct tape, leaving just a small hole for a straw to suck up his liquid food.

As far as I know this home has never had an Islamic

resident. I suspect aged Turks and Moroccans either live out their last days in the land of their birth, or are kept prisoner in the flats of their children, unable to navigate the building's stairs.

There are some Muslims among the staff, but it would never occur to the residents to engage a hijab-wearing cleaner or housekeeper in a conversation about Allah. We don't know a thing about them; they don't know a thing about us.

I may have mentioned this before, but God and I have agreed to leave each other alone. And a god who, for whatever reason, promises seventy-two virgins as a reward in the afterlife seems to me, of all the gods, one of the dumbest. If only for the fact that a virile fellow would be done deflowering his virgins within a couple of days. And besides, isn't there a reward for women?

There's going to be a minute's silence shortly. I'd like to raise a clenched fist holding my pen in the air, but I fear no one will understand.

Friday, January 9

The Taskforce for Independent Living has sent a letter to every mayor in the country to call attention to the new transition guidelines for elder care. Old people don't like change, but "transition" they don't mind as much.

The mandate of care homes used to be the three Cs: comfort, control, and companionship. Well, oddly enough, the authorities seem to have lost sight of those three Cs a bit.

The goal today is for old people to remain in their own homes for as long as they are able. That may sound like a splendid idea, but it does have its drawbacks. According to the Central Statistics Bureau, there are 300,000 extremely lonely old-age pensioners in our country. Most of them live at home, and the new directives would have them continuing to live independently and be extremely lonely for as long as possible.

That's like throwing the baby out with the bathwater. The idea of using care homes to look after the comfort, control, and companionship of the elderly is fine in principle. It just fails in the execution. What old-age homes actually stand for is infantilizing, dependence, and laziness.

You often read about groups of old people looking for new forms of communal living, in search of, well... yes: comfort, control, and companionship. Only, those old people aren't in their late eighties; they are energetic sixty- or seventy-year-olds with plenty of ideas and plenty of money.

There! That hobbyhorse can be stalled again for a while.

I have made two resolutions for 2015. The first is to make it to 2016, and the second is to get rid of one thing every day. People are magpies. Not long ago, when the staff were cleaning out the room of a resident who had passed away, they found great quantities of sugar, soap, butter, and long-life milk. In other words, everything that used to be rationed in the war. Her cupboards were also a riot of all kinds of other rubbish: vases, cups and saucers, statuettes, candles, bottles and tins. It made me cast a critical eye over my own room: it too is full of needless junk.

I ought to throw out one thing I have no use for every day. Whenever I buy something new, I should get rid of two old things. At the end of the year I ought to be at least 365 expendable items lighter.

Gonna Try This!! Favorite Idea!

Saturday, January 10

A few more words about 2014.

The Old But Not Dead Club slowly recovered from Eefje's passing and Grietje's withdrawal. In the spring we began planning club excursions again. A fresh string of pearls beckoning on the horizon. It turned out that we needed those pearls to plan and look forward to in order not to sink into gloomy lethargy. We agreed that we would never again let several months go by wasted. In our case, death, even the death of our most beloved friends, is to be no excuse.

"We'd never get to the end of it!" said Evert, and then began wondering out loud whether there might be such a thing as a coffin-decorating workshop "for a bright and creative interment."

He hasn't found one yet, although according to Evert, that's a big gap in the market. He also announced that he'd like us all to dress in loud, colorful clothes at his funeral. Even the coffin bearers. Could we please take care of that?

There is a new female resident who at teatime this afternoon devoured ten butter biscuits in a row. After about the fourth one, the room slowly grew quiet around her. Half a dozen residents held their breath watching one biscuit after another disappear into her tiny mouth. It was her own packet of biscuits, so the nurse couldn't really say anything. But when the lady started on her eighth biscuit she could no longer keep it in.

"Mrs. Lacroix, is that really sensible?"

"Shht," Mrs. Lacroix tried to say with a mouthful of crumbs. At least, that's what it sounded like.

After her tenth biscuit, she looked around the circle and asked if anyone else would like one.

"What are you *doing*?"

"I am a performance artist," she answered.

"Oh, *here* we go..." said Mr. Bakker.

"*What* did she say she is?" asked Mrs. Duits.

I wasn't actually there—I heard the story secondhand from Edward. He was there, and he loved it.

I think I want to meet this Mrs. Lacroix.

Sunday, January 11

A research study has shown that eighty-year-olds are happier than they were aged forty. Forty is the low point on the happiness scale. At that age you have to worry about both your parents and your kids, and then there's the stress of your job as well.

These are the findings of a professor who is eighty years old himself. He knows of what he speaks. But has this professor, a Mr. Vaillant, ever visited a care home like ours? If he had, he would know that the faces in here don't exactly radiate joy. That old people are very good at concealing any happiness they feel.

Perhaps he should come and give a few lectures here, to explain a thing or two. After all, it's now or never, as far as happiness is concerned.

Let me give the weather as an example.

It has been stormy for nearly a week, and after just a dip down to moderate gale force, the wind is back up to hurricane strength. If you were even just half as happy as the professor maintains, it stands to reason that you wouldn't let a stiff little breeze get you down. On the contrary: you'd go outside and let the wind whip through your hair.

But that doesn't really happen here. One mostly hears whining about ruined hairdos. As if it's so important for those last remaining hairs to be perfectly coiffed.

For myself, I have discovered that my mobility scooter is rather sensitive to crosswinds. I nearly capsized this morning when a wind gust sideswiped me, pushing me up against the curb between two tall buildings. I heard Geert shout with laughter behind me on his scooter. A few hundred yards farther on it was my turn to laugh: he got drenched by a car tearing through a puddle alongside him. Two old rascals on a quiet, stormy Sunday morning in North Amsterdam who were simply elated to be out in the wind and weather.

Monday, January 12

The members of the Old But Not Dead Club are no strangers to the travails of the flesh. Not to complain, but just to take into account: Evert is in a wheelchair with diabetes. Antoine and Ria are a classic example of the lame and the blind: he has rheumatism, her eyesight is failing. Edward has had a stroke and his speech is practically unintelligible. Geert has a colostomy and a sleep disorder. Leonie is afflicted with a serious tremor and is incontinent. I am short of breath and have trouble walking, an embarrassing dribble, and the occasional bout of gout. Graeme is the only one who is still in reasonably fine fettle.

Impressive list of ailments, isn't it?

Our club has clear guidelines about this: there's to be no whining, but making fun of one's aches and pains is allowed. That helps tremendously. We laugh a lot about our various miseries. It makes living with the restrictions brought on by the body's decrepitude a great deal easier.

A splendid new plan was born during a more or less accidental gathering of the Old But Not Dead Club. We are having a short winter hiatus from our excursion program until the end of the Christmas holidays, but none of us liked having nothing to look forward to in the interim. At teatime yesterday Ria and Antoine proposed, somewhat hesitantly, an idea for a second kind of activity.

"Something to do with food, we were thinking."

"Golly, what a surprise," said Edward.

"We thought it might be fun to go out to dinner together once a month, taking turns to choose a different ethnic restaurant to visit each time."

"Aha," said Evert, "and you thought that would be fun?"

Ria and Antoine both looked a bit taken aback. "It's just a suggestion."

"To be perfectly honest, I think it's a *great* plan," said Evert with a broad grin. "Only, maybe it should be more frequent than once a month."

And so it is decided: once every three weeks, we'll have dinner out at a restaurant of a different nationality, with the members of the club taking turns to choose the venue. Only, no Chinese or Italian—too predictable. This project won't replace our soon-to-be-revived regular excursion program, but will continue alongside it.

Tuesday, January 13

The first Dutch celebrity death of the year is Frans Molenaar. Tumbled down the stairs and never recovered. A lovely but peculiar man from the lovely but peculiar world of haute couture fashion. A world that's quite divorced from reality.

"They only make clothes you'd wear to a carnival. No one would go out wearing that," Mrs. Van Diemen decided.

"A hat like that would make a handy umbrella," her neighbor remarked when she saw a medium-sized UFO on one model's head.

"And they're always faggots, and always surrounded by the most beautiful women," said Mr. Dickhout disapprovingly.

"Only if you like skeletons, nothing but skin and

bone. Not a speck of meat," said the fellow seated next to him.

Frans Molenaar would have thumbed his pedantic nose at their point of view.

Here in the home we are not that fashion-conscious anymore. Only our droopy trousers, crotch at the knees, and floppy braces put us in the "with-it" bracket, as those also happen to be fashionable with hip youngsters in the "real" world. You might even say that we were trendsetters in that regard.

Yesterday Evert came around for a drink before dinner because he'd run out of supplies and didn't feel like braving wind and rain to go to the liquor store.

Evert has asked the director time and again why our mini-mart can't carry alcoholic beverages. "No, impossible, for licensing reasons."

"When I die I expect Gall & Gall to send a lovely wreath," Evert told me, "because I've remained such a loyal customer, despite my diabetes. A shining example of stubborn tenacity."

Miracle of miracles, my best mate was spared any further amputations or related indignities this past year. He actually looks the picture of health in his wheelchair. Sharp as a tack.

It is imperative that he doesn't die before I do. The drinks I pour for him are therefore rather stingy. Evert has rigged up a bottle-holder on his wheelchair, but I insist on putting the gin bottle back in the fridge every time. "Not that I have any intention of saving you from yourself, my friend."

"Ah, go jump in the lake, Groen."

Wednesday, January 14

A mystifying series of events is keeping the residents all agog.

For the fifth time this week an apple was found in a bizarre location. A few days ago the first apple turned up in the elevator, then someone discovered one by the front door, two were found in different hallways, and this morning a Granny Smith was seen floating in the aquarium. Fortunately no fish were harmed. Since for want of more pressing matters molehills tend to grow into mountains around here, the fact that someone is leaving apples "all over the place" becomes the topic of the day.

Honesty compels me to add that the fifth apple was originally lying *next* to the fish tank. I dropped it in. It was almost a reflex. There was no one else in the corridor to see me do it. To be clear: I am not the apple-spreader. I hope that it has thrown the real culprit for a loop, now that an apple has turned up in the aquarium.

According to Mrs. Schaap, five apples can hardly be a coincidence. Well done, Sherlock Schaap.

People have begun inspecting each other's fruit bowls.

Took my scooter out in the wind and rain and saw the first daffodils in full bloom on a strip of grass at the end of Kamperfoelie Way. I had already spotted a few snowdrops last week; it isn't all that unusual to see those, but daffodils blooming in January—they must be a bit confused, honestly.

I would like to see a sturdy layer of ice on the ponds,

thick enough to bear the weight of the scooter. It would allow me to venture out on the ice again for the first time in years. Provided I can find a good spot to get on and off. It would be capital, to scoot from Volendam across the Gouwzee to Marken, for example. Geert has promised to come with me on his Ferrari-mobile.

Thursday, January 15

Today someone found a tangerine in the elevator.

"We were just getting used to the apples, and now this." Mrs. Schaap sighed.

The fruit whodunit is the top topic of conversation over tea and coffee. It's turning some of the residents into Nervous Nellies. They think it's an omen that something terrible is going to happen.

"It's only a tangerine, dears. Not a bomb," one of the nurses reassured them.

I have a running bet with Evert. I think it is a staff member who's secretly strewing fruit about; Evert is convinced one of the residents is responsible. The stake: a book of the winner's choice. Evert had to solemnly swear to me that he wasn't the fruit sneak himself. At first we wanted to bet on the kind of fruit that would pop up next, but I don't trust him an inch, and vice versa. Had he predicted, for example, that the next find would be a banana, you could bet that a banana would turn up in a planter somewhere within the next fifteen minutes.

Meanwhile Stelwagen has ordered the staff to keep

its eyes peeled. I gathered as much from Mrs. Morales, who recently started working here as a caregiver. A Spanish chatterbox with a soft spot for yours truly. She invariably starts her sentences with "Don't tell anyone, but..." Think of her saying it with a charming Spanish accent.

In her I may have found a useful new "well-informed source" on the inside again. That role used to be filled by my good friend Anja Appelboom, the long-time administrative secretary in Stelwagen's office, who would occasionally provide me with information not meant for residents' ears, but a year and a half ago Anja was put out to pasture by Stelwagen on early retirement.

When it comes to keeping the residents informed, our esteemed director's motto is: ignorance is bliss. I have the feeling that Stelwagen honestly thinks you shouldn't saddle the inmates with information that would only make them anxious. She doesn't really think of old people as competent human beings, and she isn't the only one. I often have to agree with her. If you keep treating people like little children, in the long run most of them will start acting like little children too.

Friday, January 16

The vigor of the residents hasn't improved this past year, sadly. The weakest and oldest have left us, and instead of hale and hearty seventy-year-olds taking their place, we've welcomed into the fold several old crocks well into their late eighties.

The record for the shortest stay is held by a lady whose name we never even came to know. A day and a half after arriving through the front door in a wheelchair, she departed again through the back door in a coffin. Perhaps the excitement of the move was too much for her.

"She drank one cup of tea, *one*!" Mrs. Duits must have said at least four times.

"Yes, and so what?" asked Bakker. At least four times as well.

Someone wondered if the deceased would have to pay the whole month's rent anyway.

According to the new directives, people may only move to a care home if they are incapable of looking after themselves, and therefore need a great deal of care. Upon arrival, the new residents are only a short step away from either the grave or the nursing ward.

Healthy residents are in the minority. The average age is creeping up to ninety and the turnover rate keeps accelerating. It doesn't make for a very jolly atmosphere.

A pineapple was found in our "gym," an unoccupied office space. The culprit seems to have moved on to the larger species of fruit.

It's funny how something as inane as an unclaimed piece of fruit can cause such a brouhaha. Normally our residents have no trouble coming up with the most outlandish conspiracy theories, but in this case they've been left flummoxed. They don't know what to make of it. It's just too weird.

"I don't get it. Who would do such a thing?" is the most common reaction.

It would enhance the mystery if the fruit caper stopped without the instigator ever being found out. It would be a pity about our bet, however.

Saturday, January 17

The stricter criteria for care home admission will inevitably lead to vacancies. By 2020, 800 of the 2,000 care homes will have to close. That is 40 percent. Which also means that within the next five years a considerable number of residents will have to move to another home, since no board of directors will wait to close an institution until the very last occupant is obliging enough to kick the bucket.

Here in our home the alarm was raised a year and a half ago, when we were informed about "renovation" plans. Everyone gave a sigh of relief when the plan was called off. But our relief may well be premature. My own instinct tells me that if this old building isn't going to be renovated, it could well be because it has been moved over to the "slated for demolition" column.

I intend to accost Mrs. Stelwagen in the near future to apprise her of my concerns.

We may like to complain about all the niggling no-nos we have to put up with here, but it could always be worse. The *Algemeen Dagblad* reports that a Sientje van der Lee (91) has been told to remove her houseplants from her sheltered housing windowsill because the window washer, who comes twice a year, complains they're in his way. And also because the plants sometimes shed a few of their leaves. Sientje was a farmer all her life. She protests, "I need to have some green about," and has taken defiant action: she's hung out a banner that says KEEP YOUR MITTS OFF MY PLANTS. Problems such as these put all the uproar about the terrorist attacks in Paris and Belgium in the shade.

Sunday, January 18

We are having an Old But Not Dead Club meeting tomorrow evening. On the agenda: drawing up the restaurant plan and the new excursion schedule.

The hibernation has lasted long enough. It's time for action. We are meeting at Geert's, who, in his words, is "engaged in making exhaustive preparations."

Besides being a way to save money, turning over eldercare from state to local authorities was meant to bring control closer to home for those on the receiving end.

The money-saving aspect has been reasonably successful, but decentralizing seems to be misfiring on many cylinders. Lots of the councils that were put in charge, you see, have decided to *de*centralize again. To cut expenses, dozens of local authorities have joined hands, working together to drive down the cost of eldercare even further.

So instead of a single minister or secretary of state,

the "care sector" now has to deal with—count them—thirty-seven aldermen from thirty-seven towns and villages. These are overseen not by 150 members of Parliament, but 500 local councillors, ones who have only the best interests of, let's say, Lutjebroek at heart. I can't wait to see what that will mean for us.

My friend Edward was wondering why, exactly, the prophet Muhammad can't be depicted. A good question, to which no one knew the answer. Evert's suggestion—"Maybe the prophet was as cross-eyed as a melon"—was politely discounted when he had no retort to the counter-question, "How can you tell if a melon is cross-eyed?"

Which brings me in a subtle segue back to the fruit affair: yesterday a banana was found in the pantry. There are rumors of a staff posse out on the hunt for the culprit. To no avail, for now. The director has appealed to the residents to remain calm. Such appeals tend to backfire; surely Stelwagen ought to know that by now.

Monday, January 19

The National Bird Count Days took place this past weekend. It made me think of my late friend Eefje, who would spend an hour at her window patiently and devotedly counting tits and sparrows.

She never let me help her. "Only serious birders are allowed to participate, Henk. You're just a novice, you'll only distract me. You can come back in an hour." And then she'd give me a radiant smile. I'd melt completely. I miss her. Love seldom knows a happy ending.

* * *

I heard from Mrs. Morales that our director is considering forbidding the use of mobiles in the dining room at mealtimes. Not that many people do make calls, but when someone does, the entire room has the pleasure of listening in.

"WHERE ARE YOU?...AT DINNER...ENDIVE AND MEATBALLS...OH, FINE...NO, DREADFUL, NOT A WINK...WITH THIS WEATHER DEFINITELY...ARE YOU EVER COMING TO SEE ME?"

And so on.

Old people and modern telephone technology don't get along very well. All those confusing bells and whistles make them nervous. They'd much prefer to drag along a cordless Bakelite phone that would allow them to dial the old way. All those little keys and knobs now inevitably get the number wrong the first time. "WHO IS THIS?"

A mere slip of a phone that can contain an entire telephone directory—oh, my! Even the extra-large keys meant for aged eyes and trembling fingers don't really do the trick.

A kiwi fruit was found in the toilet.

Stelwagen is not amused. She doesn't know what to do about something as daft as pieces of fruit turning up where least expected, and it feels like a prank meant to undermine her authority. Especially since the residents have talked of nothing else for days.

It does fascinate me enormously. Evert says he'll present

the mastermind with a basket of fruit if his or her cover is ever blown.

Tuesday, January 20

Yesterday was Blue Monday. This, the third Monday of January, has been declared the most depressing day of the year. By whom? No idea. But the Old But Not Dead do not ascribe to it. We had an exuberant members' gathering hosted by Geert. It was the first time Geert had us around, and he had gone out of his way to put on a lavish spread. I think he must have enough alcohol left over to last until summer. He had bought so much of everything that, for instance, if we had stuck to beer all evening there would still have been plenty to go around. The same goes for the red, white, and rosé, the soda water, cordial, orange juice, gin, eggnog, and brandy. There was even a bottle of black-currant gin. I didn't even know that still existed. Plus heaps of food, as if we'd just come through the Hunger Winter of 1945. Everyone went home with a doggie bag. Evert with an extra-copious one, since he's the only one who actually has a dog. His dog Mo is a prodigious omnivore. It doesn't matter what you put in his dish, it all comes out the other end. Evert has offered to help Geert finish off any bottles that might go past their sell-by date.

"Just so as not to waste it," he says with a grin. He, like Mo, isn't picky, he'll drink anything you put in front of him.

Food, drink, laughter... We hardly had any time for serious discussion.

We did manage to draw up two schedules, one for the restaurants-of-the-world plan, and one for the new club outing lineup. The intention is to sally forth at least once a fortnight this year.

We have set up a fund for impecunious members, to be dipped into as the need arises. No one raised any objection. I was appointed treasurer, and have taken it upon myself to put in the seed money, anonymously, of course. I am, after all, a man of some means. Club members may discreetly apply to me for monetary support. For it looks as if this could cost a pretty penny.

"*Make sure you're in the red by the time you're dead!*" is our first official club motto. We're on the lookout for other appropriate slogans. And a club anthem. Yes, it was a rather raucous evening.

We had warned Geert's neighbors beforehand to expect a bit of noise. If that did occur, would they be so kind as to tell us first, before alerting management? Evert had insisted on being the one to "take care of it." I don't expect we'll be hearing any complaints.

Wednesday, January 21

The day of my little girl's passing. A child's little bike weaves a couple of feet too far to the right or left, on a steep hill by a canal. I was occupied marking students' homework, and my wife was hanging out the washing. Each thought the other was watching her.

Lifelong grief, lifelong senseless self-reproach.

Thursday, January 22

Yesterday no errant fruit was found, and its absence was the subject of much speculation. Strange, really; for years not even a single unclaimed grape was ever seen, and nobody said a word about it. Now, after just one day of neither a rogue apple nor pear, people are already bereft. I hope it doesn't remain an unsolved mystery forever.

Next Thursday is our first dinner excursion. Edward is choosing the restaurant. Evert is betting ten-to-one on Argentinean. Only he won't make the bet with Edward.

Mirrors have been installed in the corridors at certain dangerous corners and intersections after two scooter crashes in one week. Fortunately only minor scrapes and dents ensued. A traffic death in a care home would most definitely make it into the papers, and that's to be avoided at all costs. So the director decided to boost safety with these convex traffic mirrors, although they don't take into account the vagaries of the elderly. The mirrors have already led to several inadvertent accidents, even with no oncoming traffic in sight. Some of the oldies were so fixated at seeing themselves in the mirror, you see, that they ran straight into a wall. And the walls here sport a coat of the rough sanded beige paint that was so fashionable back in the 1970s. Which usually means a nasty abrasion or two. Forgive me for being a bit gruesome, but the sanded paint makes it hard to scrub blood off the wall. So one can see traces of accidents in a number of spots. Some of these distressing marks were painted over, only in a slightly different shade of beige.

Stelwagen has no intention of removing the mirrors for now. To do so would mean admitting she'd made a bad decision.

Friday, January 23

Yesterday was my annual check-up with the geriatrician. To my surprise my old doctor, Dr. Jonge, had retired. He was about seventy, and so he knew his stuff. The new geriatrician doesn't have his experience. She's a woman of about forty, Dr. Van Vlaanderen.

"Just call me Emma."

I'm a bit old-fashioned sometimes. That's permitted, if you're eighty-five. I'd rather not call a doctor Emma, even if that really is her name.

She seemed kind, with a willing ear, but I think I'd rather still have my old doctor. He was short and to the point, clear and witty. Dr. Emma treated me rather like a deaf toddler. She talked just a bit too loud, in a Dick and Jane voice.

"I'm not deaf, nor dumb either, Dr. Emma," I thought of saying, but then I decided it was a bit too blunt for a first acquaintance. Another negative was that I had just been making a little headway with my old doctor on the subject of euthanasia, and now I'll have to start all over again. I didn't feel like broaching it this time.

The numbers, by the way, aren't very hopeful for getting

a GP or geriatrician to help you there: only very few requests for euthanasia are granted. The end-of-life clinics do hardly any better: the clinics are true to their name in just 4 percent of the cases. The Euthanasia Society seems to offer the best solution. One simply orders pills from the Internet, or so I've heard. That shouldn't be too difficult, now that I am growing increasingly computer-savvy. At first I used the thing only as a typewriter, but now I know how to look up all kinds of things. I shall look into it shortly. After all, the decision is in my hands, and my hands only; that's what *I* think. The greatest danger lies in gradually and imperceptibly—or precipitously—getting to a place where you are no longer capable of making the decision yourself. That's what happened to Eefje. The point is to be prepared, and to have the pills on hand. Hidden in your home, someplace known only to yourself and perhaps a friend you can trust. If, heaven forbid, you are no longer in a state to take the pills yourself, then that friend may be able to give you a little (illegal) hand. As long as he or she has arranged for a watertight alibi, naturally.

I am going to take care of it. First I'll acquire the pills and then I'll instruct Evert on what to do. The right man for the job: heart of gold, and doesn't give a hoot about the rules.

Saturday, January 24

Yesterday afternoon, at teatime, the dining room was humming, and Mrs. Lacroix rose to her feet. She has only been here a month, but in that short time has managed to make herself quite unpopular. All she had to do to earn her fellows' scorn was to dress rather flamboyantly. Flowing dresses in bright floral patterns, shawls and hats, red lipstick and purple nail polish. She also has a rather posh accent.

She started tapping her teaspoon against her cup until everyone looked up. She cleared her throat.

"As everyone here knows by now, I am a performance artist." Whispering and muttering all around her. Many people had no idea what that was. "As such, for the past two weeks I have been creating a performance piece by leaving pieces of fruit in various locations. To symbolize estrangement. And to show that to give is better than to receive. And because it's healthy too."

The mutters now swelled to an indignant din.

"You gave me the willies with those apples of yours," was how Mrs. Slothouwer gave expression to the general malaise. Many nodded in agreement.

"Well, *I* thought it was very funny," said Leonie, our new Old But Not Dead member, and I was proud of her. Two camps formed immediately: those in favor of performance art and those against. A minority, those of us not immediately scared off by the unfamiliar, was in favor, and the rest were against. Evert, unfortunately, wasn't present to state his strong, uncompromising position in favor of errant fruit.

Slowly the room calmed down again. With all the commotion, some residents had even forgotten to eat the biscuit that came with their tea.

Mystery solved: a satisfying denouement.

I lost the bet with Evert. The fruit caper was the work of a resident, not one of the employees. I owe him one book. A book about fruit salads, I should think, if such a thing exists. For his part, Evert, as promised, will buy Lacroix a fruit basket.

Sunday, January 25

I visit Grietje in the locked ward on a regular basis. She always greets me with great joy, although she no longer knows who I am.

"How very nice of you to look me up. And on such a nice day, too. Lovely."

She is genuinely happy to have a visitor, and that's the reason I often stop in on the nursing floor. She has become the woman with dementia she had hoped to become: cheerful and carefree. Sometimes I catch her gazing at me a little longer, with an almost invisible little smile at the corners of her mouth, and a quick, friendly nod. As if she's thinking: I'm sure I know that bloke from somewhere... There's an entire life still buried somewhere inside that head. She can't access it anymore, but I cherish the little piece of that life I was privileged to share with her.

We chat a bit. The same old small talk mostly, since she doesn't remember a thing about my previous visits, and tomorrow she won't remember today. After fifteen minutes I've run out of things to say and take my leave. Then she'll usually say, "I'm so sorry you have to go, but never mind. I have so much to do." Then she waves goodbye.

It's Grietje's fellow patients who make the visit difficult. Many of them are anxious, angry, sad, confused, or all of the above. Or they haven't any emotions at all, and just sit there huddled in a chair. When they can no longer even sit, they lie in bed, turned every so often by caring hands to prevent bedsores.

I can't bear having to see the humiliation of it, and the helplessness.

Monday, January 26

In France it is against the law to name your pig Napoleon. In the American state of Alabama you're not permitted to drive a car blindfolded. In our care home you are not allowed to keep an insect hotel on your balcony. The first two prohibitions are hearsay; the third one was recently issued by the management of our institution.

You can purchase these contraptions, made of wood, cork, straw, and other natural materials, in the home improvement shop. They're meant to attract all sorts of flying or crawling bugs. Yes, there are people who find insects fascinating. Mrs. Bregman is one of them. She bought an insect hotel last summer, and installed it on her balcony. According to some of her neighbors, all sorts of flies, mosquitoes, and wasps would come flying out of that rooming house and into their own windows. Stelwagen was flooded with complaints.

The home's rulebook had all kinds of restrictions against pets, but the sheltering of insects hadn't yet been considered. It required a separate ban, and, lo, last week said ban appeared on the noticeboard. Bregman had to put her hotel up for sale, and Stelwagen promptly bought it from her, in order to nip any eventual unrest in the bud. Billed to her expense account, naturally. We also learned that there's to be only one bird feeder per balcony. "On account of the bird droppings."

Saturday's newspaper had an article about a care home in Rijssen. The nurses and patients there run the place by themselves, in accordance with the residents' wishes wherever possible. The story didn't say if the management, board of directors, and supervisory board had been scrapped altogether, or if they just operated in the shadows.

People who will voluntarily give up their own jobs are few and far between. I don't see our Mrs. Stelwagen declaring herself superfluous anytime soon.

Tuesday, January 27

Feta cheese and Nana Mouskouri. That was about all people here could think of when the subject of the Greek elections came up. And two dead Greeks: Zorba and Demis Roussos, the latter only because he died very recently.

"Nana Mouskouri may be dead too, for all I know. That leaves only feta, and I don't care for it myself," was how Mrs. Van Diemen summed up the significance of Greece.

And today, as if the devil had a hand in it, we learn that a Greek F16 fighter jet has crashed in Spain.

"Ten dead," Mrs. Duits read to the assembled.

"Was it a passenger fighter jet?" someone wanted to know.

"Probably a question of poor maintenance," Mr. Bakker supposed.

No, there were very few reasons to keep Greece in the EU. That was enough to lay the matter to rest.

It is high time for something exciting to happen. It's lucky our restaurant project is to be launched on Thursday, because the walls are beginning to close in on me. I have been going for my daily walk, and take my mobility scooter out for a spin several times a week, but those are just short lulls in the daily inertia.

My friend Evert is also less cheerful these days. I don't know the reason. There is no point asking him.

"Henk, *if* there was anything wrong, I wouldn't have any desire to talk about it with you."

"No, my good chum, of course, talking about yourself... What a silly idea!" I retorted, in a cautious attempt to get him to open up. "It's just that you've been a bit of a bore, lately."

He growled something along the lines of "I suppose," and then, resorting to his usual diversionary tactic—"What shall I pour for you, Henkie?"—changed the subject.

After that we played a game of chess and pretended there was nothing wrong.

Wednesday, January 28

My remark to Evert that he was a bit of a bore may have rankled a bit after all, because at dinnertime he was back in top form.

He asked the server in an unnecessarily loud voice if this "hamburger" was the kind that had maggots in it, pointing to the meatball next to his mash.

That made the others look up.

"What do you mean, Mr. Duiker?"

"Well," said Evert, "I read in the paper that Jumbo supermarkets have now started selling insect burgers." Pulling a crumpled piece of newspaper from his pocket, he read: "'*The burgers contain fourteen percent buffalo worms, freeze-dried larvae of the buffalo dung beetle, which is comparable to the mealworm.*' I thought I tasted something of the sort in this hamburger. A bit bitter. Quite tasty, really." And, without waiting for a response, he went on chewing contentedly. The same contentment, however, had fled from the other diners who overheard the conversation.

Somebody picked up a meatball with fork and spoon, holding it at a safe distance, as if it were still moving. A lady who had just taken a big bite of her burger stopped chewing, although it was clear she was reluctant to spit it out. She just sat there frozen for a while with her mouth half open.

"What's the matter?" people at the neighboring tables began inquiring. In short: utter consternation, which ended in the cook having to come out in person to announce that this was perfectly ordinary mince, without worms.

But the damage was done. Quite a few half-eaten hamburgers were left untouched on the plates. Only those who had ordered the stew instead polished off their plates with exaggerated gusto. "Mmmm, delicious brisket, I must say." People in here rarely pass up the chance to make others green with envy, as the occasion presents itself.

After dinner Cook had a few words with Evert, who wore an expression of beatific innocence. I had to compliment him later: "That's more like you, old chum."

Thursday, January 29

Departure time: 5:00 this afternoon. It will take some time to get there.

That's all we know. I am skipping lunch just to be on the safe side. I'm not a big eater, but an enthusiastic one. My sense of taste is still excellent, I am happy to report. I have contemporaries who can barely tell the difference between a pickle and a strawberry.

For them, there goes one of the joys that shouldn't, in principle, have anything to do with age: deriving pleasure from eating and drinking. It is astonishing to me that people who have little left except the enjoyment of food and drink are still not very discriminating when it comes to eating. Stale bread, cheap chocolate, bad coffee, reheated leftovers, bone-dry cake, sour wine; anything goes. We've all been through the war but, my God, what completely unnecessary deprivation! "You should spend your money freely on the few things that you're still able to enjoy!" I'd like to shout at them.

The Old But Not Dead Club motto concerning money: spend it but don't squander it.

Friday, January 30

The waiter wore a tartan skirt, there were bagpipes displayed on the walls and hundreds of whisky bottles lined up everywhere. Guess which cuisine we had the honor of sampling last night?

An exceptional repast in the Scottish restaurant–whisky bar, Highlander. We did have to travel to Alkmaar for it, but that only made it all the more fun. Edwin, Edward's nephew, was our designated driver. He enjoys transporting us in his passenger van. All he asks for in return is a full tank of petrol every once in a while.

The restaurant owner, a man with a broad Scottish accent and a potbelly full of whisky, had a warm welcome for his aged guests. We entrusted him with the decision of what we should eat. It was delicious, but I couldn't really tell what was Scottish about it. At our next restaurant, the organizer should provide us with a little explanation of the specialties of the cuisine in question. The only Scottish dish I know of is haggis, but I don't think we had it yesterday. I just looked it up, and saw that it's made of mutton heart, lung, and liver, and some lard to bind it together. I don't know if it was a missed chance or not.

Evert almost lost his mind over the fantastic whisky menu.

"I can't choose. I really don't know how to choose!" he cried, in a veritable panic.

Toward the end of the evening, having poured something like six different whiskies down his gullet, he was unable to speak, aside from the occasional groan, "Paradise, paradise!" He even allowed Leonie to pat his head fondly every so often. Sweet.

The restaurant project is already a resounding success.

Upon coming home we woke the porter from his slumber in order to wish him a good night. Geert informed him we would overlook his minor dereliction of duty "unless there should be a reason not to." That Geert, such a blackmail artist.

I slipped under the covers at 11 p.m., blissfully satisfied.

Saturday, January 31

Every winter we hear a lot of griping about the flu shot.

"Is it called the flu shot because it gives you the flu?" Mrs. Quint wondered. Almost everyone gets vaccinated, yet the flu hits us hard every year nonetheless. A concert of barking and coughing has been going on for weeks, and rumor has it that it has claimed two victims, one gentleman I don't know, and Mrs. Schreuder, whose only claim to fame was that her Hoover once sucked up her canary.

Which brings me to the subject of pets.

There is a new resident, Mr. Verlaat, who on moving here had to leave his puppy with his sister who's even older than he is, because pets, with the exception of birds, are prohibited.

He has threatened to sue; he believes that keeping a pet is a fundamental human right.

I think Stelwagen is a bit worried about the publicity. She's already visited Verlaat twice in his room.

If Verlaat were to get his way, this place could become quite a zoo, going by the recently published list of pets allowed in the Netherlands. African pygmy hedgehog, steenbok, kangaroo, porcupine are all defined as domestic animals. It would make the place quite a bit livelier, I can tell you.

The barking deer has been removed from the list, however. When I read the reason why, I got tears in my eyes. That poor little deer's legs are so frail that they could break if it tried to run away. So sad. Although one has to wonder how the barking deer managed to survive for so long on its own in the pitiless wild.

When I watch nature films I never know who I should root for: the innocent baby zebra or the lioness doing her best to procure some meat for her cute, famished little cubs.

Sunday, February 1

"The Netherlands has the best healthcare in Europe."

According to the Swedish Think Tank Health Consumer Powerhouse, our healthcare is far superior to that of our European neighbors. And who am I to contradict a think tank?

I clipped the article, enlarged it on the photocopy machine in the supermarket, and pinned it on the noticeboard in the conversation lounge. Just to make a point.

"Huh! It says more about all those *other* countries," was the only sour comment Bakker could come up with after having a long think about it.

The fact that we're not that badly off here compared to the Republic of Kalmykia is no surprise, but compared to all our European neighbors...

As soon as anyone else complains about the care again, I'll turn my head to look pointedly at the noticeboard, and a number of my friends will do the same. That should stop the irritating whiners.

"Why do you keep glaring at that newspaper clipping? It's not as if I don't know what it says!"

Monday, February 2

I don't believe in God, but I do like peace and quiet every so often, so I visit the Quiet Center from time to time. Preferably on a Sunday afternoon, because that's when it's quietest. The devout have already had their ecumenical service in the morning and are too busy in the afternoon waiting for their visitors.

Yesterday afternoon I spent half an hour enjoying the peace and quiet, and at the end of my visit I lit a candle for my little girl. A slight rustle behind me alerted me to the arrival of the old vicar.

"May I ask who you're lighting it for?" he asked with a friendly nod.

"For my little girl, who died."

"You never attend services, do you?"

"No, I'm not a member of your flock. I don't belong to any flock."

The vicar stood there staring into space for a while. "I'll confess something to you," he finally said, "on the condition that you keep it to yourself."

I said I'd always wanted to hear a priest's confession. He laughed heartily.

"I may have a flock, but I'm actually an unbelieving shepherd," he said. "I haven't believed in God in years. One fine day, I saw the light: either God doesn't exist, or He is unknowable. In practical terms, there isn't really much of a difference."

"I agree with you about God, but it would seem to me that for your calling, it would be more practical to believe in Him."

"It's easier than you'd think. I mean, I manage. I love being able to offer support and consolation to others. I wouldn't know what I'd do in my old age if I wasn't a pastor. Besides, no one ever asks me if I believe in God myself."

We sat and chatted for an hour and a half. A fascinating bloke.

Tuesday, February 3

By some weird fluke, today there's a long article in the paper about a priest in Nijkerk who has come to the conclusion that Jesus Christ never existed.

Our home's pastor has chosen to keep his agnosticism to

himself, whereas this other preacher wrote a book about it. To each his own disbelief. I intend to slip the clipping discreetly into my friend Doubting Thomas's hand.

Yesterday I bumped into Mrs. Stelwagen in the hallway.

"Good afternoon, Mr. Groen, how is life treating you?"

It took me a fraction of a second to decide on a little bluff. "Well, perfectly fine, really, except for one minor thing: I hear our home is slated for demolition."

Momentarily taken aback by my frontal approach, she gaped at me in feigned surprise for just a tad too long.

"Where did you hear that?"

"From well-informed sources close to management." I tried to accompany it with an inscrutable smile. I must say I was surprised at my own gumption.

"So... you still have one?"

That was an unforced error on Stelwagen's part. She has stoutly denied Anja Appelboom's forced early retirement had anything to do with her role as informant.

"How do you mean, *still* have one?" I inquired.

"Uh, no, nothing... But as far as demolition plans are concerned, if there *were* any such plans, it would be up to the board."

"But all I asked was if our home was slated for demolition. Not who makes the decision."

"No matter how dearly I should like to be open with you about this, I cannot. Not to mention the uproar if some residents were to start fanning speculation about possible demolition. That would be extremely unfortunate, Mr. Groen." Cocking her head slightly, she stared at me stone-faced.

"Unforewarned demolition would be even more unfortunate. Some people would not survive it, I fear," I said, staring back.

There was a brief silence.

"If I have something definite to report, I will tell you as soon as I have it, naturally."

"Naturally."

"I must get going, Mr. Groen. A very pleasant afternoon to you."

A shot across the bow, I think. If it happens to be true that we are on the list of homes slated for the scrapheap, Stelwagen will now try to hunt down an informant who doesn't exist, mark my words. We're in for some laughs.

Wednesday, February 4

I was proud to be able to give a full report of my exchange with Stelwagen to Evert, Graeme, Edward, Leonie, Ria, Antoine, and Geert. I received some pats on the back, and a firm whack from Evert. "Well done, Henkie!"

We decided that we'll keep adding a little fuel to the fire whenever the occasion presents itself. Evert was thinking more along the lines of a whole barrel of oil; he wanted to start distributing flyers straightaway saying DEMOLITION IS DEATH. We threatened to take away his booze. It did the trick.

I have finally taken the first step. I have downloaded the euthanasia declaration form from the Euthanasia

Society's website. The very idea of it does give one pause, but the thing's lying on my bedside table now. It'll just have to stay there for a while until I fill it out. For my own peace of mind, I have to deal with it at an elderly pace.

I do think it wouldn't be a bad idea to acquire a handy "out box." A box for everything you need for your last voyage. The euthanasia pills, of course; important papers, a wish list, the music you want played at your funeral, items you want to have with you in the coffin, and certain other personal effects. Plus, my old organ donor card, although I suspect most, if not all, of my parts are long past their expiry date.

I still have to find out what kind of pills you need, and how to get your hands on some. For that I'll need to gather a fresh dose of courage.

Thursday, February 5

I've had a dream about freeze-drying. The designer of that handy "out box" I read about yesterday also suggested freeze-drying, cryomation, as an alternative to cremation or burial. In my dream they dunked me into a bath of liquid nitrogen of minus 320 degrees Fahrenheit, but I wasn't completely dead yet. Then I woke up, shivering.

Cryomation is better for the environment than burial. After being frozen, you're given a good shake, to shed the heavy metals, and then all that's left is fifty-five pounds of powder that can be used as compost. At least that way you're still good for something. Dust thou art, and unto compost shalt thou return. Murderers, I imagine, must be very interested in freeze-drying, since it would make the crime very hard to trace.

There is one problem with freeze-drying, however: it is still illegal in the Netherlands. As well as in most other countries.

A resident who tends to get a bit confused went out in his pajamas and slippers to fetch some cod liver oil from the pharmacy.

"That's no longer sold, sir," said the salesgirl.

He returned home disappointed. His slippers were covered in snow as he shuffled into the entrance hall. A nurse sounded the alarm, and the porter was reprimanded. He isn't only supposed to keep an eye on *who* leaves the building, but also *how* they leave the building.

"Yes, but I can't see what they're wearing on their feet when they walk by my desk, can I?" he said, in an attempt at self-defense.

Now management has ordered him to stand up to get a better look in case of doubt. The porter doesn't like it one bit. He is one of our best chair-sitters. It shows in his dull, uninterested gaze: he won't take one step too many. He's on a permanent contract, with fifteen years of chair-sitting yet to go.

Friday, February 6

"Look," said Evert, a bit too loudly, "invalid or no invalid, you can still take good aim and rinse off the poo dregs in the toilet bowl." And took a bite of his sandwich.

"Yes, but how?" Edward inquired, pretending to be interested. Evert was prepared to demonstrate on the spot.

"Yeah, yeah, Mr. Duiker. Very funny, but there are people trying to have their lunch here. Please save the piss-and-poo stories until you're back in your own flat." It was the head of housekeeping, Mrs. De Roos, who decided to intervene.

Evert is his rowdy, boorish self one day, and the next he's silent and brooding. I'm starting to be rather worried about him.

There's a bit of a door-tussle going on here. The staff are in the habit of leaving the residents' doors open when they are in. It makes it easier to keep an eye on them, and more convenient for the housekeeping service. Some of the inmates like it; that way they can alternate gazing out the window and staring into the corridor. Others don't care one way or the other. And then there are some like myself, who don't enjoy having everyone brazenly peering in. I value my privacy and want to keep my door shut. It took quite a bit of doing, let me tell you, to get the personnel to close my door without being asked, but after almost three years of polite entreaties, I finally got my way.

When a door's been left open, I too will glance inside without thinking. I see the inhabitants sitting at their little tables at the window. Sometimes with a book, less often with a piece of embroidery or knitting, but mostly with nothing in front of them. Practicing for the great nothingness to come.

Saturday, February 7

We grew up in the time of pen and ink and the telegram: two letters or a couple of clicks per second. One letter after the next, one by one, from sender to receiver.

Today, at AMS-IX, Amsterdam's Internet exchange, it's two terabytes per second on the digital speedway. That's like scanning every book in the world's largest library three times per second. A concept beyond the comprehension of old people from the analogue age.

I read the article about AMS-IX in the paper and realized how much has changed in over half a century. On the other hand: we still have violence. People are decapitated, children are blown up, women are raped, and people are torched. So, on balance, can one really call it progress . . . ?

Parallel worlds are everywhere, having hardly anything to do with one another. In our care home we find ourselves somewhere on the very outer edge of it all. Until we tumble off.

Well now, Groen, in a bit of a philosophical mood, aren't you?

Mrs. Smit had a spot of trouble with a tin of Smac, which I believe the English call Spam. One of those tins shaped like a skating rink, with a key that opens it by rolling back the lid so that you can lift the top off. Watch out for the sharp edges.

Inside there's some kind of greasy salted ham. You can dice it and add it to pasta, or slice it, fry it in a pan, and eat it on toast. I'll have a look in the supermarket to see if they're still selling Smac, or if Mrs. Smit's tin came from a stash she's had since the 1970s.

The story goes that the ham was just sizzling on her illegal electric hot plate when the phone rang. She didn't remember it until the fire alarm went off. Moments later the attendant caught her red-handed, tossing the blackened contents of the frying pan into the waste bin.

Sunday, February 8

I've switched dates with Geert for the first Old But Not Dead Club outing of the year. I have come up with a plan to take the club to the Parent and Baby Show at the end of February. Just for a brief visit, though, just long enough to enjoy the astonished faces of all those pregnant mummies seeing eight old crocks pushing their way through the phalanx of high-tech prams. After that the real goal of our visit will be the Home Show next door. I think we'll have a competition to see who can collect the most freebies within half an hour. It will be judged by weight. You're only allowed one of each item; you can't just shove a whole stack of brochures in your bag.

There are still details to be worked out. I should really

go on a reconnaissance mission, but that's overdoing it a bit, I think. I've never been, but I imagine we'll find plenty of things to marvel at.

It's a winter that hasn't amounted to much so far. It's been more like a five-month autumn. No snow or cold of any consequence. A pity. I think the chances of trying out my scooter on the ice this year are remote.

Not that it's necessary, but I wonder if there are snow tires for mobility scooters?

Monday, February 9

"OLD AND HOMELESS" was the headline in *Het Parool*, the paper that never hesitates to throw more oil on the fire. Mrs. Zwiers (eighty-one) is soon going to have to move for the fourth time because every care home she lives in gets razed as soon as she's grown used to the place.

The home she now lives in has "first-rate attendants." They take her to IKEA and, when they bring her back, the photo shows them waving goodbye to her as she stands at the window when they leave. What more could you ask for?

The uproar Mrs. Stelwagen was so afraid of when I asked her if our home was slated for demolition has now, thanks to *Het Parool*, spread like a flu epidemic among the residents. The collective fear of having to move dominates every conversation. The newspaper is being passed from hand to hand.

"We have very nice attendants here too, even if they don't wave goodbye or take us to IKEA."

The upshot, after all the talk and handwringing, is that out of Amsterdam's original seventy care homes, half a dozen have already closed. Remaining unmentioned is the fact that they are building new independent housing units for the elderly, although those may be a bit pricey for most of us. There are also smaller institutions in the works, for people with "complex" needs. That's probably something like lots of arts and crafts, to keep people with disabilities busy.

Here in North Amsterdam we have a total of seven care homes.

There's been no announcement about this place being torn down, but Mrs. Schansleh was already sure of it: "The wrecking ball is on its way."

Our only hope, expressed by many at coffee time, is that all the other old-age homes in North Amsterdam will bite the dust before it's our turn.

"It won't matter anymore," said Mr. Bakker, "because we'll all be in our coffins by then."

"I'll be in my *urn*," Mrs. Duits corrected him.

The director did not show her face today, but I expect that we'll shortly receive an empty, meaningless announcement meant to reassure us.

Tuesday, February 10

Stelwagen did not disappoint me. The day after the alarming report in *Het Parool*, there was an announcement from the management on the noticeboard saying, in so many words, that we could all sleep in peace.

"There is no immediate plan for your home to be demolished in the near future."

That "in the near future" did raise some questions. "That's not saying much. What's it supposed to mean: 'in the near future'? To me, the 'near future' is a week, but to a mountain, it's a million years," said Mr. Pot. He'd probably read that bit somewhere, about the mountain.

After a discussion over coffee with a few club members, Leonie was deputized to waylay Stelwagen with her most innocent smile and ask her when the "major renovations," which were announced two years ago, will finally start. We haven't heard a word about it since. Demolition on the heels of a major renovation: it doesn't seem very logical to us.

"Oh, Mrs. Stelwagen, I *do* hope the renovation plans haven't been canceled because of..." Leonie, the woman with the trusting, guileless eyes, thought she'd say something along those lines.

Wednesday, February 11

Tomorrow the Old But Not Dead have another dinner date. Geert is the organizer. It is his first time, and he was too impatient to wait, even though we'd had a dinner out just twelve days earlier. He seems a bit nervous; he is usually the picture of unflappability. We are gathering in the entrance hall at half five.

* * *

I have now studied the papers of the Euthanasia Society. I see that there are a few problems remaining. In the first place, euthanasia pills aren't legally available, and it seems they're not easy to obtain via the Internet either. Legal euthanasia is done by a series of injections. For that I will need a euthanasia declaration signed by a doctor. I don't have great faith in my own doctor. Perhaps the Euthanasia Society will provide the physician; I will have to check that out. I suppose I'll go ahead and order the booklet, *A Self-Determined Death with Dignity.* For a nice, peaceful death, €9.50 isn't too much to pay.

I'll also have to find someone to be my healthcare proxy. That's the problem with having no family. All I have is a few very old friends whom I'd rather not saddle with the burden of my euthanasia and last wishes. I wonder if the Euthanasia Society could provide me with someone who'll be my deputized proxy, for a small fee.

I may talk a good game about self-determination, but putting your money where your mouth is, that's another matter. It's making me feel a bit on edge.

"Know what? You could just put it off for a bit," my trusty old procrastinator whispered in my ear.

Mrs. Van Dam asked me this afternoon if I would play Rummikub with her. In a panicked reflex I said Rummikub always gives me a migraine. But then I felt so ashamed about being such a wimp that I added, "No, just joking. I don't really like Rummikub. You should ask someone else. Why don't you try Mr. Duiker?" I was already snickering inwardly at the thought.

But apparently Van Dam wasn't as desperate as that. She

looked as if she'd rather be buried alive than play a game of Rubbikub with Evert.

Mrs. Van Dam loves board games, but nobody will play with her. She is afflicted with Parkinson's disease, and the pieces or counters are always sent flying in all directions as a result. She spends more time *under* the table picking up the pieces than at play. A sad case. I once played klaberjass with her, but that was really an exercise in patience. In the time it took for her to more or less arrange eight cards in her hand, you had more than enough time to finish a cup of coffee. And then she often couldn't help turning over two or three cards at a time. It does give her opponent a bit of an edge.

She is very despondent. Rummikub, Scrabble, and card games were practically the only activities that still gave her life meaning, but she can't get anyone to play with her anymore. "Frustration, then?" she pleaded recently, unaware of the sad irony of her words.

Thursday, February 12

Mr. Bakker and Mr. Pot are worse than the two cantankerous old geezers in *The Muppets.* Everything's going to the dogs; gangland murders are the only thing that has them rubbing their hands in glee. They have therefore had a splendid time these past few weeks. There have been so many mob killings in a row that it's almost impossible to keep up with them all. Criminals won't get much pity in here. No matter how sweet the bumped-off crook may have been to his mother.

My speculative take on this: the older, the more reactionary.

It's sad, but the residents can also be very mean to one another. Some of them refuse to look at us Old But Not Dead chaps, or exchange pleasantries with us. And why? Envy is the only reason I can come up with. Envy because they've been left out of something. Behind our backs, spurred on by Pot and Bakker, the gossip runs rampant.

We, the club members, have agreed not to react. It isn't always easy in practice, but it's quite effective. It leads to strict separation at mealtimes between the envious and the Old But Not Dead. In between the two camps sit the neutral parties, who behave in a normal, friendly manner toward us, and so are regarded as traitors by the sourpusses who, at age eighty, still can't stand seeing other people happy. Whereas we are all, in the end, in the same, slowly sinking boat, where harmony and fellowship would make so much more sense.

Friday, February 13

At 6 p.m. we were dropped off in Albert Cuyp Street. Empty cardboard boxes and sheets of plastic drifted across the deserted market. The driver of a street sweeper pretended to make a beeline for our procession of elderly citizens. Edward pretended to be given such a turn that he fell down in the street. He can be very convincing, and is admirably limber for a man in his eighties. The driver, alarmed, jumped down from his vehicle. "Oh, sorry, so sorry! I meant it as a joke. Are you hurt, sir?"

"Hoist with your own petard, friend," said Edward, getting up with a laugh. We had to explain it three times to the street cleaner before he finally understood that Edward had taken the mickey out of him. Then he couldn't stop laughing.

We ate in Barra, a tapas bar, and I must say we did the Spanish cuisine proud.

We were presented with a choice of tasty morsels—delicious ham, of course, and tortillas, fish, shellfish, lamb, grilled vegetables. Served by the owner himself, a very friendly devotee of his own cuisine. He also had a lot of patience for old people.

"Oh how I regret spending my whole life on meat, potatoes, and veg," said Leonie. "We've deprived ourselves, haven't we dearie, for eighty years," she mused, caressing Evert's cheek. Upon which Evert choked on his Fundador, spraying the Spanish brandy all over Leonie's dress. She took it in her stride, seizing the opportunity to slap Evert lengthily and assiduously on the back.

Leonie does it on purpose. She knows Evert can't bear being fussed over. Touching to behold.

After an entire bottle of Fundador, we tottered outside even less steadily than when we came in. The worry of falling was left behind in the empty bottle, and if you're not worried, you tend not to fall as easily.

Graeme howled at the moon.

Saturday, February 14

I am to play Cupid on Leonie's behalf. She has bought Evert a cat calendar for Valentine's Day and wants me to deliver it to him anonymously.

"Yes, Henk, I know, it's a very tacky calendar, and I bought it at discount, since we're already a month into the year."

"You do like to tease our ornery friend, don't you?"

"Yes, I'm having fun!"

"I shall deliver it for you with pleasure."

A great many of the latest breakthroughs are coming too late for the inmates here to enjoy. Some aren't too pleased about that. Take the onion that doesn't make you cry, for example. Mrs. Smit was visibly annoyed. Indeed, she was downright furious. "For seventy years I've been bawling my head off over every onion, and now, now that I'm no longer allowed to cook my own food, they come up with a new bloody onion."

"So? Nobody's stopping you from dicing up some onions," Mr. Dickhout suggested.

"What for?"

"No idea. Maybe try some minced onion in your coffee."

Her anger about the new and improved onion speaks volumes about the emptiness of her existence.

Could it be genetic—that some people are predisposed to getting angry about all kinds of things? It does seem to be the case. On the other hand, there are people who take everything with a smile. That's much more pleasant, for their own sake as well as for the sake of others. Although the smiling people tend to make the people in the anger category seethe. Which makes the others smile. And so on.

Sunday, February 15

Yesterday I delivered Leonie's Valentine's gift to Evert. He looked startled at first, and when he'd unwrapped it he said, "'Fess up, Henk, it's from Leonie, isn't it?"

"My lips are sealed."

"What am I supposed to do about that woman?"

"If, and I repeat, *if* it's from Leonie, what does it matter? She's a lovely girl, isn't she?"

"That's the problem, Hendrik Groen!"

I told him I didn't understand, but he wouldn't say any more.

I just don't get Evert these days.

"Feeling all right, old chum?" I've asked him several times now. He just says he's "tolerable" and refuses to divulge any other information.

"Are your toes on your good leg turning black, then?"

"My good leg? I only *have* one leg, Henk. And I sometimes ask myself what they've done with the other leg. What do you think they do with those amputated parts? Maybe they donate them to the zoo, for the lions? That would be a hilarious sight, a lion with my leg in its mouth. And as long as we're on the subject of bones..." Evert went on with a gleam in his eyes, "The Duke of York and the Earl of Suffolk both died at Agincourt. The English king wanted to take his noble friends back to England, but realized they would start to smell rather badly on the long voyage home. So they boiled the corpses until they fell apart, and brought only the bones back home. Neatly done, eh?"

And after that story, what was I supposed to do, return to discussing his mental state?

Actually, Evert is extremely well read, although he doesn't show it often. His knowledge of the Battle of Agincourt proves it.

Monday, February 16

One in four old people who break one or more hips die within the year. That number seems high to me, but it's in the newspaper, so there *is* room for doubt. What is undeniable is that a hip fracture is an inconvenience, and here comes the Wolk Company with just the ticket: the hip-airbag, for falling oldies. It's equipped with movement sensors that detect a fall as it happens, prompting the airbag to inflate. I expect it's a bit like a swimming ring.

When I see the way many of the elderly collapse heavily into their chairs, I hope that airbag has been through some thorough testing and fine-tuning, because otherwise we'll have great numbers of old people pinned into their armchairs by their deployed airbags, or, even more embarrassing, stuck fast on the loo.

Besides, there are a few other wrinkles. The folded airbag mustn't show a bulge under your clothes, since any reasonably vain oldster would rather break a hip than walk around all day looking pear-shaped. In view of the danger of falling out of bed, it has to be comfortable enough to sleep in as well. Although you could just as well put an inflatable mattress next to your bed, of course, or sleep in a bed with side rails. But if they manage to iron out these bugs, I think the hip-airbag is a great solution, especially for people with epilepsy. It's supposed to become available in 2016.

The article suggested another use for the airbag as well: tipsy café patrons. I would suggest making it absolutely mandatory for all epileptic geriatric pub-crawlers.

Tuesday, February 17

"I can't really complain," is the frequent reply to the question of how someone is, "but I *am* bothered by my..." and then you get a whole litany of woes. I get it, that people feel the need, every now and then, to vent their aches and pains; after all, there are enough afflicted old people hobbling along the corridors here. I would only plead for a set time and place for it, from ten until eleven, for example, in a screened-off corner of the conversation lounge.

Actually, isn't what I just wrote a complaint about complaining?

I'm quite well myself, as a matter of fact. For the past two years, time has been kind to me. I do tend to forget quite a bit, but that's easy to live with once you get used to it. What you forgot can't have been all that important anyway. I also find myself getting slower, although, compared to the average resident, I still belong in the fast lane. I would guess that the average speed in our corridors is about 2 kilometers per hour. I can easily make 4 kph on a short distance. I am truly the cheetah of the geriatric world. If I were really tech-savvy I'd put one of those grinning little suns here, but if you have to resort to little yellow balls to explain that something's supposed to be funny, then the joke's already on you.

Early this morning Edward realized that the Old But Not Dead Club has been in existence for exactly two years. He immediately decided to knock on everyone's door to tell us we can't possibly let the date go by unnoticed. A general meeting is called for teatime today.

Wednesday, February 18

Allowing the Old But Not Dead Club's second anniversary to pass without fanfare would have shown scant respect, so something had to be organized without delay. All the members showed up for the hastily called meeting yesterday afternoon. Not thinking it through, we had convened in the conversation lounge, which happened to be filled with a great many uninvited co-residents. Just about half of the home's entire population, crowding as close to our table as they could, were all ears. A few of them went so far as to sit down at our table, announcing they wanted to join the club. That was not the idea. Our little society is strictly closed, you can only join if you're nominated, and even then you have to be voted in by unanimous consent. We now have eight members, and that's the maximum, because the minivan doesn't hold any more than that. Only if one of the Old But Not Dead members unexpectedly dies will there be room for a new member.

We escaped to Antoine and Ria's room in the end.

There it was decided to postpone the celebration by one day, to give us a chance to organize a proper blowout in Evert's flat. Antoine and Ria were given the culinary leadership role, and, after a brief tête-à-tête, they gave each of us an assignment. All members are asked for a small contribution in the form of a dish, or perhaps a song or dance of our choice.

I am tasked with providing a cold appetizer: pears in blue-cheese sauce. They've given me the recipe, which is so simple that even I will be able to make it. I do have to go to the posh greengrocer's some distance away for it, since the supermarket only has rock-hard pears for sale. I'll also dig up my old magic kit from the back of my wardrobe and prepare a trick or two.

A very long time ago I was "The Great Magician" at children's parties. Have I mentioned that?

Thursday, February 19

The pears have been bought. The posh greengrocer lives up to his nickname and charges a very posh price for his fruit. What an old Dutch skinflint I am; I did have to swallow a few times when the time came to pay.

Speaking of money: it turns out that the sale of REAAL Insurance Corporation to some jovial Chinese businessmen has run into a little snag with regard to its parent company's bookkeeping. Even though the Central Bank of the Netherlands had done some thorough vetting of the company, they seem to have missed a huge skeleton in the closet: a debt of a cool €700 million had been "overlooked." You can hardly blame those Central Bank officers or accountants, with their measly six-figure salaries, for that little oversight, can you? It seems the Chinese lost no time spotting that skeleton.

We did not get around to telling the kitchen about missing tomorrow's dinner until yesterday.

"That really is very little notice," Mrs. De Roos grouched. She glared at us as if the potatoes had already been peeled and the meat was already stewing. "Ah well, I shall see what I can do at this late stage."

As head of housekeeping, she likes to give herself airs.

We're gathering at 6 p.m. this evening at Evert's for the gala dinner. Edward has fabricated a small banner for over the door that says OLD BUT NOT DEAD LIVES! I am going to take a little nap beforehand, so that I'll last longer.

Friday, February 20

I woke up late this morning at half past nine, feeling very satisfied, although I did have a bit of a hangover. It was a splendid celebration. The Old But Not Dead members have decided to make these feasts a yearly event; we can't afford to wait five years, as is the custom, because of the risk that one or more of us will be dead by then. So it's official: instead of a five-year anniversary, there will be an annual feast.

Evert proposed that we should likewise observe the Chinese New Year with a copious meal from now on. Unfortunately, he had the date wrong; the Chinese New

Year was...yesterday. The Year of the Goat has already begun.

"I love goat. In the form of saté skewers," Geert suddenly blurted out. Geert is a man of few words; he plays it close to his chest.

A festive evening like the one we just had uses so much energy that I am forced to tap the reserves, and need at least a day to get over it. Today I am taking it easy.

Which I shall do by stirring the old bod as little as possible; I'll confine myself to nodding off in front of the telly or the radio. That's how I'll get through the day. There are inmates here who get through entire years that way, until they nod off for good.

After the mildest horror winter ever, spring has been in the air for the past several days.

Saturday, February 21

Leonie walked up to Stelwagen and in her most innocent voice asked when the renovation work was going to start.

"Which renovation do you mean, Mrs. Van der Horst?"

"I heard that two years ago, before I came to live here, it was announced that the place was to be refurbished."

"That's right, but not long after that the plan was postponed."

"So then when will it start?"

"That is not yet known."

"But it *is* happening?"

"That is not yet known either."

"Then is it known when something will become known?" Leonie was just coming into her stride. "I'm only asking on account of the boxes."

"The boxes?" Stelwagen was starting to lose the thread of the conversation.

"The moving boxes. For when we might temporarily have to switch rooms."

"Mrs. Van der Horst, don't worry, you won't have to temporarily move into another room."

"Do you mean the home is to be torn down?"

"Oh... that won't happen, but if you'll excuse me..."

"But it's logical, surely—either it's a refurbishment, or it's a tear-down."

"I really am sorry, but I have someone waiting."

"Refurbishing a building just before it is slated for demolition would be a waste, wouldn't it?"

"I'll be happy to discuss it with you another time," said Stelwagen. She nodded goodbye, turned, and strode hastily to her office.

I witnessed the entire exchange because Leonie had announced she was about to do it. "Stick around, Hendrik, here she comes."

In asking Leonie to join our club, we gained a brilliant actress who promises to be a great asset to us, and a barrel of fun.

Sunday, February 22

At teatime yesterday it was decided: the Old But Not Dead Club will take a trip abroad in May.

It's to be canceled only if one of the members is on his or her deathbed, or being laid to rest. Otherwise we're going. At our age, everything needs to be provisional; it's best not to make too big a deal of it. There are old people who tend to overemphasize the adverse outcome. Every "See you tomorrow" addressed to Mrs. Quint is answered with "Yes, if I'm still here, that is." According to Evert, I shouldn't be surprised if Mrs. Quint's body is found floating in a ditch nearby someday soon.

Several destinations suitable for elderly travelers were suggested for the springtime trip. We put three of them to a vote—Luxembourg, Maastricht, or Bruges—and Bruges emerged the winner. A committee was formed to look into the feasibility. Now you see how "with-it" the Old But Not Dead Club is, how keen we are to give a professional impression. Everyone expressed full faith in the committee. I am its one and only member. When I put myself forward as a candidate, all the members nodded in agreement and smiled at me fondly.

There are a few provisos attached to the trip:

Not too long, and not too short.

Not too expensive, and not too cheap.

Not too serious, and not too trivial.

The committee has already googled Bruges and established that one of the city's main attractions is a Belgian fries museum. Then I rang Edwin and asked him if he'd be our chauffeur for three days for a modest fee.

"No, I won't do that," he said bluntly, to my dismay. But he added, "I will gladly drive you, but without the modest fee."

* * *

A pamphlet entitled *A Dignified, Self-Determined End of Life* from the Euthanasia Society came through my letterbox. I shall read it at my leisure sometime when I find myself in an upbeat mood.

Monday, February 23

A man has moved in on the fifth floor who plays the violin, but badly. And often. The director received seven complaints within the first week, six of them from a single neighbor. The violin, or rather the concept of "noise nuisance," has become the topic of the day in the lounge. We can state that the tolerance level is rather low here in general. If someone with Parkinson's happens to splash a little coffee into his saucer, some will shake their heads in disdain. People are quick to whisper behind one another's back about sweaty feet, dawdlers who take too long getting into the elevator, people who hack and wheeze too much, or other important matters.

When Graeme suggested that each should "look to the beam in their own eye," it drew mostly puzzled looks. "What's he on about now, talking about beams?"

"Mr. Gorter means that perhaps we should pay a bit more attention to our own actions, and less to that of others," the tea lady piped up. This was greeted with nods from the good-natured among us. A more or less equal number looked away, scowling. You could tell what they were thinking: How's it any of *her* business? They're the ones who always stick their noses into everyone else's affairs.

There was nothing specific in the house regulations about violin playing. Musical instruments are mostly allowed, "as long as the player does not cause a nuisance." Whether this was indeed a nuisance was up to the management to decide. Mrs. Stelwagen came up with an elegant Solomonic solution: from now on, musical instruments may be practiced for a limited number of hours in the space that is home to "Feel-Good-Fitness" and the watercolor class. It's located downstairs, between two storage areas.

The man who plays the violin and the lady next door are not reconciled. He now resorts to playing his radio extra loud. She has already made several complaints about it to the director. Meanwhile the building supervisor has been roaming the halls with a sound level meter. It's expected that the noise regulations will shortly be modified.

Tuesday, February 24

"The slavink is being demonized," said Evert, "and not entirely without justification, in light of its ratings."

The Consumer's Association has subjected the charcuterie delicacy we call "slavink," a bacon-wrapped burger that is still popular among the elderly, to a thorough investigation. It turns out that it not only contains far too much fat and salt, but is also often spoilt and past its expiration date.

"The best slavink scores a 5.6, and the worst a 2.5," Evert said as he read the results of the pork product test. "It's practically a bacteriological weapon, especially in senior care homes."

He said it loud enough for everyone to hear.

"Time to stir the pot a little, Henk," he whispered to me later. "Next time Cook puts slavink on the menu, he'll be left with a mountain of spoiling meat."

On Friday the Old But Not Dead are off to the Home Show. Our first outing of 2015, not counting the international dinners. I sense a healthy excitement among the club members. The minivan is coming to pick us up at eleven. I had considered organizing a meal afterward, but have decided against it. I have learned from experience that the activities should be kept on the short side. Otherwise we won't make it to the end. The average over-eighty citizen has to be frugal with what energy remains.

I wish I could try one of those newfangled pills that make it possible for youngsters to dance and rave for hours on end, but I don't dare. Not that I want to rave for hours on end, but I *would* like to spend a little more time partying at an acceptably dignified and serene pace.

I once asked my former GP for one of those pep pills. He was hesitant, but finally wrote me a prescription. I suspect they were placebo pills. I tried them, but felt just as tired as usual.

Wednesday, February 25

It should be a comical sight: Evert in his wheelchair, buried under eight enormous shopping bags of Home Show freebies. I'm going out later today to buy the shopping bags. The Old But Not Dead Club currently travels with a slew of rolling equipment: one wheelchair and three rollators. Graeme, Edward, Leonie, and I are the only ones still walking without support, or in my case, just a cane. Evert always insists on remaining self-propelled for as long as he can, but at the end of an outing is often grudgingly forced to ask for a push.

"Oh, fine, don't ask for help, then!" Leonie once nagged him as he lagged behind, panting and wheezing. "We'll just let you have a heart attack. More room for the rest of us in the van."

Evert gave some thought to having the heart attack, then changed his mind and asked if someone could please give him a little push.

A mini-scandal: Mrs. Slothouwer "fell" in the corridor, and another lady just stepped right over her into the elevator without looking. It's lucky she wasn't on a mobility scooter.

The staff are looking for the heartless hit-and-run offender, but there is some doubt that she actually exists.

"First she pushed me and then I fell and then she stepped right over me."

"What did she look like?"

"It was Mrs. Van Diemen. She hates me."

At the time of the incident, however, Mrs. Van Diemen was at the hairdresser's in the shopping center a mile away. When the staff later informed Mrs. Slothouwer of Mrs. Van Diemen's watertight alibi she said, snidely, "Then it was Mrs. Smit. She hates me too, that one."

Thursday, February 26

"If you believe what they said about Sir Cliff Richard, then there's no hope for this world." Mrs. Smit threw her hands in the air and sighed in despair.

"Yes, all very dreadful, wasn't it . . . such ridiculous allegations . . . " Mrs. Van Diemen nodded back.

They make a good team.

"It wasn't true, even he himself said it wasn't true. It was just sour grapes."

Yes, Cliff has quite a few fans in here. He's one of the last living idols. Almost all the rest of our heroes are dead. Being old is a lonely road in that regard too. Mark Rutte is no Winston Churchill, Ali B. is no Frank Sinatra, and Linda de Mol is no Sophia Loren. Come to think of it, is La Loren dead, or not?

Brigitte Bardot is still alive, but the bloom is off the rose a bit there. I used to wish I could hang a big poster of her in my bedroom, but I didn't have the nerve. It just wasn't done. Besides, I was just married. My wife definitely would have taken it the wrong way.

I can taste the spring out there in the great outdoors. With gorgeous Dutch skies that every once in a while let the sun through. Later today Geert and I are going out for a long ride. The batteries are fully loaded. We'll stop for pancakes in Broek-in-Waterland, a lovely name for a lovely village. Life can still be so beautiful.

Friday, February 27

I am quite nervous about what my friends will think about my Old But Not Dead Club outing. It is my first Home Show, but it's entirely possible that Ria and Antoine, for instance, have already seen it fifteen times. In which case they'll show us where to go, anyway.

Mrs. Van Diemen had the hairdresser dye her hair a reddish purple, and enthusiastically asked me what I thought of it.

It isn't easy to avoid lying sometimes. I think I may have mentioned this before, but people tell fifteen lies a day, on average. I have been paying attention lately, and it's true that little white lies keep tripping off my tongue. Surely it must be possible to get by with fewer lies than that per day. The simplest solution is often just to keep one's mouth shut. In the case of Mrs. Van Diemen's hair, I just nodded brightly but said nothing. She was satisfied with that.

"I think it's an ugly color and it doesn't suit you at all," would have been the only correct answer. But you can't say that to her. Sometimes lying is just the decent thing to do. An elegant evasion that doesn't actually distort the truth doesn't always occur to me in time, you see. Difficult, difficult. I really ought to try it sometime: going a whole day without lying. And avoiding human company in order to accomplish it doesn't count.

Saturday, February 28

Let's just say it was quite fun, my outing. And informative.

It was incredibly crowded, for a start. Thousands upon thousands of rather tubby women had descended on the show from every village and town in the country. They all had that healthy shopping impulse in their eyes, or was it greediness? Endless queues for the Boursin on toast samples, hands grabbing free candy, a bottleneck for the mini-soaps. Our procession of Old But Not Dead rollators threaded its way through the throng, with Evert's wheelchair in the lead clearing a path for the rest of us. Graeme brought up the rear and made sure we didn't lose anyone. Fortunately there were plenty of places to sit and rest, with massage chairs and all.

"I think you're absolutely delightful people, and I'm all for having you put up your feet, but you've been sitting here having a chat for twenty minutes," said an exhibitor with some desperation in his eyes.

After that our strategy was to coffee-crawl from café to café, watching the endless parade of women from the provinces, heavily loaded with freebies, traipsing by with the occasional downtrodden husband shuffling along behind. Evert and Leonie kept up a running commentary. Whenever we happened not to be sitting down, it was impossible to drag Ria and Antoine away from all the kitchen appliance and pot and pan demonstrations.

Edward feigned a great interest in the streak-free glass-cleaning shammies. The girls had their nails and makeup done, giving the men a head start on the beer and wine. By 4 p.m. we were knackered. We decided to skip the Parent and Baby Show because we couldn't wait to go home.

That may have been the biggest blessing of yesterday's trip: our home isn't all bad. On the ride home we broke into song. Evert turned out to have brought a bottle of port and some plastic glasses. We raised our glasses to a lovely and informative day. The driver stared at us wide-eyed in his rear-view mirror but didn't say anything.

Sunday, March 1

Today is the start of the meteorological spring, and yesterday, when it was still winter, I sat out in the sun for the first time. In the little park up the street, on a sheltered bench, my face tilted to the light, Eefje's headphones on my ears, listening to her music. Joy and sadness all at once.

I could have sat on the bench by the front door of our home. But then I'd have had someone pulling the headphones off my ears every five minutes to say, "Lovely weather, isn't it?" People assume that you should be eager for a chat at all times.

In advance of the provincial elections, I took the online Stemwijzer survey to find that the D66 party comes out on top with a narrow margin of 58 percent, only slightly ahead of PvdA and GroenLinks. I don't know . . . D66 is a bit boring. 50Plus is somewhere down at the bottom, next to the Pirate Party. That's just as well. I have been sounding people out but have found no one who has any idea what the "States-Provincial" elections are about. It's mainly a horse race between Rutte, Samson, and the rest of the pack anyway.

Let's not forget to thank God for Mark and Diederik. Even a confirmed atheist such as me is forever grateful. Just imagine if we had Putin as our president. He filches about 10,000 times our own leaders' annual salary cap from Russia's coffers. Here someone will get kicked out for embezzling a €127 bottle of wine. I'm not an alarmist, but Putin is a dangerous bloke. Mark Rutte is a saint in comparison, enjoying his cheese sandwiches in his ivory tower in The Hague, phoning his mum every day, loving his job and enjoying the occasional tiff with Diederik over a few marbles.

"Putin could put away a million biscuits a day if he wanted to," Mrs. Schaap remarked shrewdly.

"If only he would," grunted Graeme.

Monday, March 2

Yesterday I saw several residents intently studying the escape route maps. After two nursing home fires in one week, some of us are feeling a bit worried.

"That fire will have to be an extremely slow-smoldering one if I'm to reach the exit in time," said Mrs. Duits, who employs an old-fashioned Zimmer frame to get around. "From my room on the fifth floor, I'll need about half a day to get down the ten flights of stairs. There will have to be a chair on every landing to rest my poor legs, or I won't make it."

There was loud agreement. Some of the oldies started bragging that it would take *them* even longer.

Mr. Pot announced he would write to the Residents' Committee, demanding that management be made attentive to fire safety.

"Great idea, Pot," said Evert, "only we haven't had a committee for the past year and a half."

That is so. After a fierce quarrel about the scheduling of the annual day trip, the Residents' Committee was "disbanded" by the director. The subsequent election of a new committee was canceled for want of candidates. No one was willing to work together with anyone else anymore.

I shall ask Stelwagen to call an election again. There's a plan brewing, see.

Tuesday, March 3

"In light of the rat and mouse infestation, feeding bread to the birds in the common gardens is no longer permitted." The new prohibition, underlined in red, was pinned to the noticeboard.

"There goes yet another of life's little pleasures." Mrs. Bregman gave a deep sigh. She is in the habit of buying an entire loaf of bread every day, three-quarters of which she feeds to the birds. Bread from Aldi, but still.

"That's five hundred euros a year you're just throwing away," a thrifty nurse calculated.

"But I get a thousand euros of pleasure from it—so what?" That "so what" was a rather surprising retort, I thought, coming from her.

Besides, the rat argument does not persuade me. Dozens

of sparrows and starlings, a good number of pigeons and even a couple of herons mill about in the garden every day waiting for Bregman to dump the meticulously cubed bread from her second-floor window at 2 p.m. sharp. There's not a crumb left over for the rats. She also trots to the poulterer's twice a week for a pound of kidneys and gizzards, for the herons.

"Did you know that in the seventeenth century herons were considered a delicacy?" Evert once remarked. Bregman had put her hands to her mouth in dismay.

I'm not that fond of herons myself, with their beady little eyes and razor-sharp beaks for spearing frogs and ducklings. So I wouldn't be averse to trying roast heron someday.

There was good news for animal lovers as well: the panda is making a comeback. According to the newspaper, there are now 1,864 living specimens. What kind of journalist decides to take such a precise head count, it didn't say. The panda scores high on the list of old people's favorite animals. It's one of the many issues on which young children and the elderly agree.

Wednesday, March 4

Joep Peeters, the singing half of the Two Pints duo, is no more. The other Pint died a while ago. I don't know, actually, if Joep was still performing, or if he was now calling himself One Pint. Or the Last Pint. In tribute to Joep, Mrs. Lacroix, in a high soprano, performed (she is a performance artist, after all) the Pints' greatest hits:

"On Our Kitchen Door" and "I'll Take the Love and the Wine." Bakker stuffed his fingers demonstratively in his ears. As Lacroix warbled the line "You take the money and the slime," she pointed spitefully at Bakker. Well, that led to a little dust-up, as you can imagine, with Bakker calling her a "shit-artist." The staff had to step in, and Bakker, who refused to apologize, was made to move to a table at the far side of the room.

It has been two years since the staff first determined that Bakker's ranting and raving was out of control, but they have yet to find a good place to park him, apparently.

Bakker often makes me laugh. I try to suppress it, naturally, to avoid getting the entire morality posse on my back.

There is also reason to rejoice: Exota is back. Exota was once as popular as Coca-Cola is today. Until the little mishap of some bottles spontaneously exploding. The oldies can't wait to see Exota sparkling juices on the supermarket shelves again. Hopefully the bottles will be sturdier this time. In its absence, people remembered Exota as some sort of heavenly nectar. The brown "champagne-pils" in the tubby little bottle in particular was, according to Mr. Dickhout, "the *appellation contrôlée* of fizzy drinks." I'm afraid it could turn out to be a disappointment.

Thursday, March 5

Very bad news. I received a death announcement: our old lawyer Victor has passed away. He'd been ill for a while. A kind, warm, intelligent man. Until a few months ago he'd been hard at work attempting to have all the rules, protocols, and regulations of this home released under the Governance Transparency Act—with a great deal of enthusiasm, but little success. Portions were unsealed every so often, but with all the interesting passages blacked out, supposedly on account of sensitive privacy issues. Victor was determined; if it were not for him, I'd have given up long ago. He wasn't in it for the money; all he asked for in return was a weekly bottle of wine from a different corner of the world. I soon ran out of countries, although I did my best. Be that as it may, we finished many a bottle between us. This evening, in memory of Victor, I will open a nice bottle of wine. Perhaps the board and Stelwagen will do the same, but for a different reason.

"I think this is the pin you pull..." Mr. Verlaat said, studying the instructions of his newly purchased fire extinguisher and proceeding to spray foam all over his room. It took hours to clean up the mess. Verlaat kept getting in the cleaners' way, whimpering, "I couldn't help it, could I?"

"Oh yes you could," said the head of housekeeping. At teatime she informed the residents that, by way of setting an example, Mr. Verlaat is required to pay for the damage out of his own pocket. I wouldn't be at all surprised if there isn't a bit of revenge there on the part of management, because of Verlaat's threat to bring a lawsuit over the prohibition against pets. The inmates' fear of fire is now up against their fear of having to pay for damages. And there are already so many things we are afraid of here. Which points to one striking difference between the very young and the elderly: children aren't afraid of anything; old people are afraid of everything.

Friday, March 6

Tonight the Old But Not Dead are eating out, in furtherance of our exploratory tour of the kitchens of the world. So I shall have an abstemious lunch.

A friend of Mrs. Schaap's, who had been on this home's waiting list for two years, had just moved up to second place when she unexpectedly passed away last week. Schaap was in tears, because she had so looked forward to her best friend's arrival. The world is often not kind to the elderly.

In Norway they also have a waiting list. That wait is never long *enough* for the parties concerned. "No, please, you go first." It's like a waiting list for convicted felons, who must wait for a prison cell to become vacant.

I am taking note of Mrs. Schansleh's quite extraordinary idioms and proverbs. "They make a mountain out of every elephant in the china shop" was the first one to catch my attention. It concerned a bomb attack in Iraq, if I remember right.

Today she uttered these words of wisdom: "The path to the graveyard is paved with tumors." It was meant as solace for Mrs. De Gans, who at teatime yesterday told anyone who would listen about the benign growth in her stomach. "As big as a pigeon egg. From a small pigeon, though."

Someone wanted to know the exact size of that pigeon.

The entire conversation was deadly serious.

Saturday, March 7

The best part was that you were allowed to eat with your hands. Evert made a bit of a pig of himself with the sauces, and he wasn't even doing it on purpose. After some practice, eating without fork or spoon became the most normal thing in the world. The Ethiopian world, that is. Because last night we dined in a charming Ethiopian restaurant in Marnix Street. Since none of us knew anything of that country's cuisine, we asked the chef to surprise us. The result was a huge round platter for four, with an equally huge pancake on it that was garnished with all sorts of tidbits. You were supposed to tear off a piece of pancake and use it to mop up morsels of meat, fish or vegetable. Graeme took a rather big bite of something mysterious, and promptly commandeered Evert's banana-beer to quench the fire. He is to be commended for sparing the white wine. Evert used the pretense to switch over to coconut-beer.

"You like to drink dangerously, don't you, dear," said Leonie, lovingly tousling Evert's last remaining locks. It was rather dark in there, but I thought I saw him blush.

The food was delicious, and it was great fun. After doing an initial double take when they saw the geriatric parade file into their restaurant, the African host and hostess seemed very taken with us. Normally our group can expect to be met with surprise at first, and then warm sympathy.

"How nice, that you're still trying new things. At your age! We may sometimes get a grandpa or grandma in here, but eight at once...well I never." If you can think of this pronounced in some sort of African accent, it becomes a charming statement.

It took a little longer than planned, and Leonie had to bribe the Connexxion minibus driver to wait for fifteen minutes. She wouldn't tell us how she'd managed it.

Today is a day of rest.

Sunday, March 8

Mrs. Smit had forgotten to put on a diaper. When she got up from the table after dinner last night, there was a rather large wet spot on the back of her skirt. It didn't even show that much because the pattern served as camouflage. Had someone whispered in Mrs. Smit's ear that she should go to her room and change into a clean frock, no one would have been any the wiser. But she had the misfortune of drawing the attention of Mrs. Slothouwer's evil eye.

"Oh, I was just thinking: what's that smell?" Slothouwer exclaimed, much louder than necessary. She pointed at Mrs. Smit's skirt. Mrs. Smit slowly looked down. When she looked up again, she encountered ten pairs of eyes staring at her. She tried covering her backside with her hands to hide the wet spot.

"Forgot your diaper, didn't you? And now *we* have to deal with the stench. And that chair will have to be recovered; the smell will never come out."

Mrs. Smit began to cry quietly, shielding her skirt with one hand and her eyes with the other.

"Crying doesn't help," said Slothouwer.

"If you don't shut your trap now, I'll punch you in the nose," Evert hissed, looking around for something with which to carry out that threat. Geert posted himself between them and, addressing Slothouwer slowly and quietly, said, "Get out. Now."

I took Mrs. Smit's arm and walked her to her room. "Don't worry, it can happen to anyone," I comforted her. Halfway down the corridor, Nurse Morales took her over from me. I heard her say, "We'll make sure it doesn't happen again, won't we?" She kept nattering away, but I could no longer hear what she was saying.

Tuesday, March 10

I generally manage to make it through the day, but yesterday I had a bad day. Dog-tired, short of breath, and queasy.

"Growing old is a shipwreck," President de Gaulle once said, and *he* only made it to eighty.

"We're on the ropes sometimes, aren't we? The ropes of life," Graeme said recently with a big grin. I pictured two geriatric boxers wearing boxing gloves far too big for them in their corners, too spent to come out.

I could, of course, turn to a Mr. Banfa for help. I recently found his pamphlet in my letterbox.

"World-renowned clairvoyant medium with great experience. Very well known for his excellent work and effectiveness. Will solve many of your problems, even the most hopeless: return of affection, tenderness, restoration of security, exams, clients,

faithfulness, all physical and moral problems healed, reversal of evil spells, etc. Speedy outcome guaranteed."

There was a phone number underneath. Maybe we could start with the evil spell reversal.

Wednesday, March 11

Yesterday Ria, Antoine, and I went to Victor's funeral. It was very impressive. It turned out, unsurprisingly, that he had hundreds of friends and acquaintances. Everyone was very sad. Nobody said or thought, "It's best this way."

A German wolf has been spotted roaming the streets of Hoogezand.

Mrs. Bregman: "How can they be so sure it's a *German* wolf? Maybe it came from Czechoslovakia."

"In that case it left home quite a while ago, because that country no longer exists." Evert snickered. "Maybe they can tell because it howls in German?"

"Anyway, why Hoogezand, of all places?" Bregman wondered.

Topics of animal interest tend to do well in the conversation lounge.

Another important topic of the day is the mini herb and vegetable seed garden you get if you spend €15 at Albert Heijn. They're a big hit with the elderly. Grandparents will usually save their supermarket freebies as gifts for the grandkids, but they're keeping these for themselves. The plot (two inches square) is easily managed, the heavy work can be done sitting down, and it isn't all that taxing. People compete as to who can grow the tallest leek, celery, or spring onion seedling. Measured in millimeters for now. For want of other pastimes, some residents spend their time watching for the seedlings to sprout. All right, I confess: eleven of those little pots have pride of place on my own windowsill.

A judge in Utrecht has decided that people who are old and sick need no more than an hour and a half of cleaning help per week. Another judge, in Friesland, found that it takes at least three hours to clean a house properly.

Most of the ladies agreed that ninety minutes per week isn't even enough to keep the lavatory clean.

"*Really* clean, I mean."

The ladies nodded, unanimous, but I must say I have visited some less than spotless toilets...

Thursday, March 12

Justice Minister Ivo Opstelten and his under-secretary Fred Teeven have tendered their resignations. They were very popular here, these two heroes of the war against both organized and disorganized crime. Our residents are worried that starting tomorrow the number of muggings of the elderly will go through the roof. Okay, I'm exaggerating, but not terribly.

Minister Opstelten had sworn that there was no evidence of any bribery, and then some proof turned up that there was, in the form of a receipt. Government ministers don't often get caught telling little white lies. Teeven resigned too, out of solidarity; that was nice of him. Although the receipt that was found did happen to be his; a receipt for a pay-off to the underworld figure Cees H., in exchange for information that would put some other crooks behind bars. Cees is allowed to keep his €4.7 million criminal compensation, thanks to Teeven.

Crime ought not to pay, we think, and you must admit that €4.7 million is a rather generous stipend.

I caught a glimpse of myself in a shop window yesterday, and it wasn't an encouraging sight. I was shuffling. There is no other word for it. I was shuffling slowly and rather uncertainly in the direction of HEMA, where I was headed to buy new socks because my old ones have holes in them. They get holes because I am no longer able to cut my own toenails, and so they get too long. There's nothing else for it but to have the pedicurist come. I always thought it rather over the top, and a bit embarrassing, a stranger coming to fiddle with my old, rather grotesque toes and hacking at my rock-hard, fungus-infected nails. He or she had better bring some heavy equipment.

Friday, March 13

There was a story in the paper about a physiotherapists' racket in the athletics club world. Claims for treatments that were neither necessary nor ever performed. May I give the ladies and gentlemen of the papers a little tip?

You should investigate physical therapy fraud among the elderly!

There are residents who have been going to their physical therapists twice a week for years, for an ailment that is in fact incurable: old age. One time it's for an achy old arm, the next it's got to do with a dodgy old leg, but the upshot is: there's not much that can be done about any of it. Most people just have physiotherapy for the length of time it will take for their complaint to go away on its own. Not in the case of old people. They have very few ailments that will resolve themselves eventually. Talk about a complete waste of time! Most of us have supplementary insurance that covers an unrestricted number of PT treatments. Which means that it's free; therefore nothing stands in the way of countless more useless visits. The therapist doesn't care, he's quite happy to send over his bill. Sometimes he gets paid just for walking the patient from one corner of the room to the other.

"Yes, but it must be doing something," someone said recently.

"Yes, such as keeping the therapist in business," Graeme scoffed.

Saturday, March 14

Royal Dutch Shell is patching the hole in CEO Ben van Beurden's pension package to the tune of €16.8 million. That must have been quite a hole, requiring such a pricey repair. When he retires, that Van Beurden could use his pension to buy himself three entire old-age homes.

I wonder if Ben feels any embarrassment at all?

Forgive me for riding my hobbyhorse a little longer. The following gentlemen were not so long ago voted Executive of the Year:

Sjoerd van Keulen—let SNS Bank go bankrupt.

Ad van Wijk—drove green energy concern ECO into bankruptcy.

Cees van der Hoeven—chairman of Albert Heijn. Convicted of fraud.

Dirk Scheringa—drove DSB Bank into bankruptcy *and* was convicted of fraud.

I don't think, frankly, that these gentlemen will ever have to depend on welfare benefits to survive.

"My mouth and my brain don't seem to understand each other these days," Mr. Bakker, always the bellyacher, announced. He is an annoying, negative fellow, but as he said it, he looked deeply troubled. I felt pity for him for the first time since I've known him.

The people around the table stared at him, but nobody said anything.

"I also don't know why I'm always cussing and swearing," said Bakker, after a short silence.

"I don't either," Mrs. Van Diemen concurred.

It was the first time in ages that anyone had agreed with him.

Sunday, March 15

Last night I dreamed I was driving one of those nifty little Canta Cabrio autos, one arm hanging nonchalantly out of the window, the other hand loosely on the wheel, puffing on a nice cigar. The sun was shining. Eefje was sitting next to me. She wore a lovely red hat, which she had to hold tightly so it wouldn't blow away. She smiled at me.

On Sundays we are usually served an egg at lunch. It's really a delayed breakfast egg, to deter residents from cooking eggs in their rooms on Sunday morning.

Last week a new resident, I think her name is Mrs. Hoensbroek, peered at her egg dubiously for a long time.

"What a small egg, I must say," she said.

Yes, indeed, on closer inspection a number of other residents thought so too.

"Should we ask Cook to give us larger eggs?" someone suggested.

That prompted Mrs. Bregman, who likes to remind everyone that she's a member of the Party for Animals, to protest.

"When they buy those extra-large eggs, nobody ever thinks of the chicken's poor little pooper."

"Those battery hens are bred to have a big bumhole, they don't feel a thing," Mr. Pot proclaimed.

The room split into two camps: one for the chicken, and one for the extra-large eggs. We haven't yet heard the last word on this one. Where there are no major concerns, minor ones can create great division.

Monday, March 16

Mr. Verlaat has dropped his iPhone for the umpteenth time, this time into the toilet. It fell out of his pocket when he was having a piss. Splash. There's no protective case that will stand up to that. Verlaat should have been prepared, however, since the excuse he offered was that until now the phone had always landed *next to* the pot. That wasn't enough reason to take it out of his pocket when going to the toilet, it seems.

He plunged his arm in up to his elbow—"Luckily I hadn't wee'd yet"—and was just able to retrieve it. His phone no longer worked, not even after being left on the radiator for some hours to dry.

The main reason Mr. Verlaat is upset is that it means he can no longer Wordfeud.

"What can't you anymore?" asked Mrs. Smit.

"Wordfeud," said Verlaat.

"That's just Scrabble. A pretentious kind of Scrabble," Mrs. Slothouwer sniped.

"Oh, I'll gladly play Scrabble with you, Mr. Verlaat," Mrs. Van Dam said hopefully.

He did not take her up on the offer.

There are a few residents who stare at their iPhone or iPad all day, observed by the mystified rest. Usually they're only checking their screens to verify that nobody is trying to reach them, but occasionally they'll Skype or chat with their children or grandchildren. They prefer to do this when there are as many people in the vicinity as possible. In making the others listen in, they wring from their audience not only admiration, but also envy of all that modern hoo-ha.

Tuesday, March 17

The States-Provincial and Water Boards elections are tomorrow. The Water Boards have created even more confusion than the Provincial States.

"It's about the dikes," Graeme told Mrs. Duits.

"And what does the 50Plus Party think about the dikes?" Duits asked him.

"Like everyone else, 50Plus probably thinks we should have dikes that are nice and high. There aren't many political parties that would press for lower dikes and more floods, I shouldn't think," Graeme explained patiently. "So it doesn't make a blind bit of difference how you vote on the Water Boards ballot. Just fill in one of the little boxes—any one—with a red pencil."

That was most reassuring to Mrs. Duits. She decided to color in the box corresponding to her favorite number: 7.

"And in the case of those Provincial States, I can just vote for 50Plus, can't I?"

"You can, but it wouldn't be very sensible," Graeme replied, then walked away, leaving Mrs. Duits more bewildered than ever.

It's a beautiful spring day. I'm taking off for a ride with Geert later. Seeing us on our scooters, people have already given us some fine nicknames: Chip and Dale, Laurel and Hardy, and the best one, if you ask me: Urbi and Orbi.

We are fond of our monikers.

With the wind at our backs, we can gun it to fifteen

miles an hour. "Not until we're out on the open road, of course," Geert says with a grin.

Wednesday, March 18

We're having another of our international dinners out tomorrow. Leonie has made a reservation and refuses to give even a hint, and that's how it should be. The minibus is ordered for 6:00. Which means there's plenty of time to rest beforehand, so that later we can give it our all.

The world 200-meter sprint record has been broken by two seconds. It now stands at 55.48 seconds, and Charles Eugster is the current record holder. I'm talking about the speed record for people over ninety-five. Eugster began training when he was ninety-four.

"I want this to prove that you can take on challenges at any age," the newly minted record holder declared. Wise words, Charles.

I've worked out that on average, his speed was eight miles an hour. After the race he did need a little nap.

It seems there's also a ninety-year-old pole jumper, who has cleared 2.18 meters. I don't know if I'd dare to watch him do it.

When I told Evert, he said he wouldn't mind trying to smash the world white wine drinking record.

I have to go and vote, but I'm still undecided.

Thursday, March 19

A couple of weeks ago I quoted De Gaulle, who said, "Growing old is a shipwreck." The honorable Henk Krol of the 50Plus Party, whose talent for subtlety is without compare, has come up with another naval metaphor: "The cabinet is a sinking ship trying to stay afloat by tossing the elderly overboard." Henk Krol, you may remember, is the man who cheated his own employees out of their pensions. I have become a political activist for the first time in my life these past few days, touting the slogan: BE SMART. DON'T VOTE FOR KROL. Evert thought BLACKBALL KROL was stronger.

I once saw a sign in a snack bar that said BE SMART, EAT APPLE TART. Now *there's* a catchy slogan!

Fortunately, 50Plus and the other seniors' parties haven't garnered many seats. If the geriatric crowd had a voice on the Water Boards, they'd squabble over every little ditch, and within a year half the country would be under water.

We're not too concerned in here about election outcomes threatening the good governance of this country.

Mrs. Quint thinks someone sabotaged her miniature seedling gardens. When one of the caregivers suggested that watering them five times a day might be too much of a good thing, Quint said it was nonsense. She watered her seedlings no more than three times a day.

"But they aren't aquatic plants, Mrs. Quint."

"I know that. I think someone else overwatered them."

Friday, March 20

We had a Belgian meal, but to be honest I don't really know what was so typically Belgian about it, except for the tasty chips and the extensive beer menu.

Not that it made much difference, because we had a most enjoyable evening at Restaurant Lieve in Amsterdam. Leonie blushed as we showered her with compliments on her choice. "Your cheeks match your scarlet frock perfectly," Evert complimented her.

In order to get the club members a little excited about our upcoming travels to Bruges in the spring, I informed them that we will be paying a visit to the world's only museum dedicated to fries. The news was enthusiastically received.

Belgium has recently decided to name the chip shop a national treasure.

Mrs. Schaap's Canta mini-auto was defaced with illegible black graffiti. Schaap was terribly upset and just sat there sobbing and sniveling for at least an hour, now and then pulling a hanky from her sleeve. She must have been carrying that same hanky around for weeks, by the looks of it; the sound it made gave it away as well. It crackled a bit the first time she unfolded it to blow her nose, before wiping her eyes with it. The nurse offered her a packet of tissues, but Schaap declined, declaring them unhygienic.

Bakker tried to cheer her up: "There's not much you can do to that old Canta that will make it look worse."

After an hour listening to her sobs, Geert got fed up and

stomped downstairs. In five minutes he'd got rid of the graffiti by rubbing it with a special paste. Good as new. "That spray paint was inferior," he diagnosed. "Clean as a whistle again, Mrs. Schaap."

Snorting with joy, Mrs. Schaap flung her arms around Geert. I saw him shudder, and I don't think it was with delight.

Saturday, March 21

The Old But Not Dead are staging a coup.

I was at Evert's for a game of chess when Ria, Antoine, and Edward stopped in for a chat. The conversation turned to the Residents' Committee, which has been moribund for almost two years, ever since it was annulled by internecine warfare. The members of the committee had been ready to kill one another over such momentous issues as the bingo prize policy, or the timing of the annual outing. Two of them have since kicked the bucket, but no one knows whether there was any direct correlation between their demise and the committee's internal feud.

A few weeks earlier I'd had the bright idea that we should ask Stelwagen to call for new elections.

"I sincerely doubt," I told my friends, "that any of the other residents are still willing to serve on that committee. So if we'll all throw our hats in the ring just before the application deadline, the Old But Not Dead members will be positioned to take over the Residents' Committee lock, stock, and barrel."

There was great enthusiasm for this plan, and so the missing club members were rounded up. A small technical problem remained to be solved, however. Evert can't technically be part of the committee because he's in sheltered accommodation, and besides, there's only room for five members anyway. The problem was easily solved—we'll just appoint an advisory board of three. That way the whole club will have a say. Once elected, we can make use of the amenities to which the committee is entitled, such as a place to meet, a budget, and administrative support. Moreover, Stelwagen will have to meet with us at least twice a year and provide us with information about the board of directors' decisions. I already look forward to the subtle power struggles that are bound to ensue. Evert said he was primarily interested in seeing the other residents' faces when they hear that the mandatory residents' fee has been quadrupled.

"That should bring about a few conniption fits," he said.

Geert and Leonie were delegated to approach the director about calling a new election. They're the two least likely to rouse suspicion.

We are already high-fiving one another over our imminent coup. I understand that nowadays one doesn't high-five anymore, one fist-bumps. But that, from the sound of it, may require a bit too much exertion.

Sunday, March 22

The outrage! A ninety-six-year-old woman walking with a Zimmer frame in South Amsterdam was mugged and stabbed in the stomach. Between sips of tea, many a call for the reinstatement of the death penalty was heard.

"And preferably administered very slowly," Bakker said.

I think a psychiatric institution is a better solution, myself.

The old lady was able to flee and call the police. That she did so was a source of wonder and admiration. It also speaks volumes about the mugger's fleetness of foot. He surrendered to the police not long afterward.

The result of this deed on the part of a presumably extremely disturbed individual is that you'll see even fewer old people daring to go out at night.

Man often suffers most
From the adversity he fears
But never actually appears.
Thus has he more to bear
Than God in His wisdom thinks fair.

I didn't think it was the right moment to recite this little verse.

I popped in to see Grietje. She has become a sort of senile Florence Nightingale, ministering to the others on the ward. She seems content and happy in the chaos of confused, anguished, and angry old people all around her.

I have great respect for the nursing staff, who, armed only with angelic patience, try to keep the patients' lives bearable. Although out of the corner of my eye I did glimpse a nurse confiscating a teddy bear from a lady. Who then proceeded to caress the biscuit tin instead.

Every time I visit Grietje's ward, I think: let me not forget to get cracking on my own death-with-dignity ending.

Monday, March 23

In Flanders they have come up with an idea to solve the problem of elderly housing: a shipping container in the back garden of their children's house. These can be erected in one day, and removed in one day too. Upon removal, don't forget to check if Gramps or Granny is still in there.

The containers are prefab and ready to go; all they need are a few of old Dad's or old Mum's favorite knickknacks. Nice and close by for the caregiver, yet you maintain your privacy. It won't work if you live in a flat, unless you can install the container on the strip of lawn down below. But you'd risk having kids from the neighborhood kicking their soccer ball against it all day long.

The Belgian plan was discussed at teatime with many a shake of the head.

"A storage container instead of a house. A storage unit for people who are deemed superfluous." Leonie gave a deep sigh.

Evert remarked that a food hatch might come in handy.

Quizzical stares all around.

"That's poppycock," said Mr. Verlaat bombastically. He loves that word, poppycock, and employs it often. So often in fact that nobody bothers asking him what he means by it.

"Indeed. Very poppycock," the lady sitting next to him said, nodding.

This afternoon Geert and Leonie are going to Stelwagen's office to put in a request for a new Residents' Committee election. The Old But Not Dead members are on tenterhooks. We have already decided that once we are the Residents' Committee, we'll hold the management's feet to the fire about the renovation or demolition plans.

Tuesday, March 24

The director agreed to consider the request for a Residents' Committee election and will give us her answer within a week. Geert didn't get the sense that any suspicions were raised.

After procrastinating for weeks, I have finally turned my attention to the pamphlet from the Euthanasia Society, *A Dignified Self-Determined End of Life*, which I've had lying around for over a month. It isn't easy to be actively engaged in your own death, leaving as little as possible to chance. An uneasy and complicated pill to swallow, and I don't feel like writing about it right now.

Wednesday, March 25

Stop the press! Care homes can now rent a time machine. Some young people have fashioned a transportable room furnished in the style of the 1960s, with a kitchen, screening room, and dance hall attached.

The idea is to give old people a chance to rewind and reset. People who insist on just sitting there silently nodding dully over their cup of tea must be encouraged to revisit the years of their youth. Once they see the old Philips radio, the dresser with photos, and a cross-stitched rendering of a Vermeer street scene on the wall, they'll automatically perk up. Let them dwell on memories, gaze at old photos, play an Elvis record, or prepare a pudding with the skin on top. Maybe even dance a waltz. What they can't do, sadly, is light up an unfiltered Caballero with a genuine Ronson lighter.

Visitors to the nostalgia room are further stimulated by volunteers asking engaging questions such as: "What did you do back then?" and "What did you like best?" and "What do you wish you could still do now?"

It appears that the room usually does manage to give them a bit of a lift, but the problem is how to keep them animated once they're back in the year 2015. They'll probably sink right back into their old funk, complaining even more loudly than before that everything was so much better in the old days.

The nurse did think Mrs. Strikwerda's wheelchair seemed to be dragging a bit, which made her have to push harder, but actually Mrs. Strikwerda's hand was caught in the spokes.

"She was making this high-pitched sound, but I thought she was *singing*," the nurse wailed. Strikwerda was taken to the emergency room for an X-ray. Luckily nothing was broken.

"I'm fine, really," she said over and over again, waving her bandaged hand. She found it quite funny herself.

Thursday, March 26

I am waiting for a warm, sunny spring day to go fishing with Geert. It's been at least sixty-five years since I sat on a riverbank with a fishing rod. As a boy I'd often fish in the canal behind our house with a friend. We competed all summer long, and I remember the end score was 57–55, but I don't know which of us caught the most. The fish we hooked were almost always undersized or even smaller. Removing the hook was my least favorite part. Sometimes it was caught in an eye, in which case I'd leave it to my mate to get it out. We used bread as bait because the thought of threading worms or maggots on the hook disgusted us.

What fascinated me about fishing was the intense indolence of it. I would like to see if I would still enjoy that. Geert has a rod I can use, and he's promised to remove the fish from the hook for me. I'm curious to see if blissfully staring at a float bobbing in the water is as much fun as I think it will be.

Some of the ladies are against fishing as a sport, but Geert just shrugs.

"It's a sport that doesn't require you to move a lot, and that suits me just fine."

"Yes," said Mrs. Bregman, "but fish feel pain, it's been proved."

"What goes on inside a fish's head will no doubt forever remain a mystery," Edward said with a doleful grin and a wink.

"Fish do cry, but you can't see it because they're under water," Mrs. Smit declared.

Geert said he would bring a handkerchief for the fish next time.

Friday, March 27

The royalists are rather disappointed in our king. He has shortened his birthday celebration: it's to last from just 11 a.m. to 1:15 p.m. A two-hour party; Dutch frugality at its best. Willem doesn't want any *koekhappen*, or cake-biting, at his birthday; nor does he want to have any other traditional Dutch party games. And there are to be no gifts from his loyal subjects.

Pieter van Vollenhoven, always the most enthusiastic *koekhapper*, is staying home. In protest, perhaps? The old Queen Mother isn't going either, but at least that's something we can understand. She's had it with waving. I bet she's staying home to work on a lovely King's Day drawing.

This year the city of Dordrecht has been chosen to host the festivities, and they are honoring the king with a maritime parade. Nostalgia for the Soestdijk Palace parade of yore grows by the year. Stuff your maritime parades; give us a sixteen-foot-long spice cake graciously accepted from her subjects by our favorite queen, Juliana. In those days three policemen were enough to patrol the grounds. In 2015 the security preparations need a tome as thick as the telephone book. At the risk of sounding like a tiresome old bore, is this progress? Can we ever go back to the time when no one was afraid of terrorists, and the spice cake didn't have to go through the metal detector?

Scientists are busy trying to coax a living specimen out of a dead mammoth's remains. The believers among us think it is blasphemous: "Never place thyself upon God's throne to reinvent Creation." Those of us who don't believe in God, or believe in a God who's a bit more easygoing, were quite taken with the idea of a couple of mammoths roaming the heathlands of the Veluwe.

Mr. Bakker could also see the possibilities, as far as coming back from the dead.

"If they can do it with a mammoth, why not with me?"

"If I had my druthers, I'd choose a mammoth over you," said Evert.

Bakker started swearing like a banshee, until the attendant threatened to have him moved to the nursing ward.

Saturday, March 28

Mrs. Stelwagen has sent out a letter to all residents announcing that there is to be an attempt to set up a Residents' Committee again. The election will be held on Friday, May 1. Candidates may apply until April 14.

So Part One of our plan is in the bag. Now we can only

hope and pray that no one else steps forward. If necessary, we'll strongly dissuade any prospective candidates by pointing out all the wrangling that went on with the last committee. Evert is even prepared to resort to pressure tactics involving physical violence. That's because he'd enjoy being able to say, "They sometimes call me *The Nose Senior*," in reference to Willem "The Nose" Holleeder, the Netherlands' most famous crook with the prominent nozzle. After his sisters and ex-girlfriend testified against him, the ladies here knocked The Nose off their list of ideal sons-in-law.

Crime is always a very popular topic of conversation. If I were to make a Top Ten list of subjects most often heard over a cup of coffee or tea, it would look like this:

1. The weather
2. One's own ailments
3. Other people's ailments
4. Other people in general
5. All that's wrong in our care home
6. What's on the telly
7. What's wrong in the world, with emphasis on crime, both major and minor
8. How expensive everything is (compared to before)
9. Children and grandchildren
10. The food

New residents who arrive with a cheerful and positive outlook have to stay firmly planted on their orthotic-supported feet if they're not to get sucked, slowly but surely, into the slough of grievances and complaints.

The Old But Not Dead's first action, once we represent the Residents' Committee, will be to establish complaint-free zones.

Sunday, March 29

Stormy weather: rain and cold. No sign of spring. I think I have an attack of gout coming on again. Antoine had a fall and bruised a couple of ribs.

There, I have just given you the top three from yesterday's list.

I shall get nice and drenched later today on my Sunday scooter ride with Geert. We have made a bet: whichever of us spots the first duckling wins a chocolate Easter egg. I've already bought an Easter egg, to be on the safe side, since if the first baby duck doesn't show up until Easter's over, it will be too late to buy one. We didn't think of that when we agreed on the wager.

"It's a bit like the Catholics and the Protestants in the old days," Mr. Dickhout said in summary of the conflict between the Sunnis and the Shiites. That did bring some clarity, because people found "all that business with those Arabs" very hard to understand.

"One faction is for Ali, and the other for Abu," Dickhout went on. He must have looked it up on Wikipedia (he belongs to the small contingent of iPad owners); which sect was which, he'd already forgotten. "Yes, well, nobody really knows. Not even those folks themselves."

I am very happy that the Catholics and Protestants

buried the hatchet a good while ago and that we in the Netherlands don't have to deal with the most extreme of the Christian Bible-thumpers. In Zeeland and the Veluwe region we still have some strict Calvinists who are forbidden to watch the telly except in secret, but they don't really bother anyone. I have no use for Islamic fundamentalists, and Ali and Abu can get stuffed as far as I'm concerned.

Monday, March 30

In spite of the stormy weather, Geert and I went for a drive through Waterland once the worst downpours finally let up a bit. We scanned the ditches to see if we could spot the first mama duck with her ducklings all in a row. Since I was paying more attention to the ditch than to where I was going, I swerved off the bike path, coming to an abrupt stop in the deep mud on the verge. I almost went flying over the handlebars into the muck, but was just able to hold on. Got off scot-free, though a bit shaken, but my steed was stuck fast in the mud. Thirty feet ahead, Geert nearly split his sides laughing at my flummoxed face as I looked around for help. In the end I was forced to climb off my perch and wade through the sucking clay to the path. There we stood, Geert and I, staring helplessly at a stranded scooter.

After a few minutes a car drew up beside us. A farmer, from the way he was dressed—boots, overalls and cap—got out.

"It's a good thing I'm wearing my wellies," he grunted.

I started on a longwinded explanation of how it had happened, but that didn't interest him much. Without further ado, he began pushing and pulling.

"That's good and stuck, that is."

In the end he attached a chain to my scooter and used his car to pull it out of the mud very carefully.

"There you are, then," he said, nodding at my steed. I started thanking him profusely, but he didn't consider it necessary.

"Yeah, it's okay now. Cheerio." He raised a hand as big as a shovel, climbed back in his car, and drove off.

"It would have made a better photo if he'd been in a tractor," Geert chuckled.

We turned and rode home. I was still a little shaken. At home we raised a glass of cognac to the fortunate outcome. Evert almost fell out of his wheelchair laughing when I told him. He pointed at my feet: tell-tale mud tracked all over the carpet, and my good Sunday shoes hardly recognizable under all the sludge.

Actually, I have no idea when the first ducklings are supposed to emerge from their eggs. Not until May, maybe?

Tuesday, March 31

Old people have an above-average fondness for *vla*, or custard pudding. It's nice and sweet, inexpensive, and you don't need your teeth in order to eat it. Vanilla and chocolate custard are high on the list, but the indisputable favorite is *vlaflip*, which is like trifle. All those new-fangled puds, if you ask us, are just stupid fads.

In many a room the little fridge always contains a carton of custard, for when you're feeling peckish. And the kitchenware drawer always has an old-fashioned bottle-scraper spatula. It's a pity that the custard doesn't come in glass bottles anymore, but in cartons. If only the cartons were round; then you'd still be able to flick out the last remnants, but they're square, so there's always some custard stuck in the corners. True penny-pinchers will cut the carton open to scrape up the very last spoonful.

These important aspects of the pudding conundrum were raised at teatime, in response to a report about a new coating for the inside of food cartons.

"Won't it leave bits of lubricant in your pudding?" wondered Mrs. Van Diemen.

The word "lubricant" generated some appalled looks; Mrs. Van Diemen blushed.

No, we're not that keen on those new cartons. Especially not if everything tastes of lubricant from now on.

People are longing for warmer weather, but the spring is hesitant. The bulbs are starting to push up everywhere, but they're not in much of a hurry. Young sunlight on old bones is one of the best antidotes to depression. It's as effective as the pills many of the residents swallow to keep their spirits up a bit. Too much sun isn't desirable either, of course. It's a delicate balance; the window of happiness is but narrow.

Wednesday, April 1

"Right, I know, I know, my shoe is untied. I still know what day it is, you know." Two minutes later, Mr. Dickhout tripped over his shoelace. His fall was broken by a planter, but his collision with the sansevieria left him with a nasty cut.

The sansevieria, or "mother-in-law's tongue," has brilliantly outlived every plant fad of the past forty years here. You can't kill them. Evert once experimented with killing a sansevieria in an orange pot dating from the 1960s, but with little success. He tried putting it out of its misery by feeding it coffee, soy sauce, and bock beer, although in inconspicuous amounts, to avoid detection. The soy sauce seemed to have the most effect, because a couple of those long pointy leaves did turn brown, but it went on sending up new shoots all the same. Evert gave up in the end. This mother-in-law wasn't worth risking a temporary banishment from the home. That was the punishment he once received for sticking some cups and saucers together with superglue. It created a huge mess, because people tried pulling the cup and saucer apart with the coffee still in it. Mrs. De Roos, arriving on the scene, spotted a tube of superglue sticking out of Evert's pocket. Even Evert saw no point in trying to deny it. He was banned from the premises for a week, forced to spend seven long days cooped up in his sheltered flat.

I went to visit him several times, of course. Even he had to concede the joke had gone a bit off the rails.

"It was never my intention for anyone to burn themselves on the hot coffee, naturally," he admitted.

"But it *was* rather to be expected," I said primly, letting out the schoolmaster who forever resides inside me. I wasn't headmaster of a primary school for thirty-five years for nothing.

Thursday, April 2

Mrs. Hoensbroek leaves at 9:30 sharp every day for the HEMA down the street. There she buys one napoleon. Snow, ice, or Code Orange or Red are the only reasons she'll stay home; for those rare occasions she keeps a couple of napoleons in the freezer compartment. At 10:15 a.m. she sits down at a table in the lounge and unwraps her little cake. Then she waits until the tea lady arrives with the coffee, about 10:30 a.m. Only after she's had her first sip of coffee does she pick up her cake fork and start tackling a corner of her napoleon. The pink top layer fails to give way, so that the pudding layer is squeezed out on all sides. Then she tries the other end, with the same result. Next Mrs. Hoensbroek decides to pick up the cake with her fingers and takes a little nibble. That works, although it does dribble blobs of yellow pudding all over the tablecloth and her dress, which she calmly proceeds to scrape off with her coffee spoon. Finally she licks the pink icing from her sticky fingers. Sedately, one finger at a time.

"You just can't win, can you, with a napoleon," said Mr. Helder. And after a short pause, "The same goes for mimeo machines." He's right: you always end up smeared with either pudding or ink.

Mr. Helder is a wise man, and a nice bloke too. The next time someone in the club dies, I'll propose him as a new member.

There are some inmates who get frightfully annoyed at the daily napoleon ritual. They could, of course, go and sit at another table, but it isn't that simple; it's *their* table, after all. They were sitting there every morning long before Hoensbroek first decided to join them. Earlier this week one of them asked, "Can't you take your napoleon and go sit somewhere else?"

"I certainly can," she answered with a tight little laugh, "but I won't."

On Queen's Day the residents used to receive a festive orange napoleon. The filling would squirt everywhere, all over the carpets, and get stuck in the gray hair. Shortly after Willem-Alexander was crowned king, the director discontinued the napoleons. People are still expressing outrage about it, but not when she's within earshot.

Friday, April 3

"Have you heard? The English queen's palace staff are going on strike."

No, I hadn't heard. The loyalists among us are terrified that Elizabeth may soon have to clean her own toilet-throne and mop the floor on her royal knees.

I wonder if she's ever carried a pail of soapy water? Fetched a loaf of bread from the bakery? Maybe she's never even had to make her own sandwich.

It appears that the exorbitantly wealthy British queen

pays her staff below the minimum wage. I mustn't rush to judgment, however, since all this information comes from the gossip in the lounge, hardly a reliable source.

On Good Friday you don't see very many gaily colored frocks. The prevailing mood is dark. This afternoon there's a special service in the meditation room, which draws many of the residents every year. I may even join them this afternoon. On religious holidays the old priest and the old vicar team up. Ever since the vicar confessed to me that he no longer believes in God, we've had a special bond, atheists among ourselves. We'll occasionally get together over a bottle of wine, with art and food the main topics of discussion. He is extremely well versed in both. His specialty is films dealing with food. Sub-specialty: glamourous film stars. Most of his favorite leading ladies are dead, which sometimes makes him a bit melancholy, but the most beautiful one of all is still alive.

"Claudia Cardinale would be a reason to start believing in God again, if I were permitted to spend just one afternoon in her company when I got to heaven."

After the service, we have a special activity: Easter egg painting in the recreation room. The eggs are rather on the small side for the shaky motor skills of most of the artists, but the participants are kind when they judge one another's work. Someone will say, "Very whimsical," not, "What's that supposed to be?"

Saturday, April 4

Yesterday afternoon a little girl was wandering down the corridor with her doll and pram. She opened my door, stepped inside, and said, "Hello, Mr. Grandpa."

"Hello, miss, what's your name?"

"I'm not a miss, I'm Frida."

I said I thought it was a beautiful name, and asked if she had come to visit me. No, she was just giving her doll a tour of the home. Picking up her doll, which turned out to have just one leg, she carried it about the room, pointing out things it should look at.

I asked her how old she was, and who she was visiting. She was six, and Mrs. Quint was her granny.

I would have liked to ask how such a delightful little girl could possibly have such an old sourpuss for a granny, but I didn't, naturally. We spent a little while chatting. Silvia was her favorite doll, and she loved pancakes.

I said I loved pancakes too, and that my best friend also only had one leg. It didn't bother Frida.

"What do you like best about yourself?" she suddenly asked.

"Well, uh, I've never really given it much thought, to tell you the truth."

She cocked her head sideways and looked at me quizzically. To give myself some time to think, I asked what she liked best about herself.

"That I have a little brother. Do you have a little brother?"

"Oh, *here* you are!" Frida's mother stomped in through the open door with a great deal of noise, grabbed the child by the hand, and dragged her off. A little nod in my direction was the least she might have done. But no.

"Well, Frida, I very much enjoyed your visit," I said as the girl was being tugged out of the room. She looked over her shoulder and waved.

"See you next time," she sang out.

Sunday, April 5

It's Easter and we have Easter brunch later this morning. Every deviation from the daily routine causes a great deal of upset and confusion. A meal that's neither breakfast nor lunch, for instance.

"When exactly are you supposed to eat, then?" asked Mrs. Smit.

No one really knew.

"How about just eating whatever you like, whenever you feel like it?" Antoine suggested.

Well, nobody had thought of that option, but it might be a good idea.

The prohibition against eating too many eggs was recently lifted. It appears that whole cholesterol thing isn't all it was cracked up to be. One egg more or less doesn't make that much of a difference, according to the latest guidelines. Convenient, isn't it, coming so close to Easter. Mr. Bakker has announced that he will attempt to beat his personal best of six eggs in one sitting.

Yesterday I spotted my first two ducklings. Which means that I won the bet. Geert presented me with a chocolate

Easter bunny. We finished it between us. At this stage we aren't too worried about our weight. Geert is fat and I am thin, and that's unlikely to change very much anymore.

What do I like best about myself? The question has been preying on my mind ever since Frida asked me yesterday, although it has never in my eighty-five years occurred to me before. An important question nonetheless. Especially when combined with the opposite: What do you like least about yourself?

I'll ignore external features, such as big ears or bow legs. Or even nice gray hair. I'll confine myself to character traits. It isn't easy to give an honest answer. I wish I had a chance to talk it over with Frida.

Monday, April 6

This afternoon, Easter Monday, I'll take off when all the children and grandchildren come to visit their relatives. I shall go for a ride by myself, since Geert is expecting his daughters. The weather is nice enough to stay away for a good while. I'll head for the Twiske, a modest but bucolic nature reserve between Oostzaan and Landsmeer. I'll have to be careful, however: the bicycle paths will be congested. There's a café to the north with a waterside terrace, where I'll treat myself to a cup of coffee and a slice of Easter cake. So as not to feel sorry for myself. It's a bit lonesome, really.

It is high time for another Old But Not Dead outing

again, and fortunately there's one in the pipeline for next Wednesday. Antoine and Ria are the organizers. An endearing pair. After fifty-eight years of marriage, you'll still find them side by side on the sofa, holding hands. Sometimes, seeing that happy couple, their bond undiminished by age, I worry about the day one of them dies and leaves the other behind alone and broken-hearted.

I am in a bit of a funk these days. Maybe I should ask the doctor for a pill to jolly me up a bit. Maybe all I have to do is wait for the season to change. It's not unusual for me to feel tired and low in the spring.

I really find myself a bit stumped by that question: What do I like, or dislike, most about myself? I'll bring it up with Evert this afternoon, over our paschal cocktail. The best thing about Evert is that he always gives it to you straight. Less pleasant is his tendency to overdo it a bit when he's had a few too many. So it's a question of timing.

Tuesday, April 7

Diederik Johannes Maximilianus Govert baron van Slingelandt is a name that does not give one an immediate sense of kinship, of being one of us.

"We should ask him to spell it for us," said Leonie.

Diederik is the banker who wanted to give the directors of ABN Amro, the national bank, a raise of €100,000. Most Dutch people consider €100,000 a bit over the top.

But there are always bigger fish in the sea: the American

financier Stephen Schwarzman made over a billion dollars last year, Graeme informed us.

"For doing what, for God's sake?" Mr. Pot wished to know.

Something to do with "private equity."

Graeme, who likes playing with numbers, then calculated that this Schwarzman could spend in one day what the residents in our home, all taken together, would spend over the course of three years. "Approximately."

Schwarzman thinks his salary is totally justified. I think he should be locked up in a loony bin as a megalomaniac. Let him have as much bread and water as he wants.

When I asked Evert yesterday what he liked most about me, he frowned.

"Hmm . . . Well, your genuine interest in and consideration for others," he said at last, having pondered the question for quite a while.

I could live with that.

"And least?"

Evert didn't need any time to think that one over. "That you can sometimes be a gutless, slobbering brownnoser."

Gulp. And here I was under the impression that I'd been making such great strides in that regard.

"And what about *my* worst and best qualities?" Evert asked.

"You're a great boorish lout who cares about other people."

Then we drank a toast to our flaws.

Wednesday, April 8

Devout Mrs. Van Dalen, following in her Lord's footsteps, gave up the ghost on Good Friday. Her death created a bit of a scandal, since she'd been out cold in her room for four whole days before she was found. Her neighbor had noticed she was missing on Easter Sunday, and finally decided to check on her on Tuesday morning. Van Dalen had slipped off her chair, and was lying on the floor "as if she'd decided to take a nap under the table."

Since the rooms don't get cleaned during the holidays, and since Van Dalen was quite independent otherwise, no one had been in her room for several days. An attendant did knock on her door twice, but when no one answered, she assumed Mrs. Van Dalen was downstairs having coffee. Mrs. Van Dalen was one of those residents who, like me, never had visitors, or the alarm would have been raised sooner.

There's nothing in the regulations about leaving residents dead in their room for four whole days unnoticed. Stelwagen has "paid a few friendly visits" to try to hush it up and contain the gossip.

She acted as if it was the deceased's fault, and not the staff's. I briefly considered making a stink about it, but on second thought I didn't think it would help anyone. The attendants may have been a bit remiss, true, but in the big bad world outside, old people are sometimes discovered in their own homes months after they've died. With some 200,000 old people living by themselves in the Netherlands, it's rather to be expected.

This afternoon there's another Old But Not Dead Club outing. Ria and Antoine are the leaders, so I am expecting something to do with food.

Such a shame about Gertrude Weaver. She was able to enjoy her status as the oldest person in the world for just one short week before she died. She was 116. That's a record which, by its very nature, you can't hang on to for very long. We'll all just have to learn to live with that fact.

A hundred and sixteen, please don't let me live that long.

Thursday, April 9

Yesterday's Old But Not Dead outing was a sweet-treat extravaganza. Ria and Antoine had organized a truffle-making workshop for us. There's actually quite a lot that goes into making those posh chocs. Rather fiddly work, not our strongest suit. A good number of the delicacies wound up looking like chunks of peanut brittle, where a nice smooth, symmetrical shape would have been preferred. And the creamy filling would sometimes squirt out in unintended directions. It didn't really matter, since the best way to clean up the mistakes was to pop them in your mouth. After two and a half hours of fiddly mess-making, we were left with a rather nice collection of about twenty reasonably competent creations. Of course for what it cost us, we could have bought twenty pounds of chocolates at the confectioner's, but where's the fun in that?

By the end of the afternoon we were all more than ready for some alcoholic refreshment. But after eating all that chocolate, we decided to skip the usual order of *bitterballen*.

Thanks to the lovely weather, the garden will be unlocked "as an exception" a week early. Thanks a lot, Mrs. Stelwagen. It's not at all clear why it's locked in the winter in the first place. Perhaps they're afraid of residents freezing to death out there unnoticed. The garden belongs to the home, so blame for a frozen oldie would be laid at the director's door. There's a big difference between wanting to be in charge, and wanting the responsibility. A thick book of rules and regulations was devised to shift the blame for any accidents on to the lowest-rung employees. One of those rules stipulates that the garden is to be opened to the residents on April 15. And here we are a week early! How wonderfully flexible on the part of management! This afternoon the outdoor temperature is expected to be sixty-four degrees, little chance therefore that anyone will freeze to death.

Friday, April 10

During yesterday's Old But Not Dead outing it struck me that Evert has lost weight. I mentioned it to him in the evening, over coffee, but he said looks were deceiving. He was feeling fine.

Fifteen minutes before the doors to the garden were slated to open yesterday, a small throng of residents had already gathered there. There was some pushing and shoving. No sign of elderly courtesy. The nurse with the key had to squeeze her way through to the doors. When these were flung open, the residents charged, like old cows that have been shut in the barn all winter being released to frolic in the meadow. The crowd swarmed into the garden at a geriatric trot. I assumed it was out of enthusiasm for sun and nature, but it turned out that they were racing to capture a spot on one of the park benches. Mrs. Slothouwer pushed Mrs. Schaap into the bushes in order to snare the last free seat. Schaap was close to tears. She wasn't the only one: five other residents were likewise too slow to score a seat for themselves. Crestfallen, they paced back and forth in the vicinity of the benches. Slothouwer, to the great delight of her many enemies, had miscalculated, however: she'd forgotten to visit the toilet first, and she suddenly needed to go urgently. She was forced to choose: get up and lose her spot, or wet her pants. She stood up, gnashing her teeth. Mrs. Schaap was awarded the vacated spot and plopped down in it, beaming. Slothouwer did not return.

Mr. Helder thought he had found a solution to the bench shortage: he started lugging a dining room chair outside, but Mrs. De Roos of housekeeping stopped him.

"Where are we going with that chair, Mr. Helder?"

"The garden?" he squeaked.

"No, out of the question. Imagine, if everyone started dragging chairs about."

"I'll bring it back, I promise," he tried.

But that wasn't the point, said De Roos.

Saturday, April 11

I find myself increasingly unable to come up with words I *know* exist and express precisely what I want to say. Not until long afterward, when I've had to resort to "*you* know," will the right word pop out of its cubbyhole in my brain. By that time I no longer have any use for it.

It's even worse with names.

Little kids who don't know another child's name will simply say, "Hey, boy," or "Hey, girl," but if I want some lady who's been living down the corridor from me for years to pass me the sugar, I can hardly say, "Hey, you," can I? The fact that many residents have the same problem is scant consolation.

As his presidency wore on, Ronald Reagan resorted more and more frequently to fillers like "you know" or "thing." Researchers have closely analyzed his speech patterns in hundreds of his off-the-cuff answers to journalists' questions. The conclusion is that linguistic rustiness may be a precursor to Alzheimer's disease. With Reagan, the Americans very nearly had a president with dementia. And we may yet see the first granny president, because Hillary Clinton is about to announce her candidacy. Nearly seventy! What *is* that woman thinking?

For my next turn at planning the Old But Not Dead outing, I am thinking of a visit to the Kröller-Müller Museum in High Veluwe National Park. My favorite museum; has been for years. Haven't been there in years either. It's a scenic ride, and as far as I can recall, wheelchair- and elderly-friendly. And it has a wonderful sculpture garden. Since the success of the latter is rather dependent on the weather, I shall ask to have flexibility for the date at our next club meeting. In the meantime I'll ask Edward's nephew Edwin if he'll sacrifice a day to act as escort for the Old But Not Dead gang, in exchange for food, drink, and gratitude. And a strictly no-whining busload guaranteed.

Sunday, April 12

"No Dutch celebrities seem to be dying this year," Mr. Pot remarked.

"What about Hugo Walker, then?" I said.

"Who's that?" someone asked.

"See? That's what I mean," said Pot. "If a celebrity does happen to die, we've never even heard of them."

Last week we had two funerals and one cremation at the home, so it's not as if we're slowing down in that department. I no longer attend these. I'm not in a mood to sit and watch my own funeral. I prefer to stick my head in the sand. Some of the other residents can never seem to get enough of it, they have to say goodbye to every single dear departed, even if they've never exchanged so much as a word with them when they were alive. I suspect some of them only go for the cake. Not long ago I heard someone complain that they served Bastogne biscuits instead of cake at the cremation. Not very surprising, really, but it does show there's something that's even worse than funeral cake.

"They were rock-hard, those Bastognes," the complainer

added. "I always let them sit in the cupboard until they get soft, myself."

Nods of agreement around the table.

I have left written instructions that after I am laid in the ground I want the wine and liquor to flow freely. I've entrusted the document with my last wishes to Evert, and am sure that he will carry out that part, at least, to the letter. For the financial arrangements I have opened a joint account in his name. Evert has a son and daughter-in-law who will arrange his funeral, but I have no one. I'd rather Stelwagen not be involved; if she were, chances are the cake would be past the expiration date. Evert may be a bit of a loose cannon, but when it really matters, he can be relied on to take care of business, in this case my business. He has vowed to get plastered after I'm laid to rest, raising glass after glass to my health. At my expense. He's more than welcome to it.

What I just said about the cake being stale if Stelwagen arranges my funeral—that's taking it a bit too far. I take it back.

Monday, April 13

I must get a move on planning that trip to Bruges. Early June would seem to me to be a good time to go, which means I have just six weeks to pull it all together. Yesterday I asked Leonie if she would be my co-organizer, and she promptly agreed. We're having our first meeting this afternoon. Bruges, prepare thyself for the arrival of the Old But Not Dead Club!

* * *

When Mrs. Langeveld takes a bite of something, she opens her mouth long before the spoon is anywhere near it, exposing a bubble or thread of spit. Then she sticks out her tongue. This is the surface upon which the food lands before being pulled inside. Next commences the slow chewing. The mouth opens briefly every so often, allowing me to check on the mastication progress of, say, the meatball. All accompanied by slurping sounds. She sits hunched back in her chair, stretching the distance from her plate to her mouth, as well as multiplying the chances of spills along the way. For that reason a large napkin spans the area from her neck to her knees as a protective shield. Her frock stays clean, but after the meal there's usually quite a bit of spillage under the table.

Mrs. Langeveld hasn't been here for very long, and she was sitting across from me at dinner yesterday. I kept being drawn to look at her, whether I wanted to or not. This would be quite convenient if I were interested in losing a little weight, because it does spoil my appetite. I already find it hard to concentrate on my food in the company of six noisily chewing tablemates. Sometimes I think I should sit down to dinner with ear plugs in and blinkers on.

I, myself, am chewing my food extra carefully of late. I read an article in the newspaper where a scientist advised old people to keep chewing as long as they're still able. Supposedly a weakened chewing ability is linked to a weakening memory.

Free chewing gum for everyone!

Tuesday, April 14

Grandma Clinton has indeed announced her candidacy for the U.S. presidency. China was for many years ruled by men in their eighties. Since Clinton isn't even seventy yet, shouldn't I give her the benefit of the doubt? On the other hand: it's better not to trust a senior citizen who's still striving for that much power.

Yesterday, Leonie and I spent three hours trying to find the most elder-friendly hotel in Bruges. It used to be that you'd go to the Belgian tourist office, pick up a few brochures, and call it a day, but now you've got hundreds of hotels scrolling by on your computer screen, and it's hard to see the wood for the trees. Or, rather, the wood makes it impossible to spot the best tree.

We finally decided on one, and Leonie immediately picked up the phone to gauge their initial reaction to the arrival of eight elderly travelers.

"Ah, well, that's fine. Lovely," they said, and didn't seem to have a problem with it.

That was encouraging. We took the leap and reserved seven singles and one double room from the 2nd to the 4th, the week after Whitsun.

I do like Leonie. She is very thorough and great at organizing. For our trip we'll rent Stef's luxury minivan, with him as our driver. Stef is the grandson of our honorary member Grietje, who is cognitively no longer with us. Stef regrets not seeing us anymore and has offered to continue to be an Old But Not Dead Club driver, even now that his aunt is no longer able to join us. Now we have the luxury of a second chauffeur, we don't have to ask Edwin every time.

We'd like to have another person come along and lend a hand as well, because we have our work cut out for us: the lame helping the lame. Evert will ask his son Jan to sacrifice those three days and join us "in order to give me the last unforgettable days of my life." He thought that was a sufficiently persuasive way of putting it.

His son is a nice bloke, very like his old dad, so I'm sure he'll come.

Wednesday, April 15

Jan is coming along to Bruges. That's a relief. I've been acting as if it's perfectly normal for eight senior citizens to go on a little trip, but in my heart I know we mustn't be too optimistic: we're a decrepit bunch, and we need help. When we take to the road we bring a load of ailments and handicaps with us, and a whole fleet of rolling equipment. Just getting in and out of the coach takes twenty minutes. But between Jan and Stef, we'll have two helpers to keep us from careening off the rusty rails.

I'm looking forward to it again, confident that it will be a success. I had begun dreading my own plan a bit. That's a dangerous thing, dread. Dread is only a small step from the inclination to postpone something, which in turn is unpleasantly close to canceling it altogether. And, if you're looking for it, you can always find a reason to do nothing, and then before you know it you're sitting in your room staring out the window. Once you stop, you'll never get on track again. Keep moving, both literally and figuratively, until you drop dead—that's the motto.

"Bach is quite a good composer, granted, but his tunes aren't the greatest. Give me Connie Francis or Petula Clark any day."

Does Mrs. Duits think Bach is still alive, perhaps?

Someone had accidentally turned the radio to a classical station in the lounge.

Come to think of it, is Connie Francis still alive? I decided not to ask. I was afraid someone would start singing "Arrivederci Roma." There are very few people over the age of eighty who are still able to keep a tune. None in here, in any case. I am not looking forward to the opening rounds of the Elder Song Festival, starting less than a month from now.

Thursday, April 16

People still have over a week to put their names in for the Residents' Committee. No one has come forward so far. The Old But Not Dead members have done their best to dissuade potential candidates, as unobtrusively as possible.

"Oh, my, that Residents' Committee is a real wasps' nest. Nothing but aggro. I'd never want to sit on it, if I had a choice." Leonie was most persuasive. Even Ria and Antoine have temporarily dropped their principled stand against lying and deception, and given a little negative advice here and there.

I don't expect many residents will realize what's happening when, at the last moment, five members of our club suddenly put themselves forward for the position and, for want of opponents, are all chosen.

At some point Stelwagen will of course realize that the Residents' Committee has suddenly become an extension of the Old But Not Dead Club. But by then it will be too late. She'll have to put up with us for two whole years.

Friday, April 17

When, yesterday afternoon, I popped into Evert's for a glass of something or other, I caught him fiddling laboriously with a pair of red braces. I asked him why he needed braces when he was in a wheelchair.

"Even sitting in that chair, my trousers fall down," he grunted, and, quickly changing the subject, asked me what I'd have.

"How come you're losing so much weight?"

"No idea."

I suggested that he see the doctor, but according to my friend there was no need. Evert and doctors are not a good combo. During the consultation they'll sooner or later ask him about his eating and drinking habits, and that's always a bit painful.

"I'm still drinking quite a bit and I'm still eating what isn't good for me," he informed the GP as soon as he'd sat down for his last session.

"That doesn't seem very sensible, in light of your

diabetes. How much is quite a bit?" Then Evert had confessed to several bottles per week, to get it over with.

To the doctor's follow-up question as to what he meant by "what's not good for me," Evert had, he told me, "prettied it up with some fruit and veg."

I commented that it was a remarkably sensible and adult way to handle it, in light of the fact that he was losing so much weight.

"Are you starting on me now too, dear old nag? I won't hear another word about it. And now I'm going to crush you at chess."

I kindly allowed the game to end in a draw. Evert is terrible at chess. He plays the way he lives: instinctively. He just gives it a wild guess. But chess is a thinking game, not an instinctive game.

Life is also a thinking game, some of it, anyway. A good helping of instinct is vital too. And a little happiness can't hurt either.

Yes, there's the headmaster again. The headmaster is getting rather worried about his best mate.

Saturday, April 18

The shishamo, ebi yaki, and yasaka agreed with me, the maguro sushi too. Next time I'll pass on the sake and the plum wine. They gave me a spot of trouble in the night. Now, after two aspirins, I'm functioning again.

Easy on the drink next time, Groen! Drunks aren't much fun to start with, but old drunks are beyond the pale.

I have to give it to Evert: he drinks like a fish, but it's never annoying.

Our club had dinner at the Japanese restaurant Otaru somewhere near the Heineken brewery. With the exception of Ria and Antoine, it was our first introduction to Japanese cuisine. "Quite edible," was the average rating. After eighty years of Dutch fare, our palates have grown a bit dull, and no longer as open to new tastes. But it was a great evening nevertheless. Our initial attempts at mastering those fiddly chopsticks sent a few pieces of sushi flying through the air, but once we were done laughing, we politely asked for some ordinary forks, and then we didn't have any more trouble. It isn't really necessary to teach eighty-plus-year-olds too many new tricks.

"And anyway, forks, knives and spoons are just easier to handle than those little sticks. The Japanese know it too, of course, but they're too stubborn to admit it. So let them keep their chopsticks. They lost the war, after all," Graeme summarized, as he ordered a bottle of white to rinse away the taste of the sake.

The night ended on a bit of a downer, because Leonie missed a step getting out of the bus and twisted her ankle. She's been sitting with her leg up. At nine this morning Evert brought her breakfast in bed. He put it down next to the bed, red as a beetroot, then made a hasty retreat.

"Oh, Evert, how very sweet of you!" Leonie was simply beaming.

"Yeah, no trouble," and he was out the door.

So cute.

Sunday, April 19

A tidbit I never knew: there is a National Elder Trust, and there is an Ombudsman for the Aged. They don't exactly shout their existence from the rooftops; no one else had ever heard of either of them.

Perhaps they're only meant to serve the 200,000 old Dutch people living in extreme solitude. According to the newspaper, you're an extreme solitary if you don't see visitors more than a couple of times a month. (Yet you always have coffee and a biscuit on hand just in case you-never-know-who turns up.)

Elder Trust volunteers are there to pick up the lonely and take them shopping, or out for a coffee. It breaks up the month a bit. It's a pity, however, that they can't think of anything more interesting to do than take them shopping. The Trust's volunteers operate about eighty "Plus-Busses." A quick calculation tells me that each Plus-Bus driver has to take some 2,500 senior citizens shopping every month, if they're to serve all 200,000 solitary oldsters. Which means they're probably always in a rush, so you'd better not bring a long shopping list.

The increasingly restrictive criteria for admission to a care home are bound to make the number of lonely senior citizens grow. The policymakers make it sound so positive and benevolent, "to allow the elderly to remain independent for as long as possible," but what it really means is abandoning the aged to their lot as long as possible.

In our care home there's a lot of carping and complaining, but all things considered, there's more to it here than sitting at home all month long, just waiting for the Plus-Bus to take you out. If you take some initiative and are lucky enough to find a few agreeable fellow inmates, then life in an old people's home beats living independently, in lonely isolation, any day.

In a little while Geert and I will set out for our Sunday mobility-scooter spin. The sun is very bright, and spring is deliriously chipper.

Monday, April 20

Yesterday I was on the point of going for a ride with Geert when my door burst open and little Frida walked in.

"Hello, Mr. Grandpa, do you remember me?"

"Yes, you are Frida. You paid me a lovely visit two weeks ago."

"You were going to think about what you liked best about yourself," Frida said gravely.

I told her I had thought it over at length, and that the best thing about me was that I liked having lots of friends, and finding out how they are.

She nodded. "That fits you."

Frida had told me the last time that the best thing about her was that she had a little brother. I asked her what the worst thing about her was.

"That I don't have a little sister."

That made sense to me. I said that the worst thing about me was that I can be a bit of a bore.

"Oh, you're not *that* boring," she consoled me. That was kind of her.

She decided she had earned a biscuit. Fortunately I always have biscuits and chocolates on hand.

We were just contentedly nibbling on a biscuit with pink icing when her mother walked in. She nodded at me and grabbed Frida's hand.

"Come on, Granny was starting to get worried."

Out in the corridor I heard her grumble, "I *told* you not to go into other people's rooms for no reason."

"It wasn't for no reason. We had to finish talking."

"Still, I won't have it."

"But that grandpa *liked* me being there."

"That's not the point."

That little girl's visit gutted me. She brought back my grief over my own little daughter.

Apparently they are working on coming up with a forgetting pill. You can't change what happened, but you can manipulate the memory of it. I wish I had a forgetting pill so that I wouldn't have to think about my little girl's death quite as often.

Tuesday, April 21

"Imagine what would have happened if the men who escaped across the Channel to fight in the war had been sent back by the English. If the English had said: 'Take care of your own.'" Mrs. Van Diemen looked about triumphantly. It was a novel take on the boat people in the discussion about the Mediterranean migrant crisis.

Bakker, as usual, was heartless: "If they're so keen on jumping aboard a leaky old boat that's much too heavily laden, then I say it's their own fault. Tough luck if they drown."

Most of the other residents have a milder view, fortunately.

Besides, the argument that the boat refugees are being foolhardy doesn't really hold water. If the numbers in the newspaper are to be trusted, it's only about one or two percent of all the people who make the crossing who end up drowning. I expect that if they'd stayed in the terrible war zones they left behind, they'd be far more likely to die.

Besides, I don't imagine that when they're scrambling on board, the smugglers give them an honest account of their chances, or that they admit that if it becomes necessary they'll just let the boat sink.

I've noticed that two of the rooms here have been vacant for some time now. That's since Mrs. Van Dalen passed away, and her neighbor was moved into the nursing wing. The rooms were always expected to be cleared out and turned over within days of a death or departure, so that a new resident could move in promptly, usually within a week. In this case, however, it has been a few weeks and the rooms are still empty. Perhaps I'm being unduly leery, but the vacancies could signal that this home will be shutting its doors in the not-so-distant future.

I'm keeping my mouth zipped about it at coffee time. I don't want to be responsible for setting off a panic among the inmates.

Once we have taken over the Residents' Committee, we'll ask the director for clarification. The application window for a seat on the committee closes in three days.

Graeme, Geert, Leonie, Ria, and I will throw our names into the hat on April 24.

Wednesday, April 22

There are some residents who visit the Albert Heijn supermarket on a regular basis. Not to do any shopping, mind, but to partake in the free coffee they have there. The coffee at home in the lounge is also free, but drinking the supermarket's free coffee makes it doubly so. There they'll take a seat next to one or two Moroccan housewives, the odd vagrant, or some neighborhood bag lady. You really have to want it badly, that free cuppa. No matter how much I may be in the mood for a coffee, I don't see myself ever sitting with that lot.

The trip to Bruges is taking shape. I've taken a book out of the library about the city, and we should have no trouble at all filling up two whole days. An important stop on the tour will be the world's only *frites* museum, where I have no doubt we will be served the mother of all chips, or *frites*, in the traditional paper cone.

We will also attempt to fold our creaky old bodies into a small sightseeing boat. I saw photos of those boats in the book, and couldn't help thinking of the boat refugees, with such a crush of tourists on board. I shall keep that thought to myself when it's our turn. I can't guarantee, however, that the same thought won't occur to Evert, or that he won't discuss it at length with his Japanese fellow passengers.

Mrs. Lacroix, our self-described performance artist, has

announced her candidacy for the Residents' Committee. That's a bit of a spanner in the works. If she ends up being chosen, the Old But Not Dead Club will no longer have a monopoly. But that may be all for the best, "for appearances' sake," said Graeme with a grin.

He is right, it's better for there to be one board member who isn't in our club. Just one; no more, please.

Thursday, April 23

At coffee yesterday, Mr. Verlaat let slip in passing that he has decided not to sue the home about its refusal to let him keep his little dog. It was his elder sister who'd put him up to it, but in the end it would have cost too much in lawyers' fees. It isn't clear if the sister was simply motivated by wishing to see justice done, or if she saw it as the only way to be rid of her brother's dog, which now has to live with her.

"There must surely be a cheaper and easier way to get rid of a dog," I said to Evert later, grinning. That touched a nerve.

"Shut up, Groen, or I'll set Mo on you."

From the corner where Mo was lolling came a deep, almost human sigh. As if the dog was keen to underscore the hopeless futility of that threat.

"An ape, if I'm not mistaken, was recently deemed by some judge to have the same rights as a person, so why can't a dog have human rights?" Evert went on.

I asked him how he felt about human rights for mosquitoes.

"You are right, it isn't clear where we should draw the line," he admitted.

It's fine by me if old people want to bring their dog or cat to the care home, as long as they don't bother the other residents, but I am sure there are some people here who would insist on a place at the table for their pet. Next thing you know, you'll find yourself seated opposite several dogs and cats and their proud owners, who can talk about nothing else but their four-legged friend. It's ludicrous, the human traits dog and cat lovers ascribe to their animals.

"No, Rover's a bit sad right now because the ginger biscuits are all gone."

I keep hearing dog owners in the park tell joggers they meet, "Don't be scared, they can smell it on you if you're scared."

And then the runner will of course think, "Oh fine, in that case I just won't be scared!"

Friday, April 24

I try to avoid the rush hour as much as possible. The one thing people here have too much of (leaving aside physical ailments for now) is time, yet they are constantly checking their watches: time is time, after all. Time for coffee, time for lunch, time for tea or dinner. In order to be on time for a meal, they have to give themselves at least twenty extra minutes, to allow for having to queue for the elevator. Until recently I too tended to live by the clock, but with some application, I have managed to let go of it. Now I stick my head out the door to see if there's a queue for the elevator. If not, I'm on my way, otherwise I just pick up my book or newspaper and wait it out.

Evert comes and goes when he feels like it.

"I don't have a watch, I have the time," he likes to say—a bit too often.

He doesn't mind if the coffee hour is over by the time he trundles in. He's just as happy to come upstairs to my room for a cup of instant. He has also stopped asking for "something extra" during the day, and that doesn't mean a ginger biscuit. He knows I don't drink before 4 p.m. He does sometimes steal a glance at my watch. If I catch him doing it, I turn my wrist away.

"You have time, don't you, Evert?"

"I have all the time in the world, only sometimes more thirst than time."

"Just half an hour to go, mate, then I'll pour you a shot of lemon gin."

That's the only drink he doesn't like.

During the discussion about rejected asylum seekers being entitled to "bed-bath-and-bread" assistance, many residents objected to the "bath" part.

"I have never in all my life had a bath, and now they're saying all those refugees are entitled to one."

Graeme explained it could be a shower instead.

"What about a washbasin, wouldn't that do?" Mrs. Van Diemen wanted to know.

Someone else was of the opinion that before any bath, bed, or bread, they should be given life vests, for when they're sent packing in those dodgy boats.

Saturday, April 25

Our plan has for the most part succeeded!

Yesterday at the last minute five Old But Not Dead members threw their hats in the ring for the Residents' Committee. Mrs. Lacroix was the only other person who had applied. I don't think we'll have too much trouble getting her to go along with our plans. We had a celebratory meeting last night at which Geert volunteered to withdraw his own candidacy.

"That way there doesn't have to be an election. And it's not my thing, really, sitting on a committee."

Geert is right about that. He is a man of few words. So few that he'd just be sitting there like the sphinx. Geert is more of a doer.

Now there are exactly five candidates for five seats on the committee; therefore everyone is elected. Evert brought the bubbly, Ria and Antoine supplied the refreshments, and I contributed a speech that consisted of snippets of famous orators' speeches, including Obama's, which I had plucked from the Internet and pieced together. My fellow club members were at first very impressed by my eloquence, until I tossed in "I have a dream . . . " That's when they began growing suspicious. By the time I'd started on "*Ich bin ein Berliner*," Evert threw a cushion at me.

I can't wait to see Stelwagen's face when she meets the new Residents' Committee for the first time. There is already a buzz of conspiratorial excitement in the air. We're ready for our first sting operation or, rather, a pinprick operation. But still.

The first action items, in no particular order, are:

1. A monthly high tea, provided for and by the residents. Evert wanted to call it "Death to the Ginger Biscuit!" but his suggestion was voted down as being too provocative. We're going to ease into it calmly.
2. A special table in the conversation lounge where the weather and physical ailments are off limits.
3. Investigation into the room vacancies. Are there plans afoot to close this institution?
4. Streamlining of rollator traffic to prevent bottlenecks.
5. More garden benches.
6. Discussion with Cook about the possibility of more adventurous fare once a week.
7. The pet policy.
8. The rules and regulations. For instance, we believe it is a fundamental human right to be allowed to decide how many hooks are needed to hang stuff up on the walls in your room.

The list of action items is bound to grow longer. I hope we aren't biting off more than we can chew.

Sunday, April 26

Some orange napoleons have been spotted in shopping bags. As well as some orange cream cakes. The home used to distribute orange pastries on Queen's Day until the queen abdicated two years ago. Now we have King's Day, and a king who happens to be a descendant of the House of Orange as well. The director's decision to end the orange pastry tradition has given rise to some bad blood.

It was a rare dumb move on the part of the normally strategic Stelwagen. Stocking up on those napoleons from the HEMA will only set you back a few euros; you can't buy goodwill cheaper than that. Tomorrow, many a resident will come shuffling downstairs with one orange napoleon on a plate in their rollator's basket. There are also some who, fortunately, aren't as stingy, and are charitable enough to share their orange cakes with some of the others. Afterward everyone gathers in front of the telly to watch the king. Secretly hoping against hope that he'll break his vow not to have any *koekhappen* at his party.

"Cake-biting is such an important royal family tradition," someone sighed yesterday.

"Indeed," said Leonie, "if there's to be no *koekhappen*, what else is there to do?"

I think I'll go for a nice long ride tomorrow.

Monday, April 27

I've decided to join my House of Orange–loving compatriots downstairs later to watch the royal family's procession through Dordrecht for an hour or so after all. I am no great supporter of the monarchy, but I still can't help gazing with a mixture of tenderness and pity at the king and queen, princes and princesses, for having to put up with all the nonsense. I'll make sure I sit next to Evert, who always enjoys the opportunity to enrage as many fellow residents as possible. Never deliberately, it goes without saying.

I am for an elected monarchy. Elections held every five

years to choose a new king or queen. No one should be allowed to serve more than one term. The winner would have just five years to cut ribbons, ride in a golden carriage, read the King's or Queen's Speech, and live in a palace. I suspect the Dutch populace, having no imagination, would just plump for Willem Alexander and Maxima, our current pair, again.

Mrs. Van Hooidonk woke up the other day and said to her husband, "Cor, Jan, you're so cold!" He did not answer. He was dead.

She's been telling everyone who'll listen: "I says to my husband, 'Cor, Jan,' says I, 'you're so cold!' "

Mrs. Van Hooidonk has dementia. Her Jan had been keeping her in check and out of the locked ward with great patience and devotion. He used to have one night off a week, when his daughter came to babysit so that he could play billiards. That's how I know him. He was a nice, modest chap who never complained.

Mrs. Van Hooidonk is hopelessly confused and will probably be given a one-way ticket to the locked ward very shortly.

Tuesday, April 28

Evert had two names for Princess Alexia: Princess Dyslexia or Princess Anorexia.

People kept throwing him dirty looks.

"Those little princesses seem to have inherited their daddy's chubby cheeks too," he remarked.

"So in that case you shouldn't call her Anorexia," the lady seated next to Evert snapped, scooting a little distance away from him.

I took a good look at our king. Willem Alexander looked pained. The smile wasn't real. The waving wasn't real. Nothing was real. The same went for the rest of the dignitaries. Not only was every hat, every dress, every shoe a deliberate calculation; every step they took seemed rehearsed.

Those little princesses are the only ones for whom there may yet be hope. Their waving was a bit lackluster, their heads turned the other way. Their childish honesty will be knocked out of them soon enough though, mark my words.

And for the first time in sixty years, the Queen Mum, Princess Beatrix, is putting her feet up in front of the telly at home. From time to time she waves at the screen. It's a reflex.

Yesterday afternoon Geert and I rode our scooters over to Ransdorp and all of a sudden found ourselves slap bang in the middle of the Orange parade. A moment of inattention and we were hemmed in between two festively decorated farm vehicles and had to follow the procession. We promptly acquired some fans, who insisted we try our hand at jousting on our scooters. And so we did. The spectators loudly cheered us on. Geert captured a respectable fourth place, and of course we had to drink to that. We had quite a few drinks, in fact. It was lucky we didn't encounter any police checkpoints on the way home. Geert and I agreed: this was the best Queen's Day we'd had in many years. Long live the king.

Wednesday, April 29

Last night I asked Evert where he was yesterday afternoon, as I'd stopped by for a game of chess and found only Mo. He replied that he'd gone for a little constitutional in his wheelchair.

"Aren't you fibulating a bit, Evert?" (I just made up a new verb: *to fibulate*.)

"Huh?"

"Are you fibulating me?"

He stared at me, nonplussed.

"Fibulating is telling fibs you even start believing yourself. It's a common condition in Alzheimer's patients," I said.

"What *are* you talking about?"

I told him I happened to have seen the Connexxion minibus drop him off, wheelchair and all, at about 4 p.m. There was a brief silence.

"Okay, Henk," he finally said, "since you insist: I went to see the doctor."

After a great deal of insistence on my part, he finally admitted that for the past few months he'd been losing about two pounds every two to three weeks, and if that were to continue, he'd be down to zero pounds eighteen months from now.

The GP had referred him to an internist.

"That will set me back a few pounds," he said with a grin.

He made me promise to keep my mouth shut about it.

I did not sleep well.

Thursday, April 30

"We live in a land of milk and honey," said Mrs. Hoensbroek.

"I don't like milk, and I don't like honey either, come to think of it," said Mr. Bakker.

Bakker is an eternally dissatisfied fellow. Mrs. Hoensbroek is a woman who is always content. She once tried to return the portion of her state pension that was left unspent at the end of the month, slipping two twenty-euro bills in an envelope addressed to the government and putting it in the post. It created bureaucratic mayhem. It took months for those forty euros to find their way back into Mrs. Hoensbroek's bank account. The entire operation must have cost the state hundreds.

As far as the land of milk and honey goes: we have dropped from fourth to seventh place in the ranks of happiest countries in the world. Overtaken by Finland, Canada, and Iceland. Switzerland is number one. All of Scandinavia is in the top ten. Africa isn't doing so well. Of the twenty unhappiest nations in the world, seventeen are in Africa. It's no wonder, then, that quite a few Africans come looking for happiness in Western Europe. The numbers are from the 2015 World Happiness Report.

I don't know which politician I trust less: Bram Moszkowicz or Henk Krol. It's amazing how many votes they stand to receive, going by the latest polls. It's always astonished me to see the wide support clowns and crooks are able to muster. Watching old newsreels of that loudmouth Mussolini, you'd think, now *there's* a bloke only his mother could love. But no, millions of Italians loved him.

Friday, May 1

> The Director's Office and Board of Trustees are pleased to congratulate the new members of the Residents' Committee:
>
> Mrs. L. Van der Horst
> Mrs. R. Travemundi
> Mrs. E. Lacroix
> Mr. H. Groen
> Mr. G. Gorter
> We trust that we will have a fruitful collaboration.
> Mrs. F. H. Stelwagen, MA, Director

This brief missive was distributed to all the residents this morning. Mrs. Stelwagen, MA, did not bother wasting too many words on us. We are having our first official meeting this evening at 7:30 and have been assigned a conference room downstairs. I'm especially curious to see what E. Lacroix has to say for herself. What kind of ideas does our fifth committee member have? Is she good for a laugh? Does she enjoy a glass of wine or two? And what does that E stand for?

There's all sorts of gossip about the new resident. Our first Turk. They say he's a Muslim. A rumor immediately started going around that from now on there would be a halal choice on the menu.

I did a quick Internet search on halal (good) and haram (forbidden) food, and came to the conclusion that it's all a bit complicated. All kinds of things are prohibited: pork, of course, but they're not allowed to eat any carnivores either. Or any animal that has died a natural death, hasn't been bled to death, is nursing, or is an insect (a Muslim on a bicycle had best keep his mouth clamped firmly shut). Shrimp are problematic; one Muslim sect says you can have a shrimp cocktail, another says you can't. Not all Muslims agree about roasted mule either. One thing is certain: Cook won't know his way around all those rules.

What is it about gods and their daft diet restrictions? Don't they have anything better to do than to make food preparation more complicated than necessary? Let them pay more attention to the commandment against murder and manslaughter for a start. And get *on* with it please!

"My god forbids me to eat Brussels sprouts," Leonie likes to say when they're on the menu. See, now *that* is a sensible god. I can't eat oysters, but oysters are never on the menu here, so He doesn't have to go to the trouble of issuing a commandment about that.

Saturday, May 2

The E is for Eugenie, she enjoys a glass of rosé, she's good for a bit of a laugh, and her suggestions are somewhat self-serving.

Mrs. Eugenie Lacroix, besides being an artist, is a very

strange bird. She actually had no idea what kind of committee this was, but did hope that "something to do with art" could be made to happen for the residents. Her first notion was to have an art show to exhibit her own work, and then, once everyone was sufficiently inspired by that, an exhibition of the other inmates' artistic efforts.

The Old But Not Dead members exchanged glances. It couldn't do any harm. And it would buy our committee one very happy artist...

"Good idea, Mrs. Lacroix," said Ria, "that's definitely something we'll consider."

After that Eugenie didn't have much to say for herself, but, smiling benignly, managed to drain a bottle of rosé. Edward raised a glass to her more than once: "To art!"

Great. For once we don't have Evert, but find ourselves saddled with another sponge. At the end of the night she proposed a toast: "To arssht!"

The Old But Not Dead members, on the other hand, drank sparingly and had a serious discussion. An invitation has gone out for our first meeting with Stelwagen. We decided it was best not to weigh down the first agenda with too many items at once. Three is a good start.

1. The vacancy rate, and its possible consequences
2. Art exhibits for and by the residents
3. A monthly high tea to be organized by the residents

We expect quite a bit of resistance in the form of rules, regulations, and statutes. And if those don't do it, the director can always hide behind "objections made by the board."

The Turkish gentleman whose arrival had been met with some concern isn't Muslim at all. He can eat everything, halal or haram, he doesn't give a damn.

"Pass me that ham, please. Allahu Akbar."

He's Christian-Orthodox something or other, but only at Easter and Christmas, he says. The rest of the year he keeps his worship to a minimum. Nice bloke. His name is Okcegulcik, but it's possible I've got some of the letters mixed up.

Sunday, May 3

There's been yet another eavesdropping scandal. At first the Germans were spied on by the Americans, and now the Germans have helped the Americans by listening in on the French. It's France's turn to be outraged. The Russians are even more brazen. They gave the G20 heads of state a little present each: a USB stick loaded with sightseeing tips, as well as a bunch of secret hacking-thingies.

"Everyone listens in on everyone else, given the chance," was Edward's take. "And in fact the most worrying part is that we hear about it so often," he went on, "because that means there's much more of it going on which never comes out."

"If you can't see the tip, you don't know where the iceberg is," Mrs. Schansleh sighed, queen of the creative proverb.

Our home is not immune to eavesdropping or spying either. A great number of the inmates are profoundly curious. Whenever the Old But Not Dead gather around a table, some old biddy invariably comes shuffling along whose support hose just happens to need pulling up right beside us. The fact that most of the spies around here are a bit deaf and myopic makes the espionage rather less subtle than it might be. We definitely don't have any Mata Haris in here. I don't want to sound like a misogynist, but the surveillance of fellow residents is largely a female occupation. The ladies form a close-knit intelligence network of independently operating spies, out to collect juicy material for gossip and scandalmongering.

To these intelligence professionals, we are a problematic stronghold to conquer, since bugging phones or hacking computers is tough when there are so few phones or computers to break into. Lucky bastards, really. Because listening in on us would be very boring work.

Evert has been ill for several days. This means I have to take his dog out. He is being looked after by a sister from the nursing floor. I bumped into her this morning and asked how Evert was. She wasn't permitted to say, "but he's not very well."

According to Evert, it's just a touch of the flu.

Monday, May 4

The municipality of Alphen aan den Rijn has refused to provide a ninety-year-old citizen with a stair lift.

What it really means is that the council is saying that he "should have moved to the ground floor long ago, shouldn't he?"

That hasn't gone down very well here. Three of the residents have sent the mayor of Alphen aan den Rijn a stern handwritten letter. Therefore I'm sure those people in the town hall will soon see the error of their ways.

We are blessed! At least we only have to deal with Mrs. Stelwagen. If an independently living senior wants to have his windows washed, he has to deal with the Social Insurance Bank, the Central Administrative Office, various local agencies, and the Tax Authority. All for one measly grant request. With the result that one washed window may easily wind up costing €100, if you count all the bureaucrats' salaries.

Thousands of caregivers have been waiting months to be paid, courtesy of the new Health Care Law.

So: hooray for the old people's home! We enjoy a wonderfully carefree existence—at least as far as window washing goes.

Edward has asked if I'll come with him to the WW2 memorial ceremony at the war monument here in our neighborhood. I said it sounded like a good plan, but then asked him why he wanted to go. He tried his best to explain, but his aphasia is becoming more and more trying. Finally he wrote it down on a notepad: it's because he's getting so annoyed at the residents always going on about their own trivial deprivations in the war. They seem to think the poverty of their childhood, with nostalgic war stories about bicycles with wooden tires, is more compelling than Auschwitz.

Tuesday, May 5

It was a good idea to escape the home on Remembrance Day and attend the memorial ceremony in the square instead. Out in the open air (the chirping of birds and the shouts of toddlers notwithstanding), the two minutes of silence seemed quieter and far more affecting, as well as more hopeful, thanks to the considerable turnout. Afterward the local brass band played the national anthem. I was genuinely moved. Edward thanked me, but I had just as much reason to thank *him.* Back home we raised a glass to freedom, and, as if he'd smelled it, along comes Evert in his wheelchair to join us in our toast. He was still looking a bit pale, but "There's nothing that kills the bugs like a wee dram," he said. It wasn't long before our artist friend Eugenie wandered over and asked us if we wouldn't mind if she joined us for a glass of rosé.

"I have my own bottle."

We weren't that keen on her joining us, actually. Edward and I are too well brought up to tell someone she's not welcome to sit with us, but Evert has no such compunction, fortunately.

"My dear Lacroix, we do mind terribly. We're talking shop, men's business, you know. You're welcome to join us tomorrow. That is, if we happen to be discussing women's business then."

Eugenie was rather taken aback, and shuffled off.

"Isn't that a bit mean?" I sputtered.

"Stop whining, Groen; if you don't put your foot down now, you'll be saddled with a crazy artist with a drinking problem for the rest of your days. And one alcoholic in the bunch is enough. Pour me another." Evert leaned back, contented, in his wheelchair.

Wednesday, May 6

This morning I had another visit with Grietje.

"Oh, how nice! Have you come to see me?" she said, cheerful as ever. She is always happy to receive visitors, which makes it easier to bear. But a little problem has arisen of late. The moment I set foot in the nursing wing and Mrs. Van Tilburg spots me, she's all over me. She'll sit down on my lap given half a chance, so I am forced to remain standing until a nurse gently steers her away. Sometimes it takes a while, and I'm standing there having to undergo her caresses.

"Come, Mrs. Van Tilburg, you'll make your husband jealous," says the sister when she finally shows up. Then, sending me a wide, toothless smile, Van Tilburg toddles out of the lounge on the nurse's arm. Sometimes she'll turn and look back at me with a sly wink.

Grietje watches the whole performance with solemn interest.

Then we'll have a cup of tea and a macaroon. They're her favorite, and I always bring her some when I visit.

"How did you know they're my favorite?" she says every time.

"You just seemed the type who likes macaroons," I say, likewise every time.

Grietje thinks that's very funny. After twenty minutes or so, it's time to go.

"See you next time," I say.

She nods and stares at the floor, thinking.

"Yeah, see you later." She turns and picks up her magazine again. The same one she's been reading since she's been there.

Thursday, May 7

Yesterday afternoon Stef unexpectedly appeared at my door.

"Surprise! Come, let's go."

One has to use extreme caution: old people and surprises aren't a safe combination. We need time to prepare ourselves for the surprise. Mentally and physically. To be picked up on a random afternoon for an impromptu little trip can lead to stress. Not because we're so busy, mind, but because when you're old everything takes time, including getting used to the idea that you're suddenly going to *do* something. Stef, Grietje's grandson, happened to have a day off and thought to himself: "Why don't I go and fetch my old friends in the care home and take them to see the tulips? I'll just go and see who's home and who wants to go."

We were all home, and after some hesitation, we were all game. Some had to change their clothes or finish their lunch first, others had to cancel a pedicure or, in my case, change a diaper, but forty-five minutes after Stef had rung our bells, we were ready to push off.

The trip took us to the North-East Polder. We didn't even know that was bulb-growing country, but Stef had thoroughly researched this tulip route. Great expanses, larger than soccer fields, filled with tulips—red, pink, purple, yellow, and white. The oohs and aahs never died down. We stopped at a pick-your-own-tulip garden, but that was rather a stretch for us; all that bending... We only managed to gather two rather untidy bunches between us. It was also a bit of a tourist trap, as it turned out when we went to pay. The tulips were rather pricey, and even if you didn't pick any, you still had to fork out the €1.50 entrance fee. Fortunately, to make up for our sense that we'd been had, Evert and Edward smuggled out at least €15 worth of stolen tulips in the basket under Evert's wheelchair, which they produced once we were all back on the bus, and presented to Stef. The gesture was met with loud cheers.

"Where have our standards and morals gone, friends? Your layer of civilized veneer is but gossamer thin," Evert said with a wicked grin.

On the way home we made a quick stop for beer and wine and were back in time for our potato dinner at 5:45 p.m. sharp.

We were a bit dazed at having had such an unexpected holiday.

Friday, May 8

In the St. Jacob Nursing Home here in Amsterdam, university students can rent a vacant room for €350 in return for some community service, such as helping with errands, pouring coffee, accompanying a resident to church, and so on. It's only ten hours per month, and the young people are even paid two-fifty an hour, not a fortune exactly, but better than nothing. But staff have been cut since the number of residents has declined and now the students sometimes have to do night duty. They don't like that.

Could this be in store for our home as well? We've had a number of unoccupied rooms for a while now. The conditions for accepting new residents are so stringent that they can't find enough candidates. One foot in the grave, yet still too healthy for the nursing home; you don't get too many who fit into that category. The student housing shortage would be a way to solve the vacancies here and a heaven-sent gift for our treasurer when he balances the books.

Next Monday, at the Residents' Committee's first meeting with the director, we intend to bring it up with her. I am very much looking forward to it, but also a bit nervous. I can just imagine how the conversation will proceed:

"Is there a move afoot, Mrs. Stelwagen, to turn this old-age home into student housing a few years from now?"

"Most astute of you, Mr. Groen, that is indeed the plan. The board expects in the long run to see greater returns from students than from the elderly."

Saturday, May 9

I very much enjoyed sitting by the water's edge yesterday. But I'd have preferred not to catch any fish, an unusual attitude for a fisherman, naturally. Nevertheless I caught three fish on my hook, the last one by accident; I was just reeling in my line because I wanted to sit in the sun a few feet farther along, and oops, I had a shiny little fish flapping about at the end of my line. Once again Geert had to come to my rescue and pry the hook out of somewhere, I think its tail. I didn't even dare look. After that, I proceeded to dangle my line without any bait. I was finally able to relax a bit. I was just as happy watching Geert, who actually produced the biggest fish of the afternoon when his float was pulled under as he took an apple out of his bag.

"You've got one, Geert."

"I'll be damned."

A few moments later, a gorgeous fish at least nine inches long was thrashing about on the bank.

I asked Geert what kind of fish it was.

"A silvery one," my fishing chum replied.

I'm not sure if I'll go fishing with Geert again very soon.

Sunday, May 10

The temperature rose a smidgen above the sixty-eight-degree mark for the first time this year, and I overheard someone say, "It always gets so terribly muggy here in the Netherlands."

"Yes, in Spain it's different," said Mr. Pot, "that's a much more pleasant sort of heat." Pot was in Torremolinos just once in his life, back when Franco was still in power, and Pot could not rule out that that was the reason the heat wasn't as oppressive then.

I've grown more aware lately of a loss of sensation in my hands and feet. Especially when it's cold. The blood isn't reaching the old body's extremities. Either the arteries are clogged, or the pump just isn't putting enough effort into it anymore. I'll have the doctor check it, just for form's sake, but I'm afraid there isn't much to do about it except to add it to the long list of ailments I already have.

Until recently, I always thought having to wear diapers was crossing the line from a life of dignity to a life of shame. A reason to seriously consider ending it all. I have been wearing a diaper for more than a year now. It isn't something one ever gets used to, but I have moved the goalposts. That's what tends to happen: after a while, every new ailment eventually leads to acceptance. And then you cling even more tightly to the small pleasures that remain.

The day after tomorrow we dine in a Swiss restaurant. Evert has made the arrangements and told us about it this morning. If you ask me, it's his way of making himself feel a bit better.

Monday, May 11

I read somewhere that everyone makes five hundred choices or so in a day. When I looked it up on the Internet, it turns out it's actually five hundred *million*. Of those, only a few are conscious choices, but still...

It seems to me that since everything is already decided and arranged for us in here, we hardly have any choices to make. It's probably just a question of definition. If you consider the decision to stir your coffee clockwise or counterclockwise to be a choice, then the number of choices increases exponentially, but their importance does not.

It promises to be a beautiful summery day. This afternoon Ria, Antoine, and I are going to try an ice cream parlor that's just opened. We may not sample all twenty-eight flavors on this first visit, but we'll have tasted all of them by the end of the summer, and then we'll decide which was the ice cream of the year. A great project. Here you have another point of agreement between little children and old people: we all scream for ice cream.

"I can't eat another bite," you often hear people say after they've managed to work down the last bit of potato with a great deal of huffing and puffing. Wasting food is a sin, after all. Upon which the same diner will proceed to devour, with no problem and much gusto, an enormous hot fudge sundae.

Mrs. Smit's freezer compartment is full of strawberry cornettos from Aldi. She eats at least one a day. But not when she has company, because she doesn't like to share.

Tuesday, May 12

At 3:00 on the dot Mrs. Stelwagen came waltzing in. Impeccably dressed as always. Amiable as always. After shaking everyone's hand, she sat down at the table her secretary had set up.

"Welcome, everyone. I am extremely happy that, after

more than a year, this care home once again has a Residents' Committee. And not an inconsequential one either, if I may say so."

"We thank you for your kind words. As the representative body for the residents, we suggest you take up the gavel first. After all, you are most in the know about what's going on. Next time the Residents' Committee will appoint the chair. That way we can take turns." Leonie looked around the circle. If you'd listened carefully, you'd have heard our jaws drop. This hadn't come up in our preliminary discussions. Leonie had seized the initiative in order to make sure that the director would not always be chairing the meetings going forward. I thought I detected a slight pursing of Stelwagen's lips.

"It has always been customary for the director to run these meetings," she said after a brief silence.

"But in order to delegate the tasks and duties more fairly, and so to relieve you of some of the burden, we are proposing to rotate the chairmanship," said Leonie. We all nodded innocently.

"Well . . . I suppose I can accept that proposal," Stelwagen said. The noncommittal little smile was already back.

After the meeting I complimented Leonie at length on her quick-witted, astute intervention. Not having the director always in control was a great tactical move for our side. When I wondered how she'd thought of it, it turned out that Leonie has an impressive background in the care sector.

"I was a professional committee member for many years," she said, "and after a seventeen-year sabbatical, I'm in the mood again."

That promises to be good.

After that initial confrontation, the meeting proceeded in a most friendly and civil fashion. The Residents' Committee inquired about the possibility of a monthly high tea for and by the residents, and whether a space could be found to hold an exhibition of committee member Mrs. Lacroix's artwork. Stelwagen said these were "very interesting ideas" and that she would bring them to the board.

I predict that's what we can expect: we come with proposals, Stelwagen hears us out willingly, shows enthusiasm for our ideas, and then says she needs to "examine them more closely" or "bring them before the board." It's her way of stalling. I don't for a minute think that she needs the approval of the board for the high tea idea, or for an art exhibition. The Residents' Committee will have to keep up the pressure and hold her feet to the fire. Stelwagen will remain largely passive, and whenever possible put off what we ask her to do. She is a leader in the traditional conservative mold, convinced she knows better than anyone else what's good for the residents. It promises to be a long, tough, subtle fight. Only: we are in a hurry, whereas she has time on her side.

We'd saved the most important topic for last. I inquired, as nonchalantly as I could, about the vacant rooms. What was happening with those?

"I am still in discussion with the board about that."

"Could we hear about the results of your discussions at our next meeting?"

Stelwagen was certainly going to do her very best, but

she couldn't make any promises. Leonie made sure that all our points made it into the minutes.

It was decided that we would meet four times a year. The next meeting is set for August. We don't intend to stay quiet that long, however. The request for the high tea will be sent out in a couple of weeks, to test the waters.

Wednesday, May 13

The restaurant wasn't Swiss, but the dish was: cheese fondue. The minibus dropped us off at Het Blaauwhooft, a popular Amsterdam café that finished first place in *Het Parool*'s cheese fondue competition. When I asked the impressively large bartender about it, he said a prize like that can have unexpected consequences.

"It's left me with fondue-arm."

"A fondue-arm?"

"Yeah, from stirring the cheese."

It turned out he was the owner. Nice chap. He told us he'd been serving prodigious quantities of fondue for a long time, but never to a group of such respectable advanced age. We all had to drink to that. The first bottle of wine was on the house.

The cheese fondue was absolutely delicious and the wine flowed abundantly.

There was one problem: the bathroom was up a few stairs. That's quite a challenge for most of the members of our club, and an insurmountable obstacle for Evert. But patrons and staff joined forces to heave the doddering among us up the steps.

"One of the services we provide," the owner said with a grin.

For Evert, however, another solution had to be found. One of the regulars, who lived up the street, invited him to use his own home's facilities. As for me, I had fortunately remembered to put on a clean diaper before setting out.

"I'd love to go back another time, but not with a bladder infection," Leonie puffed, recovering from her trip to the ladies'.

Still, it's important not to let practical considerations such as daunting toilet facilities stop you from venturing out. Experience has taught us that sad lesson: once old people stop doing something, they are unlikely ever to do it again.

The moment you stop riding your bike, driving a car, going out, moving, grooming yourself, taking the bus, or visiting friends, it means giving that activity up for good. Although there are exceptions: I knew someone who got rid of his car when he turned eighty, regretted it, and bought another car the following year. A month later, to prove how wrong that decision had been, he crashed into a delivery van that had the right of way, and totaled his brand-new car.

At 11:30 p.m. we tumbled out of the minibus to our front door. Almost all the lights were out.

"Long live Evert's Swiss restaurant," whooped Antoine, slurring a bit. A cheer of agreement went up. In a few of the rooms the lights came on, and curtains were parted slightly.

Thursday, May 14

Yesterday, on my ten-minute stroll (plus time out for a rest), I ran into my old neighbor Antje. She was walking along the bicycle path, carrying half a loaf of bread.

"Antje, how nice to see you. How are you?"

She looked at me pensively. "Oh, fine. I've just been to the baker's."

I asked her what she was doing so far from home.

"I thought to myself, why don't I go to the baker's and have a nice little walk," she said.

"But don't you still live in Amsterdam-West?" I asked.

Yes, she was still there.

The distressing truth hit me: Antje had walked all the way from Amsterdam-West, at least an hour and a half away, and wanted to get home, but had no idea where that was. I don't think she knew exactly who I was, either.

"Don't you remember me? I'm your old neighbor. I lived next door to you for twenty years."

"Yes, yes, the neighbor." She gave me an empty little smile. "Normally I take the car, but the weather was nice, so I thought, why don't I take a walk."

I asked her how long she'd had a car again.

"Oh, well, a while now."

I invited her in for a cup of tea, and we walked back to the home arm in arm. She held on to me tightly. When we reached the lounge she collapsed in a chair with a sigh of fatigue. A phone rang in her coat pocket. She did not respond.

"Don't you want to answer it, madam?" asked the caregiver who had brought her a cup of tea. Antje looked at her pocket, baffled.

"Shall I answer it?" I asked.

"Yes, by all means." By the time I'd retrieved the mobile from her pocket, it had stopped ringing. I asked the caregiver to assist me, since I don't know my way around these modern telephones.

"Someone has been trying to reach you twelve times, madam."

"That'll be my son, he doesn't like me going out alone," said Antje.

"Shall I ring him for you?" I suggested. She nodded.

Twenty minutes later her son Bert arrived in a car to pick her up. He said he was glad to see me again. With a friendly nod, Antje took her leave and obediently climbed in.

Bert promised to come back for tea on Saturday afternoon.

"To catch up."

Today is Ascension Day. Evert is stopping by this afternoon. We'll raise our glasses to the Good Lord Jesus's safe ascent.

Friday, May 15

Evert was quiet and uncharacteristically calm. My best mate wasn't feeling well; I could see he was in pain, although he pooh-poohed it when I mentioned it.

"Hendrik, chum, may I just sing a brilliant ditty for you?" And Evert sang, off-key and as harsh as a crow:

It's always something, is it not
Sometimes it rains
And sometimes it's too hot.

"In spite of these profound words by the great philosopher Duiker, I nevertheless worry about you, Evert."

"Come on, Groen, you old pessimist. The worst thing that can happen is that you snuff it."

He said it with a laugh, but he was bluffing; I knew it. Evert is honest and trustworthy, except when it's about his own well-being. Then he's a terrible actor and an even worse liar, depriving me of the opportunity to console him or show that I care.

Saturday, May 16

Geert bought eighty-four packets of Cup-a-Soup at the minimart. For every three packets you buy, you get one free Artis Zoo stamp. Twenty-eight stamps fill two stamp booklets, which gets you one free ticket to the zoo. And enough soup to last 252 days.

"Come on, Henk," Geert growled on Thursday, "tomorrow we're going to Artis."

I wasn't looking forward to it. I prefer to avoid crowds when I'm on my scooter.

"You can just ram your way through," was Geert's suggestion, and it's hard to argue with that.

So yesterday afternoon we rode to the ferry dock, which was even more congested than I'd feared.

"Stay close behind me," Geert ordered. That helped. He elbowed aside a bicycle here and a moped there with a friendly smile for the victims. There were some indignant glares, but also some approving nods.

I was very chuffed to receive a sexy wink from a pretty woman. It may even have brought a blush to my cheek.

Once I got used to it, I even began enjoying the hectic bustle of downtown Amsterdam.

Artis was spectacular. In zoological gardens the emphasis these days is more on the garden, and less on the creatures. Lots of beautiful flowers, bushes and trees, and fewer animals. They are no longer confined behind bars but hidden somewhere in the greenery where two myopic senior citizens can barely spot them.

In the ape house we were proud as monkeys when we spied the world's tiniest primate: a mother monkey carrying a baby the size of a matchbox on her back.

Geert had brought a thermos of hot water to make himself a nice Cup-a-Soup, but he hadn't screwed the lid on tightly enough: the water had leaked out. Making the best of a bad bargain, we bought ourselves a salami sandwich.

"I don't really like that soup anyway," Geert confessed. "Those eighty-four packets were a bit of an impulse buy."

"They have a long shelf life," I consoled him, "so you can keep them for a long time before throwing them out."

On the way home I almost landed under a tram, but aside from that it was a successful trip. My worry had been groundless. I was pleased with myself for not using some feeble excuse in order to get out of it. I often think of my wife's words of wisdom: it's the things you *haven't* done that you will regret the most.

It's time to visit her again—I'm going the day after tomorrow.

Sunday, May 17

Bert, the son of my former neighbor Antje, came for tea yesterday. To catch up on what's happened in the past five years. He was well, but his eighty-seven-year-old mother had been wandering off and frequently getting lost, both literally and figuratively. She had been brought home four times by complete strangers, the last time on the back of a Moroccan paperboy's moped.

"That put a big dent in my prejudices," Bert was forced to admit.

"Lucky he wasn't stopped for having a passenger without a helmet. Or did he happen to have one for her?"

Bert gave a wry chuckle. "If the situation wasn't so tragic, it would make you laugh till you were blue in the face."

Mother Antje wasn't just getting lost, she had also spent hours wandering around the shopping mall in search of her bicycle, which was parked in the shed at home. She had also lost her purse. Bert had stopped giving his mother any money as a result; but then she'd walked out of the supermarket with a loaf of bread under her arm without paying. The geriatrician, the gerontologist, the social-geriatric care visitor, and case manager had all advised him to give Antje back her purse. Wise decision: within a week she had lost it again, and someone had withdrawn €500 four times from her bank account, since she conveniently kept her PIN number with her bank card.

"What a farce. Anyone with a grain of common sense can see she should be in a nursing home, but a foursome of overqualified, overpaid social workers think it best to wait until she's run into a few more mishaps. *Four* of them said so!"

I said it's difficult to make people go into a nursing home against their will.

"And so we should just sit back and watch her break a hip? Or get run over by a car?"

See, that's what's wrong with the welfare state, in a nutshell: the only way for a woman with dementia to get the protection and rest she needs is via the hospital or the police station. And that's leaving the undertaker out of the picture for now.

Bert was a bit down when he said goodbye.

"Sorry, neighbor, I haven't been very good company, but I am really at the end of my rope."

I couldn't think of what to say to make him feel better.

Monday, May 18

I went to visit my wife yesterday, the trip I make twice yearly to the psychiatric institution where she lives. I no longer dread it. I have made my peace with it.

She softly says hello, but doesn't recognize me, or barely; it's hard to tell. We'll have a cup of tea, she lets me hold her hand, and if the weather is nice we'll take a little turn around the garden, arm in arm. I like to point out the prettiest flowers. She seems content with what life still has to offer in the form of slight pleasures. Every once in a while a little smile, every once in a while a friendly nod.

An hour later I'll say goodbye, and board the train from Brabant back to Amsterdam. All in all it's quite an undertaking. Fortunately I can have the home's transport pick me up from the station.

Home again, I reward myself with a snifter of brandy and a game of chess with Evert. On days like these I let him have a draw. Unless he goes too far and sacrifices his queen. Then that's his business and he's checkmated in thirty minutes or less.

Tuesday, May 19

It's nice when old people take some interest in their appearance—if not for their own sake, then for those who are obliged to look at them.

Traipsing around all day in threadbare slippers and the same old pair of shabby trousers does not signal much in the way of self-respect. (By the way, I saw a picture in the paper the other day of Fidel Castro in a baggy Adidas training jacket, a messy beard, and hair that had obviously not seen the inside of a barber shop for quite some time. The revolution isn't what it used to be.)

I myself take pride in my appearance. Polished shoes, clean shirt, jacket, tie. I frequent the barber's on a regular basis, and also have them see to the unruly eyebrows and the bristles spouting from my nose and ears.

Most of the Old But Not Dead are quite vain. Ria and Antoine look as if they're ready to walk down the runway in a geriatric fashion show. Edward and Graeme are quite civilized-looking, and even Leonie is rather with it. Only Geert might be encouraged to change his clothes more frequently, and Evert too has to be reminded occasionally that it wouldn't hurt to have a wash every once in a while. Since joining the club, Leonie has taken to wielding the fashion and hygiene cudgel. In her most charming manner, she gently steers those two gentlemen, who've lived as bachelors far too long, in the right direction. She recently took Evert to buy a new jacket.

"The collar of that jacket won't come clean anymore, I'm afraid, Evert."

"That's fifteen years of neck grease, that is," Evert grunted. Well, Leonie thought that might be sufficient reason to pick out something new. And, miracle of miracles, Evert docilely followed her to C&A and came home with a spiffy powder-blue jacket.

Leonie also gave Geert a lovely scent for his birthday.

"You should wear it often," she said. It was the first time in his life that anyone had ever given Geert an eau de toilette. Cool Water, by Davidoff.

"Coal water?" he asked, surprised.

Wednesday, May 20

Sad, sad! Our national songstress Trijntje did not make it.

"It was the pantsuit. She looked like a scarecrow," said Mr. Pot.

The Eurovision Song Contest has attained a new apogee: four Finnish mongols. Here in our home most people still refer to them as "mongols" and not "people with Down's Syndrome." They also talk about "negroes" and "foreigners." It isn't because they don't respect the people belonging to those groups; it's because the concept of politically correct language has passed them by. Here language is frozen in time.

There was quite a bit of complaining about the lightning pace of the songfest, as well as the rather enervating light-show.

"It'll make me have an epileptic fit, all that flashing and flickering," Mrs. Quint feared.

"Huh! *You'd* get an epileptic fit from a red traffic light," said Pot. He was in top form last night.

Every year Eurovision leads to nostalgic ruminations about Ted de Braak, Corry Brokken, Teddy Scholten, and, yes, even Udo Jürgens and Charles Aznavour. Although no one is sure whether or not they were all contestants.

Halfway through the Finnish punk rock band, the sound on the conversation lounge set was turned to mute. After the bearded transvestite, those Finns were the last straw.

"We had Russian grannies once, but never any Dutch grandpas," Antoine mused. "That may be an untapped opportunity."

Evert thought an Alzheimer's band would fit the bill.

"I can just picture some of them taking a nosedive off the podium, trying to escape."

"Now, now, that's enough of that, Mr. Duiker," the nurse reprimanded him.

The sound was turned up again for the results.

Even though we'd heard only five of the sixteen songs performed, it was of course a downright scandal that Trijntje wasn't going through to the next round.

"We just can't win against so many Eastern bloc countries," people fumed. Now we won't have to watch the finals on Saturday. If "we" aren't in it, "we" won't watch it. So there.

Thursday, May 21

Circus Magic comes to North Amsterdam once a year. Since the weather was nice and we had nothing better to do, I proposed to Geert that we go there on our scooters. All too often we have nothing better to do. Having tea or coffee, or bellyaching about this-that-and-the-other: those are the core activities of our existence, so any excuse to break free of the daily grind is a plus.

Circus Magic was a gift.

On a small stretch of lawn in the middle of a housing estate, we found the blue tent and its circus wagons. Driving up, we were met with the usual expressions of amazement at the sight of two old chaps out and about with neither a kid nor a grandkid in tow; but then you could see them think, "Whoa, how cool is that, two old geezers out on their own."

We bought tickets for the wooden bleachers in the second circle, but were treated as special guests and led to even better seats: molded plastic chairs down by the ring. And if we preferred to remain seated on our scooters, that wasn't a problem either.

The circus family's Dutch contingent consisted of a charming young ringmaster, a big fat clown, and a blushing blonde. A strongwoman from Spain, a juggler from the Eastern bloc, and a pretty acrobat from... I forget where, made up the international complement. Two mute Ukrainians were in charge of the props, and there was also a portly man wearing a sweater that said "Security."

It was a lovely, poignant, and festive performance. The strongwoman's sweat flew in all directions, the clown high-fived everyone, a goat stepped through a hoop, the pretty girl dangled from a contraption high in the air, the juggler juggled, and six ducks all in a row waddled ahead of the blonde duck-tamer.

Afterward all the artists came over to shake our hands.

"That was fun," Geert grunted, "and you still have some popcorn in your hair, Hendrik."

Impossible. I don't have enough hair for anything to get tangled up in it, but I ran my hand over my head anyway.

"Joking."

Friday, May 22

Evert had to go to the doctor's this afternoon. He was nervous, I could tell. He had his usual swagger on, but it wasn't convincing. I have a bad feeling about it.

We're leaving for Bruges in a week and a half. Quite an undertaking for folks who, for years, haven't been away from home for more than a few hours. Some of us might spend a night at a son's or daughter's house at most. Ria and Antoine have their bags packed and ready at the door, and Leonie's table is littered with constantly changing little piles of clothes. Geert is keeping a close eye on the weather in Bruges, and Graeme has drawn up an itinerary for the entire three days. As for me, I have rung the hotel to make sure that everything is in order. I was politely reassured that it was.

"Don't worry, Mr. Groen, we'll make sure that everything is ready for your arrival."

It is now 9 p.m. I just left Evert's. He wouldn't tell me anything. He also turned down my offer of a game of chess.

"You'd better go, Henk, my head's killing me."

Tuesday, May 26

On Saturday Evert came to my room before morning tea. With some very bad news.

"I decided to sleep on it, but there's no point going on

pretending nothing's wrong: I have cancer. I have only a few months left. Half a year, maybe."

I think all I did was shake my head or maybe I said something feeble, like "Impossible."

Evert was shown the results from tests that were done two weeks ago, and it was clear: advanced-stage colon cancer.

Evert is refusing chemotherapy or radiation.

"The most they can do is slow it down a bit, and I don't feel like subjecting myself to that."

I protested a bit more, against my better judgment.

"I won't think of it, Henk. It would only prolong the agony."

He did ask the internist for the best painkillers and pep pills that exist, and the doctor agreed not to make a big fuss about one pill more or less.

I was a basket case for two days. Yesterday I was given a stern talking-to by Evert himself.

"Hendrik Groen, chum, you *must* go on with your life the way you have lived it for the past couple of years: with joy and gusto, and let the chips fall where they may."

That was a clear order.

He'll wait until we are back from Bruges to inform the other Old But Not Dead Club members. He had wanted to keep it from me until then as well, but he had to tell someone, and decided that his "best mate would just have to be the poor sucker to have to hear it."

"You've had only fun and games out of me long enough," he added with a grin. Evert himself had needed just one day to adjust to the new reality and resume his devil-may-care attitude.

I realize that, for the moment, he is supporting me more than I am supporting him. I don't think that was supposed to be the idea. This will be one of your life's last great challenges, Groen: to do everything in your power to give a beautiful friendship a suitably upbeat ending. I *must* pull it off, there's no second chance.

I'll start tomorrow, when the Old But Not Dead Club gets together for a festive conclave to discuss preparations for our trip to Bruges.

Wednesday, May 27

Death is always looming over our Old But Not Dead Club. With eight members well into our eighties, we can expect one and a half funerals a year, statistically speaking. It's just like waiting for the bus: the longer you wait, the greater the likelihood that it will eventually get here. To make life bearable, we ignore the statistics. Old ostriches, we are: we bury our heads in the sand as the Grim Reaper saunters among us with his scythe in search of his next victim. It would make a great cartoon, that.

If an ostrich next to us keels over, we look up in alarm and then quickly stick our heads back in the sand.

To Evert, it's a relief to have clarity. Now he knows what he must do: face the final curtain with pluck and bravura.

Yesterday evening he popped around again.

"Life has always been too short for cheap booze, but even more so now." He pulled out a bottle of twenty-year-old Scotch. We drank to a grand finale.

He is probably planning to be well into the red when he dies; in fact, he came to discuss his intentions in that regard. This week he will transfer half of his nest egg into his son's bank account, to be used for arrangements for a decent funeral. The other half will be paid into my account.

"Yes, I decided I'd rather give it all away while I'm alive," he said. "It's for the whole club, but they don't need to know. Not yet."

Seven thousand euros. We'll see how fast we can spend that in the coming months.

"The other seven thousand should be enough for Jan to buy a cheap pine coffin and a nice spot in the Noorder Cemetery." He prefers to be buried beneath a tree, since he isn't fond of sitting, or in this case lying, in the sun. He wonders if cemeteries offer a choice of cheap or expensive plots, as in the theater. He wanted me to go with him tomorrow to check it out, but that's a bit too soon for me.

"Can't you let me get used to the idea first?" I protested.

We'll scope it out after Bruges.

Thursday, May 28

It wasn't as difficult as I'd thought, pretending nothing was the matter. Especially since, for the first time in weeks, Evert was in the jolliest of moods. We had an Old But Not Dead meeting to discuss the trip to Bruges.

We leave next Tuesday at 10 a.m., and return Thursday afternoon before the evening meal. We thought two nights away from home was enough for the club's first big trip.

Expectations are high, but so are the nerves. We look forward to having new adventures, but at the same time there's the natural inclination to want to cling to familiar routine. We love surprises, but then again we don't. You know what to expect at home, and there's no telling what may happen when you're away. We run the gamut of human emotions.

Evert and Geert are the ones who are always ready to forge straight ahead imperturbably and without hesitation. Ria, too, if somewhat less so. She's the one who sees to it that Antoine doesn't stay at home reading a book; she gets him off his backside.

"Stop spending so much time studying life's instruction manual. Just *do* it! Yes, you may fall down a few times, but so long as you get up again, you'll be ahead of where you were." Ria casually spoke these words of wisdom not long ago, as if asking someone to pass the sugar. She amazes me.

I've drawn up a detailed list of what I have to pack. The schoolmaster in me is never far away. I caught myself dithering over whether to take three pairs of underpants or four. In the end, cross with myself, I tossed five into the suitcase. And an extra pack of diapers.

The program for Bruges is on the light side and not too taxing, suited to old age, you might say. Each of us will bring along a nice bottle of something, for eventual postmortems in one of the commodious single hotel rooms. Evert asked everyone to refrain from falling or breaking any bones over the next three days. I did find myself having to swallow when he cheerfully made that request.

Friday, May 29

"Goethe said: beware of the man with nothing to lose." Evert looked very solemn as he said it.

"I never knew you'd read anything by Goethe," I said, astonished.

"Someone once gave me a book of quotations for Sinterklaas."

I asked him if he had any funny business in mind. Not at all, he just thought it was a good line.

"But you've always lived like a man with nothing to lose." Strangely enough, he briefly seemed overcome by what I'd said.

"It's a splendid compliment, Groen, that you so casually let slip there. One of the nicest compliments I can think of, even."

That, in turn, made me clear a lump from my throat.

Two sentimental old fools.

A number of residents here in our home think that we're taking unwarranted risks with our trip to Bruges.

"You could get diarrhea," said Mrs. Smit, shaking her head.

Embroidering on that subject, Mrs. Ligtermoet advised us to pack a big cork, then almost fell off her chair laughing. She is new here and is already reputed to have the loudest, most booming laugh of any resident. She would make a jolly addition to the coffee table if you wanted to lift the mood. When someone else recently complained about a mole that had grown 2 millimeters, Mrs. Ligtermoet confessed herself to be a walking bill-board for melanoma (great guffaw), but that in the coffin it wouldn't show anyway (throaty chuckle), unless you were Snow White (infectious giggles).

I bought some extra-strength diarrhea pills at the pharmacy. You can live dangerously, but not stupidly. Thanks for the tip, Ligtermoet.

Saturday, May 30

Yesterday it occurred to me to wonder why some of the rooms are being left vacant, and yet Mrs. Ligtermoet has been admitted as a new resident. I can't make sense of it. Perhaps there are certain obligations that remain to be filled. I, for one, am more and more convinced that our home is slated for closure. Last week we had people here from a company that does the maintenance on the awnings, and Edward heard the head of the technical department tell them they needn't do a very thorough job of it.

"As long as it lasts another year or two."

An urgent task for the new Residents' Committee: to obtain some clarity about the future plans for our home as soon as possible. It also makes me feel good to know I still have a role to play, and that the committee can make a difference.

Sunday, May 31

"It's tempting fate, you know, taking old people on a long trip!" Mr. Dickhout exclaimed every time he saw me. In the end I'd had enough.

"We're just going to Bruges, you know. That's Belgium, not Syria. The likelihood of getting beheaded in Bruges is minuscule. The likelihood of my dropping dead of old age is about ten million times greater. And I don't have to go anywhere to do that, I can drop dead right here in your presence."

Dickhout is keeping his disagreeable mouth shut, at least for now.

The greatest danger you'll encounter in cities popular with tourists is being trampled to death by Chinese travelers. Over the past few days, ninety coaches carrying 4,500 Chinese have been crisscrossing the Netherlands, creating all kinds of havoc. It could be worse, however. Tiens, a Chinese corporation, held a company outing in Nice, France: a herd of 6,400 staff members running roughshod all over the Riviera for four days. I hope the Asians haven't discovered Bruges yet, at least not in great numbers.

And that's just the tip of the iceberg. In China there are at least a billion more would-be tourists who can't wait to visit the Anne Frank House. The queues to get in will reach all the way to the Martini Tower in Groningen. And don't discount the Indians; there's a billion of them as well. First they'll have to get a bit richer, but as soon as they do, they'll troop to Europe on vacation en masse, mark my words. It's lucky I won't be alive to see it.

Monday, June 1

So many things to make a body nervous: a one-day heat wave is forecast for the end of the week, and it's already causing great consternation.

Some residents only feel good when the temperature is between seventy and seventy-three degrees, so long as it's not too muggy, or windy, or rainy. So on the other 355 days of the year, there's always something to complain about. Today, at fifty-nine degrees, it's much too cold, naturally, and the day after tomorrow, at eighty degrees, will be unbearably hot. Maybe, just maybe, tomorrow will be just right.

We are looking forward to sitting on a sweltering outdoor terrace in Bruges, with sun for the sun-worshippers and parasols for the shade-lovers. Evert intends to concentrate on the two cornerstones of Belgian patriotic pride: chips and beer. He claims the Belgian chip stand is on the list of UNESCO World Heritage Sites. That sounds too good to be true, and too good to risk verifying.

My suitcase is packed. I am a bit nervous, I must admit. I'm taking today off to rest, to save up energy for the trip. That's necessary, because at my age I tend to run on empty sooner than I'd like. I wish I had a little pill to give me a pick-me-up, but I wouldn't know how to go about getting some. I did ask my GP, but he brushed me off. He prescribes antidepressants by the boatload to morose seniors, but he won't even think of giving me one of those pep pills.

"They call them 'uppers,' and they say you can dance

and rave on them for hours, Henk," Leonie said with a sly smile. A smile that was most becoming.

"In that case I wouldn't mind trying one of those pills myself," said Evert from his wheelchair, "but I may need a double dose, since I have only one leg."

Evert has recovered admirably. For the past few months he had been rather quiet and reserved, for him; now he is his cheerful self again, the biggest loudmouth of us all. There's nothing fake about it. The prognosis has ended the uncertainty. The brakes are off. It grieves me to see it, but it also lifts a weight off my shoulders and, more than anything, fills me with admiration. It may be selfish of me, but it does make his approaching end much easier to bear.

Tuesday, June 2

By an unhappy coincidence, today's *Volkskrant* has a big front-page story with the headline: "Why aren't the tourists in overcrowded Bruges a problem?" I am not going to read it, and will leave the newspaper at home.

The temperature in Bruges is forecast to be sixty degrees, and grandson Stef is driving up to the front door in half an hour. I am sure that Edward, Ria, and Antoine are already waiting downstairs. I think I'll join them.

Friday, June 5

Dear Sir or Madam Director of the Frites Museum,

We were sadly disappointed in the chips at your museum, the only museum of its ilk in the world. We were counting on a masterful fry, but it was limp, too pale, and made from an inferior, tasteless spud. We are giving this chip a minus 4 out of 10. The classic paper cone was okay, but the contents were worthy neither of your museum, of Bruges, or of Belgium. Belgium, the only country whose chip stall is on the National Heritage list! This is unacceptable.

There may have been an extenuating circumstance, of course, a cook out sick, or a new trainee having to step into the void, but if not, we should like to have our money back (10 times €2.60 = €26.00).

In anticipation of your response, we remain disappointed but sincerely yours,

Graeme, Ria, Antoine, Edward, Evert, Geert, Leonie, Jan, Edwin, and Hendrik (chips connoisseurs par excellence)

We had great fun writing this letter. It's going out the door this afternoon, and we're very curious to see if they reply.

The priciest chip stall in the world is in Bruges' Great Market—that's to say, its location is what's priciest, for it is said that the spot rents for €100,000 a year. But the chips there taste like it too: we gave them a 9 out of 10.

We headed over there after the Frites Museum for a few portions, to help us over our disappointment.

Mrs. Schansleh might say, "You really painted that town yellow, didn't you?" It was a very successful experiment, our first Old But Not Dead holiday. Although it must be said that yesterday, on our arrival home, eight catatonic elderly citizens were a sorry sight. Ria and Antoine did not even make it down to dinner, Geert fell asleep halfway through pudding, and the rest of us drooped off to bed right after dessert. Evert was the only one to stay for a thimble of brandy with the coffee. But he has to make up for lost time.

We set off on Tuesday morning after coffee, with quite a few of our fellow residents enviously watching us go. Edward intoned, "And we're not yet going home"; at least, I thought I recognized the old marching song from the melody. His speech is growing less and less intelligible. The journey went smoothly, with just one lavatory stop—not bad—and we were at our hotel by 2 p.m. A gracious welcome, very pleasant rooms and, for the first time in years, no waiting for the elevator! Half an hour later we were out on the terrace, the men quaffing their first Belgian beer and the ladies sipping tea or wine. A rather conventional division of roles, I'll give you that. Under the outdoor heat lamps it was perfectly bearable. A short siesta was planned from half past three to half past four. To get the most out of our adventures, we have to be careful about energy conservation. At a quarter to five, two horse-drawn carriages drove up. Great plaudits for the program committee, which consisted of Leonie and Graeme. We were conveyed like kings and queens around the beautiful city. Traveling rugs on our laps, roll of peppermints on hand.

"Should we wave?" Ria suggested, doing an excellent imitation of Queen Mum Beatrix.

The horse-drawn carriage is the ideal mode of transportation for the elderly tourist no longer all that nimble on his feet. Some philosopher once said that the mind travels at the speed of a horse; the aged mind travels at the speed of an old nag.

It was quite a job hauling Evert in and out of the carriage, but we had Jan and Stef with us for that. They aren't daunted by having to hoist him up another stair tread or foot board. The coachman gave us a running sightseeing commentary, but his Flemish dialect was almost impossible to understand. We did our best to nod politely at the right moments, and he usually nodded back amiably; a good sign. At the end of the tour we were dropped off at a restaurant serving Belgian specialties. It was delicious, but don't ask me what we had. I suspect Evert of slipping the coachmen €100, because any time we had to go somewhere or had to be picked up somewhere, they were waiting for us. Most convenient, because pushing a rollator or a wheelchair over the cobblestones is no doddle.

It was quite a bit hotter on Wednesday, perfect weather for a canal tour of Bruges.

"We're like those refugee boat people, packed in like sardines," Geert grunted as the boat pushed off.

"One-way to Lampedusa, please," Leonie said to the

captain. Evert's empty wheelchair was left behind on the dock, a poignant sight. It was chained to a lamppost in true Amsterdam style, in spite of the fact that Bruges is so nice, spotless, and honest. A little less spotless or honest wouldn't hurt, if you ask me. It wasn't as crowded with tourists as I'd feared. No Chinese corporate outings, anyway. Fortunately.

The disappointing visit to the Frites Museum has already received a mention. Then a siesta, drinks on the terrace, and a bite to eat. It all went off without a hitch, except that a plate of fish soup spilled all over Antoine's suit—a clumsy maneuver on Graeme's part.

"I think there's no point complaining that the soup wasn't hot enough," Antoine remarked laconically. True; at least he did not receive a nasty burn.

The rest of the evening Geert and Evert took turns saying, "What's that fishy smell?"

The next morning we headed to a museum that wouldn't let our cabs inside. One gets used to a horse and carriage all too quickly. Without our conveyances, the tour of the museum ended a mere twenty minutes later on the terrace of the museum café, in the bright sunshine. A chat and a little snooze; exhaustion was beginning to set in.

One last horse-drawn ride, a quick pit stop at one of the city's 700 chocolate shops, and an elaborate lunch in the hotel. And, once in the minivan, a final pick-me-up when Evert's bag suddenly produced two bottles of ice-cold champagne and nine plastic glasses. The bottles were soon empty, upon which the bus grew quiet. When, on reaching the border at Breda, Stef glanced over his shoulder, he saw that most of his passengers had nodded off. Edward and I were the only ones still awake, contentedly silent.

Saturday, June 6

Yesterday the temperature climbed to over eighty-six degrees, and today it's down to sixty-six. Dangerous fluctuations for the elderly population.

"Oh, if only my heart holds out," said Mrs. Quint. She was breathing heavily, more like an incessant throaty wheeze, which got on my nerves a bit.

"You look like an earworm with a toothache," Mrs. Schansleh said, pointing at me. Schansleh must spend every night in her room dreaming up fantastic new idioms and proverbs, as she comes out with these pearls so often. I am a great fan of her patter. But that's as far as my sympathy goes. She has the annoying habit of announcing what she's about to do before she does it.

"I'm going for a wee," she'll say, for example. Or, worse still: "I have to poo." I don't have to know that! And when she comes back from the loo ten minutes or so later, she'll even inform you if she succeeded in her mission or not.

"I'm going to my room, I'll have one of those lovely biscuits, I'm going to read the new *Margriet*, I'm taking off my shoes, I'll have another cup of tea, I'll just run up and put on a cardigan."

"It doesn't interest me a goddamn bit, Mrs. Schansleh, can't you keep it to yourself?" No, that is not what I said;

I said, "You do like to tell us what you're going to do, don't you, Mrs. Schansleh?" Which didn't help at all.

We bought vouchers for dinner for two at a nice restaurant for Jan, Evert's son, and Stef, Grietje's grandson. A bribe that we're hoping their wives will appreciate so that they won't mind sacrificing their husbands from time to time in the future. Without a couple of sturdy fellows to help us, we wouldn't be able to go out anymore. They fetch the rollators, push the wheelchair, bring the drinks, help us into our coats, carry our bags, find lost spectacles, hoist a bit here, and give a helpful little push there. And they take us where we want to go. It's lucky that they seem to enjoy it. We *are* a jolly bunch for our age, naturally, even if we say so ourselves.

Sunday, June 7

The staff member who deserves the most sympathy in our home, I think, is the pedicure lady. Anyone who chooses that profession is already a bit mad, but if you then go and apply for a job at an old people's home, you must really be desperate, or else have some rather peculiar inclinations. Choosing to become a dentist and having to peer into people's open mouths all day long is understandable because it's a lucrative profession, but I once cautiously asked what the pedicurist was getting paid, and she said it wasn't exactly a king's ransom. The residents have to contribute €5 of their own if they want to have her come, which for many is reason enough to postpone her services as long as possible. Just slip on a pair of socks, and no one will see it. Not yet. But overgrown toenails will eventually start poking through socks or slippers; they'll even gore holes in battered shoes. The poor pedicurist then has to use pruning shears to tackle those overgrown nails. Trimmings fly everywhere, if you'll excuse the gruesome description. I do have to say it's a phenomenon largely seen in men. For myself, I have decided to have her come every other month. The first time she ministered to my feet, I kept apologizing, saying I was sorry I could no longer do it myself. It's simply that I can't reach my toes anymore. I also have trouble putting my socks and shoes on, but I have a gadget for that, luckily. I hate being dependent on anyone. Standing on my own two feet is literally what I have to do.

There are plenty of residents who think if anything requires even the slightest effort, you may as well call the nurse.

"That's what they're here for, isn't it?" is the reasoning. It's for people like that that I'd like to see tarring and feathering brought back.

Monday, June 8

Yesterday afternoon the opening round of the Old People's Song Festival, a yearly torment for the ear, was held in the recreation room.

"Last year you had a migraine, I seem to remember," said Mrs. Van Diemen just before it began. "I hope you don't have one again this year."

"I hope the reverse for you," I said under my breath.

Van Diemen is one of the ladies who always confidently signs up for the first round. She thinks that in the past few years her voice has got better rather than worse. Actually, she's right, but only because her voice has lost some volume and shrillness, thank God. Yesterday she sang a simple French song in the style of an Italian coloratura soprano. She sounded like a giant canary; she was wearing an appropriately yellow dress. I took a seat as far back as possible but didn't dare leave, since I suspected that several of the artists were keeping a close eye on me. Ria and Antoine are very polite, and kept me company, but the rest of my so-called friends from the Old But Not Dead Club failed to show up.

"I propose that once a year on this day we change our name to Old But Not DEAF," said Evert when I went to see him in the late afternoon.

He handed me ten €50 notes. He has decided that instead of transferring his savings into my account, he'll give it to me in cash, €500 at a time.

"That way they'll never find out where my money went," he said in a conspiratorial whisper. "And Jan knows about it."

I don't think it's against the law to give your money away and if this is how Evert chooses to go about it, that's certainly up to him. Next week I'll open an Old But Not Dead account at the bank, into which I'll deposit our advance-inheritance from Evert.

Tuesday, June 9

Mrs. Smit was convinced someone had stolen her false teeth.

"But what would someone want with your teeth?" Sister Herwegen asked for the third time.

"Well—to put them in," Mr. Bakker said, although it was none of his business.

"Put them in?"

"Into their mouth, of course. Where else would you put a set of teeth—up your arse?"

"I can see that Mr. Bakker is in fine fettle again," said the nurse.

The teeth were found shortly thereafter in the cutlery drawer.

Sister Herwegen is a very nice woman. She is nearing retirement age and doesn't let herself be pushed into making the "targets" imposed on the staff of late. So many minutes to help someone shower, so many for the tea rounds, and however many to hoist an old biddy into her support hose. No room in the schedule for a nice little chat. Herwegen doesn't take any notice of all the directives from above. If she wants to stop for a little chat, then she'll stop for a little chat. She's the last of the old guard; she knows Stelwagen can't be bothered to tell her off.

Herwegen told us a great story, a classic. Forty years ago she worked in a mental institution, on a ward for the aged. They still had dormitories back then. At night the false teeth were kept in glasses lined up on a shelf. One of the old women wore someone else's teeth for the entire day once. When the victim had looked a bit alarmed when they were being put in, the nurse simply jammed them in more firmly.

"They did think her speech sounded a bit funny that day," said Herwegen.

The shrewd reader may remark that someone else should then have had the wrong set of teeth in too, but no. One of the women happened to be ill, and not wearing her teeth that day.

It wasn't until the evening that the nurses found that the teeth wouldn't come out. The victim made high-pitched squealing noises as one of them tried pulling them out with a pair of pliers. After that they'd had the teeth engraved with the owners' names.

"Yes, those were the days, Mr. Groen," said Sister Herwegen with a smile.

"You are a treasure," I said.

"Thank you, so are you."

Wednesday, June 10

The day after tomorrow is slated to be very hot, so that will be a good time for Ria, Antoine, and me to apply ourselves seriously to our great Italian ice cream test. Evert asked if he could join us, and of course he can.

Yesterday was a lovely day too, as a matter of fact. Geert and I went for a long scooter ride. Geert was lucky I had come along, because his battery died toward the end. Sputter, sputter, stop. We had to ask a shopkeeper for a length of rope and then I towed him the last few miles.

People laughed to see us go, and the children waved at us. Waving children warm the cockles of my heart.

Eugenie Lacroix, the fifth Residents' Committee member, is French by birth. She is affronted by the fact that the Netherlands has issued a coin commemorating the battle of Waterloo.

"That's a sensitive subject, for us."

"But there's a hat on one side of the coin, and the other side shows our king," I protested. "Who gets angry about a hat?"

"It's the hat of Prince William of Orange, who defeated our Napoleon."

"That was two hundred years ago, my love," Evert interrupted. "High time you swallow that turd once and for all."

France's President Hollande, reacting to a Belgian Waterloo coin, said: "Circulating a coin that has negative connotations for a segment of the European population is offensive. Especially in the context of the Eurozone governments' push to strengthen unity and cooperation in the fiscal union." Waterloo was 200 years ago! How petty can you get?

It turns out that Napoleon can claim a small posthumous victory after all: in order not to hurt France's feelings, the Belgians have melted down all 180,000 coins depicting the Waterloo monument. The greatest problem facing European unity is chronic narrow-minded chauvinism. So says H. Groen, your old-age home correspondent.

Thursday, June 11

More French politics: French Prime Minister Valls was at the Champions League final in Berlin to cheer on Barcelona. Yes, that is indeed a Spanish team. He flew there on a government jet and his little escapade cost the French some €14,000. Many French citizens are up in arms about it. The statesmen of this world let no opportunity go by, it seems, to bring down the wrath of the common people upon themselves. One of those Furious Frogs was MEP Rachida Dati, who not so long ago charged €6,000 worth of scarves and perfume to her government expense account.

That's one good thing about our home: everyone is the same, everyone is equally rich (or equally poor, depending on how you look at it) and everyone is equally powerless. The one exception is the director. This place is her modest little empire, even if she, in her demure business suits, does not yet possess the dazzling allure of a sun-queen.

The yo-yo weather is still with us: fifty-nine degrees the day before yesterday, tomorrow it will be eighty-six degrees and Monday it's back to fifty-nine degrees. Early tomorrow morning the awnings will be lowered and most of the curtains closed in order to keep out the heat. There are still signs of life as people come down for a cup of coffee, but after lunch the corridors and lounge are deserted. All the inmates are nodding off in their favorite armchair in their own rooms. One rests her weary head on a jigsaw puzzle; the other drops off in front of the telly; a third conks out staring into space. There's no sign of the staff. The home is drained of every last drop of energy. I always make a concerted attempt to resist it. Sometimes it works; sometimes it doesn't.

Friday, June 12

"James Last is dead," Leonie said.

"About time too," Evert replied.

Leonie patted him gently on the head. "Didn't you like his music, you old curmudgeon?"

Evert gets flustered by loving gestures, and when he tried to answer, all that came out was a kind of croak. Then he launched into a lengthy coughing fit.

"Frog in my throat," he excused himself.

"I'll kiss it," Leonie offered, and promptly planted a kiss smack on his lips. "Oooh, the frog has turned into a handsome, one-legged old prince!" she cried.

I almost died laughing, Evert, turning red, chuckled along sheepishly, and Leonie stood there beaming. For one split second we were in touch with perfect happiness.

Saturday, June 13

It's all over the newspapers and the telly: the economic crisis is over. The final proof is the fact that sales of caravans are back up. I've heard the first politician say, "After the bitter times, here come the sweet." We may in all good conscience partake of an extra biscuit with our tea. It's just a shame that the staff who were laid off are never coming back, at least not in my lifetime. Somehow I suspect that they'll first boost the salaries of the management and board, to keep them in line with market-level compensation.

The ice cream salon "Ice Cold Best" boasts twenty-eight different flavors. And I'm already so bad at decision-making! After our first visit, we had decided on the following game plan: we'll work down the list of flavors from top left to bottom right. Since there were four of us yesterday (Ria, Antoine, Evert, and I), we sampled the first four flavors on the top row. Feeling the pressure of fifteen customers behind us, we made a silly mistake: we ordered four times four scoops instead of two. The ice cream chef, poker-faced, doled out four scoops into each cup. The top scoop rolled off the top each time. Settling up, I pretended not to be aghast at the cost. Then we ate ice cream until we thought we'd burst. Scrumptious. Since it was eighty-six degrees out, we slurped, rather than ate, the last spoonfuls. But we discovered an error in our game plan of sampling every flavor in seven visits. For the trays were set out in a different order than on our first visit.

This time we did write down the flavors we tried—melon, pistachio, cookie, and wild berry—but it means that on our next visits we'll have to pore over an ever-growing list of eliminated flavors. I don't know if the other patrons will be amenable to the delay. We took a taxi there and back, and attracted a certain amount of attention: four doddering oldsters going for ice cream by taxicab. There was plenty of time to gape at us, since loading and unloading so many creaky limbs can take a good ten minutes. We told the cabdriver to run the meter until we were all out. Evert insisted on paying both ways. I know why, but Ria and Antoine objected.

"I've won the jackpot in the State Lottery, and that money has to be spent. You can pay me back by pushing me to my room when we get home, Antoine, then we'll be quits," Evert said with a big grin. Antoine, frowning, gave a reluctant nod.

Sunday, June 14

Sometimes I am overcome with sadness when I look at my friend Evert and think that within a few months he'll no longer be here. Of course anyone who is over eighty could kick the bucket at any time, but there's a big difference between the *chance* of dying and the *certainty* of dying. A chance isn't something to worry much about, but certain death is impossible to ignore. It gives you an entirely new perspective.

A steely stoicism has taken hold of Evert. He seems to be enjoying life more intensely than ever before. But who knows what it's like for him when he lies awake in bed at night? I went over there for a game of chess and spotted a newspaper cutting on the dresser. It was about the most straightforward euthanasia method that exists: simply to stop eating or drinking. Evert saw me reading it.

"Hendrik, do me a favor and set out the chess pieces instead of delving into my secret time-out tactics, won't you?"

I muttered, "Sorry."

"I am at peace with it, Henk, so don't bugger it up, will you? Be a man."

"Yes, easy for you to say once you're gone," I said.

"See, that's the kind of retort I like to hear from my old chum."

I couldn't resist looking up the article in question later. It seems that more and more old people who are done with life are deciding to just stop eating and drinking. It spares them the trouble of trying to arrange a proper euthanasia through the offices of uncooperative physicians. If you're healthy, starving isn't the most pleasant kind of death, but if you're old and sick, stopping your intake of food and drink is just a little nudge off the edge of the cliff.

Monday, June 15

Sunday afternoon; no shopping to be done, and not very nice weather.

"It's been a while since we've been to visit my dad..."

"We went to see him three weeks ago, didn't we?"

"We're not around next week, on Father's Day, so I think I should go and see him today. Coming?"

"Must I?"

"Oh, come on, we won't stay long."

That's the conversation I imagine people having before visiting their old parents in a home for the aged. I don't even blame them. Old dads and mums gratefully exploit the visit to discuss a litany of physical and mental ailments with their kids. After a whole week of being surrounded by fellow inmates focused on their own aches and pains, it's nice to have a willing ear all to yourself for once. Although if it's sympathy you want, you may have to look elsewhere.

"Just try it for a week, why can't you? If it's not for you, I'll go back to talking to you on the phone. But I can't ring you every day, I simply haven't got the time." It was Mr. Helder's son who said this. I couldn't help overhearing their conversation; they had sat down at my table because there was nowhere else to sit on a crowded Sunday.

"Yes, but what am I supposed to say to a complete stranger?"

"Well, the same things you would tell me."

"But you're my son, that's different."

The discussion was about the Hello! Service. For the price of €65 a month, an organization based in the Achterhoek region will provide a care worker to talk on the telephone to an aged parent for five minutes a day, or half an hour per week, if the son or daughter is unavailable. Children outsourcing filial love by arranging for a phone call from a stranger, how sad!

"You can decide for yourself what to talk about," Mr. Helder's son explained.

I couldn't stand having to hear any more of this. "I'd cut him out of my will immediately if I were you," I advised Helder. The son glared at me. I refused to avert my gaze.

Tuesday, June 16

"It's time for another restaurant visit," Evert said this morning, "seeing that I'm a bit pressed for time, as surely you must understand."

I did understand, and I promised to arrange something soon. I then asked Evert when he was planning to inform the rest of the Old But Not Dead about his illness. He told me that after giving it some more thought, he had decided to put it off a bit longer.

"So as not to spoil the mood. Not everyone will be able to handle it as well as you, Henk."

I took it as quite the compliment.

Wednesday, June 17

Dr. P, the stage name of Heinz Herman Polder, the singing poet, viewed old age as a punishment. He wouldn't have minded if he'd kicked the bucket by the age of eighty. He would have been spared not only the physical discomforts, but the world's sorry decline as well. When on the occasion of Dr. P's death a few days ago I mentioned this at the coffee table, almost everyone there disagreed with him completely. The only one I saw nodding almost imperceptibly was Edward. Dr. P immediately plummeted in the popularity stakes.

"Well, he lived to ninety-five, so he had fifteen years of tough luck," was Mrs. Bregman's conclusion.

To burnish his dented image somewhat, I quoted another thing I'd read in the newspaper about him. Dr. P considered the time he'd lived as a "man of means" in colonial Indonesia his "Golden Age." "*I didn't have to do any number of annoying tasks because there were people who were paid to perform those services for me with a cheerful demeanor.*"

"Which is not unlike living in our care home," I added.

I'm afraid that confused my fellow inmates a bit. Were they now to view their own lives in here as their Golden Age? And what was the Golden Age again, was it the one they'd learned about in school?

Mrs. Hoensbroek saved face by changing the subject to that poor crooner Albert West. The second famous Dutchman to die this week. And how he died!

"He was calmly riding along on his tricycle, because there was something wrong with him, I don't know exactly what; and then another cyclist fell on top of him. Racing bike and all. And then Albert landed on his head. Dead. Stone cold."

Everyone was shocked. The pressing question was: what had caused that cyclist to crash into him? Some people are better at digesting disaster if the blame can be pinned on someone.

"Now there's no closure," Mrs. Hoensbroek complained.

Then the conversation took a sharp turn: to a flood in Tbilisi, that had led to all the zoo animals escaping. Photos of a hippopotamus waddling through the streets and a bear snuffling about on a balcony had made a deep impression.

"There's also a couple of lions still missing," Mr. Verlaat said.

"How far is Tbilisi from here anyway? Can you get there on foot?" Mrs. Schaap asked somewhat anxiously.

Thursday, June 18

The Residents' Committee has received a letter from Mrs. Stelwagen.

Our director is granting us permission for an art exhibition in August to show the work of one or more of the residents. Just as an experiment, and subject to further consideration.

Our Eugenie was beaming. She is the "one or more of the residents," and the committee member who put this proposal on the agenda. It seems she had already worked out a detailed plan for the exhibition, and has submitted it by return post, that is to say by her own hand, to the director's office. It lists exactly where she wants to hang or place each piece of art.

"For I am a multimedia artist, I should tell you," Eugenie told us over coffee.

"Puts on airs, that one, in that ridiculous garish dress," I heard Mrs. Slothouwer say to the lady seated next to her. Slothouwer has harbored a seething grudge against Eugenie Lacroix since the moment she first walked in. Slothouwer despises everyone, but she despises eccentric people even more. The one she despises most is Evert, but she doesn't dare say anything to him, because he'll only accidentally spill his vanilla pudding and strawberry sauce all over her trouser suit again. Last year that exploit caused Evert to make several friends for life.

As for the request for a monthly high tea, the director was able to inform us that the board was, in principle, sympathetic but that it necessitated further investigation, just to make sure it did not contravene any statutory labor laws. There she goes again, forever hedging her bets! If it turns out that there are indeed grave dangers lurking in the concept of a high tea, she has an elegant way to wriggle out of it. The greatest risk, actually, would reside in residents with Parkinson's pouring their own tea. You'd have to have plenty of burn ointment on hand. But pouring the tea and coffee is already a job reserved for the staff, and will remain so even if there is a "high" in front of the "tea."

It could, of course, turn into a bit of a shambles, all those shaky oldies juggling scones, pastries, and strawberries and cream, but crumbs or clods of whipped cream strewn about everywhere should only add to the fun. A previous request by the Old But Not Dead for permission to use the kitchen was thwarted by the labor laws. Residents are not permitted in areas with hazardous machinery, kitchens and the like. So we are proposing that preparations for the high tea will take place in a corner of the conversation lounge. Let's just hope that the whipped cream dispenser doesn't fall under the "hazardous machinery" category.

Friday, June 19

I have made a reservation at Hotel de Goudfazant for Sunday. Not a hotel, as the name suggests, but a restaurant. Evert was pleased, although he wishes it could have been today.

"Well, well! I just read that the first Syrian refugee has washed up on our shores, on the island of Texel. Dead, so for that one no bed, bath, or bread. It even rhymes!" Ghastly Bakker guffawed at his own wit.

With the best will in the world, I just can't understand some people. They're indifferent to hundreds of refugees drowning in the Mediterranean, yet they'll shed tears over a ladybird with a broken leg. Great tragedy is impossible to comprehend, it seems, whereas small tragedies can be mended.

The tragic story of Mouaz: fled from Syria to Jordan, then set out for the promised land of England via Algeria, Libya, Italy, and France. After nearly five months on the road, he arrives in Calais and sees the white cliffs of Dover on the other side. It must be possible to swim that last leg, Mouaz thinks to himself. Three weeks later his body washes ashore on Texel. And what do some of our fellow residents say? It's your own bloody fault, mate, tough luck.

"It could have been your son," I said in response to Bakker's reaction.

"Me? How could *I* have a black son?"

Where even to begin with such sheer stupidity?

Saturday, June 20

A girl of about six playing hide and seek with her little friends in the park yelled, "The king's hat, on one leg." That was the cue for the other kids to hop on one leg and put their hands on their heads. The one who got there last was "It." I was sitting on my bench watching them and was moved nearly to tears. I have become a sentimental old coot. Perhaps he was always in there somewhere, and is only coming out now. I don't mind, it feels good, actually, those rather over-the-top emotions. My bench overlooks a playground for little kids. There's always something to see. I wish I could hand out sweets to the children, but I don't dare. People are so suspicious these days. Some things really were far better in the old days.

I am still just managing to make it to my park benches, although painfully and with difficulty. If I grow even less steady on my legs, I shall have to stop going to the park on foot, and ride my mobility scooter to my bench instead. Then I can always take a very short walk from there.

In early July I'm to accompany Evert to Uden for a few days, to stay with his son Jan and daughter-in-law Ester. After the success of our first visit, it has become an annual tradition. The division of roles requires me to thaw out the dour Ester with my most engaging grandpa-charms, while all Evert has to do is not push the boundaries with his jokes or create a mess. We were there almost a week the first time; this time it's down to four days. That's best for everyone. I look forward to Wii-ing with Evert's grandson and granddaughter. Last year Evert surprised everyone by being extraordinarily good at Wii baseball. When we'd finally had enough of his showing off, we switched to ski jumping. You need two legs for that sport.

Evert has decided he'll wait to tell his son about being terminally ill until the day of our departure. That's quite soon enough, he thinks.

Sunday, June 21

There were no outright cheers, but Mr. Bakker died suddenly yesterday.

"I hope Slothouwer's next," Graeme heard Mrs. Smit mutter under her breath.

"I did not hear that," he told her pleasantly. She jumped in alarm, apologizing profusely.

"There's no need, I totally understand. But when you're whispering something to yourself, you should try to keep it down, just to be on the safe side. Especially when Mrs. Slothouwer is about."

Bakker's death is no loss. It's not often one encounters so much negativity in one person, although to be honest, his tirades did sometimes make me laugh. He had a rich repertoire of impressive invective. The only one Bakker could sort of get along with was Mrs. Slothouwer. Now she's the last one left to deliver spiteful commentary on just about everything that goes on in here. Maybe she'll control herself a bit more now. Her life can't have been such a bed of roses either.

"What was your childhood like?" I once asked her, without any malice.

"None of your business," was the answer.

Dining out tonight. The Old But Not Dead are obligated to keep each other active and on our toes. At our next general meeting I'll propose that we add keeping each other on our toes to the rules and regulations. It is often easier to get someone else moving than yourself. Also, you tend to be more amenable to another's suggestion. If a friend proposes an activity of some sort, you think, "Ah, why not?" Whereas if you'd thought of it yourself, you'd be more inclined to think, "Ah, why should I?"

Monday, June 22

The first veal cheek of my life was delicious, and my first smoked duck was also divine. You're never too old to try something new, even if many old people don't seem to think so. There's nothing tastier than a meatball if you never choose anything but meatballs.

Now, the mention of that veal cheek may give the impression that we had dinner in some snooty dining establishment, but that's not the case. Hotel de Goud-fazant is located in an old factory along the Ij River. Not posh at all, the floor is barely swept. Normal, cheerful youngsters serve you. All incredibly friendly and patient. Patience is already a virtue, but when it comes to dealing with the aged, you're talking about double helpings.

When the young man came to take our drink orders, Geert was in the bathroom, which took him fifteen minutes, and a little later, when we were ready to order from the menu, Ria had disappeared. She got lost on her way to the coat rack to retrieve her handkerchief from her coat pocket. She was brought back to our table on the arm of a handsome young fellow. Then Leonie declared herself eager to get lost too, but we were hungry, so we forbade it.

"You can go after pudding, pet," said Evert.

We are usually among the first to arrive in a restaurant, being reluctant to give up the Dutch golden rule of "dinner at six." But because we do everything so very slowly, we're also often the last to leave.

Of course we aren't the only old people who go to restaurants, but it's usually just a couple, or as part of a much larger family gathering: Opa and Oma, their children and grandchildren, celebrating someone's birthday or an anniversary. They tend to sit there looking a bit lost, waiting for one of the children or grandkids to make an attempt to draw them into the conversation. A conversation they have trouble following because of the ambient noise, and anyway, what the others are talking about is often way over their heads. They're sitting there, but they don't really belong, not really.

You seldom see a whole contingent of eight doddering oldsters trooping into a restaurant. We belong together, although we often have trouble understanding each other. The acoustics are a problem. It's even worse for the other guests, since we are so loud that they can even hear us in the kitchen. Fortunately we are past caring or being embarrassed, and what we talk about is rarely offensive, even if Evert does tend to come out with the occasional piece of toilet humor while we're eating. This is met with fond slaps or kicks under the table from several quarters, until he stops.

Tuesday, June 23

I already miss old Bakker. Senior citizens are the new taxation plan's biggest losers, the prime minister has admitted to the man who represents us in Parliament, Mr. Krol of the 50Plus party. A newspaper report like that would have sent Bakker into a complete tailspin. He wouldn't have known who to start on: should he execrate Prime Minister Rutte, "who always screws us," or reserve his best invective for "that pancake-eating poofter of the 50Plus Party"? Bakker possessed an astounding repertory of profanities to describe our homosexual friends. I often found myself laughing at these in the most politically incorrect way.

"What a horror-summer," I heard someone say even though summer is only two days old. With a temperature of fifty-seven degrees and pouring rain, it hasn't been particularly toasty these past few days, that's true. The weather is mainly observed through the window here. A little stroll outside, to experience it in person, is the most one can be expected to do. As for me, I like to set out on my mobility scooter in the summer rain and get drenched to the skin; the others think I'm crazy. If the director could think of a way to forbid it, she would definitely consider it. A rather sorry sight, that, a dripping wet old codger in his motorized chair.

"Do you really think that's sensible, Mr. Groen?" she once asked me, frowning dubiously at the trail of water I was leaving in the hall.

"Oh, a little rain won't do me any harm."

"You don't exactly look... presentable," she said with faint disapproval in her voice.

"What, or who, am I supposed to present, then?" I asked with feigned nonchalance.

That question did stump her somewhat.

The Women's World Cup doesn't get much traction here.

"You're just watching a game of rubbish men's soccer, and there's quite enough of that on the telly already, but still, it's nice there's women's soccer as well," was the verdict from an unexpected quarter, namely Ria. When someone asked what she could possibly know about it, she was able to name fourteen players on the Netherlands Women's Team, causing some jaws to drop. Tonight Ria is going to watch the Netherlands vs. Japan match. I knew Ria was a big soccer fan; I'm also sure she'd have had a better shot at managing Ajax than Frank de Boer.

Wednesday, June 24

"Did someone in here just fart?"

Mrs. Slothouwer isn't shy about asking that question. Then she'll look around with a sneer on her face, ostensibly in search of the embarrassed culprit. Everyone at the table will then turn and stare at Mrs. Langeveld.

"She has a disorder that makes her rather gassy," Sister Herwegen once explained.

"As if that's any excuse," Slothouwer had said as soon as the nurse was out of earshot.

That disorder, combined with her rather unappetizing dining habits, means that Mrs. Langeveld usually sits all by herself at mealtimes. No one ever joins her, and if she sits down with another group, they'll get up one by one and move to another table. The odor she produces is rather strong, I have to admit. Although it's tragic to see how she is made to suffer by such a minor affliction, I too can rarely make myself sit down at her table. Only when I have a stuffy nose.

The Dutch table tennis champions Li Jiao and Li Jie have won gold and silver respectively at the European games. It's possible that "we here" are too stuck in the past. Chinese or African athletes competing on behalf of the Netherlands takes some getting used to. Another thing that takes some getting used to, actually, is the European Games being held in Baku. Nobody realized that Baku was in Europe. Or that Baku even existed.

Thursday, June 25

Yesterday Evert went to the internist, to go over treatment options. Metastases have been discovered in the liver and lungs. The doctor, substituting for Evert's own internist, nevertheless suggested another operation, to remove a portion of the intestine.

"Save yourself the trouble of explaining why an eighty-six-year-old should subject himself to an exorbitant and pointless operation, because I won't have it. Save your energy for prescribing painkillers and pep pills for me, the strongest there are, please." Evert must have put on a convincing show, because the doctor didn't argue.

"He's told me I have another three months or so in an acceptable state, and then it's downhill for me very fast," Evert said matter-of-factly.

I finally agreed to visit the cemetery in North Amsterdam with him "to choose a nice little spot." We'll have a look one day when the sun is out and the tombstones will look so much more jolly.

"If you're planning to stop by once in a while, I'll have them put a bench at the foot of my grave," he offered. I told him I'm not really one of those grave-sitters. He quite understood.

"But I'd consider it an honor if you chose to be buried near me when the time comes," he said.

I have been sleeping poorly ever since knowing about my friend's impending death. The doctor gave me some sleeping pills, but they only seem to work during the daylight hours, so I've flushed them down the toilet. I do a great deal of reading at night.

Evert has given me back my little list of last requests. He had promised to make a few arrangements for me when I died.

"Forgive me, old chum, but I don't think I'll be able to do it." His voice sounded a bit croaky.

"Oh go ahead, wimp out on me as usual, you gutless old git. And what does one have to do to get a drink around here?" I just managed to get out.

"Oi, now you've gone too far, Groen, that's supposed to be *my* line."

Friday, June 26

Besides billiards, there is another sport that is popular here: shuffleboard. Not every player has a competitive mentality. There are ladies and gentlemen who just muck about a bit, some of the pucks barely making it to the end of the board; and there are some who play as if their lives depended on it. It can even lead to minor scuffles.

"You bumped the table," Mr. Pot barked at Mrs. Van Diemen.

"But it was by accident."

"If you hadn't, the four would definitely have gone in."

Pot demanded a chance to do it over, but Van Diemen objected, upon which Pot stomped away in a fury.

Mr. Helder lobs with great force but rather inaccurately. Recently a puck sailed off the board and slammed into a biscuit tin on a table across the room.

"If it hadn't been for that tin, I'd have been a goner," Slothouwer declared. She was sitting near the biscuits. "Or I'd have needed stitches."

Since that near-death experience, players are only allowed to aim toward the wall.

In billiards, too, there are considerable differences in the way the game is played. Some players are happy for their cue just to strike any ball; others are good for a whole set. Dickhout is the home's billiards champion, and he thinks it gives him star status. He doesn't whip off his shirt after the winning carambole, but almost.

During an informal gathering of the Residents' Committee yesterday, Graeme suggested it might be a good idea to have a boules court in the private garden. We are going to request one from the director. We will need a magnet on a string, just like old Frenchmen, to pick up the balls. Having to bend down and straighten up again would slow down the game too much.

Mr. Helder is banned. One doesn't want to make the front page with a fatal boules accident. I predict the director will first want to know who would be held responsible in the case of a mishap, and whether boules victims are covered by insurance.

Saturday, June 27

I found out this morning that we have a resident who has his head in the clouds. It is our Turkish friend, Mr. Okcegulcik. His is a hobby that is well suited to life in an old-age home, preferably if you live on one of the higher floors. For Okcegulcik is a member of the Cloud Appreciation Society, an international club for cloud aficionados. He scans the sky daily for unusual cloud formations. Blankly staring out the window is a common pastime here, but Okcegulcik has made a virtue of necessity: he peers at the clouds and photographs them. This morning he came in waving a newspaper article. For the first time since 1951, a new cloud has been officially identified: the bubble cloud, or the *Asperitas.* There were pictures of bubble clouds that looked a bit like undulating ocean waves. He proudly showed us his own pictures of a fantastic bubble cloud. "May 16, 2012" was written on the back. I went with him to his room to admire his wall of cloudy skies photographs.

Most of the residents are not interested in Mr. Okcegulcik's hobby.

"Sodding clouds. I'd rather have sun," is the predominant feeling. These people would rather sit staring blankly out the window with the awning down. From now on I intend to pay more attention when I'm looking out. It would be something, wouldn't it, if I saw a bubble cloud before I died.

Edward gave me a copy of the handbook *Staying Young and Growing Old*, by a professor of geriatrics, Prof. Olde Rikkert.

There's a dedication from Edward on the flyleaf: "For my friend Hendrik As a fellow founder of the Old But Not Dead Club you have made my life so much more enjoyable for which many thanks Your Edward."

That "Your Edward" moved me, and the fact that Edward doesn't seem to believe in commas or full stops, as well as the postscript: "No need to stop by to tell me *you shouldn't have* but do stop by for a drink."

Sunday, June 28

Suppose you alone had a telephone that allowed you to hear the first thing your interlocutor said after hanging up, would you want to use it? Would you want to know what they said?

The reason this occurs to me is that there are some

residents who will sweetly say goodbye to their sons (in-law) and daughters (in-law) and then, upon hanging up the phone, promptly start complaining.

"No, don't worry, I quite understand. We'll just skip it this time. No problem," I heard Mrs. Van Dam chirp, and one second later, after putting down the receiver: "Going out of their way for their aged mother is just too much effort."

I have also heard: "bastard," "nail in my coffin," "hypocritical witch," "I'll disinherit him," "I'd rather die," "nasty scumbag," and "I could strangle her." I wouldn't mind seeing the look on those children's faces if they'd overheard what was said.

But it's not all carping and spite. Mrs. Ligtermoet just cooed, hanging up, "Such a dear, that one."

I don't know to whom I should entrust my funeral wish list, now that Evert has given it back. Who should be saddled with it? I can't make up my mind. I don't want to wait too long to decide either, because you could die before you know it. Which would be a blessing in disguise, actually. But I don't want them playing Mieke Telkamp's warbled version of "Amazing Grace" at my funeral. Even though at that point I won't be able to hear it, I am entitled to my posthumous pride.

Monday, June 29

Next Friday Evert and I are off to Uden, to visit his son Jan and daughter-in-law Ester. I am sure it will be fun, but I rather dread having to witness Evert telling them he is terminally ill. It isn't right, I know, but I am an ostrich and prefer to hide from the truth.

In Greece the ATMs are empty and the country is on the verge of bankruptcy. The newspapers are urging people who've booked a Greek holiday to bring plenty of cash. I imagine that every Bulgarian pickpocket under the sun must also be planning a working holiday to Greece. Never before has so much loose cash been expected to traipse along Greece's shopping streets.

Actually, Mrs. De Roos is leaving for a Cretan holiday next Saturday. We're hugging ourselves with glee, and not only on account of the felicitous pun (Cretan/cretin). De Roos, the head of housekeeping, is a spiteful woman who doesn't like people, has no sense of humor, and very little patience. It's a mystery how she ever chose a career in the service industry, and then, to make matters worse, ended up in a home for the aged. Let's just put it this way: she isn't exactly doted on here. The fact that she's now fretting about her holiday on Crete does not elicit much sympathy. We wouldn't wish her to be mugged, but a lengthy air traffic controllers' strike, once she is stuck on that island, would be met back home with muffled cheers.

A heat wave is in the offing. On Friday it will get to ninety-one degrees.

"There will be deaths," sighed Evert with a wicked grin. "Every time there's a heat wave, our population is decimated." His table companions stared at him in horror.

Tuesday, June 30

It's getting serious: the National Heat Wave Plan is going into effect!

I didn't even know such a thing existed, but what a sense of security it gives me! With a plan like that in place, surely nothing bad can happen to us.

France is another country that could use a heat wave plan; I read that during the last heat wave, in 2003, 20,000 people died within two weeks. (It didn't say how many of them would have died anyway, but the consternation was sown.)

The Heat Wave Plan is aimed largely at the elderly, the sick, and the obese. We have a good number of residents here who are old, sick, *and* obese, so getting them through the heat all in one piece is quite a job. The body's air-conditioning doesn't work very well in the elderly, nor for that matter does the body's central heating system. Many oldies are therefore always too hot or too cold.

The main thing is to have plenty to drink, but we sometimes forget, because we're so busy sitting at the window. We tend not to feel thirsty. What makes it even harder is that drinking a lot also means having to go to the bathroom a lot. Peeing is a strenuous undertaking, which we like to postpone as long as possible. Some people just do it in their diaper, whether by accident or on purpose. It doesn't make the air smell any fresher, especially when it's hot, but it does save a laborious trip to the bathroom.

Other National Heat Wave Plan recommendations: don't sit in the sun, and avoid unnecessary exertion. Well, there you are! Finally, people are advised to open their windows at night.

"So I didn't sleep a wink because of all the mosquitoes," Mrs. Slothouwer complained.

"Mosquitoes are very fond of sour blood," Evert cheerfully explained.

Wednesday, July 1

The heat has claimed its first victim: a zebra finch. Mrs. Bregman had withdrawn to her sleeping alcove, with the curtains closed and the fan going, but she'd left the birdcage out on the windowsill in the sun. The poor zebra finch couldn't take it. Sister Morales, whose Spanish blood makes her more able to resist the heat, took it upon herself to take a temperature reading: right inside the window, it was 135 degrees. A case of slow cooking.

"But it's a tropical bird, isn't it, so shouldn't it be able to take the heat?" Bregman blubbered to anyone willing to listen. It could be that it simply died of old age, of course. The parakeets in the hall downstairs are still alive. There's a sign on the cage saying they shouldn't be fed prawn crackers. Apparently someone once did.

"It doesn't say you can't feed them any other Indonesian food, such as rijsttafel... or sambal..." Graeme once remarked.

The trip to visit Evert's son in Brabant has been postponed for a fortnight. Management has advised us not to travel on account of the heat. According to the

National Meteorological Institute, on Friday it will be eighty-eight degrees, and Saturday ninety-five degrees. Not the most pleasant weather for outings or socializing. If you're trying to move as little as possible, you might as well do it in your room, with the blinds drawn. Our home doesn't have air-conditioning; too expensive, probably, or it wasn't standard when this place was built back in the 1960s. Which means that during the day the temperature in my room fluctuates in the region of eighty degrees. Management did make a fan available for every resident, and downstairs in the conversation lounge there's a portable air-conditioning machine. That helps by a few degrees. Other than that, there isn't much to do about the heat wave but calmly sit it out. Literally.

Thursday, July 2

The branch manager of the supermarket yesterday wanted to have a word with Mrs. Duits.

"Good afternoon, ma'am, may I help you with something?"

"Help me?"

"My colleague tells me you've been sitting here all afternoon."

Mrs. Duits had gone to the Albert Heijn supermarket after lunch because it's so nice and cool in there. She sat down at the little table where customers are invited to enjoy a free cup of coffee or tea. It's become a gathering spot for people down on their luck and women in headscarves. One wonders if that was what old Albert had in mind. After three cups of free tea, Mrs. Duits had nodded off a bit, until the manager came along to wake her up.

It must be said: in the Albert Heijn it's a good forty-five degrees cooler than in our home.

Mrs. Van Dam is especially affected by this heat. She suffers from the chills, and so possesses only winter clothes. She pays for it during a heat wave. Yesterday afternoon she was a pitiful sight. After perspiring all day, white salt stains had formed under her armpits, and the heavy synthetic material had given her neck a nasty red rash. Since she's already all black and blue from her Parkinson's, she looked like a walking national flag.

"You'd better watch out that your dress doesn't spontaneously burst into flames in this heat," Leonie said.

"Oh, could it?" Van Dam squealed in alarm.

Friday, July 3

Life in here never offers a wide range of exciting events to start with, but now it all boils down to one thing: the heat wave.

"Oh, I wish I was dead," Mrs. Slothouwer wailed.

Ha, if only you were, I couldn't help thinking after hearing her say it for the tenth time. "You might perhaps consider expressing your death wish just a little less insistently," I suggested as genially as I could. She stared at me in surprise, and then sent me a look that intimated she wouldn't mind seeing me keel over first before her own departure for the happy hunting ground.

I received support from Mrs. Smit: "I wouldn't mind

either if Our Dear Lord came for me now, but there's no need to shout it from the rooftops."

Nicely put, Mrs. Smit.

Tomorrow is the start of the Tour de France, in Utrecht. The forecast says it will be ninety-three degrees.

"The Pope continues to surprise us," said Graeme. "This time he's going to try chewing coca leaves when he visits Colombia. It seems the Father of the Church is keen to sample the pleasures of this world. Maybe he should try a woman too, some time."

"Tssk," came the sound of indignation from nearby. That was the Catholic sector.

"Sorry, that wasn't very respectful of me," said Graeme, who was on a roll. "I mean, in regards to the poor woman."

Saturday, July 4

I had a restless night, with little sleep and lots of mosquitoes. I am too slow now to swat and kill them. The slipper kept landing uselessly against the wall, and I had no citronella. I'll have to go out and buy some.

I plan to have a morning siesta right after coffee, then back downstairs for a light lunch, after which I shall install myself in front of the box at 2 p.m. Blinds lowered and curtains drawn, glass of water and pack of biscuits within reach. When it's over eighty-six degrees, there's nothing more soothing than allowing the Tour de France to wash over you gently for hours, like a cool footbath. I like to change the channel every thirty minutes, switching back and forth between the Dutch and Belgian sportscasters. I don't need any company, they'll only drown out the commentary with misinformed observations. There are very few cycling experts here; Mr. Pot is the only one who's quite knowledgeable on the subject, but he's a fount of cranky opinions, so I'm not inviting him. If anyone knocks on the door, I won't answer.

Besides, there's very little chance that someone will be dropping in. During this heat the corridors are deserted in the afternoon. Everyone's in their room dozing in the dark. Every ounce of strength is frugally saved for breathing and for withstanding the high temperatures. Sometimes we don't even come down for tea. We don't even have the energy to talk about the weather. The nurse looks in on us twice a day, just to check if we're still alive. If we are, she urges us to stay hydrated—drink and keep drinking!

Sunday, July 5

Another similarity between little children and the elderly: they can't eat without making a dreadful mess. Bibs are de rigueur, and plastic tablecloths too. Not a meal goes by without trails of gravy stains from the pan to the plate. Potatoes are dropped onto laps, peas roll off the table, and pudding drips onto trousers and skirts.

Our champion food dribbler is Mrs. Langeveld, the time she ate a magnum at ninety degrees. It was fascinating, and also rather disgusting, to see her doughy tongue extend slowly toward the ice cream, then pull in again equally slowly, only to have most of the ice cream and chocolate coating land on her chin, hands, neck, and frock. You couldn't make a bigger mess if you tried. After that ice cream she really needed a shower.

To be honest: I am not a stranger to clumsiness myself. In the past three days I have knocked over one container of yogurt, spilled one cup of coffee, and found myself sharing a seat with a potted plant.

"Groen in clover," was Edward's reaction to that last mishap. The plants in here are luckily quite used to that sort of thing. I have the sense that the hot weather is making me even slower and more ungainly than I normally am.

Monday, July 6

It's become a great new tradition: half an hour after the end of each stage of the Tour de France (there have been two so far), I join Evert in a glass of something very good, actually, something that's the finest of the fine. The money must be spent as quickly as possible. Then Evert asks for a short summary of that day's Tour.

"I'm not a big fan of cycling myself, but I do like to hear you talk about it."

Then I'll tell him what happened that day, and we drink a toast to the winner, no matter what nationality he is. Then we'll play a game of lightning chess, in order not to be late for the evening meal.

The Greek population's "No" has not gone unnoticed here. Extra cash is being stuffed into socks, more biscuits and sweets are being squirreled away, and people are expressing a great deal of sympathy for poor Nana Mouskouri. The threat of a shortage of feta or raki, however, is unlikely to affect most of the residents that much.

On to the order of the day: the weather. Fortunately the heat has died down somewhat. Except for the zebra finch, there are no victims to mourn.

"Stelwagen said it's all due to the precautionary measures she took," Sister Morales confided to me. "That's what she told us in the staff meeting. Well, isn't that something! She didn't do a thing!"

Morales is growing less and less enamored with Mrs. Stelwagen. Something to do with a less than stellar performance review. Since that happened, she has been gossiping even more enthusiastically than before. I don't really like it, but I haven't yet wanted to confront her with it. Add to that the fact that even though I dislike gossip, I do want to find out as much as I can about Stelwagen.

Tuesday, July 7

The director has informed the Residents' Committee, in a letter, that there is no financial leeway in the 2016 budget for the construction of a boules court, but she will do her best to clear the necessary financial decks for 2017.

"Therefore the court could be ready as early as the summer of 2017."

AS EARLY AS!?

I am considering writing back that, statistically speaking, a third of the current residents won't be able to use the court because they'll be dead by then.

"We may live slowly, but with death snapping at our heels, haste is of the essence." I think that's a rather good ending for my letter to Stelwagen; that "of the essence" sounds elegant, although I'm not sure if that's the right use of it.

Mrs. Schansleh recently put it this way: "Time is slipping through my fingers like a ripe banana."

Several fights that have recently broken out at a German swimming pool have led to security screenings. I suspect it's to prevent people from trying to smuggle in baseball bats in their swimming trunks.

I would love to go swimming again. After a thorough memory search, I came to the conclusion that it must have been about eighteen years since my last foray into a pool.

"You never forget how to swim, same as riding a bike," someone remarked recently. I would suggest that the person in question, if he's thinking of climbing on a bike again, start off not far from the Emergency entrance. He'll never stay on for more than 65 feet. And so now I'm told that one doesn't forget how to swim either. Yet I would advise someone in his eighties against climbing up to the high diving board. Best stick to the paddling pool instead.

Actually, maybe swimming would be something for the Old But Not Dead. Surely they must have an hour reserved for the elderly at the local pool? Not as one of our mystery tour outings, but simply as an activity for anyone who'd enjoy it. I'll find out if there's any interest. Meanwhile I shall have to dig around to see if I still have a bathing costume somewhere.

* * *

Twenty-six years ago the wall separating East and West came down, to great jubilation. Now Hungary has started building a ninety-three-mile-long fence along its border with Serbia. There's a great call for new walls and fences. Even here in our care home, despite the fact that, for many of the residents, the outside world is already an impenetrable fortress.

Wednesday, July 8

I stare, amazed, at all the tattoos one sees in the shopping center when the weather's nice. Modesty and good taste have flown out the window a bit: eagles, snakes, flags, hearts, cars, naked women. I have to ask myself what one of those great big eagle tattoos will look like when it's soaring across the mottled, wrinkled skin of an eighty-five-year-old grandpa. A most bedraggled sort of raptor, I expect. Nor will the inked portrait of a loved one be a spitting image fifty years later. No, pity the nurses who some fifty years from now will have to wash the wrinkled creases and hides of the garishly tattooed in their dotage.

For that matter, you see more and more people who even in their forties and fifties seem to think they're improving their appearance by adorning their bodies with tawdry cartoons. I have yet to see anyone tattooed with a lovely reproduction of Vermeer's *Girl with the Pearl Earring*. Or with Paulus Potter's *Young Bull*—nice and macho.

Ria's take on it: blame it on the soccer players, who are the role models for the young. They don't train hard enough, and so have too much time to spend at the hairdresser's and tattoo parlor.

I have also seen youngsters with great big holes in their earlobes. I wonder if those saucers in the bottom lip favored by some African tribes could also become fashionable in the Netherlands? I can't rule anything out.

Thursday, July 9

The resident with the longest track history here has left us: after ninety-eight years, Mrs. Schepers yesterday breathed her last. She lived here for twenty-four years, longer than she had ever lived anywhere else. When she first came here in 1991, the rules about moving in were far more lenient. You could apply when you turned seventy, if I'm not mistaken, and there would be a place for you. Mrs. Schepers outlived hundreds of other inmates, and saw dozens of attendants come and go. She also outlasted five directors and seven cooks. She kept a close eye on everything and never expressed any dissatisfaction. On the other hand, she never let a day go by without remarking, "Such a shame my husband can't be here to enjoy this." She came here as a widow, so she must have said it at least 8,500 times since then.

This past year she'd become a ghost-resident: the ones who seldom leave their rooms. Meals and beverages were brought up to her. She had just barely enough energy for the transfer from bed to chair and back again. There are about twenty others in here whiling away their last days that way. On weekdays they see no one but the nurses;

on the weekend they see only their offspring. If they're lucky they die peacefully in their own beds, and so never have to go into the nursing home.

Friday, July 10

Greece possibly leaving the EU, the Chinese stock market slump, a new tax plan, refugees on the high seas; it doesn't make us eat one ginger biscuit less. The influence of the world outside our cocoon is largely limited to the seasons. The cocoon has started to show some cracks, however. Even the most introverted residents are starting to notice how many vacant rooms there are. It is rumored that some people are being asked to move to another room, so that a whole section can be emptied. Can't the Residents' Committee do something about that?

The Residents' Committee is meeting this afternoon to discuss it.

Mrs. Hoensbroek just ate a chocolate still in its foil wrapper. Her tablemate looked on in astonishment, but waited until Hoensbroek had laboriously managed to work it all down to ask, "Why didn't you take the wrapper off?"

"Wrapper?"

"Yes, you just ate the foil as well."

"Did I?"

Mrs. Hoensbroek picked up another chocolate and studied it. Ah, indeed, it was wrapped in foil. She called the nurse over. Who told her not to worry.

Well, at least something of interest to report.

* * *

Omar Sharif is dead. Ria cut his picture out of the newspaper and pinned it to the noticeboard.

She said she'd seen *Doctor Zhivago* at least seven times, the last time just a couple of months earlier, on the telly.

"I cried all seven times. A bit less every time, but still."

Antoine gazed tenderly at his wife. He is still in love with her. If you really love someone, it's okay for her to love Omar Sharif as well.

Saturday, July 11

Many people prefer to watch the Youth News rather than the regular news. At least the Youth News always has something cheerful to report on: a newborn polar bear cub, a dog that plays the trumpet, the return of a parrot given up for dead. It's often something to do with animals.

That's the sort of thing they ought to show on the Eight O'Clock News. It should end on a positive note is the widely shared opinion, and I must agree. After the weather report, a little levity to signal: come on, people, it isn't all doom and gloom.

We were *this* close to having to bury our friend Antoine. Not that it wouldn't have been a fitting end for him. "He died while eating," the obituary might have said. He'd been enjoying an illicit homemade tartlet with his eyes closed so as to savor it more fully, you understand. In this case, it meant that he couldn't see the wasp he was biting into as well. A second later his eyes flew open wider than wide; he'd been stung in the cheek. Sister Herwegen, always on her toes, promptly came up with an old-fashioned antidote for wasp stings: a cut onion. His cheek nevertheless swelled up to worrisome proportions and the doctor was called in.

"You are very lucky, Mr. Travemundi, a few centimeters further in, and you could have been a goner," he said after a brief inspection of the puffed-up interior of Antoine's mouth. Ria started to tremble—retroactively, since she had at first thought her husband was just putting it on.

"Well," said Edward, chuckling, "I suppose that for the time being, at least, there'll be no more of that la-di-dah with your eyes closed." Antoine's appetite is temporarily spoilt. And every resident now inspects every biscuit from every angle before taking a cautious nibble. Mrs. Hoensbroek has totally sworn off biccies. Actually, it's all for the best. She tends to buy dresses that are one or two wishful sizes too small, XL instead of XXL, or even XXXL. Perhaps her clothes will start to feel a little less tight now. She doesn't consider herself fat. She claims heavy bones and water retention are responsible for her girth. The daily cream cake and all the biscuits and chocolates with her coffee should certainly not have much to do with it.

The wasps, by the way, are very early this year.

Sunday, July 12

"It's high time we began working on our international restaurant project again," Antoine said at our last-minute convocation of the Old But Not Dead Club. "We'll fall behind on the culinary front if we're not careful. Does anyone have any ideas?"

Edward put his hand up. He volunteered to reserve somewhere for Tuesday evening.

I have again asked Evert when he is going to inform his Old But Not Dead Club friends that his membership is soon to expire.

"When they ask me about it, not before," he replied. I must have looked puzzled. "When people start noticing of their own accord that something's not right with me, that'll be soon enough to confirm it. Until then, there's no reason for anyone to know I'm dying. I'd rather not have to face the blubbering and lamentation, or chums who don't know what to do or say."

It took me a night to think it over, but Evert is right: it's often best to put off announcing the bad news as long as possible. Especially if the victim in question, in this case Evert, won't exactly be overjoyed if his nearest and dearest start mourning his departure while he's still alive.

I see now that I am the one chosen to share the preliminary awareness of his impending death. For even Evert needs someone to confide in and exchange black humor with. He knows I won't indulge in weeping and lamentation.

"You can blubber in your own good time, Groen. Not while I'm alive."

I think Leonie can tell he is doing poorly. She tends to stay close and looks after him discreetly but tenderly, almost intimately. And Evert allows himself to be coddled and seems even to be enjoying it in his own oafish way.

She's allowed to straighten his jacket, to brush crumbs from his cheek. Whereas Evert disparagingly refers to most elderly women as "old biddies," his name for Leonie is "pet." That's how he expresses his fondness for her.

Monday, July 13

"You've got to hand it to that El Chapo chap," Mr. Pot remarked. The fact that the drug lord was responsible for bumping off quite a few people is less significant in Pot's books than his escape from one of Mexico's highest-security prisons.

"Through a tunnel a mile long! They even had a motorbike waiting for him down there so he wouldn't have to walk the whole way." Pot was all hopped up about it. He grew even more excited when someone else mentioned that, back in 2001, Chapo had escaped prison in a laundry basket.

"I don't suppose that in Mexico they'd ever heard of the chest of books Hugo Grotius hid in to escape from prison," said Graeme, "otherwise that enormously heavy laundry basket of dirty underwear would have set off some alarm bells."

Tuesday, July 14

No, no, we definitely should not view the vacancies as a prelude to the home's closing, but as a step of a much broader process of optimization and transition.

"What does that optimization and transition look like, then?" Leonie demanded.

These matters were still subject to a more narrow decision-making process by the board; as long as they were still "under discussion," the director could not, to her great regret, give us any further information. Although, naturally, she would like nothing better than to be allowed at this time to discuss these matters with the Residents' Committee.

"I do get the sense, nevertheless, that this committee is not being taken entirely seriously, I feel like we're being kept dangling," said Leonie curtly.

"Oh, no, not at all," Stelwagen insisted with a condescending smile. "Fortunately, I did manage to get two other very important matters resolved by the board," she went on, informing us that our proposals for a residents' art exhibition and a high tea had both received board approval.

Leonie could not help remarking that those two requests were on quite a different level to whether or not the institution would close for good.

"You're absolutely right about that. But he who doesn't appreciate the small things..."

Fingernails on a blackboard. Stelwagen is like an arrogant tyrant and a patronizing nursery school teacher all rolled into one.

The permission for the art exhibition was actually a bit of a con, since it was granted six weeks ago. Eugenie has been busy at work on her paintings and Stelwagen can count on her support until the end of time. The art show won't cost the institution a thing except for the wall hooks to hang the paintings. The maintenance department did make a big fuss about those hooks at first, citing the strict no-holes-in-the-walls policy. Stelwagen then stepped in personally, magnanimously declaring that with the director's consent, the prevailing no-holes policy may be waived in exceptional circumstances.

The high tea, however, does come with a few stringent conditions attached. We are not allowed to go near any electrical appliances or slicers. (To prevent anyone finding a piece of finger sticking out of their cream cake.) And we're not allowed to serve hot drinks. Not an unreasonable restriction, but an unnecessary one, since it is already in effect. The high tea project must be "cost neutral"; the director therefore suggested charging a small monetary contribution. We were completely against it at first, but during a brief adjournment, Leonie helped us to see it differently.

"Asking for a contribution from participants will bring its own natural selection. All the sour skinflints will drop out, and only the bons vivants will be left."

Upon which the proposal to collect a modest contribution from the high tea-totallers was passed by unanimous consent.

Wednesday, July 15

Yesterday it was the turn of Restaurant Mount Everest to receive the Old But Not Dead Club.

The Nepalese hostess spent a great deal of time on us, which wasn't such a problem, since we were the only patrons. It was extremely enjoyable, as usual; if you're in good company, not much can go wrong. Even if the Nepalese wine did turn out to be rather disappointing. The beer from Nepal was quite palatable, however. We ordered a few mystery specialties and gave the old taste buds a thorough workout. Mindful eating isn't an easy thing to do. At home I often catch myself barely tasting what I'm eating. You put something in your mouth while looking around and listening to your table companions, you rearrange your napkin, chew mechanically, and then you swallow. It's a good thing you look down and see what's on your plate, otherwise you wouldn't even know what it was that you ate a minute ago.

But when we eat out, it's not like that. Ria and Antoine are strict with us, and make sure, with expert questions and remarks, that we don't just thoughtlessly stuff our faces, but pay close attention to what we are tasting.

During the meal I was watching Evert out of the corner of my eye. He seemed to be enjoying himself immensely, but hardly ate a thing. He's lost a lot of weight.

Farmers will soon have their own TV channel, a twenty-four-hour broadcast, no less, with documentaries and profiles of farmers and growers. Interesting. That news item led several people here to argue that what's needed is a twenty-four-hour channel for the elderly. It would bring us fascinating profiles and documentaries about old age.

Why don't you just gaze at all the elderly profiles around you, I was going to suggest, but decided it wouldn't be nice. In hindsight, I realized I was being far too well-behaved again, for a change.

Thursday, July 16

Jan is picking us up for a pleasant weekend in Uden at 10 a.m. tomorrow morning. I'm looking forward to Wii-ing with his kids. Last year I beat them at tennis on several occasions, and even at ski jumping once, but in the intervening year I haven't had an opportunity to practice, and they have. I also expect that my young opponents may have let their jolly grandpa-guest win now and then, and trust that they'll do so again, preferably as discreetly as possible.

It might be a better idea to postpone our stay once more, since it is going to be very hot. It's like trying to cross a busy street. You stand there waiting for an opening. Suddenly there's a chance you could make it to the other side, but you decide: don't risk it, best wait a bit. Then, if it's taking forever and you're starting to run out of patience, you cross just when it's far more dangerous than the time you let the opportunity pass you by. You're always moving the goalposts.

Not to mention my elderly brothers and sisters who, when they cross the street, tend to rely on respect for their advanced age. I have yet to see the stubborn and rather deaf Mr. De Grave do anything but point his cane to the other side just before stepping out, looking neither left nor right. He walks at an angle, with the traffic, to give the cars a chance to swerve around him. One time he even caused a small pile-up behind him, to which he remained completely oblivious. It happened very close to here, and a short time later the police came to "ask a few questions."

"No idea what you're talking about, Mr. Officer," Mr.

De Grave said, "it must have been another bloke with a hat and cane."

Even within these walls De Grave has caused a number of accidents with his completely unpredictable changes of course. It's never his fault, naturally. His wife, Rietje, is the opposite: she cops to everything immediately, even if she's not in the least to blame. It does in a sense balance out their relationship. But I wouldn't be surprised if, in her heart of hearts, she sometimes wishes she could very slowly strangle him to death.

Tuesday, July 21

The overnight visit was not a success. Worse than that, it was a pileup of minor and major miseries.

I already wasn't feeling that well when we departed. My stomach and intestines were rumbling. I didn't want to be a spoilsport, however; the weekend trip had already been postponed once, and I hoped it would blow over. It did not blow over, it just blew. Upon arrival in Uden, I was in urgent need of a shower. Fouled my diaper in the car, and some of it had run out the sides. I could have died of embarrassment. Ester, Evert's daughter-in-law, did her best to conceal her disgust as she got rid of my diaper and tossed my pants and underpants into the washing machine.

The entire house is polished to a T, everything tidied up and shoes have to be left at the front door. That's the kind of housekeeper Ester is.

"Not to worry, Mr. Groen, it can happen to anyone."

I muttered my apologies for the fourth time.

That same Friday night I again failed to make it to the bathroom in time. There I was at 3 a.m., trying to clean up the poo as best I could, when Jan knocked on the door. Was anything the matter? He helped me without saying a word. When everything was sort of clean again, he put his arm around my shoulders.

"It's not easy, sometimes, is it?"

No, it's not easy sometimes.

The following afternoon, as Evert and I sat sweltering under a parasol, my friend asked me when I thought would be a good time to tell them about "it."

"There isn't a good time," I said after giving it some thought for a while.

"Then I'll just put it off a while longer, as I've done with the Old But Not Dead gang," said Evert.

I remarked that there might not be another opportunity to inform them of it in person. He sees his son, daughter-in-law, and grandchildren only once every four or five weeks. I suggested that he tell them that evening after supper. We were quiet for a while.

"Well then, after pudding, I suppose," said Evert, "otherwise it's a waste of the strawberries. Then we'll still have Sunday to get a bit used to the idea, together."

I could tell that he dreaded it enormously.

We spent the rest of Saturday unable to do much except sit in the garden in the shade. I had swallowed a good handful of anti-diarrhea pills, but still did not dare stray too far from the toilet. Even playing Wii with the children, which I'd been so looking forward to, seemed to me too dangerous an undertaking. We were all doing our best to act cheerful, but even a lunchtime libation did not do much to lighten the rather depressed mood.

The meal passed in relative silence. After the strawberries, I saw Evert looking at me. I nodded. He coughed a few times.

"My dear family, I am sorry to have to inform you that I am going to die quite soon. I have cancer."

For a moment it was as if a film had been put on pause. Then Evert's grandchildren began to cry. Jan said nothing, and grabbed his father's hand. Ester put her arms around both of her children. I sat there mute. Jan asked about the medical details. Evert told them that the doctor, with some hesitation, had said that they were "running out of treatment options."

"He wanted to try a few things to buy some more time, but I told him I'd had enough. Once the body is finished, it's finished. If that's the case, I'm not interested in prolonging the agony."

They took turns hugging Evert. He let them, possibly for the first time in his life.

"And now I wouldn't mind a nice nip of brandy," he concluded.

To complete a weekend of disasters, when we got home Sunday afternoon, Mo's back legs suddenly crumpled as he was getting out of the car. He managed to get back on his feet half an hour later, after Evert had jammed a few aspirins down his throat. The emergency vet on call couldn't come because he was out on an emergency.

Wednesday, July 22

Couldn't he just take a cab and bring the dog in?

In simple but pointed wording, Evert explained to the vet's assistant that in this case it would be a lot simpler for the doctor to come to the patient.

That morning Mo hadn't clambered out of his basket. He was looking even sadder than usual, and even refused a treat.

Once the vet arrived, it turned out that Mo had also wet his basket.

"How old is Mo?" asked the doctor, after peering here and tapping there.

Evert reckoned he was about sixteen.

"That's a ripe old age, for a dog."

"That's why he lives in a sheltered basket, doctor."

The vet pronounced a diagnosis in Latin, wrote a prescription, and gave Mo an injection.

"I haven't much of a clue about what you just said; I just want to know if there's anything that can be done about it," said Evert.

"We'll do our best."

In cases like this, I don't think it's a good sign when people use the word "we." As if they're willing to share the responsibility for the blow that's coming with unnamed others.

It must be said that an hour after receiving the shot, Mo, with a great deal of groaning, did hoist himself back on his feet and drank some water. After a walk from the front door to the curb and back again, he collapsed into his basket again with a grunt.

Thursday, July 23

Two pythons were found in a Dumpster just a few hundred yards from here. Their owner apparently wanted to get rid of them. Mr. Dickhout breathlessly reported that he had walked past that Dumpster just yesterday, as if he'd narrowly escaped death by strangulation.

"Oh, Indiana Jones, stop exaggerating," Evert sneered, "those baby snakes were only half a yard long. They wouldn't even stretch round your fat neck."

I have never really understood people who love snakes, and even less so since seeing a documentary about a pet shop in North Amsterdam. There was a bloke who came every week to buy a live bunny to feed to his snake. It may have been a hamster, I don't recall. Snap, gulp; bye-bye, sweet little bunny. I can picture the owner gazing contentedly at the bulge in his pet's body, maybe still squirming a bit? Wouldn't you think the fellow should sit in the crocodile pit in the zoo for a while, to make him see the error of his ways?

Mo seems to be doing a little better.

The Alps stages of the Tour de France are providing me with a most necessary diversion. Whiling away a few hours watching men toiling up mountains on their bikes, in an unashamedly chauvinistic frame of mind, does me good. *Go Holland Go!* "We" aren't doing too badly, with two Dutchmen in the top ten. Okay, we haven't yet won a stage, but I'm sure it will happen.

Friday, July 24

At morning tea a difference of opinion arose on an important question: should you be disqualified from the Nijmegen Four-Day March if you're doing those twenty-five miles on crutches? The debate was set off by a photo in the paper showing an official mercilessly cutting through the wristband of a lady on crutches. Ha! Now she could kiss that medal goodbye.

Everyone could agree, however, about another marcher who was caught covering part of the distance by taxi: he should be debarred for life. This year there are mobile brigades whose job it is to sniff out cheaters. Do you really think the other marchers could give a hoot if a handful of participants win one of those silly medals without actually deserving it? The answer, probably, is a thousand times yes. People who enjoy marching with the herd are people with a highly developed sense of discipline and honor.

There are people who watch the televised coverage of the march every day.

"My, my, five thousand blisters yesterday!" I heard someone mutter, aghast.

There are over 40,000 marchers this year, and the organization is expecting a million spectators, I read. That's twenty-five spectators per marcher, which does seem a bit much. I used to love walking, but I think I'd have taken a cab from start to finish so as not to drown in such a sea of humanity.

Mr. Verlaat came down for coffee this morning with his own Four-Day medals pinned to his lapel. Eight of them, collected between 1973 and 1984. He was eager to tell us all sorts of stories, such as the fact he'd have two pieces of gingerbread toast for breakfast before setting out each morning.

"To prevent blisters."

There were some skeptical frowns, because it's not often you hear such rot, even in here.

"I never had any blisters myself, so it had to have been the gingerbread."

"A watertight argument, I must say, Verlaat," said Graeme.

Saturday, July 25

Did you know there's an old-age hip-hop troupe? Evert's granddaughter showed us a clip of this club on YouTube last week; they call themselves Hip Op-eration (or something like it). I am a great proponent of old people staying active and keeping up with the times, but there are limits. Hip-hoppers of over seventy overstep those bounds. It hurt my eyes to see this sad demonstration of "look how with-it we are." I'm willing to listen to all sorts of music, but hip-hop isn't one of them. My rather old-fashioned verdict: amateurish doggerel with a lot of "fuck" and "shit" chanted to a computer-racket beat. When you get twenty oldies dressed all in black doing a wooden little dance to it, quite out of step with one another, I think they are a disgrace to our generation. I can get all hot under the collar about it. If I'd been there and had access to a water cannon, then that YouTube video would have had quite a different outcome.

In the same old-people-trying-far-too-hard category: British housewife Mrs. Doris Long, 102, has broken her own rappelling record. Daredevil Doris, the oldest abseiler in the world, sailed down a building 103 meters high.

Sunday, July 26

Mo is dead. The vet gave him an injection yesterday afternoon. Mo was stretched out on the table, Evert held his head, and I held Evert. The dog groaned softly, gave his owner one last sad, glassy gaze, shuddered, and died. There were tears in my friend's eyes. And in my own.

"Will you take care of the burial arrangements yourself, or should I have someone come for him?" the doctor asked. "It would incur certain costs."

"You can go now. We'll take care of the rest ourselves," Evert snapped.

First there was the little matter of settling the €130 bill, in cash. I took care of it with the vet out in the hall.

Evert immediately rang Jan. He's driving the car up from Uden today. We have wrapped Mo carefully in his own old blanket, and this afternoon we'll drive to the woods to bury him. I don't think it's allowed, but we'll just risk the fine. Evert wants it done this way.

"On the one hand, I'm glad he died before me. I don't know what would have become of him. They don't accept dogs this old at the shelter, do they? I'd have had to give him an injection myself."

He gave a deep sigh.

"It's best this way."

Monday, July 27

In order to avoid the Sunday strollers, we had waited until the late afternoon to load Mo into the car. Then we hoisted in Evert, then the wheelchair, and finally yours truly. Jan had brought a shovel from home. It was raining, which was lucky, because that meant very few walkers in the woods, with or without dogs. It took us quite a while to find a suitably secluded spot. There Jan dug a big hole, not an easy feat because of the tree roots. He was drenched in rain and sweat. Evert looked on in silence from his wheelchair with the dead dog wrapped in the old blanket on his lap. At one point a jogger disturbed us. We pretended we were very interested in trees, which didn't seem so farfetched, since we were in the woods. The young man stared at our strange little group in surprise, nodded, and ran on.

When the hole was deep enough, Jan and I picked Mo's blanket up by the edges and carefully lowered him in. Evert muttered, "Goodbye, Mo," and then Jan filled the hole, covering the grave with twigs and leaves. Back in the car, Evert gave a deep sigh.

"There, that's done. Now a drink, before anything else."

A little later we were sipping brandy, waiting for the pizza delivery.

"You know, an old dog barely stirs all day long. Some grunts and groans, a few farts, and a waddle three times a day to and from the patch of turf where he does his business. And yet—it's company. You talk to him, at least I do, and he'll cock his head as if he's listening. You won't see a goldfish doing that."

Jan and I nodded. It was true.

Tuesday, July 28

It's something you might not expect to hear, but even here a juicy sex scandal is greatly appreciated. Especially if an elderly English lord is implicated. And, better yet, not one, but two prostitutes, a line of cocaine snorted through a rolled-up banknote off a naked female breast. A film with that many tired clichés would get terrible reviews. But truth is always better than fiction: this Lord Sewel also happens to be the chairman of a committee in the House of Lords that's supposed to make sure the gents behave themselves. He was paid £119,000 per year for that post. Sewel had written a few weeks ago: "The actions of a few damage our reputation." And: "Scandals make good headlines." Not one word was a lie. And the cherry on top: a picture in the paper of this lord modeling an orange bra.

Old people and sex are not a happy combination. Sex is only discussed here in extremely couched terms. Mr. Dickhout is the only one who likes to boast of his former prowess.

"Women used to call me Tyrannosaurus Sex," he bragged.

"Well, isn't *that* a coincidence," said Leonie, "I just read in the paper that Ted Kennedy used to say the same thing."

"Well, then he must have got the idea from me," said Dickhout, his face red as a beetroot.

What I can never understand is that even men of the highest rank can't seem to keep their salacious details out of the papers, with Clinton's horny cigar in Monica's humidor the high (or low) point. The exception was our assassinated would-be prime minister, Pim Fortuyn, who didn't think it necessary to hide the fact he had frequent sex in the "darkroom" with Moroccan boys. That wasn't offensive, apparently, because he wasn't trying to hide it.

Wednesday, July 29

People are mourning two deaths that are by no means run-of-the-mill: Cecil the lion, and Hitchbot the robot hitchhiker. The lion was shot dead by an American dentist who'd paid $20,000 for the privilege. The first attempt was with bow and arrow. Perhaps the hunter had some Native American blood in him. When that failed, he used a rifle. The dentist has gone into hiding, and his practice is suffering. Before Twitter and Facebook nobody would have given a hoot about a dead lion. Besides, it hasn't even been that long since American cowboys and Indians cheerfully bumped off forty million buffalo. I'm sure there was at least one dentist among the buffalo hunters.

The other dear departed also received much commiseration here: Hitchbot. It was an experiment—a little robot that held up a sign by the side of the road saying where he wished to go. His creators wanted to know what would happen. He'd already thumbed rides all over the place, and was treated with great kindness, until the day he was found lying in a ditch somewhere. Someone had decapitated Hitchbot.

Speaking of robots, there are some that should count on

far less sympathy: the killerbots. The paper reported that it may not be long before death and destruction will be sown on the battlefield by mechanical combatants. I bet it won't take long for a robot to decide to join a terrorist organization, either, or start one by itself. Scientists and technicians will fail to take responsibility for it, as usual.

"Let's hope we won't be around to see it," was the fervent wish.

Robots in the care industry aren't jubilantly welcomed by us either.

"If a robot ever comes to help me get dressed, I'll yank the batteries out," someone said. A ghastly prospect, to be cared for by a machine. Yet there's a lot of research being done on robots in the care industry. The rationale is that if those tasks can be done by a robot, the human staff will have more time to pay some *real* attention to the inmates—in the form of a chat, for example. I predict, however, that management would decide that little chats weren't one of life's important necessities, and would cut costs by sacking the superfluous employees.

Thursday, July 30

Has Mrs. Slothouwer overplayed her hand? She has been spreading the story that she's been abused by her son on several occasions. Slothouwer is by far the least sympathetic resident of our home. Opinions about the abuse are threefold. There are those who believe what Slothouwer is saying, but think her son is completely justified in treating her harshly. A second group of the residents think she's made it up to make her son look bad. A third camp thinks that the apple doesn't fall far from the tree and that the son could well have caused the bruises Slothouwer showed one of the nurses. For many residents, proof, or at the very least some evidence, are not necessary for them to reach a verdict. I myself am keeping an open mind for now.

According to police statistics, elder abuse is probably very common, but it is rarely reported. Old people are often completely dependent on their children or caretakers, which makes them extremely vulnerable. They're afraid that filing a complaint will only make matters worse for them. A classic tip of the iceberg.

I would guess that here in the home it isn't too prevalent, but I wouldn't bet my life that even here there's no hitting, pinching, or stealthy emptying of bank accounts going on.

Friday, July 31

The director first had a long talk with Mrs. Slothouwer, and then announced there will be an investigation, in consultation with the GP. In case it's necessary to press charges. Since that talk Slothouwer has kept her mouth shut about the whole affair. We don't know what tactics Stelwagen used to make her shut up, but that too may well verge on elder abuse. I am not suggesting anything like waterboarding, but I wouldn't rule out a veiled threat about a transfer to the locked ward.

Meanwhile the son has signed an affidavit saying that he never hurt a hair on his mother's head. Which isn't saying much. I don't call that news—unless he'd confessed straight out to dragging his mother across the room on a regular basis and beating her black and blue.

With that, the peace is restored, at least for the time being, and, knowing Stelwagen, that was her primary and most important goal.

Saturday, August 1

"We should think about procuring ourselves a ring, from Perry Sport."

"Ring?"

"A rubber ring, you know, for swimming. The climate scientists have updated their calculations, and they're predicting the sea level is going to rise by ten feet."

"Well, I'm on the fifth floor, so by the time that sea level reaches me . . . I won't be around to see it."

Mrs. Smit was growing visibly irritated at our flippant remarks. She thought we should be thinking of her grandchildren, who in that event would have to move to South Limburg.

Having weathered four heat waves, we are all finally agreed that the climate is out of whack. It's quite possible that the consequences of global warming will turn out to be a much greater disaster, and also happen much sooner than we think. Homo sapiens is an animal that is not too concerned about the species as a whole. And it's the only animal capable of annihilating the entire planet, whether by accident or on purpose. Thinking about it doesn't make me happy. The fact that I am standing with one foot in the grave, with no children or grandchildren to worry about, doesn't make it any better.

There have been lots of articles in the papers again lately about preventing dementia. As of now it still comes down to healthy eating and keeping the body and mind fit. You don't have to be senile to know that those things are good for you.

Sunday, August 2

We, the members of the Residents' Committee, have sent the director a letter demanding that something be done about the elevator congestion. Yesterday Graeme broke another record: it took him all of twenty-four minutes to get from his room on the fifth floor down to the dining room.

One of the elevators was being used for a move. The room of a lady who passed away on Wednesday had to be cleared out by yesterday at the latest. The lady in question hasn't even been laid to rest yet, but rules are rules. The equipment provided for a move of this sort is one laundry cart, and a trolley from the kitchen. If you insist loudly enough, you're allowed to borrow these if they're not in use. Emptying a room with such inadequate means takes at least half a day. Which means that one of the two elevators will be full of boxes and other rubbish. At the rush hour before lunch, some sixty residents have to make their way downstairs. There are only two residents who take the stairs; all the others depend on the elevators, which can hold four fat bodies in a pinch, or five thin people equipped with rollators or other equipment. Taking into account the aggravating amount of time it takes to load and unload, and the fact that the elevator moves at about the same pace as its passengers, it isn't hard to work out that there will be long queues.

Graeme had to let three full elevators go by before managing to squeeze into the fourth one. Then it stopped at every floor, and at the second and third floor, the passengers at the back had to get off. So everyone had to step out. Someone dropped a handkerchief as he was getting in again; by the time he'd picked it up, the doors had closed and the now almost empty elevator continued on its way. Then Graeme had to let two crammed elevators go by again before he was able to continue on his way to his lunchtime sandwich.

We had timed our last ten trips and informed Stelwagen of the outcome. At rush hour, the average time it takes to travel by elevator is more than fifteen minutes.

"The time we have left is scarce, and therefore too precious to spend an average of fifteen minutes doing something as simple as riding up or down a few stories. Moreover, we worry what would happen in an emergency. The sign DON'T USE IN CASE OF FIRE isn't very reassuring. We ask ourselves, "Who's going to carry us downstairs one by one?" That was our letter.

The question, in a nutshell, was: what she was going to do about it ASAP? It is curious that when they built this old-age home, they did not think of installing a third and fourth elevator at the far end of the corridor, where there's only a stairwell, which is also the emergency exit.

Ah well, it's just for old people, and they have all the time in the world, the architect must have reasoned.

Monday, August 3

"What a vain little man you are, Hendrik," Edward said to me yesterday as we sat under the sun umbrella in the garden.

I had to agree. Eighty-five years old, and still sharp.

"Well," Edward granted, "I suppose it's better than turning into a mingy old derelict. We have enough of those here."

I had to agree there as well. It's often all or nothing: you have the residents who eke out their final days immaculately groomed, and you have those who can't even be bothered to disguise their threadbare slippers and moth-eaten clothes.

"What difference does it make now?" the frumps say.

Self-respect, dear senior citizens, it's a question of self-respect.

A bit later I glanced at my reflection in the glass of the patio door and saw a very neat gentleman wearing pale-colored shoes, beige trousers, a short-sleeved blue shirt, immaculately pressed, and a coquettish straw hat resting upon sparse but neatly trimmed hair.

"Hmm, nice-looking gent, if I may say so myself," I muttered.

Yes, what a vain little man you are, Hendrik. Too bad about the diaper. I always worry it shows under my trousers, even though Evert swears you can't tell.

Speaking of Evert, tomorrow he is venturing out with Leonie to buy a new suit. She spontaneously offered to go with him when my chum publicly announced that he needed a new suit. Deliberately, I expect.

"It's the suit for the coffin," he confided to me in a whisper. "But of course Leonie doesn't know that."

I didn't say it, but if I were him, I wouldn't be so sure. Leonie may not have had much schooling, but she is not lacking in intelligence—especially not in social intelligence. As an old head teacher, I would bet my nice new hat that Leonie has her suspicions.

Tuesday, August 4

Since they weren't able to jump in the car and race to the scene of the accident, the rollator-pushing rubberneckers were gathered around the porter's computer. What they were watching, with great excitement, was the umpteenth replay of the collapse of two huge cranes in Alphen aan den Rijn. That poor dog that was buried under the rubble—that was the worst, the residents decided. The poor thing had even barked in the end. A pathetic final death-bark.

Then the sensation seekers trooped into the conversation lounge, where the television had just been switched on for the first on-the-scene reports. These were composed, as usual, of interviews with local residents, witnesses, and experts.

"I thought, what on earth is that noise?"

"So you didn't immediately think it might be two

enormous cranes that toppled onto a bridge spanning eighty-two by fifty feet?" I wished I'd heard the reporter ask.

Equally unsurprising: the deputy mayor says it's a tragic accident.

After the umpteenth replay and yet another inane interview, I decided to take my scooter out for a spin with my unperturbed friend Geert. For him to get perturbed you'd need something more than the collapse of a couple of building cranes. It was hot. The meadows of Waterland were looking downright torrid in the heat, if that's what torrid looks like. Besides the cows there was not a soul to be seen. A sluggish breeze. We had an ice cream at the special needs farm Ons Verlangen (Our Expectations) in Zunderdorp. We've stopped there before. The folk who work there are "people with disabilities." We used to call them—no harm intended, I assure you—the village idiots. They always greet us, noisily and enthusiastically, as old friends.

I'm afraid the writing is on the wall for our ice-cream-tasting project at Ice Cold Best in Meeuwenlaan. After going three times and sampling not even half of the flavors, we feel we've seen it all, or rather, tasted it all. Ice cream parlors are popping up all over the place, like mushrooms. The main reason: ice cream parlors don't need a special food permit. A few trays of Italian gelato in a vacant storefront, a manager behind the counter, and you're in business. In order for all those new stands to thrive, every Amsterdam citizen would have to consume two ice cream cones a day.

Wednesday, August 5

We who were children during the war are outraged that our soldiers no longer have real bullets to practice with. Instead they have to yell "Bang-Bang!" or, even more cringe-worthy, "Peanut! Peanut!"

"Do you suppose that when the Germans invade our country again, they'll respond to our so-called 'firepower' by yelling, '*Erdnuss! Erdnuss!*'?" Mr. Helder wondered in despair.

An army with no bullets is simply absurd. Imagine the drill sergeant screaming at the marine to yell "Bang-Bang" louder. And we've also sold off our tanks. I'm no fan of the military, but I do think: *either* you provide the soldiers with bullets and tanks, *or* you disband the entire kit and caboodle.

I thought I was getting very forgetful, but no, it seems I just have a mild case of cognitive impairment. That's what it's called in the newspaper, anyway, so I can breathe a sigh of relief. That "mild," especially, makes me feel better. We of the old guard sometimes have trouble with the modern terminology. We'd only just got used to committees for this or that, and now we understand that it's taskforces. A Dementia Daycare Taskforce, for example, a Volunteer Caregiver Taskforce, and the Dignity and Pride Taskforce for Compassionate Care in Nursing Homes. We'd also just adapted to saying "dementia" instead of "senile," but now it's "Alzheimer's" or something "cognitive." Difficult new terms that tend to obscure rather than clarify, especially when uttered by policymakers. It often has to do with hiding something—either a budget cut, or hot air, or both at once.

Most of the residents just resign themselves to whatever new words they come up with. We no longer have the sharpness, or the energy, to keep asking ourselves what "they" really mean by it, or what "they" are trying to achieve.

I plan to visit my friend Grietje in the locked ward tomorrow. I think I'll casually ask the nurse how all those taskforces are doing.

Thursday, August 6

Yesterday I was pleasantly surprised by a visit from Frida. *Knock, knock*, a little head with a blonde ponytail peered around the door.

"Can I come in?"

"Of course, how nice."

I said I was happy to see her again after such a long time, and asked if her mother knew where she was.

"Well . . . actually, I told her I was going to play outside. Otherwise she'll only tell me not to talk to strange men. Mama is tidying Grandma's room."

Did that mean she *was* allowed to talk to strangers who were women? That, thought Frida, wouldn't be a problem.

"But you don't have to worry, because you're not a strange man anymore. I've already visited you three times."

I asked her what she would like to drink.

"Orange cordial, please."

I didn't have any cordial. I only had coffee, tea, wine, or brandy to offer her. Fortunately I knew the lady next door always has some on hand for her grandchildren.

A little later Frida and I were sipping orange cordial. The first I've drunk in fifty years. We talked about school, about growing old, and about dolls. And then she asked me, "May I call you Grandpa?"

I am now Grandpa Henk. It's about time.

On the heels of yesterday's assortment of taskforces, I have now discovered there is also an Elder Abuse Barometer, which tells us that the tip of the abuse-iceberg in Amsterdam is growing like a cabbage. Mrs. Schansleh couldn't have put it better herself. The number of reported abuse cases has doubled in five years. There is no recent data about the dimensions of the iceberg, unfortunately. An estimate from a few years back was that 200,000 old people are abused by their children, partners, or caregivers every year. Our care home isn't the kind of place where the worst abuses occur. Bruises would be too conspicuous there. Old people living alone, with just one person caring for them, are at much greater risk. When the last "care center" has closed because of budget cuts, people will think back on the good old—*safe*—old age home with nostalgia.

Friday, August 7

At tea yesterday, the Residents' Committee unveiled the ailment-free-zone initiative. Our in-house artist Eugenie had painted a handsome sign with the text: YOU ARE KINDLY REQUESTED NOT TO TALK ABOUT AILMENTS, ORGANS, OR DEATH AT THIS TABLE.

Mrs. Duits came waddling up, saw the sign, and read it aloud. (Another similarity between children and the elderly: they find it hard to read to themselves.) Her performance drew quite a bit of attention. Our idea of introducing it quietly therefore fell by the wayside.

"Why can't I talk about my ailments?" asked Slothouwer. "That's my personal right to free speech."

"Think of it as the quiet coach in a train. To have at least one place where there's no noise," I tried to explain.

"Quiet coach—I've never heard of it. I'll talk about my ailments wherever and whenever I like, thank you very much."

"You can talk about your aches and pains wherever and whenever you like, EXCEPT AT THIS TABLE! And if you insist on doing it here anyway, I'll give you something else to complain about," is how Evert decided to clear things up in his own inimitable style.

Slothouwer slunk off, and the case was settled. She is wary of Evert since she knows a slew of little mishaps will happen if she lingers too long in his presence. A loose cap on the bottle of Worcestershire sauce, an overturned glass, and salt in the coffee are just a few examples.

"Rather a good idea, actually," was the verdict of a good number of residents, and there was soon a crowd gathered around the "no-ailments table." After fifteen minutes Mr. De Grave's attention wandered a bit, and he accidentally let slip that his eczema bothered him in this hot weather. Mrs. Quint haughtily demanded his dismissal, but the

Residents' Committee pressed for leniency. From here on in, everyone is allowed one slip of the tongue. Mr. De Grave kept his mouth shut the rest of the time, just to be on the safe side.

Wouldn't it be nice if it were the other way around: so that if you wanted to talk about your ailments, your organs, or dying, you could only sit at one specially designated table, off in a corner somewhere—the table of illness, death, and organ recitals?

Saturday, August 8

Yesterday I paid Grietje a visit. When I asked the nurse what was going on with all the different taskforces, she stared at me blankly. Grietje, smiling warmly, took my arm and dragged me off to show me her new sixteen-piece jigsaw puzzle.

Today Evert and I went to the cemetery to choose a nice resting place for him. It turned out that it isn't possible to reserve a spot. One section is set aside for dead Catholics, another area has graves for dead Protestants, I expect there's also a patch for "Other Religions," and finally there's a zone saved for atheists.

"If I understand correctly, you wish to be buried in the non-religious sector?" asked the caretaker, pointing us in the right direction. "But even there you can't choose your own spot. We fill the empty spaces on a first come, first served basis."

"And what if I paid a bit more?" Evert tried.

No, that wouldn't help.

While we were there, Evert did make a decision: he wanted a plot all to himself.

"I don't want to have a coffin above me and another underneath, Hendrik. You know I rather cherish my privacy."

"Indeed! What if you and your neighbors didn't get along?" I empathized.

"Right, it's not a happy thought. Three corpses stacked on top of one another, that's Holland at its thriftiest."

The sun shone effusively, and the birds sang their little hearts out. It was a special moment, there in the cemetery. Amusing, moving, peaceful, and sad, all at the same time.

Sunday, August 9

"You people are still in fairly good shape. I can't do any of that anymore."

I looked at the fellow who said that and realized that there was no point objecting. Facing me was an emaciated, bitter little man in a wheelchair. On the table in front of him was his mug of tea, topped with a lid with a spout to prevent spillage, like a toddler's. He can no longer do anything without help, or go anywhere, but he's still got all his buttons.

That "you people are still in fairly good shape" referred to our Old But Not Dead Club. And he's right; with some reciprocal help, patience, and goodwill we manage to get ourselves out and about.

The envious bloke, I don't know his name, would love to be able to do the same. Sometimes he'll fly into a rage. He'll smash his hand onto his plate of spuds as for the umpteenth time his fork hasn't managed to make it into his mouth. He doesn't possess what for many old people is the final remedy: resignation. Stoically waiting for death while enjoying a nice cup of tea.

The Old But Not Dead are still too fit and resourceful to be resigned. That's the reason they were chosen to be members; harsh, but true. You're a member for life, but in order to participate fully, you do have to have your faculties. Grietje, for instance, is a Member Emeritus. She can't come with us anymore, even if she wanted to. And when Evert goes, he'll leave yet another hole that will be very hard to fill.

Evert is going to start a rival club: the One Foot in the Grave Club. He is looking for suitable candidates.

Monday, August 10

I woke up exhausted. I sat on the edge of my bed for a while and then lay down again. It was one of those days when you're dragging life along behind you like a bag full of sand. I did get up in the end because Antoine came to find out what was keeping me.

It's at moments like these that you need friends to rescue you from complete apathy and give you a kick in the behind: no whining! Another day the roles may be reversed and it's your turn to cheer someone up and help them to get through the day. If you're alone, you can't do it. You'll sink into total lethargy, unable to haul yourself out of your chair by the window. Then you're dead before actually dying. You have to keep yourself from falling into that trap. That's what our club is for: Old But Not Dead. It sounds a bit pathetic, but it's the truth.

Tuesday, August 11

In Flanders they've come up with a solution to the problem of the elderly living alone: the postman keeps an eye on them. There are 1,500 people over eighty in Hasselt, Belgium, who receive a monthly visit from the letter carrier. Not to deliver the mail, which they receive very little of anyway, but to make sure they haven't fallen into self-neglect, or aren't lying dead somewhere. The social services pay the postman for this job. It's cheaper than sending a social worker, since they're making the rounds anyway. After a crash course in Communicating with the Elderly, he's ready to start. It's a pity that the Netherlands has just sacked all our old-time mail carriers.

Wednesday, August 12

I never knew it, but as many as a million Dutch people suffer from some rare disease. Even rare diseases aren't all that rare, it seems. According to the newspaper there are close to 7,000 rare diseases, so it's quite likely you'll come down with one. All things considered, I've been very lucky when it comes to rare diseases.

I couldn't discuss this subject with my friends at coffee time because I was sitting at the "no-ailments table." The system is working perfectly. The sign YOU ARE KINDLY REQUESTED NOT TO TALK ABOUT AILMENTS, ORGANS, OR DEATH AT THIS TABLE has already been copied and posted at two other tables. Although for many of the residents it takes some getting used to. Now, if you're sitting at one of the unrestricted tables and happen to mention a problem with your bowels, it will seem as if you've chosen that table specially to discuss the state of your poo. It does make it a bit awkward. So on the whole there's much less talk about physical ailments.

It has also already been suggested that we should have a table where any complaining in general is not allowed. That may be taking it a bit too far. Blurting "Whew, isn't it hot?" could get you banned.

"Well, at least it's a nice heightening of the general awareness," I couldn't help remarking.

"Nice heightening of the general awareness...? Mr. Groen, what *are* you saying?" Evert chuckled.

When Stelwagen first read the sign, she hesitated, and then walked on. There has been no other reaction so far. As far as I know there have not yet been any complaints from the residents either.

Tomorrow Leonie, Ria, Edward, and I are going for a swim in the Flora Park pool. Swim time for the elderly is from 10 a.m. until 11 a.m., although I'm not supposed to call it that anymore.

"No, we no longer call it that," said the lady on the phone. "You mean the quiet hour."

"Are the elderly allowed during that quiet hour as well?"

The quiet hour on Thursday morning is reserved for people who like to swim laps at a snail's pace. Evert isn't coming.

"I can't swim laps with my one leg, I can only paddle in circles."

Even if he were allowed to swim in circles, he's far too weak for that now. He'd sink immediately.

I have dug my forty-year-old swimming trunks out of my wardrobe. It looks like they still fit.

Thursday, August 13

Just got back from the swimming pool. It was delightful, except for some minor setbacks. I couldn't wear a diaper in my swimsuit, naturally, so I visited the bathroom right before going in, and then just ignored some minor leakage.

A problem of a more technical nature was that after forty years, the elastic in my trunks had rather lost its stretch. I was able to solve the problem temporarily with two safety pins that Ria happened to have with her. Every once in a while I'd feel something dangling loose down below, and I'd stuff it back in under the water, hoping no one would notice. Fortunately the ladies all swam with their heads above the water to keep their hair dry.

All the to-do with the swimsuit hampered me from showing off my powerful breaststroke. Honesty compels me to confess that I stayed down at the shallow end. The swimming did go better than expected, in fact, but

I still did not dare venture into the deep end. I was afraid I would never manage to hoist myself up one of those flimsy little ladders to get out. The good thing about the shallow end is that you just wade in and wade out again.

Ria and Leonie were a charming sight in their bathing costumes, and rarely have I seen such orderly lap-swimming. Edward, on the other hand, displayed a rather more choppy style. There was a great deal of splashing, both above and under the water, and a lot of noise to go with it, but I couldn't tell what kind of stroke it was. Each of his limbs seemed to be doing something different. "Free-style butterfly" may come closest to defining it. A novel swimming method not exactly designed for rapid forward propulsion.

Antoine came along to keep us company. He sat on the bleachers, proudly watching his wife. He would have liked to go swimming, but, to put it in his own words, he "sloughs off" too much. When it comes to old people and swimming pools, it's best not to dwell too much on what ends up in the water.

It was invigorating, and we're going to do it more often.

Friday, August 14

"How long have you lived here?" I asked out of politeness rather than interest. Mrs. Schaap's forehead puckered. It seemed the answer wasn't so simple.

"Long," was the reply, at last.

"And how long might that be, approximately?" I asked.

She had no idea. One, two, five years? I decided not to insist.

Schaap is not the brightest bulb, but the fact that she's lost her sense of time says something about life here in this home. Many of the residents rarely venture outside, if ever. It's fear, lack of interest, or no one to push your wheelchair. And if you never go out, you lose your connection to the seasons. The days grow longer or shorter, but it happens so gradually that it doesn't really register if you only see it through the window. The same goes for the color of the leaves on the trees. Sometimes the world on the other side of the glass is suddenly white as snow. That may provoke one of them into remembering, with a little shock, winter as it used to be. Inside, each day is the same as any other day. The same people, the same food, the same room with the same furniture, the same temperature, seventy-three degrees (unless there's a heat wave, like yesterday). So then what's a week, a month, a year?

I should count my blessings, even if it's only because I can still experience summer, autumn and winter by sight, sense, and smell.

Saturday, August 15

Mr. Helder is a nice bloke who still has all his marbles, but he does have a strange habit: whenever he sees a knife, fork, scissors, anything that's sharp, in fact, he hides it out of sight. I asked him yesterday why he does that. He told me that when he was a boy of ten, he accidentally stabbed his brother in the eye with a pair of scissors while they were wrestling.

"The trauma has haunted me all my life," said Helder. "I can't bear to have anything sharp around me. Seeing knives or scissors makes me break out in a sweat, something compels me to banish them from sight. That's the reason I usually take my meals in my room. I eat with a spoon."

It's a foible to which he is resigned.

"I can hardly ask them to remove every fork and knife from the table at dinner time, can I?"

I was moved by his candor.

It's a pity, because I wanted to nominate Helder for the Old But Not Dead Club. I told him so.

"I am honored, but must, alas, decline. I fear I would be a disrupting presence. Perhaps you could involve me indirectly from time to time?"

Judging from that reply alone, the Old But Not Dead Club would have been lucky to have him.

This morning there was a dark spot on the back of Mrs. Van Diemen's frock shaped like a boat viewed from above. It reminded me of something, but I couldn't think what. Edward provided the answer.

"Mrs. Van Diemen, perhaps you shouldn't iron your frocks yourself in future."

She looked embarrassed.

"I was listening to a song by Willeke Alberti on the radio, and went to turn up the volume, but I forgot to lift the iron off my dress." She asked us please not to mention it to the nurse. No, of course we wouldn't, but why not cut that dress up for cleaning rags? Mrs. Van Diemen thought that was a waste. She'd only had the dress seven years.

Sunday, August 16

If you pinch aging skin between your fingers, it sticks together and stands up.

Now that I see it written down, I wonder if I haven't already mentioned it before.

(I frequently forget whether I've said something before. The possibility that I'm repeating myself is something I'll just have to live with; I don't have the energy to reread 500 diary entries to check if I've written the same thing before.)

A lady on the nursing ward does that all day long: pinching the old flesh on her arm, letting go, and observing that it's still standing up. She stares at it until it subsides. Then she does it again, but this time it's the other arm. It does keep her occupied.

It has been a while, but next Sunday we're off again: the Old But Not Dead Club is going day-tripping. Ria and Antoine are the organizers and refuse to lift even the very edge of the veil of secrecy. A 10 a.m. departure and home just in time for dinner.

There was an altercation at the billiards table. Mr. Dickhout was accused of cheating.

"It's possible I didn't count it right," Dickhout admitted in hopes of avoiding a lengthy discussion. But his opponent had already walked off in a huff.

"I'll never play with you again. Never."

Feuds are quick to emerge in here. There are people who refuse to look at each other for years on account of coffee accidentally spilled on a dress, a handkerchief disappearing into the wrong pocket, or a cheated card at klaberjass. How petty can you get?

Monday, August 17

Evert showed me his new bracelet, which says: DO NOT RESUSCITATE ME. His son Jan purchased about five of them for him on the Internet. So Evert has a few extra to give away. Not just to people who want one, but also to people Evert thinks ought not to be resuscitated. He's thinking primarily of his arch-enemy, Mrs. Slothouwer.

"I've offered her the bracelet twice now, but she refuses to take it, the old witch. I'm trying to find a way to snap it on unnoticed, while she's dozing or something."

I am in charge of seeing that the directive on his own bracelet is followed. I have heard from an unreliable source that Stelwagen isn't particularly fond of these bracelets. She thinks it's bad for the home's reputation if some old crock keels over and the staff just stands there watching, arms crossed, until the victim finally stops moving. According to Sister Morales, who is fond of spreading Stelwagen gossip, our director has charged the staff with making sure the non-resuscitation happens out of sight of the other residents if at all possible. And to double-check what it says on the bracelet. There's a story making the rounds that two attendants stood by as a lady wearing one of those bracelets breathed her last, but later found that she had written the names of her dead cats over the original text in magic marker.

Evert has given me one of those bracelets as well. About time too. I kept putting off getting one for myself. "Why do today what you can postpone until tomorrow?" the ostrich in me would whisper in my ear. "It's not as if today is the day you'll die of a heart attack."

Who are you kidding, Groen? If you knew ahead of time when you'd be having a heart attack, you know you'd find a quiet spot well in advance and wait for it. In your own bed, for example.

Tuesday, August 18

Yesterday was the second time the Residents' Committee met with the director. Two important items on the agenda: the growing vacancy rate and the bottlenecks at the elevators.

Sadly, I must once again tell you that we were fobbed off with much hemming, hawing, and empty platitudes.

The future plans for our home are still under discussion with the local council, the board of directors, and the supervisory board. Transition, tailored care, revenue, humanitarian considerations, structural adaptations, budget cuts in the field of Public Assistance; Stelwagen just nattered on and on.

"But does the board want to close down our home, or not?" Graeme asked when she was finally finished.

That was something to which she could not, with reference to all that she had just said, give an unequivocal answer.

"So you can't guarantee that our care home will not be closed?" Leonie insisted.

She could not at this moment make any guarantees.

As for the bottlenecks at the elevators, she was fully aware of the problem, and she was also in a position to tell us she was setting up an investigative committee to thoroughly examine traffic flow issues inside the building. She did not deem it necessary for now to have any resident representatives on that committee. However, she could definitely assure us that the residents' safety had never been out of consideration, not even for a moment.

All our objections, arguments, and suggestions were either drowned in a swamp of managerial jargon or put off until a next meeting. It was enough to make you tear your remaining hairs out.

At a certain point Leonie couldn't stand listening any longer. "Are you taking the residents seriously, or aren't you? I can't help having the sense that the management and the board tend to think that the residents are here to serve *them*, instead of the other way round."

Stelwagen did not blanch. "If I have given you that impression, I am truly sorry. I can assure you that blah blah blah..."

In conclusion she complimented the committee at length on setting up the no-ailments table. She knows: always wrap up the meeting on a positive note. Then she looked at the clock. Our time was up.

She didn't seem her usual self to me, actually. I can't

put my finger on what was different about her. A bit distracted, perhaps?

Wednesday, August 19

Evert came to tell me he'll be picking up a vial of fresh blood from the hospital every three weeks. As if it was a gift.

He has been to the internist, who found that he was anemic.

"That's to be expected, with colon cancer, so I'm not going to get too excited about it. Apart from that, given the hopeless situation, everything's fine."

I didn't know if I should say something comforting or something funny. Neither one came out.

"You *can* close your mouth again, you know, if you have nothing to say." He went on, "Death is snapping at my heels, but we shall ignore that as much as possible. I always say, in the words of my old friend Carel: Carpe diem, but...memento mori."

I was again left with nothing to say.

"Takes you by surprise, don't it, that I know Latin?"

"*Doesn't* it."

"I knew you'd say that, you old school prig."

I asked if he would like to come with me tomorrow to the Ij River, to watch the big ships come in for Sail Amsterdam. "Geert can let you borrow a mobility scooter. His son will bring one over if we ask."

I saw him flinch a bit. It's a sore spot for bigmouth Evert: he's scared of getting on a scooter.

No, he wasn't very interested in boats. And he'd already seen the sailboats, five years ago. And there would be far too many people to be driving around in one of those things.

"Just admit it, you're too chicken, old friend."

"I'm not too chicken, I just don't want to go tomorrow."

"Okay, then let's go Friday, to watch the fireworks."

He protested that he could see the fireworks perfectly well from his room, but in the end he gave in. We're going to have a scooter practice session Thursday afternoon in the park, and Friday evening we'll go. Geert is asking his son to bring us a user-friendly motor-chair.

Thursday, August 20

The reaction to two old grandpas on their mobility scooters varies. Either people think it's "cute" or you can see them thinking: "What are those two old codgers doing here? Let them get in people's way somewhere else." Yesterday, however, we were received with nothing but sympathy.

Geert and I had made our way to the banks of the Ij to watch the tall ships come in. Geert is mad about boats, and I don't mind spending an hour or so every five years watching the big sailing ships go by, even if they're not actually sailing.

The weather was beautiful, there were sandwiches, coffee, cake, and sweets in the scooter's front basket, and we set off early to find a nice spot along the water among the throng of thousands. It went off without a hitch. The people were in the best of moods. Everyone was being nice to one another. People were kind enough to let us through, and we wound up in the front row. It was a shame that the one time in years when my old binoculars would have come in handy, I had left them at home. A little boy next to me let me borrow his from time to time, whenever he had his hands full managing an ice cream cone, a Mars bar, or a Coke. The boy was already much too fat, but in this case I thought it best not to mention it.

We even joined the parade on the water for a little while. From our vantage point on the shore, I could tell that the ferry, which makes the crossing in a long diagonal line, was much less crowded than you'd expect. A few crushed toes ("Oh, don't worry, I have ten of them, one more or less doesn't matter") and a clipped post later, we managed to make our way to the ferry. We made the crossing twice, in the midst of an armada of thousands of little boats teeming around the great three- and four-mast vessels. We were made to get off when we got to the other side, but immediately joined the queue for the return trip again, taking full advantage of our scooters' tight turning radius. It astonished me that of the many thousands of spectators on shore, there weren't more with the same idea. The common herd is sometimes hard to fathom.

At night the Old But Not Dead gathered on Graeme's balcony to watch the fireworks. It was a bit of a squeeze, but convivial as always. With wine and nibbles.

"You have a better view of it from here, actually, than making the trip all the way over there," Evert remarked casually.

"Wanker! Trying to get out of your first scooter ride, aren't you?" That was Geert, who had uttered virtually nothing but monosyllables or two-word sentences the entire day: "Nice," alternating with "Very nice."

Friday, August 21

Beyond belief: Mrs. Quint complained at morning tea that she hadn't slept a wink on account of the fireworks.

"Oh, poor you! The fireworks lasted all of fifteen minutes. That's a long time to be kept awake," I commiserated. "You must be *so* tired." An angry stare was the answer. It has taken a while, but I find myself more and more often leaving the meek, polite old Hendrik behind.

Yesterday afternoon Evert tried driving the mobility scooter, but I can hardly say it was a successful effort... My chum had a bad motorcycle accident at the age of seventy, which left him with an irrational fear of anything with an engine. His fear is greater than his big mouth, and that's saying a lot. At the same time, he realizes that he soon won't be able to get out of the house anymore in his manual wheelchair. His illness is taking its toll, sapping his strength. With an electric wheelchair or a mobility scooter, he could be mobile a while longer.

Evert had helped himself to a bit too much Dutch courage before trying out the scooter Geert lent him, resulting in a rather bizarre driving style with a great deal of erratic maneuvering. He kept just barely avoiding collisions, but did finally wind up crashing into Geert, who was quite rattled by it. He tried to pretend he wasn't mad, but couldn't help cussing and swearing like a drunken sailor. Which, in turn, startled Evert so much that he forgot to be afraid and resumed the lesson as meek as a lamb and slower than a turtle. On arriving home, looking rather pale, he hopped back into his wheelchair.

"I'll just go and take a little nap."

Geert inspected the damage. It wasn't too serious. Evert had already offered to pay for it four times. "For the psychological damage as well. And the emotional." That came out sounding not quite right.

Later Geert and I went out to reconnoiter the route for this evening's fireworks. Piece of cake.

Saturday, August 22

Impressive! We had front-row seats, right under the fireworks smoke with the brilliant colors raining down all over us, so close that you felt the thuds in your belly.

Once we got home, Evert had to grant that it had all been worth it. Not just the fireworks, but rather this late-day victory: notwithstanding his fear, he had managed to ride a mobility scooter. Safe out, safe home, as they say, without one drop of alcohol. Exceedingly slowly, granted. There was one extra hurdle on the way back: the darkness. The dark makes many old folk feel insecure. In old age, it's the same as when we were kids: when the street lights go on, it's time to hurry inside.

Sunday, August 23

We are urged to be prompt. Grandson Stef will arrive with the minivan in fifteen minutes. I had my beige summer suit dry-cleaned specially. I'm also bringing my Maurice Chevalier boater.

Monday, August 24

After an hour in the van I had worked it out: we were on our way to High Veluwe National Park. It was a splendid day, the perfect temperature for the aged: between seventy-two and seventy-seven degrees. A fresh breeze was the icing on the cake. Antoine and Ria had it planned down to the last detail. There were three wheelchairs waiting for us at the entrance to the Kröller-Müller Museum, as well as three extra wheelchair-pushers: nephew Edwin, and Evert's son and grandson. The latter was persuaded to come with the enticement of a small remuneration. The wheelchair parade rolled past the magnificent van Goghs and other masterpieces, all purchased by Mrs. Müller a hundred years ago with her husband Kröller's money. I must say the woman had great taste and foresight. Apparently van Gogh sold only one painting while he was alive. Dead at the age of thirty-seven, and never aware of the millions of fans he has had since. Sad.

Then we walked and/or rolled at a calm pace through the magnificent sculpture garden, although not without some impatience from certain quarters. Art may be beautiful and all, but not at the expense of the carnal appetites.

The cry for food and drink kept getting louder. Ria and Antoine tried our patience for a while longer, only to unveil a lavish picnic spread in the park. Folding chairs, thermoses, wine coolers, cutlery, glasses, a tablecloth, all emerged from Stef's minivan.

The white wine also led to a number of minor mishaps: Leonie tumbled backward in her folding chair (minor scratches), I spilled ketchup on my beige suit (my own fault), and Evert, in one of his frequent inattentive moments, pissed on his own shoes from his wheelchair. We gave his socks a solemn burial at the foot of a pine tree.

We got home at 6 p.m. but were too full to have more than a few bites of pudding. Cook was fit to be tied. That one still thinks we're here to serve *him.*

Tuesday, August 25

Mrs. De Grave likes to darn her husband's socks downstairs in the conversation lounge. She doesn't much like to converse, however. In fact, she ignores all the other residents, except for Mr. De Grave, as much as possible.

"On the autism spectrum," one of the nurses said, by way of excusing her.

Instead of talking, she is one of the last women in the Netherlands who still darns her spouse's socks. With grim determination.

"For ten euros you can buy eight new pairs of socks at Blokker's," Mrs. Slothouwer snorted.

"Blokker's doesn't sell socks," Mr. De Grave said,

defending his wife. His hearing isn't the best anymore, but he has an unerring ear for insults.

"Well, at Zeeman's, then, what difference does it make?" snapped Slothouwer.

"My wife likes to make herself useful. What business is it of yours, what people do?" De Grave asked spitefully.

Slothouwer walked off in a huff. She couldn't resist wondering out loud how in the world anyone could tear so many holes in their socks.

"He must have very long, filthy toenails."

Every once in a while Mrs. De Grave switches from darning socks to repairing nylons, which she stretches over a glass with a rubber band. That evokes warm, nostalgic feelings in the other ladies. They wouldn't mind doing the same themselves, if only their hands didn't tremble and shake so much. Mrs. De Grave has a very steady hand for her age.

I still remember how my wife would panic at the sight of a ladder starting in her stockings, and go at it with a bottle of nail polish. I have no idea how she got the polish out again afterward.

Tomorrow will be a novel experiment for our restaurant project: we're going to McDonald's. None of us have ever been to a McDonald's. It may be a bit of a shock for the regulars and the people behind the counter to have eight old biddies peering at the menu. They do *have* a menu, don't they? Actually, I don't know what you can eat there, except for hamburgers. I did pick up a ready meal from the supermarket, in case the cuisine of the Mac disappoints.

Wednesday, August 26

"Men of the progressive or liberal persuasion are still having sex until well into their eighties, is what I'm reading here in the paper," Evert said, gazing at the circle of ladies and gentlemen respectably dunking their biscuits into their cups of tea. "Which of you is still having sex?"

Mrs. Van Diemen choked on her biscuit and began coughing uncontrollably.

"May I take that coughing to mean a wholehearted yes?" asked Evert.

Van Diemen, red in the face, shook her head vehemently.

"Ah, well, sex over sixty is still a bit taboo, isn't it," Evert sighed.

"Yes," Antoine concurred, "but I will admit that we still do it, occasionally." And he looked at his Ria, who smiled at him fondly but slightly flushed.

"Well, something resembling it, anyway," said Antoine. "What about you, Evert, does one need two legs to have sex?"

This candid conversation about a rather unmentionable subject precipitated anxious faces that didn't know where to look.

"Certainly, but in my case, that second leg sits in the middle."

The discomfort around the table now grew even more intense.

"I once read that people who wear red trousers often own a boat." Mrs. Bregman tried changing the subject.

"Yes, and people wearing pointy shoes are more likely to be musicians," Mr. Verlaat declared.

"Maybe it's just that the men in here are not progressive or liberal." Evert cut short this fascinating conversation.

"Who'd like another cup of tea?" asked the nurse.

Thursday, August 27

It wasn't busy. There were more cheerful boys and girls in blue tartan McDonald's shirts and matching snazzy caps than there were customers. They did not look surprised when we entered, but maybe that is part of their job description: never look surprised, not even when eight elderly customers come tottering in. Antoine was a bit confused: he asked one of the girls for the menu.

"The menu's on the wall, sir."

Luckily it was printed in big letters.

It took us a while to get the hang of it. Then we ordered: two Happy Meals, two big McChickens, two boxes of Chicken McNuggets, three different McSalads, and something to do with McFish.

"And two bottles of your house wine," Evert shouted to Graeme and Leonie, who were giving our orders at the counter.

Many a restaurant could learn a thing or two from this establishment, namely the speed at which everything came out: the food was delivered to our table within five minutes. We did have to unwrap it ourselves, resulting in a formidable mountain of plastic and cardboard, which we had to clear ourselves, since there were no waiters. We must have tossed out a cheeseburger with the rubbish as well, because we couldn't find it anywhere.

The Happy Meals netted two toy watches. At least, we thought they were toys, but they turned out to be real. A real watch for a meal that cost just €3.99! How *do* they do it?

"I got my first watch when I turned eighteen," said Ria, "and it cost a week's salary."

"Yes, the times have changed, especially when it comes to watches," said her husband.

Just to make sure, Evert went to inquire if we really couldn't buy any wine.

"You must have some under the counter, young lady, surely? I'll pay good money for it, I assure you."

The girl shook her head a bit anxiously.

The food, actually, wasn't at all bad. Food that appeals to children is also quite palatable to the elderly. Sweet and salty. The double burger did present a bit of a problem. Geert tried to stuff the whole thing into his mouth, but managed to get only half in. When he tried to pull it out again, his false teeth got stuck in the bun, and he had ketchup running down his chin. The few other people who were there looked up from their burgers, startled by the uproarious laughter coming from our little corner.

For dessert we tried various milkshakes and the first McFlurries of our lives. I don't think McDonald's often sees patrons lingering there for as long and convivially as we did. And all of that for under a tenner. It was Evert who finally put an end to it. He said he was having withdrawal symptoms, and invited us back to his place for an alcoholic nightcap.

* * *

McDonald's reports that 2.36 billion McDonald's hamburgers are consumed every year. Made from one million cows.

Friday, August 28

It came as rather a shock: Stelwagen is leaving. Now I know why she looked so distracted at our last meeting: in her heart she was already out the door. It also explains why she was being so amenable; she wanted to leave a pleasing last impression, and as it is, she won't be the one saddled with any negative consequences. She is getting exactly what she wants: her own personal fiefdom, consisting of fifteen or so old people's homes, sorry, care centers. This home is too small for her now.

The residents received a short announcement.

Starting on 1 November, Mrs. E. H. Stelwagen, MA, has accepted a post as Director of Regional Sector West 1. She will be leaving your care center on that date. The board is presently engaged in deliberations about finding a replacement.

We thank Mrs. Stelwagen for the inspiring and professional manner in which she has led this institution for the past five years, and wish her great success in her continuing career within our organization.

The Chairman of the Board of Directors

It did affect me, in spite of everything. One finds oneself, strangely enough, having fond feelings for the enemy. Notwithstanding her bureaucratic attitude and managerial arrogance, she was just like her crisp pastel business suits: neat, correct, and joyless. Whenever something went wrong, she would smoothly pin the blame on one of her underlings. But lurking somewhere deep inside, there was also something of a mother who only wants the best for her aged children.

I do, however, worry about the board's wording regarding a successor. Those deliberations about finding a replacement don't bode well. It would not surprise me if they appointed some tyrant charged with shutting the place down with as little fanfare as possible. The board would call that a "transition manager."

Saturday, August 29

Stelwagen's departure is the topic of the day. Not that the inmates are going to miss her very much; it's the fear of what's next that is on everyone's mind.

"You know what you've got, and you don't know what you're getting," is the predominant train of thought.

"It's not as if we have a finger in the pie in the sky," Mrs. Schansleh reasoned, applying one of her homemade proverbs.

Evert is already plotting a fitting send-off prank, provided he is granted the time on earth to carry it out. He's afraid that Stelwagen will forget him all too quickly otherwise.

* * *

We have suddenly become great fans of track and field. Last year only a few people here had heard of the athlete Dafne Schippers, but today twenty people were gathered around the telly to watch the World Championship 200-meter final in Peking. And most of them pretended to be knowledgeable about it too. Some of these "experts" were certain she would win; other pundits were convinced she would not. So we're always left with at least a couple who can say, "See, didn't I tell you?" Happily, it was the optimists who won out this time. "Our Dafne" ran a fantastic race.

"Although she's no Fanny Blankers-Koen, naturally," the everything-was-better-back-in-the-old-days brigade declared.

"Good people," said Graeme, "not that it makes any difference, but our Fanny, if she had run her personal best, would have finished almost thirty meters behind Dafne." Graeme is more of a math and statistics kind of fellow, and not so much the nostalgic poppycock type.

Mrs. Smit was given a secondhand camera by her granddaughter. There's nothing wrong with that, but the granddaughter has also taught her how to use it, and now she's photographing her tea- and coffee-sipping companions all day long. Some of them get so unnerved by it that, for instance, an entire plate of biscuits is swept onto the floor. Only to have Smit, like a genuine paparazzo, snap a picture of the mishap. Then she spends the rest of the day showing everyone photos of the smashed biscuits.

Sunday, August 30

Last Friday we, the members of the Residents' Association, received pats on the back for our first high tea. It was a great success.

The preparations began at 2 p.m. Stelwagen had ordered Cook out of his kitchen, which he did with unconcealed reluctance. Ria and Antoine directed the kitchen troops: Graeme, Evert, Geert, Leonie, Eugenie, Edward, and myself. We, the humble slicers and spreaders, spent an hour and a half following their directions meticulously. No messing about, either: the bread slices, for example, had to be carefully severed from their crusts and then halved into exact triangles. "No right angles, okay?" Ria said sternly. At 3 p.m. sharp we rolled two kitchen carts into the dining room laden with scones, cream cheese and salmon sandwiches, patés, savory pastries, strawberries and cream, chocolates, and biscuits. Aged jaws dropped at the sight of such abundance. Only those who had signed up and paid a small €3 contribution were allowed to dig in.

"Ridiculous, so over the top," Slothouwer, at the too-stingy-to-participate table, was heard sniping just a bit too loud. Evert started rolling toward Slothouwer, brandishing the whipped cream dispenser. Slothouwer suddenly needed to go to the bathroom.

Stelwagen came to have a look. She took half a scone, dispensing benign smiles at everyone. Evert had mischievous designs on her business suit, but Leonie slammed the brake down on his wheelchair just in time. When he looked around, she pinched his cheek. Instead of swearing, Evert blushed.

Half an hour later it was all gone. The floor and tables were strewn with crumbs and cake remnants, but aside from that you saw only contented faces with the odd dollop of cream cheese. The organizing committee received a generous accolade. And a request from a Catholic resident: could we have the high tea on a Thursday next time, since Friday was a fast day and she couldn't eat meat?

"Well, then, just don't spread paté on your apple pie," was Edward's ready solution. Edward is allergic to religion.

Eight people have signed up to help next time. We'll make them each take an exam to qualify.

Monday, August 31

Yesterday afternoon was the opening of Eugenie Lacroix's art exhibition. Our artist in residence preferred using the term "vernissage," but that mostly brought on puzzled faces.

"Does that mean I have to do something?" Mrs. Duits asked anxiously.

The Residents' Committee had furnished the tables with alcoholic beverages, cheese, and sausages at a time normally reserved for tea and biscuits. This created some confusion. Mrs. Duits accidentally dunked a piece of salami in her tea.

"It's because of that vernie-stage. I'm all in a muddle."

Eugenie had the maintenance department hang twenty of her pieces in the conversation lounge and the downstairs corridors. She didn't give them an easy time of it. After thirty changes and adjustments, everything was finally in the right place "as far as lighting and placement." She had chosen Sunday afternoon for the opening event because it was the busiest time of the week for visitors. She led people around on guided tours to explain the artist's intended meaning of each work. The explications were certainly not unwarranted.

"Why does that woman have a pony on her lap?" asked Mr. Pot.

"It isn't a pony, it's a cat," said Eugenie, cut to the quick at such lack of finesse.

Stelwagen also made an appearance. At one point she was standing next to me, staring at something that was supposed to be a self-portrait.

"So have you begun your farewell tour yet?" I asked.

"Not yet, Mr. Groen, I have plenty of time left. Are you sorry I am leaving?"

The question took me somewhat by surprise, and I had to think.

"In actual fact, I feel sorrier for you than for us," I said.

"How do you mean?"

"I wish you had a bit more love for the job, and a bit less ambition. I believe that's what makes one happy, you see. I'm speaking from personal experience, since I was headmaster of a school for most of my working life. You are the headmistress of a care home. There are similarities."

She thought it over.

"You may be right." Then she walked away and—uncharacteristically—did not say goodbye.

Tuesday, September 1

The poem "Insomnia" by J. C. Bloem rings true to me of late. I don't sleep well because I am afraid of approaching death. Not my own, but that of my best friend. Every time I see Evert I become more aware that, in the not-too-distant future, I will never see him again. An anticipated death is worse than an unexpected one.

It doesn't seem to bother Evert as much. His eyes still twinkle. He devours life every day, and relishes it.

When I complimented him on this, he said that I should follow his example, since he'd had enough of looking at my worried face the whole goddamn day. I didn't know what to say.

"Touché!" Evert added. It sounded funny, coming from him.

Then I quoted the first four lines of "Insomnia" to him.

"A bit naff, isn't it, three lines in a row starting with 'and'?" was his reaction.

There you go, Bloem, put *that* in your pipe and smoke it.

And then we heard, from the table next to us—putting death into perspective, as it were: "Yes, you see, I'm no longer able to hold my pee in. Well, that's the beginning of the end, isn't it."

"Beginning of what end?" asked Evert, twisting around in his seat. The ladies were embarrassed into sheepish silence.

"Oh, no need to stop talking. You are sitting at the sickness-and-death table."

It has taken no time at all for the table demarcation to become established. The happy result is that we don't have to constantly hear the many physical tribulations affecting the care home's inmates. Talking about it doesn't help, but the temptation to do so is contagious. It makes everyone eager to air his or her own affliction, thereby increasing the torrent of complaints. No, pretending everything's fine most of the time makes it much more pleasant for everyone.

Wednesday, September 2

Next Saturday is my birthday. I am racking my brain for an original way to celebrate. People appear to have high expectations.

"What kind of super-duper plan have you come up with for your Satur-birthday?" asked Ria.

Now there's an expression you don't often hear these days: "super-duper." I should have complimented her on her "waggish way with words"—now *that* would have been a snappy linguistic comeback.

When I last visited Grietje in the locked wing, I thought for a second the apparition I saw sitting there was a very old clown. Looking more closely, I realized it was one of the residents, in the process of putting on makeup. Various tubes and compacts were spread out in front of her on the table. Admiring herself in a little mirror, she decided to pile on a little more lipstick. When I next saw her, she had started painting her nails, or rather her fingers, with an unsteady hand. A nurse walked in and saw her doing it.

"Mrs. De Beer, where did you get that makeup!?" she asked in alarm. Mrs. De Beer had no idea, but she did grow stroppy when the nurse took away her toys. A surprisingly distinct series of four-letter words fell from her painted red lips. The sister went for reinforcements to help her wash the stuff off, since De Beer was putting up quite a struggle. In the end they hustled her off to her room.

All this time Grietje had been looking on with interest, every so often giving the victim an encouraging smile. In the corridor, as I was leaving, I heard Mrs. De Beer bawling her eyes out.

Thursday, September 3

Two ladies who live on my corridor have invited me to go rollator-dancing at the local community center. They saw an announcement in the local free paper and they thought it would be nice to have a man accompany them. I broke into a sweat. I had no time to think of an adequate excuse. I could hardly say that next Tuesday I'd be coming down with a migraine. Playing for time was the only thing I could think of.

"Yes, that sounds fun," I said gutlessly, "but when is it exactly?"

When they informed me of the date and time, I said I would first have to consult my diary. Now I have until tomorrow to think of a proper excuse. I'm worried they'll just invite me again the next time. I shouldn't have said it sounded like fun. It sounds hor-ri-fic to me.

I don't like to dance and I don't like rollators. To be perfectly honest, rollator-dancing strikes me as worse than waterboarding.

Geert, Evert, and I are taking advantage of the last nice sunny days to take the old mobile scooter out for a spin. Ever since his scooter debut for the Big Sail, we've been able to persuade Evert to come along on his leased motorized steed. He does have qualms beforehand every time, but once we're on our way, he is happy as a clam. We try to avoid the traffic as best we can; motorbikes in particular make us nervous.

In Het Twiske, the large nature park on the outskirts of Amsterdam, it is quiet and beautiful during the week. Our little caravan glides almost soundlessly over splendidly asphalted bicycle paths (off-limits to motorcycles) through lovely and even somewhat untamed nature. The sole danger is a potential collision with an oblivious rabbit, because the park is teeming with them. We once tried counting them, but stopped when we got to one hundred. We drive around for an hour and a half, stopping halfway for a nice cup of coffee at an outdoor café overlooking the water. Once home again, we treat ourselves to a nip of cognac. Happy days.

Friday, September 4

The picture of the dead Syrian toddler washed up on a Turkish beach has shocked me, and many of the other residents, deeply. The horrifying outside world has come hurtling with singular force into our safe little world. Some had tears in their eyes at the sight of the lonely little fellow lying there almost as if he was peacefully sleeping. Drowned innocence.

By nightfall we've forgotten the refugees' tragic plight and are tearing our hair out about the staggeringly weak Dutch team that's lost to Iceland! But in bed I saw the dead toddler again. His little shoes. His little face in the sand.

Tomorrow, on the occasion of my eighty-sixth birthday, I am taking the Old But Not Dead Club to a new pancake restaurant not far from here. I know that most of them will be pleased with my choice. I have ascertained that wine and beer are served along with the pancakes.

The ladies of the rollator-dance accosted me at coffee time: was I going to join them?

"I'm so sorry, but my doctor forbids it. I asked her about it, and she doesn't think it's advisable for my knees. Both meniscuses are in shreds, practically."

That "in shreds" made a deep impression. My rejected dancing partners didn't want to have my creaky knees on their conscience, in case these succumbed while I was dancing, sending me crashing to the floor.

Saturday, September 5

"Here you are, my dear chum, a little something for you."

Evert arrived at 9 a.m., bearing a cake and an envelope containing €2,000.

"The last two thousand, Henk," he said. "For you and the rest of the club. Use it to do something fun."

He did ask that we hold off spending it all at once, because if he should live longer than expected, he might need to ask for a couple of hundred back. I immediately pressed him to take back half.

"Just joking, I've kept some for myself."

Evert has everything arranged now with his son Jan: money, coffin, funeral, cemetery. His room has been tidied, the junk disposed of, and some of the items have a sticker underneath with the name of the future owner.

"I am ready for the Grim Reaper. Nothing to worry about anymore."

I am about to go downstairs for coffee. Armed with Evert's cake and two other cakes I bought yesterday. Happy birthday to me!

Sunday, September 6

Yesterday at 5 p.m. the Old But Not Dead Club boarded the minibus with our two chauffeurs, Stef and Edwin, for my birthday dinner at Restaurant Stroop. Stroop is a hip pancake joint housed in a former soccer canteen. And environmentally correct besides: the bacon in the bacon pancakes was still a pig rolling in the mud in the field next door until the very last moment. They also offer salads or fish for the man or woman who doesn't like pancakes. Delicious home-brewed beer, a nice little wine, a tasty dessert. In short: excellent. There was one problem, however: a steep uphill climb to the front door. Edwin and Stef had to work hard for their pancakes: there was no elevator, so they had to push us all up to the first floor. And on the way out, they had to prevent the rollators and wheelchairs from hurtling downhill and landing in the pigsty.

I was showered with gifts, and Graeme and Ria made speeches. I don't usually like being the center of attention, but I have to be honest: it was a very nice birthday. And I tried the first Japanese pancake I've ever had in my life. An experience I wouldn't have wanted to miss.

And the bill was reasonable: €300 for the ten of us.

To put that cost into some perspective: according to the newspaper, when last week China's stock exchange crashed, along with other world markets, $5,000,000,000,000 evaporated into thin air in the space of two to three days. Gone. Down the tubes. In euros that's 4.4 trillion. Newspapers tend to give the amounts in dollars first, and then convert it into euros for us. Show some consideration for old people, please, and convert those euros into guilders as well. In this case, rounded up, that would be 10 trillion guilders. Now there's a number we can sink our teeth into, to give us a clearer sense of those stock market losses.

Monday, September 7

Mrs. Langeveld has been caught stealing a spoon. As she made her way back to the elevator after dinner, a nurse asked if she could just have a peek into her basket. Well, no, Langeveld would rather she didn't. The head of housekeeping was called in, and hey presto, she unearthed a spoon from the rollator basket. Mrs. Langeveld was asked if she would be so kind as to accompany her to the office. Mr. Dickhout later reported that a home inspection turned up sixty-five dining-room spoons and forks in Langeveld's room. Dickhout, eavesdropping outside her door, heard the attendants exclaiming loudly in surprise upon finding a drawer bursting with cutlery.

I suspect the disappearance of so many spoons and forks had been noticed, and the staff was ordered to do some detective work.

"Men are hunters. Women are gatherers," Mr. Dickhout said after making Mrs. Langeveld's shameful heist public.

The pressing unresolved question was: what would anyone want with sixty-five spoons and forks? I feel sorry for Langeveld.

Others think the police should be called in.

We thought it couldn't get any worse, but no: the Dutch team has lost 3–0 to *Turkey*! A small but hardened core of soccer fans skipped dinner last night to watch the Netherlands vs. Turkey match. When it was over we were not only hungry but also down in the dumps. Evert swore he'd have managed it better in his wheelchair than those spoiled, tattooed soccer millionaires. He was furious.

"The Turkish people have been having a hard time recently. They could use something to smile about. Don't you agree, Evert?" I said. Evert suggested that I shut my trap.

It's nice for our Turkish cleaner, and of course for Mr. Okcegulcik, who out of sympathy for the rest of us kept themselves from outwardly rejoicing at the Turkish victory.

Tuesday, September 8

Three ladies were seated at a table behind me yesterday, their rollators neatly lined up in a row. One of the ladies asked me what day it was. I said, "Monday. Monday, September 7."

"It's Monday, September 7," she told the lady sitting next to her in a loud voice.

"It's Monday, September 7," that lady told her neighbor in an even louder voice.

"It's Monday, September 7," this third lady said to me. I confirmed that it was indeed Monday, September 7.

Fifteen minutes later another lady sat down at their table.

"I thought you went to visit your husband on Tuesdays," said lady number 1.

"Yes, I always visit my husband on Tuesdays. But today's Monday."

"Is today Monday? Let me ask."

"Is today Monday? Or did I already ask you?" lady number 1 asked me.

"Not to worry," I said. "And it is indeed Monday. Monday, September 7."

You just have to have a little patience sometimes.

* * *

Writing in my diary seems to take more effort these days. I fear that I may be about to get writer's block. (Personally, books about writers who have writer's block tend to give me acute reader's block.) I must make myself soldier on, because I have promised myself to carry on until December 31. In the back of my mind the wonderful (but unattainable) directive from Kafka: "A book must be the ax for the frozen sea."

What worries me more than the writing getting harder is the fact that reading is no longer as easy for me either. I keep having to go back to the beginning of the page because I don't remember what I've just read, either because I was distracted by something or, worse, nodded off for a second. And it isn't usually the book's fault.

Wednesday, September 9

In the middle of a game of chess, or rather a round of blundering, Evert suddenly said, "The whole concept of heaven seems unlikely to me."

"Huh?"

"I just hope to God that heaven doesn't exist. Every heaven turns into a hell in the long run. You could very well end up sitting next to Bing Crosby crooning 'White Christmas' into your ear for all eternity."

I asked him who he *would* like to sit next to then. Evert took his time thinking it over.

"I have no idea. I'd rather have a heaven all to myself,

somewhere where I could have friends over. I'd frequently invite you over for a game of chess, a brandy, and good chatter. About heaven, for instance."

I said I was quite convinced that there is no hereafter, and that I, too, could foresee big problems if heaven did actually exist.

"How do you keep everybody happy if, for example, Ajax is playing Feyenoord?"

"And whose job is it to take the rubbish out?" Evert wondered; yet another dilemma. But the ones we're most worried for are the terrorists in their explosive vests, who are bound to realize soon enough that in eternity, seventy virgins won't last forever.

Evert and I pop in to see each other every day unannounced. Sometimes we'll bump into each other in the corridor, on our way to the other one's flat.

"Hey, fancy meeting you here!"

Mrs. De Grave has cleaned out her closet to find clothes for the refugees.

"I like the idea of a poor Syrian woman walking around in my woolen suit," she said with satisfaction.

"It does have a little hole in it," Mr. De Grave had to admit.

"Never look a gift horse in the mouth," his wife said.

"They've stopped collecting secondhand goods from Holland, you know," said Graeme, "you might as well give it to the ragman."

"Do they still exist?" asked Mrs. Duits.

Mrs. De Grave seemed disappointed that she would never see a refugee walking around in her woolen suit.

Thursday, September 10

Several Old But Not Dead members have discreetly asked me about Evert's health. They've tried to get that information from the horse's mouth, but he is refusing to give them a serious answer.

"I'm going to Weight Watchers," was all his friends were told upon remarking that he'd lost quite a bit of weight, "and if I keep going the way I'm going, they'll make me an honorary member."

When the club members ask me about Evert, I'm forced to stay noncommittal, since I've had to promise not to tell anyone he has cancer.

"Oh, so-so," I'll say. If they insist, I tell them to go and ask Evert.

Yesterday I told him it was becoming untenable. He has lost at least thirty of his hundred-forty-five-pound starting weight. No one believes that nothing's wrong. There's probably already a great deal of speculation going on.

"Your Old But Not Dead friends have the right to be told the truth. I definitely think you should tell them now."

Evert looked doubtful but said he'd consider it.

"Besides, I don't think it would do any harm to inform the staff either," I added. Out of the question, said a steely Evert. "When I die it will still be too early to tell the nurses. So: Old But Not Dead, okay. Staff, no way." He smiled. "That's a good haiku, isn't it, Henkie?"

I had to admit it was short and strong. I do understand Evert; he doesn't want a whole slew of nurses and doctors fussing over his sick body. He's scared they'll make him go into the nursing ward against his will.

"I'll die the way I want to."

I swallowed, and nodded.

Friday, September 11

This may be a good day for it, September 11. So that people will ask, later: "When was that attack on the Twin Towers again? Oh yes, it was the day Evert told us he had cancer, September 11." Evert thought he'd come up with a rather good idea.

Tonight the Old But Not Dead Club are meeting at his place. "Meeting" makes it sound weightier than it is, it's just an excuse to get together, chat, nibble, and drink wine or stronger liquor. Sometimes we have just one item on the agenda, and that is to choose a date for the next meeting. This evening's merrymaking will therefore be brutally interrupted by Evert's announcement that his membership will soon be terminated.

I am finding distraction in cycling's Grand Tour of Spain. "We" suddenly have a new Dutch hero with a somewhat French surname: Tom Dumoulin. He has won two stages, and has been wearing the race leader's red jersey. I have been spending my afternoons for over a week watching it on Eurosport. Now that it seems there's a chance that Tom will win the Spanish Vuelta, it's suddenly all over Dutch TV. I don't like that—jumping in only when the going is good.

* * *

The Jumbo supermarket in Nijmegen was evacuated because of a suspicious container of potato salad that had been left unattended. It seemed strange to me at first, but then I read it was a six-pound tub. I've never even seen such a daunting quantity of potato salad. I'm sure you could hide quite a lot of explosives in there, and if that Jumbo market blew up, it would make a horrible mess.

Have we become so paranoid that we'll evacuate a supermarket just because someone has second thoughts about needing quite that much potato salad, and can't be bothered to cart the heavy tub all the way back to the potato salad department?

Saturday, September 12

The die is cast.

Last night Evert cleared his throat and then announced he had something to say. As if everyone could tell he was being serious, you could suddenly have heard a pin drop. Evert stared into space, opened his mouth and closed it again. He cleared his throat again, then looked at me helplessly.

"Groen, my boy, can't you help me out here? You're my friend, aren't you?" he asked in a small voice. So then I told the others that Evert was ill, very ill. With just a few months left to live, if that. The room was silent; everyone was looking at Evert.

"Yes, it could happen to the best of us," he said with a crooked grimace.

Leonie went up to him and threw both arms around him.

"That's what I was afraid of, my dear old chump," she said softly, giving him a kiss. "Well, we had better make the best of it."

"That's what I like to hear, pet. Start frying up those *bitterballen*, Antoine. And open the best bottles we have."

And so it came to pass. It turned into a hell of a night. There was gallows humor and there were tears. There were hugs and pats on the back. There was a good deal of drinking.

Now it's 9 a.m. the next morning. I expect that we're all trying to work off our respective hangovers over our breakfasts of bread and chocolate sprinkles. As the horrid new reality becomes part of our everyday life.

Sunday, September 13

Eefje is in my mind a lot again of late. She had quietly taken a back seat in my life, but now, with Evert's approaching death, she is back in my thoughts every day. I hadn't taken out her iPod for a while, but these past weeks I have started listening to her favorite music again. It makes me recall the times I used to let her listen to music in her sickbed, and she could only show me with her eyes that she loved it. Eyes that kept growing dimmer.

After her passing, the Old But Not Dead members helped one another get over it. We are close, without being overly nosy. Interested, warm, affectionate people with humor and compassion. At times sentimental, and at times a bit mad. Each one of us as old as the hills, but we try to ignore that fact as much as we can. We hope everyone has a chance to belong to such a club, but not ours. We often still hear from people who want to join, but we turn everyone down. That's because there is no room for more than eight people in the minivan we use for our excursions, in addition to the driver.

The British queen became the longest reigning English monarch ever last week: she has been on the throne for sixty-three years and seven months. Her poor son Charles is the longest heir-in-waiting ever. At the age when the Dutch now start their retirement, he's still waiting for his first job.

The longest reigning monarch in the world was King Sobhuza of Swaziland, but he was an infant when he ascended the throne. That doesn't count.

At eighty-nine, Elizabeth is a stellar example of sprightliness, according to some of us in here.

"And she still goes to work every single day," is how Mrs. Van Diemen expressed her admiration.

"If you ask me, the work isn't all that taxing," Evert remarked. "She even has a special footman to wipe her royal arse, so she can't get *that* tired."

Van Diemen was deeply shocked at such lèse-majesté.

Evert went on in that vein for a while, saying he suspected that Elizabeth had actually died a long time ago, but was stuffed after her death, with a small motor inside to keep her moving.

"I just don't see anything that's human there anymore."

I had to step in in the end, because Mrs. Van Diemen

was about to whack Evert with her purse. My friend beamed with glee.

Monday, September 14

The poet Lucebert spoke these insightful words: "All that is valuable is helpless," but there are also people who think differently about it. "All that is helpless, is without any value" comes closer to their experience. You sometimes feel, especially in young people, the contempt for our slowness and uselessness, even if it's seldom voiced.

I can get very angry about the condescension toward old people sometimes. If you speak up about it, you'll often get an aggressive reaction.

It terrifies me, to be so helpless. I can't even take a hurried step backward without toppling over. A little push is enough to decide every conflict.

And it does happen: Mr. Dickhout once rebuked a young man for jumping the queue at the supermarket checkout. He muttered something along the lines of: "Behold the living proof of a poor upbringing." The queue-jumper took it as an insult to his mother, and punched Dickhout in the face. Yelling something about "respect," the young man then took to his heels, leaving his cans of Red Bull on the counter. Dickhout was left with a black eye, eventually turning a yellowish-green, which he proudly showed off to everyone. He said he'd do the same thing again.

Not me. I am not brave. I keep my mouth shut, scared shitless and hopping mad at the same time.

Anyway, at the supermarket no one found it necessary to get involved, apart from the Moroccan cashier who jumped to her feet and yelled, "Wanker!"

Netherlands' hope in these dark days.

Tuesday, September 15

It's the third Tuesday in September, Prince's Day, time for the King's Speech and the Golden Coach. The latter needs repairs, and the restorers say they'll need four years to do the job properly, the same amount of time it would take you, for instance, to build a huge skyscraper. It's hard to imagine that refurbishing a coach, not even twenty feet in length, could take that much work. Wouldn't it be much cheaper and quicker just to make a new one? Does no one realize that? To please the Party for Animal Welfare, you could add a small electric motor so the horses wouldn't have to work as hard.

Mrs. Bregman asked herself anxiously how the royal couple would get to Parliament these next three years, without the Golden Coach.

"I suppose they'll take the tram," said Leonie.

Mrs. Bregman looked quite disconcerted.

"I was only joking," Leonie said to reassure her, "they'll be riding in a glass coach for the time being."

That sent Mrs. Bregman into even more of a tizzy. She thought a glass coach could be terribly dangerous.

It is a tradition in our home to gather downstairs to watch the King's Speech and comment on the parade of silly hats in the Ridderzaal. It's becoming more of a carnival every year. Nowadays, there's also a tall bloke dressed up as a rather corpulent king.

Ria has promised to wear a fetching hat for the occasion this afternoon. I hope she will set an example, and that by the time the next King's Speech rolls around, all our ladies will be watching the telly in their fanciest hats.

At last year's Prince's Day we already had two gentlemen watching the televised ceremony with all their badges, medals, and Four-Day March crosses pinned to their chests.

Wednesday, September 16

Ria had a brilliant hat on: a plate made out of blue cardboard, with a huge orange napoleon on top. Her lips were painted a matching orange.

The best thing about it was that her hat was edible. When the King's Speech was over, she took it off, took a big knife from her purse, cut the napoleon into small pieces, and offered those around.

"Long live the king! Hip, hip, hurray!" Graeme cried.

"Antoine baked it himself last night," Ria said proudly. "Not allowed, but all for a good cause," she added with a giggle.

The lady MPs would do well to follow her example.

A number of inmates have written to the director proposing that we shelter some Syrian refugees in the empty rooms in our home, which now number about fifteen.

When the proposal was discussed over coffee, there was

a consensus that there shouldn't be any pickpockets among the new guests. Best if those stayed in Syria, really.

It would liven up the place quite a bit, some exotic new residents from distant lands. We'd be able to make ourselves useful by babysitting from time to time, and we could teach them Dutch, as the language barrier could be a problem in the beginning. They, for their part, could run errands for us, or push the wheelchairs. I am curious to see if Stelwagen will come back to us with a serious response, or if she'll leave it for her successor to deal with.

By the way, no news yet on a new director.

The Residents' Committee is having a final meeting with Stelwagen at the end of the month. We'll definitely ask about the situation regarding her replacement.

Yesterday we thoroughly enjoyed seeing Louis van Gaal's sour expression after the humiliating defeat of his Manchester United (with a €600 million turnover) by PSV Eindhoven (just €60 million in revenues).

Thursday, September 17

Mrs. Langeveld's room has yielded a new stash of about a dozen spoons, knives, and forks, property of the home. Ten days ago another sixty were uncovered in all sorts of cupboards and drawers. The head of housekeeping, with Stelwagen's permission, performed a thorough search of Langeveld's room, and they found not only the cutlery that didn't belong there, but also towels, dishcloths, soap, cups, plates, and other items. The bathroom had an extra wall of toilet paper rolls stacked up to the ceiling. Come to think of it, it's strange that the cleaner, who mopped the floor around it, never said a word.

Mrs. Langeveld was given one last warning. It's questionable if that will help, since she doesn't seem to have any idea how those things made it into her room. She's all in a dither and spent an hour crying.

Her son proceeded to march into the director's office, incensed, but when Stelwagen showed him the loot found at the scene of the crime, he was suddenly meek as a lamb. Then he turned on his mother, to save face. Which was pointless, of course, and only made her wail even louder.

Edward has taken Mrs. Langeveld's dilemma to heart, and promises from now on to check that items belonging to the home haven't accidentally fallen into the basket of her rollator.

Friday, September 18

Mrs. Smit is driving me bonkers. A couple of weeks ago she began taking photographs of the residents with an old camera, and she just won't stop. She accosts me at least ten times a day.

"Give us a smile, Mr. Groen." The first couple of times I managed to produce a fake grin, but I have lost any inclination to smile.

"I'll be damned if she isn't stalking me, at my advanced age," I complained to Evert, who thought it was a riot. At coffee time, at teatime, at lunch, and at dinner, at least twenty times a day there she is, snapping pictures of me. A few days ago I politely asked her to stop, but it didn't help. Last night I told her point-blank that I'd finally had it with having my picture taken. That did startle her, I think. We'll have to wait and see if the message got through.

Evert offered to roll over Smit's camera with his wheelchair a few times by accident, but I thought that wasn't necessary—yet.

Another outing next week. Graeme is the organizer. He asked me, in confidence, if I thought Evert could, or would, want to come. I assured him that Evert is determined to enjoy life to the full with what strength remains to him, so he'll definitely want to come. And that he is able to as well.

"Once he's dead, it might get a bit harder."

"That's something Evert himself would say, Henk," said Graeme.

"That's right, I'm quoting him, more or less."

Saturday, September 19

Well, I must say it did have an effect: Mrs. Smit has stopped taking pictures of me. And the fact that her camera mysteriously ended up in the aquarium can't be the only reason. Now she just sidles up to me and sits down next to me ten times a day. I have remained cordial for as long as I could stomach it, have even tried getting up and sitting down somewhere else several times, have asked her not to follow me; but nothing helps.

"I can sit where I want, can't I, Mr. Groen?" she told me with the sweetest smile.

That woman is getting on my nerves. I suddenly know what an intrusion it is to be stalked. I keep getting the urge to hit her. And I have to stop Evert from doing it for me. Not only on account of the enormous brouhaha that would ensue; but I also fear there's a good chance my friend's brittle arm would break.

His weight is down to almost nothing now. Recently I walked into his room—after knocking, naturally—and saw him sitting in his wheelchair, wrestling with his shirt. His red braces were slung across his sunken ribcage. I was shocked. I could see every rib.

"Admiring the results of my exercise routine?" my friend said.

Carefully, with tears in my eyes, I helped him into his shirt, and pulled his braces up. Evert doesn't like to be helped, but the time has come when he'll just have to put up with it.

"I had rather you did it than to have some nurse barge in," he said.

"I can easily pop in every morning before coffee to help out a bit," I offered.

"Well, all right, then, Hendrik, only because it's you." And he gave me a vicious pinch in the arm.

Sunday, September 20

Twenty percent of the elderly prefer to live in the traditional sort of care home. That's what the research outfit

Platform 31 has discovered. And if a research outfit says it, it must be true. The fact that the traditional care home is so popular is a bit inconvenient, since many of them are being demolished because the authorities will no longer pay for this type of housing. Women over seventy whose sole income is their state pension are particularly partial to living in an old-age home. It's probably for the companionship and the twenty-four-hour alarm button. Yet they are precisely the demographic that can't afford the new "market-rate" fees for care, room and board. "Market rate" is the new term for too expensive. Old-age homes are closing their doors, and there are 30,000 elderly people outside waiting to be let in.

"We're still all right in here, but for how much longer?" I heard at teatime.

"Before you know it all the old-age homes will close, and *then* what?"

"Then we'll be just like a bunch of old slugs trying to make it across the A2 motorway," said Leonie with a shake of the head. She helped herself to another ginger biscuit.

Her tablemates nodded. A few of them did start to laugh, luckily, including yours truly. Then Mrs. Smit pulled up a chair next to mine.

"I'm coming to sit next to you, Mr. Groen."

"Yes, you often do, lately. It's making me rather nervous."

"Goodness, that's not necessary, you know."

"Actually, I'd rather you left me alone."

Smit nodded amicably, but remained firmly planted beside me.

Then Mrs. Schansleh decided to butt in. Why not.

"You're glaring like the man with the sour grape on his shoulder, Mr. Groen."

I fled to my room. Ria and Antoine, who saw the whole thing, stopped by a little later to lend support. They are going to help me find a solution that's short of a bloodbath.

Monday, September 21

The director has yet to respond to the proposal put forward by some of the residents to house refugees in the vacant rooms. Edward has written a separate letter on his own initiative, asking if we couldn't offer two innocent prisoners from Guantanamo a place to live as well, to make up for our government's shameful refusal to accept them. There was far from unanimous agreement on that one.

"Where there's smoke, there's fire," said Mrs. Duits. "I bet they weren't imprisoned all that time for being innocent."

On Saturday I fetched a quarter pound of Serrano ham, which goes so well with a glass of white wine. I was going to share it with Evert yesterday. The ham was in one of those resealable plastic bags, which means the bag can be closed again, as long as you've been able to master pulling apart the two slippery, tenacious halves first, and then, with your shaky old fingers, peel off the fiddly plastic strip to reveal another sticky surface. Bleeding modern technology! I wasted five minutes on it before deciding not to let it spoil my mood. Scissors to the rescue, and three seconds later, hey presto. Then, just to be on the safe side, I ate the entire quarter pound, thereby removing the need to close the damn bag again.

I'm not done yet. The label on the ham said, in hard-to-read writing: "May contain: almonds, barley, brazil nuts, cashews, durum flour, egg, gluten, hazelnuts, lactose, lupine, macadamia nuts, milk, mustard, oats, pecans, pistachios, rye, spices, sesame, soy, spelt, sulfite (e220-2270), walnuts, wheat." I am not exaggerating! It's a few ounces of ham for God's sake, not a five-course meal. Just ham, which "may" contain every nut and grain known to man, plus a dozen or so other ingredients. And perhaps even little specks of lupine! Did the ham delivery van sideswipe a flower stall, by chance?

While I'm complaining: I recently cooked pasta for Evert, one of the few things he'll still eat, and it took both of us forever to find out how long you were supposed to boil it. We finally discovered, with the help of a magnifying glass, a minuscule "6 minutes" on one side of the box. Why oh why make it so small?

Tuesday, September 22

The locked ward visiting hour was unusually busy yesterday. I suppose because it was World Alzheimer's Day, which has been widely covered in the papers. Which made the children decide to visit their neglected dads and mums again for a change. After all, parents with dementia are no longer able to pick up the phone and casually remind their son or daughter how long it has been since their last visit.

I had brought Grietje a new puzzle. She was very happy with it, but still preferred to work on her old puzzle for the hundredth time. The new one remained neatly packed in its cellophane. She made a happy impression, as always. It makes my visits more bearable, but I don't try to ignore the general misery there. It's not only the patients who often grow anxious when they have visitors, but also their children or companions. You never get used to not being recognized by someone you love or once loved. Just as you never get used to recognizing very little or nothing about a loved one as he or she once was.

I read in the paper that the Deltaplan for Dementia doctors are again claiming that a cure will "shortly" be found for Alzheimer's, but for the people here, "shortly" is too late. The same doctors wrote the book *The Mystery of Alzheimer's*. Sounds a bit like a detective novel. A novel whose denouement we, in our old people's home, won't be around to see. And if Dr. Sherlock Holmes doesn't get on with it soon, it is estimated that by 2040 the Netherlands will have half a million people with dementia. The term *dementia-tsunami* has already been coined. Another popular phrase is *refugee-tsunami*. It's a veritable tsunami of tsunamis. I propose that the word *tsunami* be restricted to tidal waves from now on.

An Old But Not Dead Club outing is in the offing! We're to present ourselves in the hall at noon.

Wednesday, September 23

I must say the Old But Not Dead presented rather a dashing sight yesterday. Arrayed in brightly colored rain gear and umbrellas, we took in the windmills of the Zaanse Schans, the wooden-clog workshop, the birthplace of the Albert Heijn supermarket, and the Verkade biscuit factory. The last Japanese and Chinese tourists of the season thought we were even more photogenic than the antique houses and windmills. As a group, we are too hardy to allow the weather to dampen our mood. I wonder what they'll think out there in the Far East when they see photos of a little team of rain-drenched elders posing in, on top of, and next to an eight-foot-long bright-yellow clog. In the restaurant Evert treated us to a round of "coffee with legs," i.e., Irish coffee. Or we could order a coffee with cognac if we preferred, he said magnanimously, or tea with rum.

Then Edward bought us another round because it was raining, and Ria yet another one while we waited for the next squall to blow over. It was warm and convivial, and Evert was beaming.

Since the Serrano ham debacle, I have been paying greater attention to product labels, including the "richly filled lasagna" I bought at the supermarket, for instance. Well! It certainly deserves its name: almost fifty different ingredients! Can't you just see the chef juggling fifty jars, shakers, and test tubes?

"Let's see... I think it needs another pinch of E339 and a teaspoon of maltodextrin. A few more drops of emulsifier, perhaps? Overdid it just a smidgen on the bamboo fiber, pity."

Thursday, September 24

Yesterday morning Ria and Antoine had a stern word with my stalker, Mrs. Smit, and it looks as if they've succeeded. She now avoids me like the plague. Which is, actually, what they advised her to do.

"We have noticed that you often seek out Mr. Groen's company, and we feel we must warn you not to get too close to him, for your own good."

They told her that I am a walking magnet for infectious bacteria, and showed her an article in yesterday's paper with the headline: "EVERYONE HAS THEIR OWN UNIQUE BACTERIAL CLOUD." The human body has billions of bacteria living in and around it. A healthy body harbors as many as 10,000 different kinds of bacteria. Ria and Antoine persuaded Smit that my bacterial cloud is very contagious. It was actually meant as a joke, but Smit is a bit gaga and extremely gullible.

"Well, in that case I'd better stay out of his way," she said nervously. I saw her sitting next to Mr. Verlaat last night and this morning too. Sorry, Verlaat. Thanks, Ria and Antoine.

"I'd never have thought it of the Germans," said Mrs. Schaap flatly.

She was referring to the Volkswagen company, which has apparently been rigging the exhaust levels in its diesel cars. Thanks to a specially designed computer program built into the car, the engine ran far cleaner during emissions tests than it did on the open road. The share price has plunged €25 billion and the company may have to fork out €15 billion in penalties. I wonder how they arrived at the decision to cook the numbers.

Boss 1: "Oh, nobody will notice."

Boss 2: "Yeah, but what if it does get out, and we're in for €15 billion in fines, and the share price suddenly tanks by €25 billion?"

Boss 3: "That's a risk we'll just have to take."

Or don't they have anybody who'll calculate how many billions it might cost, and do they all just stick their tycoon-heads in the sand? Do they simply choose to ignore the laws of probability? Dozens of people must have been aware of this scam, and the fraud is easy to prove. Wouldn't you think to yourself that it's bound to be discovered, sooner or later?

I don't think we can underestimate the honesty, intelligence, or foresight of the men at the top enough. Allow me to point to the bankers as an example of this.

The upshot is that every car will now probably be put through a proper "honest" test. I'll be curious to see if there are other makes that turn out to be much dirtier than the official allowance as well. I bet there will be folks who won't sleep well in the coming days.

The general consensus in our home is: such a shame, they were just starting to behave decently again, those Germans.

Friday, September 25

Not only have the refugees dominated the news in the papers, on the radio, and on the telly for weeks, but even in here they are frequently the topic of conversation at tea- or coffee-time. There are many Dutch who believe that Europe is getting too crowded. To put things into perspective, Graeme went over the numbers with those who were interested:

1. The number of refugees who have arrived in Europe this year is about 1 million.
2. The EU has approximately 750 million inhabitants.
3. We therefore have to accommodate one refugee for every 750 citizens. Provided that their numbers are spread out evenly across Europe.

"Well, if you look at it that way, it's not that terrible," his tablemates had to admit.

Mrs. Duits continued to insist that 1 million is too many.

Graeme went on doing the maths: "In Lebanon, a small country bordering Syria, there are four and a half million inhabitants, with a million refugees right now. *That*'s too many. If you projected those numbers on to Europe, it would come to about 150 million."

"Okay, okay, enough of politics," said Mrs. Duits. "Who'd like more tea?"

I was asked if I'd like to join the Crafts Club and make my own Christmas cards. No, actually, I'd rather not. "But it's only €2, and if you applied yourself you could have ten cards done in an afternoon, so that's just twenty cents per card."

I'd have liked to tell her that I'd only consider doing it for €10 a card, but I restrained myself.

"The Christmas cards seem to arrive earlier every year—just like the ginger nuts for Sinterklaas (St. Nicholas's birthday, December 5) appearing on the supermarket shelves in September. It's simply not time for it yet, was Mr. Helder's attempt to back me up. But whether I appreciate it is another story...for I can tell you I will *never* be ready for Christmas card decorating or Easter egg painting."

Saturday, September 26

Ria and Antoine don't complain, but sometimes they can't help sighing when confronted with the weekly menu. The starters for the next seven days: vermicelli soup, mushroom soup, chicken soup, cauliflower soup, tomato soup, oxtail soup, and vegetable soup. Or a salad of comparable originality. Not a day goes by when the main course does not include a lovely boiled potato. Flan and pudding dominate the dessert menu. Ria and Antoine, on the other hand, devoted their entire lives to fine dining. It's not as if they turn up their noses at bangers and mash, but still, it's just Dutch fare every single day...Our most exotic choice is spaghetti, or, very rarely, Indonesian fried rice.

The residents of our home belong to a generation that was not raised on going out to eat or paying much attention to the food. "Just act normal, because that's crazy enough": the same applies to meals.

Our current cook has certainly tried. At the start of his tenure the menu offered choices such as paella, coq au vin, or roti, but very few people circled those. The meatball and red cabbage won out decisively over the Indian curry. The tiramisu was snubbed for the custard pudding. Mr. Dickhout was the only one prepared to try everything. But he did drown every dish, even the paella, in a thick layer of applesauce from his 64-cent family-size jar from Aldi.

After some months of trying, Cook finally gave up. One thing I must say I did agree with: when he took it into his head to promote forgotten Dutch heirloom vegetables, they wouldn't go for that, either.

"Those vegetables weren't forgotten for no reason," Mrs. Schaap decided. "If they'd tasted good, we'd still be eating them."

My favorite vegetable that deserves to be sent into oblivion is salsify. Never think of it again! There's also a forgotten vegetable called Good Hendrik. Never tried it.

Luckily we still have our Old But Not Dead restaurants-of-the-world project. It's time we gave it another shot. I plan to make a reservation somewhere posh with Evert's money.

Sunday, September 27

Early this morning Mr. Schoute hit a golf ball right into Leonie's bedroom window. It gave her quite a turn, but once she'd recovered from the shock, she complimented Schoute on his drive: her room is on the third floor. Schoute used to head out to the golf course here in North Amsterdam on a daily basis, but over the past few years he hasn't had the stamina for all that walking. The distances became too great and he was growing too muddled. Sometimes he would accidentally hit a ball in the wrong direction. You don't make friends at golf that way.

This year he had occasionally been practicing, slowly and intently, in the garden downstairs. He does have a very fine stance. Legs apart, leaning forward just a bit, hollow back.

"Nice arse," Mrs. Ligtermoet once blurted out, then turned red as a beetroot.

After a few small accidents and near-accidents, Mr. Schoute was no longer allowed to practice his golf in the garden. He couldn't judge his strength anymore, and his technique was failing him.

This morning he couldn't help himself. He'd woken up early, grabbed his clubs, and tiptoed out to the garden for a little practice.

"Perhaps I should have used a number 9 iron: chip, putt, par," he sighed later, after the porter had taken away his clubs. "But there was a magpie in my line of sight, so I forgot to finish my swing." No one had any idea what he was on about. I felt sorry for the deflated little man sitting all hunched over at the coffee table. The head nurse arrived to return his clubs and said, "This is the last time, right, Mr. Schoute?"

He nodded, defeated.

Yesterday we took part in a nationwide event: National Good Neighbor Day. We were promised refreshments, information, and music. It was all there, except for the neighbors: only two stopped by, plus a *Homeless Journal* vendor. The other visitors were all family members or friends.

Monday, September 28

Last night the Residents' Committee met to prepare for our last meeting with Stelwagen. Leonie had visited an old friend of hers last week who lives in a rival old-age home not far from here. Leonie went there on an exploratory mission. It seems that over there they have finished "recalibrating" and "transitioning." According to Leonie, the result is not encouraging. Part of the building has been sold to a property management company, and the rooms are now called "apartments" and rent for €870 per month to people over fifty-five. Another part has become a nursing home reserved for people with serious care needs. The third remains a traditional old-age home like ours. It's to remain open until the last resident is moved into a nursing home or the cemetery. The porter has been sacked in order to save money. The independent kitchen is about to close. The clubs are moribund for want of participants.

"We are warned," said Leonie.

Stelwagen's departure is a convenient opportunity for some good housekeeping. I'm sure they've got an interim busybody chomping at the bit somewhere. Our departing director isn't sticking her neck out for anything anymore. It won't be easy, but we'll try to save what we can. We, seasoned old warriors, are sharpening the daggers.

Another important thing: the Residents' Committee has received a letter demanding nicer bingo prizes.

"It's time to replace the liverwurst. And the drip candle," it said in the letter signed by a dozen concerned residents. The committee has a simple solution: we'll propose raising the cost of the bingo cards from 50 cents to €1. If our proposal receives enough support, we can buy prizes costing twice as much. If it doesn't, then the only thing we can do is replace the liverwurst with a salami.

Tuesday, September 29

Mrs. Schansleh came downstairs with a red face and a head full of curlers. She'd fallen asleep under the hairdryer, and must have stayed under it for an hour and a half. Her hair was nice and dry, anyway. Schansleh is too cheap to go to the hair salon downstairs, and therefore prefers to use her own 1960s-era hairdryer.

We men have to go out for our haircut. The hairdresser, Gaily Grey, on the ground floor next to the physiotherapist's, only coifs the ladies. I asked the bleached-blonde hairdresser, who is well on her way to the old-age home herself, why she won't do men.

"Men? Never! What next!"

"That does seem an excellent reason," I ventured to answer. She gave me a dirty look and then turned her back on me.

We have been enjoying a lovely Indian summer these past few days. Geert, Evert, and I have taken our mobility steeds out for some nice spins. Evert is a complete convert: "I should have bought one of these things ten years ago."

Our three somewhat souped-up motors never fail to attract attention as we drive behind one another through the town or the countryside. Our steeds are red, white, and blue, like the national flag. It took someone else to point it out to us. We've been trying to ride in order of the colors of our Dutch Glory ever since. Sometimes people wave at us, especially the children. Then we wave back proudly, breaking into broad, wrinkly smiles.

Wednesday, September 30

Yesterday we had our last meeting with Mrs. Stelwagen. She has begun her farewell tour and brought us an apple tart. She announced, almost as an afterthought, that her successor has been named: Mr. Van de Kerkhof, Master of Public Administration, will be appointed as of October 15 for a two-year stint "to steer our home into a new future," as Stelwagen rather solemnly put it.

"It sounds great, but what does that future look like?" I asked.

"And do those two years mean that there won't be any need for a director after that because the care home will have ceased to exist?" Antoine wanted to know.

The director had to admit that these were not the sunniest of times. Then Leonie described conditions in the care home where she had gone to do some comparative research, and asked Stelwagen what directive her successor was being given.

"It is up to the new director to disclose those matters, not me," she said, remaining noncommittal, as was to be expected. Could she offer us anything more to drink? She brushed a crumb of apple tart from her impeccable business suit.

Stelwagen then thanked us for our enjoyable and constructive collaboration. Yeah, yeah, blah, blah, blah.

"I think it's a pity that we have seen so few concrete results from that enjoyable and constructive collaboration," said Graeme.

Well, the director was sorry, but she had to disagree: the high tea for the residents, the art exhibition, and the no-ailments table, surely those were great steps forward? We looked at each other and left it at that. We must save our energy for Mr. Van de Kerkhof, Master of Public Administration, and presumably a "transitioning" expert.

Thursday, October 1

Evert is failing fast. Brother Hendrik and Sister Leonie keep him company and care for the patient for as much as he'll let us. I help him get out of bed and into his clothes in the morning, and then prepare his breakfast: a cup of tea and a breakfast smoothie. It takes Evert half an hour to get it down. After that he wants to be left alone. Leonie comes at about 1 p.m., tries to entice him to eat half a sandwich, and does some light housekeeping. Then

Evert naps for a few hours. At the end of the afternoon I return for a chat and a tipple, and sometimes we'll play a board game. In the evening we watch television together, with Leonie sometimes joining us, until Evert falls asleep in his wheelchair. Then we'll wake him up and help him into bed. The GP stops in from time to time to diagnose his steady decline. Evert is a model patient; he always manages to cheer his visitors up. He is growing more passive, however, largely thanks to the enormous quantities of pills he gulps down to keep the pain bearable.

He has made a reservation for the Old But Not Dead Club at a chic restaurant next Saturday. He's already given me his cash card and PIN number to pay for it.

"And don't you dare to argue with a dying old man, Hendrik Groen!"

There's a great kerfuffle about two paintings by Rembrandt, a pair of portraits of Maerten and Oopjen Nogwat. Ninety-nine percent of the Dutch populace had never heard of this painted couple until a week ago, but now our country suddenly can't *possibly* do without them. "We" must have them, no matter what it costs. It seems we're now on the hook for 80 million for just one of the paintings. I hope it's Oopjen, because I like saying her name. Such a bargain! The other one is to remain in French hands, for another 80 million. Together they'll be shuttled from the Rijksmuseum to the Louvre and back again. What a funny business.

I've wondered for ages: why don't we ever see a new Rembrandt? Or an undiscovered Vermeer? Master forger Han van Meegeren once painted several nice little works in Vermeer's name, and almost all the experts waxed lyrical about them for years, until the day they discovered they were fakes. Then they were suddenly, literally and figuratively, not worth the linen they were painted on. In my opinion, beautiful is beautiful and ugly is ugly, no matter who puts his name to it.

There is a museum of fake art in the village of Vledder. I should like to visit it, but am afraid that it's unlikely now that I will.

I am a great proponent of the blind test, although in the case of art that may sound a bit odd. What you do is hang a few well-done forgeries among the "authentic" works, cover the signatures, and let a random sample of the public rate them or guess the name of the artist. I'd like to see if the real master painter comes out on top. You could also hang the modern paintings upside down, just for fun. See if anyone notices. I think most Japanese and Chinese tourists would fail this blind test. They only see most of the paintings much later on anyway, in the "selfies" they take standing in front of them.

Friday, October 2

We had two intruders yesterday. The porter was out sick, and according to the person in charge no replacement was available. Maybe the director wanted to see if we could do without a porter. In that case the porter should thank the intruders, because now there's a great outcry about how indispensable he is. As his main occupation consists of looking weary and doling out bored nods, he isn't exactly the epitome of helpfulness. On the rare occasion when he has to hoist himself off his stool to give someone a hand with something, he sighs and groans as if he's been asked to carry some bags of sand up twelve flights of stairs.

During the absence of the porter's vigilant eye, the thieves had simply waltzed in and out again fifteen minutes later with their loot: one housekeeping purse, a piggy bank, some jewelry, and one set of teeth. At least, Mrs. Van Diemen was adamant that both her bracelets *and* her teeth had been stolen. Even the most gullible residents were a bit skeptical about that one.

The scoundrels had each taken one floor. Several residents had noticed them, largely because they greeted everyone so politely. The descriptions of the suspects were not that helpful to the police, since they diverged quite a bit. The estimated age varied from twenty to about forty, and they couldn't even agree on the color of the men's skin. Somewhere between white and dark brown, that much was certain.

"It would never have happened if the porter had been there," many a resident opined, having momentarily forgotten that about a year ago, a young man had commandeered a resident's brand-new mobility scooter and ridden out of the building in broad daylight while the porter was engrossed in his *Football International*. At the time management had taken "appropriate action" against the porter. They told him he wasn't allowed to read at work any longer.

Saturday, October 3

The Rollator-Walk is on the march across the Netherlands. Today it's in Amersfoort, I read in the newsletter at the doctors'. Employees of YourHomeCareShop.nl are on hand to oil the wheels and inflate the tires to the correct pressure. I read that they'll even lend you a rollator if necessary. Am I being too suspicious if I wonder: why would someone take part if they don't actually need a rollator? What do the competition rules have to say about that?

Amersfoort's mayor fired the starting shot for the race, a 450-meter course. Some participants managed a whole six laps. It didn't start raining until the end, fortunately, since your average rollator-pusher doesn't have a hand free for an umbrella. The newsletter adds: "Everyone had fun, and in spite of the ambulance crews' presence, there were fortunately no accidents." In Amersfoort, apparently, ambulances, just by being there, often cause accidents.

"All participants received a medal and a goody-bag. Won't you join us next year?"

No, no, no, and no. And, just in case that wasn't clear enough: no bloody way.

A new nurse has been taken on as a stand-in for a colleague who is ill. She's quite a nice girl, but ends every other sentence with "lovely." It is getting on my nerves.

"Oh yes, will do, lovely."

"Nice cuppa, inn't it. Lovely."

"It's a nice day out there. Lovely."

I'm doing my best, but I just can't seem to ignore it. Recently I even overheard a faint "lovely" coming from the far corner of the lounge. And in spite of having adopted my father's motto, "Don't get mad, just marvel that it's so," I can't help myself and it's driving me up the wall. After a week of "lovelies" I screwed up the courage.

"Sister, this may be a strange thing to ask, but could you possibly refrain from saying 'lovely' quite as often? It rather touches a nerve, you see."

She stared at me in surprise. After a short silence she said, "I'll certainly try. If that makes you happy, Mr. Groen. Lovel... Oh, sorry."

She hadn't done it on purpose.

Sunday, October 4

Yesterday the Old But Not Dead Club dined at Restaurant Mario, in the village of Neck. I had the feeling that this was supposed to be Evert's last supper. He had booked it himself. And even though he is a self-confessed hater of codswallop, a word he pronounces with huffy contempt, he had chosen a restaurant with almost one Michelin star for a fancy seven-course prix fixe repast. And that doesn't mean seven variations on hearty Dutch fare, but seven delicate works of art sparkling with color and flavor.

Don't ask me what we ate. At the start of every course a lady came to explain what the bits and bobs on our plates were supposed to be, but by the time she'd listed the fifth ingredient, I had already forgotten what the first one was. Also, the waitress was in rather a hurry and not very used to old folk, since if she had been, she would have known she should speak clear-ly, slow-ly, and LOUD-ly. Not in a hurried mumble! We were all soon of one mind: no need to bother, lady, as long as it tastes good. We also had Ria and Antoine, our own culinary experts, with us to explain patiently what we were eating.

Evert ate little. He can barely get anything down these days. The body is finished, but not yet the spirit. He was obviously enjoying himself, and kept looking around our circle with visible satisfaction. I knew that he'd taken an extra dose of medicine beforehand in order to make it to the end of dinner. He has stockpiled a good supply of drugs at home, an assortment of legal and illegal pills, painkillers and pep-pills, and takes them as needed. On the advice of his GP.

With the seven courses came seven different wines. The sommelier was friendly, and he did speak loudly and clearly, but that didn't make much difference as far as we were concerned. To be honest, after two glasses we no longer cared that much which grape hailing from which region was in the bottle.

Upon departing at about 11 p.m., we did experience some difficulty climbing back into the minivan without any mishaps. By the time we arrived home, a happy chorus of snores was heard coming from the back seat. It wasn't easy to shake Evert, Geert, and Edward awake.

Leonie and I pushed Evert to his room, undressed him, and tucked him into bed. He was too tired to put up much of a struggle, even if only for form's sake.

"Bye, me darlings," he slurred.

Leonie swallowed. I swallowed too, in solidarity.

Monday, October 5

Our home's clubs are in crisis. The bingo afternoon remains as popular as ever, but the rest of the activities are ever more sparsely attended. The knitting club has only eleven members, the bridge club has already given up the ghost, and the klaberjass club, the shuffleboard club, and billiards club are all desperate for new members in order to stay in business. It isn't the cost: even the most tight-fisted resident is capable of coughing up 50 cents for an afternoon's entertainment. The real problem is that the home's population is shrinking. There are fewer residents, and those who are left are on average older and more passive.

The Residents' Committee was asked to come up with a solution. We suggested opening our home's activities to outsiders, other old people in the neighborhood. The response revealed a latent fear of strangers.

"You don't know what sort of rabble you're inviting in," said Mr. Dickhout anxiously.

"Well, hopefully, billiards players, shuffleboard aces, and knitting enthusiasts," said Ria, "because that's the whole point."

It was especially those alien billiards players that Dickhout was against. He's afraid he'll be toppled from his championship perch by "someone on the outside."

A rival old-age home in North Amsterdam had two inmates who both turned a hundred in the same week. Some people were envious. Not so much because of the mayoral visit, but because of the cake the mayor always brings on such occasions for all the residents to enjoy.

The number of hundred-year-olds in the Netherlands keeps growing. In 1950 there were only about forty. Now they are 3,500 strong. And on their hundredth birthday, each receives, besides that cake from the mayor, a letter from the king. Well, it comes with the king's signature, anyway. If this pace keeps up, Willem-Alexander will be left with no time to do anything but sign letters for hundred-year-olds.

I felt sorry for King Willem recently, when he had to read a speech before the UN General Assembly: almost everyone seemed to have chosen that moment to take a break. The room was three-quarters empty.

Tuesday, October 6

We are of the generation that thought it sensible to have all, or almost all, your teeth pulled *before* they started giving you trouble. "And then it won't cost you any more money going forward" was the second reason. You had to grit your teeth initially to get through the first phase, although gritting your teeth was the one thing you weren't supposed to do. But after that it was plain sailing. Or so everybody thought. But the reality is less rosy. Only too often here do you encounter dentures grinning at you from a saucer or a glass. The puckered mouths they belong in tell painful stories about dentures that no longer fit because of shrinking jaw bones. All in all, not a pretty sight.

(I read somewhere that in the American state of Vermont, women have to have permission in writing from their husbands to wear false teeth. Rather a strange law, wouldn't you say? Is it meant to protect the women or the men? Another strange American law: in Florida, unwed women are thrown into jail if they decide to go parachute jumping on a Sunday. No, I am not making this up.)

I myself possess, besides the odd remaining tooth, a set of dentures, or rather, two sets; one upper and one lower. I would rather die of the pain in my mouth than sit downstairs at coffee time toothlessly sucking on a dunked biscuit. Alas, some fellow residents are past all shame. They'll put their teeth down on the table for everyone to see, and then open wide to show anyone who's interested exactly where it hurts.

Another Old But Not Dead Club outing later today.

"It may well be my last," Evert said this morning.

I wanted to say something consoling. Such as "That's still a long way away, surely." But Evert looked at me, raised his hand, and shook his head.

Wednesday, October 7

"Yeah, it's still got that swing," said the drum teacher at the music school, cheerily looking around the circle. "When it comes to percussion, age doesn't mean a thing. In Africa there are drummers who are over a hundred. Although they're not always sure what year they were born, of course."

The Old But Not Dead Club outing was a djembe drum workshop, taught by a man called Jan-Dirk.

"Funny name for someone from my background, but I'm only half Surinamese," he said apologetically. An amusing bloke. He threatened to do a striptease if we didn't do our best, upon which the two ladies went about botching it up demonstratively.

It wasn't easy to beat the drum and keep the rhythm, and after fifteen minutes everyone's hands were bright red, but that didn't make it any less fun. Those whose fingers hurt too much were allowed to continue with drumsticks. Evert sat behind a drum set, as pleased as punch.

"This happened to have been on my bucket list," he announced cheerfully, producing a little drumroll.

"What's a bucket list?" asked Antoine.

After a moment's hesitation, Evert answered, "That's the list of things you want to do before you die. I've worked down my entire list now."

We were all quiet.

"Okay, let's hit it!" Evert called to Jan-Dirk.

When we were done, the teacher declared himself extremely satisfied with the accomplishments of the oldest students he had ever had the pleasure of teaching, disregarding the fact that we hadn't been able to keep it up for very long.

Afterward we headed for a café. Not for too long, because Evert was knackered.

Thursday, October 8

This morning was the new director's official introduction to the inhabitants of our home.

"Good morning, ladies and gentlemen, my name is Mr. Van de Kerkhof, MPA, and I have been appointed by the board of governance to take over as the new director of your care home."

Next came a rather bland speech about his management experience and the excellence of our parent organization.

Kerkhof means "churchyard." "The name isn't too promising," Graeme whispered in my ear. The fellow didn't seem to have a first name either, at least not one he cared to reveal to us.

My initial impression: a stiff, formal-looking man in a dark gray suit with a saucy light gray tie. This one won't have us slapping ourselves on the knees with laughter, that's for sure. After only five minutes I was already longing for Stelwagen's neat woolen suit. That suit had started the meeting by introducing the new strongman as a very capable manager with a great deal of experience in the care sector. Those aren't exactly qualifications requiring a kind heart. I would so like to see management and board members show some real affection and attention for old people, even if it's just a little. But that, it seems, isn't the qualification needed for this job. Managerial skills alone don't make for better care, it only makes for cheaper care.

No, it wasn't an uplifting meeting. Forgive me for doing what I myself detest: complaining and being gloomy. On the positive side: Mr. Van de Kerkhof can only turn out better than he seems at first blush. The Residents' Committee has its first meeting with him in three weeks. Come, I am only moderately pessimistic.

To celebrate meeting our new director, we were offered a piece of cake instead of the usual biscuit with our tea. Brilliant, I'd almost dare to say!

Friday, October 9

Oh, the cheapskates! At the end of the day, most residents have quite enough left of their meager old-age pension to put it away for God only knows what; but the proposal to double the bingo cards' price from 50 cents to €1 did not pass. Could it not be raised to 75 cents first, was one suggestion, so that people could get used to the hike?

This is the generation that never eats fresh bread because the stale bread has to be finished first, that cuts the brown bits off an overripe banana because it's "still perfectly okay to eat." A generation that thinks throwing out food is a waste, even if they have to swat away the flies or scrape off the mold first. People who would rather sit day in and day out in a chair with broken springs than buy a new one. And who are always moaning about how dear everything is, once they've converted the euros into guilders.

And the worst thing is: I belong to that generation myself. I have to talk myself into the occasional splurge, and into allowing myself to enjoy it too. But—there's hope yet—I am getting better at it all the time! Two weeks ago, for instance, I bought myself a pair of shoes costing €130. That's 286 guilders. (Sorry.)

Saturday, October 10

The leaders of the Union of Dutch Seniors are at one another's throats again for a change. "Swindler," "bungler," and "embezzler" are just some of the terms they bandy about, not to mention other insults such as "crook," "agitator," "pilferer," or "con man." Understandable, therefore, that there isn't much time left for advocacy. How is it that for as long as I can remember, there has never been peace and harmony in the senior henhouse? Surely one would expect more common sense, patience, and respect from the Netherlands' elders! With old age comes wisdom, goes the adage. Ha! Let me modify that: with old age comes the mudslinging.

Let me just quickly give the word to Mrs. Schansleh, our queen of the newly minted proverb. Her two latest creations:

You can't clap with one hand.
Clumsiness is the mother of the bull in the china shop.

Well, all right, I would be remiss if I failed to add this superb one from Antoine: A dog's breakfast is the cat's meow.

Mr. Pot won't come down to the conversation lounge any longer because of the din. He can't stand it. He brayed his resolve at the top of his voice today at coffee time.

It doesn't seem an insurmountable problem to me. Why doesn't the hearing-aid shop Hear-More, for instance, open a branch called Hear-Less? Something to do with cotton wool, perhaps. That's what *I* do, anyway.

Sometimes I secretly stuff cotton wool into my ears, because the conversation does get rather thunderous, with all the deaf and hard of hearing in our midst. It can be a torment to the people who still have their hearing. But if that's the worst thing we have to worry about…

Anyway, let's not make Mr. Pot seem any smarter than he really is. Everyone is better off if he stays in his room to enjoy the silence in solitary bliss.

The Netherlands is somewhat divided in its view of the refugee resettlement policy. I suspect the government officials who are saddling a village of 120 inhabitants with 700 refugees (after the same villagers had reluctantly taken in 700 to start with) are really supporters of Geert Wilders. Our national fear-of-foreigners-monger. If they aren't, I would say that with enemies like these, Geert doesn't need any friends.

Sunday, October 11

It isn't simple to get some eighty old codgers to agree on anything. The Residents' Committee has proposed three choices for the annual daytrip. Perhaps we shouldn't have, because it has sown great division. We now have the Port of Rotterdam Tour camp, we have the *Billy Elliot, the Musical* contingent, and the Christmas Market in Aachen enthusiasts. No matter which one comes out on top, I can predict that lavatory stops will take up the most time anyway. Finally, we also have a petition brought by a number of residents to have an extra Christmas bingo afternoon, with great prizes, instead of the trip.

"If it's the tour of the harbor, I'm not coming," Mr. De Grave announced loudly. If we hadn't offered them a choice, most of them would have signed up without grumbling. Instead, there are now several secret lobbies afoot. Many have voiced their support of the democratic vote we promised, but only as long as their own preference comes out on top.

To tell you the truth, I don't really care where we go. My own preference would be to plead a migraine the day of the excursion, but as a member of the Residents' Committee, I feel I have an obligation to go. The polls close on Saturday, October 17. For some it is the most important decision they'll have to make this year. At least the daytrip is creating some ferment, and that can't be all bad.

Monday, October 12

"Congratulations!" said the letter from the National Postcode Lottery, which I have been entering for years. The prize: a gingerbread from Peijnenburg, with accompanying Peijnenburg gingerbread tin. I had two tickets, so I won two gingerbreads and two tins. To be redeemed at the Primera Post Office shop.

Like so many others, I play the lottery mainly so that I won't be the only one who doesn't win when my postcode hits the jackpot. Although with a prize this measly, I wouldn't have any trouble overcoming my disappointment. Since all the residents live in the same lucky postcode, we must have at least fifty happy gingerbread prize-winners in here. There are some who can't resist waving their gingerbread spoils under the noses of those who did not take part. One of the inmates always takes five lottery tickets, so that she can make the less ticketed of us green with envy if there is a prize. She's got enough gingerbread now to last her half a year.

Some years ago the inmates of an old-age home in Zeeland, I believe, were the recipients of an enormous cash prize. As it turned out, most of the lucky winners were deeply distressed by all that money and the attendant fuss.

"Could they make one that's suitable for old people, I wonder?" asked Graeme, tongue-in-cheek, in reaction to a piece in the paper that said that they are working on developing a sex robot.

"Preferably a sexy female robot that likes to take it easy," Geert grunted.

"Yes, a geriatric sex robot that's got a headache six days a week," said Graeme.

Of course there was quite a bit of indignant head-shaking at this exchange, but there are plenty of oldies who enjoy the odd dirty joke or nudge-nudge wink-wink served with their coffee or tea. I have noticed that a surprising number of the ladies don't seem to mind a bit of naughty innuendo.

Tuesday, October 13

"Do you mean the nurse with the mustache?" Graeme asked me. The nurse with the mustache was standing right behind him. I blushed, Graeme looked over his shoulder and blushed even more deeply, and it wasn't hard for the nurse with the mustache to guess who we'd been talking about.

"I don't mean to be rude, you are a lovely nurse," Graeme said in an attempt to save himself.

"A lovely nurse with a mustache," she said, summing up Graeme's verdict.

"Just think, a beard would be worse," Evert put in his two cents.

Luckily it drew a little smile.

Next Evert let out a toot like a blast from a tuba. By accident. He used to do it on purpose, but nowadays he can't help it. But he still adopts the same indignant expression and yells over his shoulder, "Beat it, Rover, I haven't got any cookies!"

Over a game of chess yesterday Evert told me he had heard talk on the radio about an unorthodox approach to the problem of the skyrocketing cost of care. Someone had come up with the idea that insurers ought to offer patients in need of terminal care a choice: they could either have the expensive medical intervention or no care at all but a big pile of money, to be spent on whatever they liked.

"Then you'd have got your money's worth out of me even when I was gone, with a tidy sum for the club's coffers," my ailing friend said, "but alas, there's no time left to arrange it."

"No."

We were quiet for a moment.

"It's your move."

Wednesday, October 14

The Dutch were eliminated from the European Championship yesterday in the qualifying round. We lost to the Czechs. This summer the streets of Amsterdam will not, alas, be draped in orange. The manufacturers of orange gimcrackery are in sackcloth and ashes. They may even be considering suing the team for loss of income due to epic fail. I have heard a number of different explanations for why we didn't even make it to third place in our group. I find it strange that almost none of them concluded that our players may just not be good enough.

"We've been cast back into the Dark Ages of soccer," Leonie said with a beautifully feigned sob in her voice. "And I fear we won't make our way out again in my lifetime." Only to add, after yet another sob, that it *will* be nice and quiet for a change, a summer without all that hysterical soccer hoo-ha.

I think I'll become a follower of Albania for this championship. Or should I swallow my pride and throw my support to the Belgians?

On a visit to Grietje, I watched a man dunking an entire pack of biscuits into his big mug of tea one by one. He'd take one out, slowly dip it in and out a few times, then stuff it into his mouth. His cup had a thick scum of biscuit dregs floating on top. The nurse saw him doing it but did not interfere. Maybe because he looked so blissfully content. Or maybe she had too much to do to get into a skirmish over a pack of biscuits. Strangely enough, the man was as skinny as a rake.

Thursday, October 15

I had another think about old people and computers, and have come to the unsurprising conclusion that people over eighty, with the odd exception, are too old for new technology. Resistance to anything that did not exist in the past partly accounts for it, and partly the simple fact that it's too complicated for an old brain to understand. There are a few residents who have computers, but they employ only a smattering of the computer's infinite possibilities. I, for instance, use it as a typewriter, and I know how to look things up on the Internet. But I don't dare to click on most of the icons on the screen because I have no idea what will happen if I do. Then there are the residents who Skype with their children or grandchildren: there's always a handwritten note next to the computer with instructions for each of the steps, in the right order. If they lost that note, they might as well throw away the computer. Young people claim it's so simple, those modern media thingamabobs, but that doesn't apply to everybody. We don't understand the basic principles, and we can't remember anything in the first place. A person is said to have around 100 billion brain cells, but in the over-eighty age group to which I belong, a great number of those cells are not running on all cylinders, especially in the memory department.

Friday, October 16

Yesterday I had my half-yearly appointment with my geriatrician, Dr. Van Vlaanderen. She again insisted on being called Emma, but I refused. I may be old-fashioned, but doctors don't have first names.

She palpated me and peered at me, took my blood pressure and listened to my heart, and then made me do ten deep knee bends. Which was eight too many: while doing the third one, I got stuck and couldn't stand up again. I only just managed not to land on my backside. The doctor had to help me up from my stranded position.

"I must tell you that I don't often do knee bends anymore. It does happen sometimes that I have to pick something up from the floor, but never ten times in a row."

She pretended not to have heard me.

"For a man of eighty-five, there's no reason for complaint, Mr. Groen."

"I do try to complain as little as possible, Doctor."

All in all, it was a rather pointless visit, and those tend to be the best ones. I must have said this before, but from, say, age eighty, stasis is progress. The really serious collapse hasn't yet begun. I read somewhere that, statistically speaking, men spend the last fifteen years of their lives in poor health. So I have no reason to complain, for now: I'll either live to be a hundred, or I'll end up with having had fewer bad years than most people. The average lifespan for men today is 79.87 years. So you could say I already have a head start of a good five reasonably healthy years. Count your blessings, Groen. Although it is also true that once the fly tumbles into the ointment, it never comes out again. Our lifespan keeps getting longer, but you can't choose to squeeze in those extra ages between twenty and forty, the more's the pity. The extra years always come at the end, attended by ailments and infirmities. People therefore spend an unreasonable proportion of their healthcare costs in the last few years of their lives, when they—let's not mince words—already have one foot out the door anyway. Imagine the scandal if Prorail, to name just one example, spent the biggest part of its budget on the maintenance of obsolete railway equipment.

Hmm, not a very respectful comparison, Hendrik. But who cares; as a superannuated steam engine, I think I have a right to say what's on my mind.

Saturday, October 17

I have been a seeker of good fortune all my life. Who hasn't? And now "fortune seeker" has suddenly become a dirty word.

"Fortune seekers get out!" is the battle cry. If you were to take that literally, the Netherlands would become a very quiet place to live. Here in our home, the only ones left would be a few notorious malcontents, or *mis*fortune seekers.

The witch-hunt against fortune seekers began when thousands of refugees found their way to the Netherlands. A refugee can certainly use a bit of good fortune, especially when his home and hearth have been reduced to rubble and his family members are dead. So I say: go seek your fortune where the chance of finding it is greatest, which is not at this time Syria or Somalia. I don't mind helping you in your search. In the meantime I will go on seeking good fortune for myself every single day.

There are quite a few residents in our home who gradually become bent over. And once it's bent, you can never get it straight again. The spinal column compresses, bone crumbles faster than it can regenerate, and there's nothing that can be done about it. What I never realized before is that if you walk around in a stooped position and don't fancy looking down at the ground all day, trying to stand straight actually feels as if you're straining to look up at the ceiling all day. From now on I shall treat hunched old people with even more respect than before.

There are modern parents who name their kids Storm or Butterfly or Innocence, but you can always take it *too* far.

"It was something to do with a Cavia in the Xenos," was all Graeme could recall about the baby of soccer player Wesley Sneijder and his actress wife Yolanthe Cabau-something.

"The child is called Xess Xava," Mrs. Slothouwer said tartly.

"Is that a boy's name or a girl's name?" someone inquired.

Poor kid, it's not given a very easy start, having to go through life as Xess Xava Sneijder. His (or her) initials are XXS, extra-extra small. Which is more applicable to the dad, actually.

"If I had another child, I'd name it Whisky-Cola," said Evert.

Sunday, October 18

This morning I pinned the outcome of the annual daytrip vote on the noticeboard: the Christmas market in Aachen won it by a hair. We can go ahead and book the coach. I can see it now: six hours in the coach, and two hours of sausage and glühwein. The tour of the harbor came in at number two. Old people have a thing about boats, although in this case it wasn't enough to swing the vote. The attraction of boat trips lies in the peaceful tempo at which the landscape drifts by. It's the tempo that suits us. The musical *Billy Elliot* came in last. The extra cost must have scared many people off. They are quick to decide something is too much money.

"Left home before the war," Evert will say whenever someone complains that the price of a cup of coffee is now €2.50, or rather, 5 guilders and 50 cents.

There are always people who'll immediately tell you how much dearer something is now than in the old days. Which old days they're referring to isn't always very clear. And how much more money they currently have in their pockets isn't something the grumblers seem to take into account either.

The choice of the Christmas market gave rise to contented smirks on the one hand and long faces on the other. Can't be helped. The Residents' Committee did, however, add a Christmas bingo with extra big prizes to the schedule, as a sop to those who were left disappointed.

As the icing on the cake, we were able to announce that "THE COST OF A BINGO CARD WILL REMAIN 50 CENTS." That has boosted our popularity enormously. It was made possible by the generosity of two anonymous benefactors. Their names are Antoine and Evert. Each dropped €100 into the prize kitty. Gigantic liverwursts for the winners! We are even thinking of having a stealth round in which it turns out at the end that "everyone wins." I can already see the long faces, and hear the grumbles of inmates who were playing with one stingy bingo card: "If I'd have known, I'd have bought a lot more cards."

It promises to be a spectacular afternoon.

Friday, October 23

It isn't easy to press Ctrl-Alt-Del with one hand. Luckily one doesn't have to do it too often. But if you have only one hand, just writing a capital letter slows things down considerably.

I broke my arm last Sunday afternoon. A combination of an unanticipated step and a moment of inattention. I may have been distracted, I think maybe there was a dog nearby, and I missed the step, twisted an ankle, fell, and heard something snap. I didn't even manage the usual instinctive reflex of people taking a pratfall: bounding back to their feet again and acting as if there's nothing wrong. My arm was twisted into a strange angle and hurt like hell.

I used to wonder what the siren sounds like from inside the ambulance. I finally had a chance to find out, but I forgot to pay attention. Before lifting me into the ambulance the paramedic gave me "a little shot for the pain." Splendid stuff. My memory of the rest of the afternoon is rather hazy. It was Sunday afternoon, and the Emergency was crammed with injured sportsmen, but they let me go first. The nurse said later that I'd muttered, approvingly, about "positive age discrimination."

"We are going to invite you to spend the night here, Mr. Groen," I do remember the sister saying.

"I can't, I have someone who needs looking after."

At my request the sister phoned Antoine, who arrived an hour later with my pajamas and toothbrush, and reassured me that the Old But Not Dead would look after Evert. He had wanted to come along, but Antoine had told him he couldn't.

I woke up in the middle of the night. My arm hurt a lot, my ankle too.

I am of the generation of "no whining, and no bothering other people with your problems." It took me a while to overcome that admonition, but then I pushed the bell for help.

"So sorry to bother you," I couldn't help apologizing when the night sister arrived.

"That's what we went to college for," she said, "and we're paid for it too, so don't be embarrassed."

She gave me two cheerfully colored pills and if I hadn't had a fractured arm, I'd have awoken some hours later rested and refreshed.

I was home again by Monday afternoon.

Saturday, October 24

I have been an object of pity for some five days now, and I don't like it. Some people will ask me at least three times a day, "How are you feeling now?" It's well meant but these solicitous inquiries into my condition occur at least a hundred times a day. Which has begun to annoy me so much that I'm avoiding the conversation lounge for the time being, which in turn will lead to a concerned resident knocking on my door every so often to see if I'm still alive. If I happen not to answer, since I'm spending most of the time hiding out at Evert's, they'll panic and fetch the nurse, who will establish that I am not answering the door because I'm not in.

Evert and I are keeping our spirits up with the help of board games and, as soon as the cocktail hour rolls around, the best libations money can buy. Evert has to keep drinking in order to flush down the multitude of pills he pops out of the big automatic pill dispenser at his elbow.

I was given a box of twenty-five board games by the Old But Not Dead gang, and Evert and I are systematically working our way through them. We waste a lot of time repositioning the pieces, pawns, and tokens, which I tend to knock over with my clumsy left hand. Fortunately we are not in a hurry.

I am a rather handicapped caregiver with one arm in a cast, but I am starting to get the hang of it and between the two of us we manage. Showering is the only thing we both need help with.

"It creates a bond," Evert said.

I suggested taking a shower together.

"Perish the thought!" he said vehemently. "I'm not going under the shower with a dirty old man like you."

"Just kidding, the revulsion is mutual," I reassured him.

In the meantime, typing journal entries is getting a little easier. The first day after I got home from hospital it took me two hours to write half a piece. I was so frustrated that I did not go near the computer for several days. But I am happy to report that my left hand is doing a yeoman's job, and is allowing me to type a bit faster now.

Sunday, October 25

Many old folk are afraid of using ATMs. They are worried about getting robbed. They don't have much faith in Internet banking either, if they own a computer, that is. They've been put off by stories in the paper about all the things that can go wrong with computers.

It must be said there's no lack of worrisome examples. Take the following item, for instance: the German Bundestag's computers all went on a rampage one day, of their own accord. It led to considerable panic. Who knows what they'd been up to? Every single one of the 20,000 computers had to be replaced. The question is: who was responsible? My first suspect would be whoever is supplying the new computers. Next in the order of suspects are of course the Russians. Although the Americans' hands aren't exactly clean either. A computer security firm sold the secret keys to its own system for $10 million to the American intelligence agency NSA, which in turn used them in its pursuit of terrorist organizations such as UNICEF and Doctors Without Borders.

And yesterday ING Bank's website was once again down for several hours. So all things considered, it's no surprise, really, that we'd rather hide our pennies in an old shoebox in the bottom of the linen cupboard. A lady on the fourth floor has been bragging that she sleeps with her purse tucked between her knees. I think that's definitely a safe place for it. He who dares venture thither deserves to be richly rewarded. Evert could not rule out the possibility that the reason the woman is giving away her purse's hiding place is to invite thieves to come and check it out. Although that did sound a bit farfetched to me.

Twenty thousand computers at the Bundestag seems a bit farfetched too. But that's what it said in the paper.

Also in the paper: Johan Cruyff has cancer. Lung cancer, to be precise. The news landed in here like a bomb. Especially because always, through thick and thin, "El Salvador" has remained just an ordinary boy. Or, as he says himself, just your ordinary "savior."

Monday, October 26

Yesterday afternoon Evert, Leonie, and I took a walk in the park. The sun was shining, the colors were dazzling. Leonie was the one pushing Evert's wheelchair, not without some difficulty. Our ailing friend kept listing sideways: he'd fallen asleep just a few minutes into our stroll. We sat down on a bench in the sun, taking turns to push Evert back into an upright position whenever he threatened to slide out of his chair. A lost dog came along and started sniffing at our legs. There wasn't much to say. Before starting back we woke Evert up. He gazed at us in surprise, looked around, and then nodded his head a few times.

"Phew, quite a walk, that was."

Before we arrived home he'd dozed off again. He didn't wake up until we reached his room. I fed him a few pieces of pear and then Leonie undressed him, assisted by a male nurse, who carefully carried him to his bed. Half sitting, half reclining, he sipped a little brandy. He was all out of jokes.

"I'm going to sleep, see you in the morning." He seemed content.

I went downstairs for a cup of coffee and to watch the finals of *The Great Dutch Bake-Off.* Seated up close to the widescreen telly were Ria and Antoine. They haven't missed a single episode. They felt terrible for every failed cake. It was touching to watch them from a distance. Afterward they promised to bake me an illicit cake someday soon.

"That's an offer I can't refuse, but what I'd *really* like is if you'd bake the most beautiful cake you've ever concocted for Evert's funeral," I said. I believe that they began making preparations that same evening.

Tuesday, October 27

The animal lovers in our home are simply overjoyed: China is giving the Netherlands two giant pandas. Although it does come with a catch or two:

1. They're only on loan, or rather, for hire. At the rate of €1 million for the pair, which is quite a sum for two fat black-and-white layabouts.
2. Any eventual baby bears must be returned to China.
3. If the Netherlands isn't being nice to China, by saying something about human rights over there, for example, we'll have to send them back.

As far as I'm concerned, the Chinese can keep their gift, but I am rather alone in that opinion. It seems that the zoo stands to make a fortune, since the pandas will bring in so many more visitors. Here in the home there has been considerable interest as well. The Residents' Committee has already received a request for next year's daytrip to go to the "panda-zoo."

A British granddad in Saudi Arabia has been condemned to a year in prison and 350 lashes. His grave transgression: making homemade wine. The police found the bottles in his vehicle. Saudi Arabia—isn't that country our partner in the fight against Islamic extremism? How extreme is it, then, to flog an old man to death because he likes a little glass of wine now and again? When our King Willem Alexander, whom we used to call Prince Pils, was at that state dinner in honor of his visit to Saudi Arabia, he really should have made a point of uncorking a nice bottle of Beaujolais. If he had, I'd have changed from a hardened republican into a loyal monarchist. Although only for this particular king.

We are having our first meeting with Mr. Van de Kerkhof, our new director, this afternoon.

Wednesday, October 28

When I arrived at Evert's flat this morning I found him panting heavily in his wheelchair, clad only in a dirty pair of underpants. His excrement-smeared pajamas were on the floor next to the bed. He was trying to pull the soiled sheets off the bed, but didn't have the strength. His emaciated body was shaking. I went to fetch the ever-helpful Sister Herwegen.

"Oh, Mr. Duiker . . . Were you lying half the night in . . ."

Evert nodded.

She went to work energetically. Half an hour later the bed was clean and Evert was sitting in his wheelchair in a clean pair of pajamas. The flat smelled of cleaning products over a vague odor of urine and shit.

"Feel better, Mr. Duiker." The nurse left.

"I believe I've just about reached rock bottom, Henk," Evert said to me when she was gone.

"Yes, I'm afraid you may be right."

"I must put it off a little longer. Jan, his wife, and children are coming on Sunday," my friend said.

I couldn't think of anything consoling to say except a rather helpless "Chin up!" I made him a cup of coffee, only half of which he managed to get down. Then I found that I could assist him a bit by using my good hand, as he hauled himself painfully out of his chair and into his bed.

"Hendrik, my good friend, allow me to recover my breath a bit, in order to demolish you at Snakes and Ladders later this afternoon," he said with a thin smile. Five minutes later he was asleep. I sat in the chair by his bed for a while, trying to read the newspaper. When Geert arrived two hours later to relieve me, I had already forgotten what I had read.

Thursday, October 29

Not that I really care, but I think it is telling that at the start of his first meeting with the Residents' Committee, our new director did not inquire about the cast on my arm. Not that I don't get enough sympathy here, but wouldn't you expect someone leading a caregiving institution to make a show of caring about his residents?

The rest of the meeting was also conducted in a frosty, businesslike manner. We inquired about the situation regarding the vacancies, the eventual dismissal of the porter, and outsourcing of the food preparation, as well as the prospective closing of our institution.

Mr. Van de Kerkhof was unable to provide any information about these matters at this time. He wished, rather, to confine himself in our discussion to what he saw as the "core business" of the Residents' Committee, namely the activities, clubs, and outings.

"Actually, at this juncture we consider our home's continued operation rather more important than bingo, and we sincerely hope that the management shares our concern," Leonie said flatly, as if she were ordering a loaf of bread at the bakery.

No, of course, Kerkhof agreed with her completely, but within the institution, everyone had their own distinct responsibilities.

"The Residents' Committee would like to be involved in more than just marginal affairs," I heard myself say.

"I will certainly take that into account wherever possible," our new boss retorted stiffly. That should lead to some interesting confrontations.

Talking it over afterward in Ria and Antoine's room over a glass of wine, we all heartily agreed: in less than an hour, the fellow had managed to motivate us into standing firm and not allowing ourselves to be kicked around.

We started dusting off our networking options: who among us still had some press or law connections? Graeme, Ria, and Leonie have volunteered to visit old acquaintances who may be of some use to us. We will be keeping it under our hats, naturally. Kerkhof must be kept in the dark for as long as possible, in the misapprehension that he'll be able to drive his docile herd to the slaughter without a struggle. Stelwagen, what a sweetheart you were, compared to this butcher!

Friday, October 30

This morning Evert seemed to be doing slightly better.

"Got through the night without soiling myself anyway, Henkie."

"My nose did detect that fact."

"Those new bung-plugger pills are already helping."

His solid food now consists mainly of pills. His liquid intake is limited to small sips of some kind of astronaut-diet concoction, fortified in the late afternoon with one or two nips of whisky or brandy.

Some concerns are being raised on another front: with regard to our Christmas market trip, are we hiring a good coach, with an experienced driver? The trepidation was set off by the news of a bus accident in France. Not the accident itself, you understand, but the fact that thirty old people were killed in it. Pensioners on holiday. Funny, isn't it, that spontaneous sense of solidarity with accident victims? The first question, always, is: Were there any Dutch victims? Such a relief when there aren't. Oh well, just foreigners, then, that's lucky! But then when it turns out that the victims were fellow senior citizens, suddenly the accident takes on far more harrowing proportions.

The bus driver lost control of the wheel. I can't quite picture how that happens, losing control of the wheel. As if the steering wheel could suddenly break loose and have a life of its own.

The English fellow sentenced to 350 lashes for wine possession has been granted clemency thanks to the intervention of Britain's foreign minister. There was some discussion among the residents whether it was the cane or the whip he would now *not* be flogged with. I believe he'd already served that year in the clink.

Saturday, October 31

Yesterday Evert presented me with a beautiful book: *Old People Are the Happiest People*, the collected poems of Anton Korteweg.

"A farewell present. Chosen for the title. You do like poetry, don't you?"

I said I did.

"I don't. Although, these are all right, because they don't rhyme. I've leafed through it, it's really your kind of thing."

He advised me to read a couple of the poems every day in his memory, and if someday I found myself down in the dumps, to take the dedication on the flyleaf to heart.

I opened the book.

"No, not yet. When I'm dead."

"It's a nice hefty book, anyway," I said.

"Over six hundred poems, so if you read two a day, you'll get through another year before you even know it."

The residents are feeling a bit more empathy for the refugees than before. That's thanks to Bibihal Uzbeki, from Afghanistan, who at 105 may be the world's oldest refugee. She arrived in Croatia after a twenty-day journey, having hitchhiked a good portion of the way carried on her fellow travelers' backs.

"We had problems many times," Bibihal reported.

Rather cautiously put, methinks.

"I would never *think* of it, having my son carry me on his back," said Mrs. Quint, "not even from here to the front door."

"Is your son a weakling, then, or are you that heavy?" Slothouwer asked.

Mrs. Quint almost choked with outrage.

A little while later, Geert bumped into Mrs. Slothouwer's chair just as she was sipping her tea.

"Oh, I do apologize!"

"You again!" Slothouwer glared at Geert, furious.

"No, that was me, last time," Graeme said with a friendly nod.

"Maybe it happens because you're always so mean to other people?" asked Geert.

Slothouwer stood up and disappeared to her room.

"Ha! Good riddance to bad rubbish," Mrs. Quint noted with some satisfaction.

I know that besides his regular collection of medicines, Evert has another stash of pills somewhere. With the help of the Euthanasia Society and son Jan, he has stocked up on pentobarbital. Euthanasia pills. He confided it to me the other day.

"Just so you know, Hendrik. So that I won't have to bother anyone else when the time comes."

Sunday, November 1

9 p.m.

As if to emphasize the sadness of this day, North Amsterdam was shrouded in a stubborn mist all day. According to Ria, six miles to the south it was bright and sunny. It had to be so.

This morning I went to see Evert. He said he would stay in bed, and wanted nothing but a cup of tea. That was all. There was nothing left to talk about. I suggested a game of drafts, but he shook his head.

"I'm going back to sleep. Just stay and sit with me for a few minutes, and then when I'm asleep you can go downstairs and get back to your skirt-chasing," he said with one of his last grins.

When he'd fallen asleep, I took his hand in mine. I could feel the bones and arteries. Two hours later Jan, his wife, and the kids arrived. We gently woke Evert up. He was confused at first upon seeing such a large group standing around his bed. Slowly he regained his grip on reality.

"Hey, Groen, still here? Don't you have anything better to do than sit here holding my hand?"

I left him to be alone with his family. A good hour later they were at my door to say goodbye. Wet cheeks. I got hugs from all four of them.

Jan said, "My dad's sleeping now, but he asked if you wouldn't mind popping in at the cocktail hour. Just pop in—sounds nice and breezy, doesn't it?"

"Of course."

Jan was the last to walk out the door, and he turned back briefly: "See you tomorrow."

I went to him at 5 p.m. He was still asleep. He woke up an hour later. Shortly afterward he said, "There's a few dregs of good cognac left over there in the cabinet, Henk. Why don't you fill the glasses one more time? Pour yourself a big one, a small one for me."

We clinked our glasses.

"To a happy end, dear old chum," he said, "and many thanks for your very entertaining friendship these past few years. I have enjoyed your company very much."

I wanted to reply with something equally nice, but my mouth couldn't seem to make a sound. I had tears in my eyes.

"Don't worry about me, please; I'm actually looking forward to the peace and quiet. You're going to be around a while longer, so try and make the best of it," he consoled me. "Here's to some Dutch courage! You can have the remains of my liquor reserve. There are one or two nice little bottles left."

We clinked again. When the glasses were empty, he asked me to leave him with two glasses of water on his bedside table, and his pill box.

"And now bugger off, you." He swallowed.

We hugged. For the first and last time. Two skinny old chaps who loved each other in their own old-chap way.

"Leonie will be coming along shortly to say goodbye, so you can leave the door off the latch," Evert said.

That was an hour ago.

Now he is alone.

Monday, November 2

At 10 a.m. this morning I warned the head nurse that Mr. Duiker wasn't answering his door. Evert had planned it that way. I went in with her. He was lying there perfectly decently, except that his mouth had fallen open. He was wearing the good suit that Leonie had recently helped him buy. He was freshly shaved, his hair neatly combed. He still looked like Evert, but the real Evert had departed. For parts unknown.

Next I went around to our Old But Not Dead friends one by one, to tell them that Evert, sadly, had to give up his club membership. These were the same words Evert himself had used a few days ago.

"Hendrik, I am sorry that I'll have to end my Old But Not Dead membership very soon. Will you please thank the rest of the club on my behalf, for having tolerated me as a member for so long? Do give my apologies for leaving the party prematurely."

He had never in his life been a member of any organization for as long a period as he'd been in the Old But Not Dead Club, he told me proudly.

When I knocked on Leonie's door and she opened it, I could tell that she already knew. We just held each other tight for a very long time.

Tonight we are assembling at Ria and Antoine's.

Tuesday, November 3

On the flyleaf of *Old People Are the Happiest People*, my farewell gift from Evert, it says, in rather clumsy cursive writing:

Hendrik, friend,
Read, laugh, and love someone
'Cause what's gone is gone

Try to keep having fun
As long as there's life

Evert

P.S. For my very first stab at doggerel, not too bad, is it?

Wednesday, November 4

The funeral is on Friday, at 3 p.m.; Evert wasn't a morning person. There's nothing left to do. He arranged it all splendidly while he was alive: the undertaker, the coffin, the cemetery, the card, the music, and the strict prohibition against coffee and funeral cake. Instead we're having Irish coffee.

The Old But Not Dead members gathered on Monday evening for some support and to exchange memories. Jan was our special guest. The libations were supplied by our drinks specialist: the deceased himself. He had entrusted a number of bottles to Ria and Antoine, for safekeeping until this occasion. Food was never his strong suit. Whenever Evert was responsible for providing something hot and edible, you wouldn't get much, save perhaps a fire emergency. He cherished that reputation in order to get out of his culinary obligations whenever he was able.

We cried some, and laughed a great deal.

Jan, Graeme, and I are to speak at the funeral. His granddaughter will play a little waltz on her accordion. Ria and Antoine are baking the most beautiful cake of their lives, and Geert and Edward will see to it that, come the spring, two hundred tulips and daffodils will bloom on his grave.

Thursday, November 5

Yesterday I had a transition rituals guide at my door.

"First of all, please accept my sincere condolences on the passing of your friend. My name is Anita Veen, and I'm from the training school for transition rituals guides, The Moment."

I said I had never heard of it, and asked her how she had found me. The care home had given her my name.

"Surely Mr. Duiker, even without any official religious affiliation, must have given some sign that he'd appreciate some kind of remembrance moment?" She put a folder down on the table entitled "Inspiration Creativity Spirituality."

"You're lucky that you did not speak to the deceased while he was still alive."

Mrs. Veen looked rather taken aback.

"If you had accosted Mr. Duiker while he was alive to ask him if he'd like a remembrance moment from a rituals guide, you would probably have been a candidate for a remembrance moment yourself. Mr. Duiker was not, to put it mildly, very fond of spiritual quackery."

"Oh," said Mrs. Veen, crestfallen. "And I don't suppose you have any interest in it either?"

"You suppose correctly."

When I later asked who had given her my name, nobody seemed to know. The head of housekeeping thought it was standard procedure. She also informed me that there was growing interest in the transition ritual "from one's own home into the care home," for the last transition faced by the elderly—not counting the transition into the cemetery. Apparently the management passes on the particulars of residents and new arrivals alike to these commercial modern-day do-gooders.

It isn't easy to find the right words for a moving eulogy for Evert. He casually alluded to it a few weeks ago.

"Keep it short and try to get a few good jokes in, preferably some rude ones," was his advice.

Saturday, November 7

It may sound like a cliché, but I can't think of a better way of putting it: it was a splendid farewell. It seems that my friend, who had so skillfully cultivated his rough edges, had nevertheless managed to show many people his soft heart. For a funeral of an eighty-seven-year-old, there was quite a large crowd. Many of the residents attended, some of whom were moved to tears. I suspect only one or two of having come just to gloat about Evert's demise. Quite a few of the staff also came, including, surprisingly, Mrs. Stelwagen. Even though she no longer works here, Jan had given her permission to say a few words on behalf of the institution, and she kept it short but sweet. She said Evert was the most sympathetic troublemaker she'd ever encountered in her career. There's a heart beating under that gray woolen suit after all. It was a compliment Evert wouldn't have known what to do with.

Jan and Graeme spoke movingly and amusingly, and I believe I did as well.

Evert had arranged for a startling choice of music. "Hurt" by Johnny Cash, "If Death Must Come One Day," by Zjef Vanuytsel, and "Kraaien" ("Crows") by André Manuel. Shatteringly lovely. I didn't realize I still had that many tears.

Jan went last. "My father asked me to tell you that he wished to take his last nightcap in the grave by himself. Those were his words. So this is where we take leave of him. I think we could all use a stiff drink ourselves now. Let us begin our Evert-less lives with an Irish coffee and a slice of the most scrumptious cake his friends Ria and Antoine have ever produced, and while doing so tell each other our best Evert stories."

And that's what we did.

Sunday, November 8

In reaction to the attack on the Russian airplane that has crashed in Egypt, Geert remarked: "If I were still able to travel, I'd book myself a flight to Sharm el-Sheikh right now. It's never been as well guarded, probably very cheap *and* nice and quiet."

The ISIS bombs are a great worry to the residents. As far as I know, never in the history of the world has a home for the elderly been targeted for an assault, but still... Some of the residents think that the very fact that a care home has never been a target only increases the chances of its happening.

* * *

For the past several years, I would drop in on Evert at around 4 p.m., four or five times a week. I'd always have a cup of tea first, for form's sake, followed by a stiff drink. So as not to waste any time, Evert would skip the tea and go straight for the booze. At about 6 p.m. we'd go down to dinner. Two hours of pleasant camaraderie—a nice, old-fashioned word that suits old geezers like us. Now he is no longer with us, I thought I'd have trouble filling those afternoon hours, but my Old But Not Dead friends are looking out for me. And they're keeping an eye on Leonie as well, that strong, quiet woman who did so much for Evert in her discreet and seemingly nonchalant way. Yesterday she came around in the late afternoon. She strode into the middle of my room and stood still.

"Hold me, Hendrik—please?"

She wept quietly into my shoulder.

After a few minutes she took out her handkerchief. "Thank you. It just had to come out. Let's go to Ria and Antoine's now for a cup of pea soup, shall we?"

We have invitations from friends for the next two weeks at least, to distract us. We shall gratefully accept.

Monday, November 9

Our only foreign resident is a Turk, Mr. Mehmed Okcegulcik.

"Can't we just call you Okkie? I can't remember the rest of it," Mrs. Van Diemen had asked soon after his arrival. No problem, said Mr. Okcegulcik, so he has been

Mr. Okkie ever since. Okkie's a nice bloke, with just the right amount of self-mockery. He has publicly and gravely declared that he is not a terrorist, even if he does hail from Turkey. I'm willing to take his word for it, but I have overheard some doubtfulness from certain quarters.

"Easy for him to say, but with Muslims, one can never be completely sure," said Mr. Pot, who, sadly, has already forgotten about his intention to boycott the conversation lounge. Staying alone in his room was a bit *too* quiet for him.

"Mr. Okkie isn't Muslim, he's Russian Orthodox," Ria objected.

According to Pot they are just about the same thing.

Mr. Okkie occasionally joins us at the Old But Not Dead table. Yesterday I had a serious conversation with him about loss, in the wake of Evert's death. Okkie lost his wife and daughter within a short space of time. His two sons have returned to Turkey, they live in Istanbul, but he himself doesn't feel like going back to his village in Anatolia, and he finds Istanbul far too crowded.

"I like living here. Nice people and no worries. I speak to one of my sons every other day. I talk to them more often now than when they lived in the Netherlands."

Okkie worked as a welder in the shipyards here in North Amsterdam for over thirty years. Upon his retirement he went on living in Amsterdam with his wife and daughter.

He has been a widower for two years. His daughter took over caring for her father when her mother died, but she too died half a year later. He had been on the waiting list for a place in a home for the aged for several years, and got lucky. He was offered a room in here just before the new, stricter standards went into effect.

"It's a clever mick who'll ever get me to leave," he said yesterday.

"Clever dick, you mean," I said, laughing.

"I don't care *who* never gets me to leave," Okkie twinkled back.

The Old But Not Dead Club could consider offering Evert's spot to Mr. Okkie. Then we could present ourselves as a multicultural organization. I shall give it some thought.

Tuesday, November 10

The National Health Council has issued a new list of what you should and shouldn't eat in order to stay healthy. There's lots that's off-limits: alcohol, red meat, sugar, and sausage have been banned. Deep-fried food already had a bad reputation. It's a good thing Evert no longer needs to get all in a stew about it, because he used to overindulge in everything on the list with great gusto.

As far as sugar goes, Mrs. Hoensbroek is the uncontested champion here: six heaped spoonfuls or more in her coffee or tea.

"If you don't start reducing your sugar intake, you'll never make it to the age you are now," a nurse told her. Huh? You could hear the brains creaking. Did that make sense?

Personally, I have decided to keep eating and drinking the old way. Alcohol, red meat, sugar, sausage, and fried *bitterballen* have brought me to this juncture; I am not going to abandon them now. With some reluctance I will have to concur just this once with Mr. Pot, who at least a couple of times a day will say, "It'll wait until after I'm gone."

Sister Morales, the little schemer who would sometimes try to badmouth Stelwagen in the past, now has it in for our new director, Mr. Van de Kerkhof. At teatime she leaned over to me.

"Did you know that Mr. Kerkhof is planning to close the entire home within the next two years? I thought the Residents' Committee should know."

I asked her how she had got hold of that information, but she wouldn't say.

I don't know what to do with this. Is Morales a well-informed source or a compulsive liar?

This evening the club is going out to dinner. It will do us good in these somber times.

Wednesday, November 11

Mrs. Slothouwer thought that with the demise of her arch-enemy Evert, she was now free to resume tormenting people and spewing her malicious gossip and spite undisturbed.

"Have you washed today, Mrs. Smit?" she asked in a loud voice.

Mrs. Smit looked up skittishly.

"I did, you can ask the nurse."

"Well, not very well in that case, because you're a bit smelly."

The next instant a small pitcher of milk happened to spill—right onto Slothouwer's lap.

"You did it on purpose!" she fumed at Geert.

Geert looked at her evenly and then said, "I am the new Evert."

"So am I, actually," I said, putting up my hand.

Two more Everts came forward: Edward and Leonie.

Mrs. Slothouwer slunk off to her room and did not come back.

Yesterday we had a delicious Mexican meal. Lots of beans, corn, mince, and Mexican pancakes, called wraps. All of us, even the ladies, had a Corona beer to go with it.

"This is the second beer I've had in my life," said Ria.

You could tell from her expression that there would not be a third one.

We all drank a toast to our departed friend.

It was a great deal quieter without Evert, and the conversation was rather more polite. With Evert, it tended to veer into piss-poo-shit territory. He would have taken the presence of a dish of kidney beans as an excuse to bring up the subject of flatulence. Although he certainly wouldn't have used the word *flatulence*. If others had used that word, he'd have accused them of being foul-mouthed.

Thursday, November 12

Graeme has opened a temporary betting shop. What's the occasion? The Lower House has a committee overseeing our intelligence services. This committee has acquired the nickname "Hush Council" because the members are required to keep their deliberations secret. The committee is composed of the faction leaders of ten different political parties. At least one of them has leaked information to the press. But which one? We all tend to have our favorite suspect. You hope it's that one politician you just can't stand, but deep in your heart you're afraid it's your political soulmate who did it. Our fellow residents aren't generally all that interested in politics, but in this case they haven't been shy about pointing the finger: it must be that one, or the other.

In the interests of this new party game, Graeme decided it would be fun to bet on one's favorite stoolpigeon. The opportunity was initially reserved for Old But Not Dead members only, but now it has been opened to all. The take will be divided among those who correctly guessed the actual traitor. The stake is €2. Should the parliamentary committee charged with investigating the Hush Council fail to come up with a culprit, you get your money back. If one of the gamblers should meet an untimely end, his stake will be forfeited. For Mr. Pot that was enough reason not to participate.

"Dead or not, I want my money back."

Sorry, Pot, rules are rules.

Some of the inmates here are quite fond of snitching themselves. They'll tell on their neighbors for a minor infraction, such as cooking in one's room, or putting hooks in the wall.

"Yes, nurse, I don't know, the room next door smells of fried eggs..."

"I was in the corridor and heard a loud banging, sister.

It was almost as if someone were hammering a nail into the wall…"

It's always the same disingenuous residents who complain. No, I am not going to say who they are.

Friday, November 13

To those who are superstitious: be especially on your guard today. Friday the 13th!

Talking of superstition: Ne Win, Burma's military leader, had new banknotes printed in 1987 in denominations divisible by nine because an astrologer had told him that nine was his lucky number.

Yesterday I went to visit Grietje. One of the nurses was telling me about a care home in Weesp that's been turned into a neighborly dementia village, with streets, squares, and gardens. The demented residents can bring their own former front doors from home; there is a supermarket where they can buy soda and licorice, and a café where sentimental old songs are sung. I asked if they also have an old black-and-white television showing *Swiebertje*, *Steptoe and Son*, and *The Generation Game* all day? She didn't know.

I think it would be great if they brought back old series with the original cast, if the actors are still living. An old-as-the-hills Harold pushing a rollator, chased by a wheelchair-bound Steptoe, would be something to see—but alas, they're both dead.

* * *

Some Christian schools in the Veluwe are boycotting the *Sinterklaasjournaal* because of the fiendish "white wives" story in the latest broadcast. A headmaster in Voorthuizen: "The Bible tells us that the Lord God is distressed by those who call attention to witchcraft." Well, I know of quite a few things the Lord God and his headmasters ought to get far more distressed about than the *Sinterklaasjournaal*. If I had to choose between the Book of God and the Book of Sinterklaas, I know which one *I* would pick. There's too much unpleasant bunk in that Bible.

Saturday, November 14

Yesterday morning everyone was up in arms about silly white witches on the telly, and then last night five attacks took place in Paris with more than a hundred twenty slain. Can you think of a greater and more ghastly contrast? The bafflement and indignation exceed all description.

One resident said, with tears in her eyes, "You see: Friday the thirteenth."

We were huddled around the telly all night. All the experts and eyewitnesses notwithstanding, television is rather useless, since in light of the horrific news there's really not much to say: five bloody assaults, one hundred twenty dead (provisional toll). Heartrending. The whole of Europe is united in grief—for a while, anyway. A few days from now the differences will start bubbling up to the surface once more over what should be done about terrorism, and who's directly or indirectly to blame.

Sunday, November 15

Some residents got stuck in the elevator yesterday. It had stopped for no apparent reason between the fourth and fifth floors. A minor panic broke out.

It took a while for it to occur to the people in the elevator that there might be an alarm button somewhere; then it took a bit longer for that button to be discovered behind Mr. Dickhout's broad backside, but once the alarm was raised, a member of the staff came rushing to the scene.

An anxious "Help!" was heard.

"Please stay calm. Who's in the elevator?" the nurse called.

"We're standing, and I can't stand on my feet that long."

"Neither can I."

"Then why don't you sit down?"

"On the floor?"

"Can't you sit on your walker?"

"No, I only have my cane."

"If your legs give out, just sit down on the floor."

"Then I won't be able to get up again."

"We'll deal with that later. How many of you are there?"

The count was four people, two rollators and one cane.

I had the pleasure of being in the front row for the spectacle, since I had been about to take the elevator down.

It took a long time for someone from maintenance to arrive. Meanwhile the victims received encouragement from both the fourth floor beneath them and the fifth floor above.

"Someone will be coming to get you out any moment now."

"Mrs. Duits says she's going to faint," someone shouted anxiously.

She was advised not to, from all sides.

"Is it any moment now yet?"

"Let's just hope there isn't a fire," said one of the gawkers who had gathered, pointing to the sign DO NOT USE THE ELEVATOR IN CASE OF FIRE.

Finally the head of maintenance showed up, with a sandwich in his hand. He disappeared inside the machine room, and manually lowered the elevator a meter or so, upon which the door could be opened with a special key.

The spectators shamelessly thronged forward to see how bad the situation was in there, so that it took a while before the four victims, with much theatrical groaning, could be assisted out. As if they were mineworkers stuck deep under the ground for two weeks. Mrs. Duits looked as if she was about to faint again. Mr. Schoute pretended he had to shield his eyes against the brightness of the light. He meant it as a joke, only nobody got it. The whole thing took twenty minutes, but provided fodder for many hours of chin-wagging.

A pleasant side effect: it did distract us a bit from the Paris attacks.

Monday, November 16

At noon there was a minute of silence for the Paris attack victims.

Mrs. Bregman turned the Dutch flag into the French flag for the occasion by rotating it on to its side and adjusting the proportions with needle and thread. She tied the flag to the radiator and then hung it out the window, which means the window has to stay open a crack.

"It's a bit cold, but I felt I *had* to do something, even if it's just a gesture."

A lovely small gesture. Who knows? Millions of small gestures could, one day, add up together to overcome the power of bombs.

This morning I had to go to the hospital for a checkup for my arm. The doctor gazed at the cast and the X-rays.

"Looking quite good, Mr. . . . uh . . . Groen."

"Only 'quite'?"

"The fracture is healing nicely for someone your age, but I'm afraid there are signs of osteoporosis."

"Osteoporosis?"

"Indeed, osteoporosis, loss of bone."

He proposed having my bone density checked.

"You'll have to pop over to Groningen for it," he informed me, as if it was just around the corner.

"Pop over to Groningen . . . ?" I repeated.

"They specialize in osteoporosis there." He kept saying it faster—*ost-prosis*.

"Doctor, you want me to drag myself all the way to Groningen in order to confirm something we already know: that I have brittle bones. These bones are eighty-six years old, you understand."

"You do have quite a good chance of having osteoporosis."

"I suspect—it's just a guess—that after the doctor in Groningen finishes examining me, he'll tell me to take it easy and try not to break any more bones. As I'm sure you're about to recommend as well."

I was being very assertive, for me. But I was extremely indignant at the thought of such a waste of money and time. This wasn't even like a Band-Aid for a hemorrhage, it was like using a Band-Aid to stop Niagara Falls.

"You don't *have* to have the test," the doctor said stoically.

I have to come back on December 2, and if all goes well the cast can come off then.

As I left the examination room, the doctor said without a hint of irony, "Just be careful out there."

Tuesday, November 17

Perhaps Sister Morales was right after all; Mr. Van de Kerkhof, MPA, isn't letting the grass grow under his feet, in any case. Our new director has only been here a month, and already he's announced that in 2016 a small section of the home will have to close for "operational reasons." Not only that: he has announced he is investigating whether the kitchen could eventually be replaced by outside catering. I will ask him next time if he'd like to bet me €1,000 on the outcome of that investigation.

Kerkhof is making no secret of his intentions.

"Such drive that man has," said Leonie. "He's probably already got his sights on his next wrecking job." The mood at the hastily convoked Residents' Committee meeting was grim and determined. We are not going to be led to the slaughter like a bunch of meek, decrepit old sheep by Whippersnapper Kerkhof, MPA, who is much fonder of cleaning house (restructuring and layoffs) than of old people.

"He has thrown down the gauntlet," said Leonie, our own Joan of Arc. "He's going to have to pay dearly for our wrinkled hides."

We're trying to stay under the radar for the time being, but intend to contact the central Workplace Council and get in touch with a lawyer we know. We are going on the assumption that Kerkhof will underestimate us, and we plan to catch him unawares.

Wednesday, November 18

Leonie has contacted the secretary of the sectoral Workplace Council. That sounds important, but I'd never heard of it before. She made an appointment on December 9 for a consultation.

A mobility scooter was pulled over on the A12. The driver was drunk and had decided to switch from the bicycle path to the six-lane motorway to save time. The police told him, by way of a warning presumably, that although riding a mobility scooter does not require a driving license it can be confiscated if you break the rules. Excuse me?

So that you can then get back on your scooter without the driving license you didn't need in the first place?

Or do the police suppose that most mobility scooter drivers also regularly get behind the wheel of an actual automobile?

I did have to wonder, however, whether the scooter driver, even in his drunken state, hadn't felt a qualm or two as cars doing seventy-five miles per hour on the motorway came whizzing past his lurching little three-wheeler?

Saudi King Salman, our Islamic ally in the war against ISIS, is not a man who espouses simplicity. For his stay in Turkey for the G20 conference, he reserved 546 rooms at the Turkish Riviera's most luxurious hotel. Salman had his luggage sent ahead in sixteen trucks and he'd brought sixty-five armored Mercedes of his own, as well as hiring four hundred Turkish rental cars, since you never know. In his defense: it wasn't all just for the G20 conference. King Salman had also tacked on a little holiday.

An important topic at the G20 summit was the environment, carbon emissions in particular. I would be curious to know what the Saudi king had to say about that.

"Isn't this king also the one who orders old people to be flogged?" Graeme asked rhetorically.

Yes, the same. And he may also not be averse to ordering a stoning, as long as it's well deserved.

"Seeing him among all those gray-suited world leaders, you have to admit he's the only one wearing a lovely gold bedsheet," said Graeme, studying the group photo in the newspaper, "but I don't think that's enough to build a solid friendship on, really."

"Gaddafi was our 'friend' too for a while, or at least

he was a friend of France. They allowed him to pitch his gigantic tent in the heart of Paris whenever he took a break from torturing people back home in Libya," said Leonie.

Hey, that's supposed to be *my* hobbyhorse!

Thursday, November 19

I miss playing chess with Evert. It wasn't about winning, it was about the pleasure we took in each other's company, even if that sounds a bit naff. Sometimes, in order to make it a bit more difficult for myself, I'd sacrifice a rook "by accident."

Now I have been reduced to Rummikubing. Where I used to trundle off to Evert's sheltered flat at about 4 p.m., I now head over to Ria and Antoine's, Graeme's, or Edward's in the late afternoon. None of them play chess. Graeme does know how to play drafts, but not well enough to pull off a draw. I'm working my way through the Big Box of Games with Ria and Antoine: Snakes and Ladders, Risk, Yahtzee, and Rummikub. Once a week I challenge Edward to a game of backgammon. For pennies.

Geert doesn't like board games; Leonie will occasionally join Ria, Antoine, and me for a round.

Yes, it's a bit of a duffer's existence. Evert used to provide a bit of spice to the proceedings. I miss him, but I gave him my word that I wouldn't whine or fret.

"The point of living is the zest for life," I once read somewhere, but right now the zest is hard to find.

* * *

There seems to be a curious new vogue for terror-attack merchandise: the slogan *Pray for Paris* on baby bibs, dog jackets, golf balls, beer mugs, shower curtains, and who knows what else. All available less than a week after the attack.

The Residents' Committee has decided not to cancel bingo, to show that we are not going to let terror have the last word.

It was Mrs. Slothouwer who thought that all activities should be called off out of respect for the victims. The fact that she never participates in any of those same activities has nothing to do with it, according to her.

There are some residents who are genuinely terrified that the next target could well be an old people's home.

"We are so very vulnerable," sighed Mrs. Schaap. She would like to see a permanent sentry stationed at the front door. And at every door in the Netherlands, why not? Where those hundreds of thousands of guards were supposed to come from, she couldn't say.

Friday, November 20

There are so many books being published for or about the elderly that it's hard to keep up. It's a growth area, apparently. I myself have the following books lying on my dresser: *More Joy than Grayness*, *The Happy Granny*, *Cookbook for Seniors*, *The Hundred-Year-Old Man Who Climbed Out the Window and Disappeared* and two novels by Maarten't Hart and Adriaan van Dis, both about their aged mothers. All secondhand, passed on to me by Graeme, and not yet read. I don't really like to read about the elderly. The older I get, the more I find myself loathing old age and everything to do with it. I am rather enjoying the poetry collection titled *The Old Are the Happiest*; but it isn't really about old people. I recently spotted a poster in town that said OLD IS GREAT, but it turned out it had to do with cheese.

The last book I read: *CV* by Carel Helder. A splendid hodgepodge of a book, with nary an old person in it. And the thing I seem to be more and more partial to: short chapters. Reading, you see, is becoming a bit of a problem. I tend to nod off, even if it's a very good book. It isn't a matter of burnout; it's more like a breakdown of the faculties, I'm afraid.

Sister Morales has leaked another piece of news: the new director is shortly planning to have the porter replaced with cameras.

"I thought you should know," she said in a whisper, in her lovely Spanish accent. "I saw it in Mr. Kerkhof's office. I 'tidy up' in there," she added with a conspiratorial wink, glancing over her shoulder to make sure no one could see or hear us.

I'm rather of two minds about this informant, since I suspect she likes to tattle because she hates bosses. I shall give her the benefit of the doubt for now. There's no need to be more Papist than the Pope, after all, and last time her information did turn out to be true. I hinted that it might be better to have these things in black and white.

"Black and white?" Morales didn't understand.

"On paper, I mean."

Oh, that was no problem.

This corporate espionage does make me a bit jittery. Leonie was over the moon when I took her into my confidence. We decided not to involve the others for now.

"That way, when they're cross-examined, they won't spill the beans," Leonie said with a sneaky grin.

Saturday, November 21

I have made a list of things I will henceforth no longer allow myself to get annoyed at. It's going to be a matter of persistence, since these are things that have been irking me for many years. But I believe that at my age I should be able to rise above them.

In no particular order:

1. A cup handle too small for your finger.
2. Dogs with bandannas around their necks.
3. George Baker's laugh.
4. Teapots that leak when you pour.
5. "The Winner Takes It All" by ABBA.
6. Minuscule illegible lettering on packaging.
7. Packaging impossible to get open.
8. Nordic walking.
9. Tiny wastebaskets (e.g., in a train compartment).
10. People who boast that they're real people-persons.

There are many other irritants, of course, but these ten will do for now.

* * *

Since Evert's death I find myself drinking less. Every cloud has a silver lining. And the tidbits I'm served at Ria and Antoine's are also rather more refined than the hunks of liverwurst or cheese Evert used to serve with the brandy. Pieces so big that they required you to tear at them with your teeth.

I miss my uncouth friend terribly.

"Don't mind me, I just have to dredge the boogers out of my nose," he would say just as you were about to help yourself, and out would come a huge red handkerchief, into which he'd blow his nose with a great deal of noise.

"Bon appétit, Hendrik," he'd say when he was done.

Sunday, November 22

"A woman is like chewing gum," Mr. De Grave said to me under his breath. "After a while both lose their taste." He had looked around first to make sure his wife wasn't back from the bathroom yet. She won't leave him alone for a second. When she has to go to the toilet, she'd like nothing better than to have him wait outside the door, but that is taking it a bit too far, even for her rather docile spouse.

"She's always on my tail, not literally of course, but it's what she would really like, to be glued to my back." Mr. De Grave gives a martyred impression. I had nothing to offer him. I can hardly advise him to give her a little push when they're standing at the top of the stairs. He's a prisoner until one of them dies.

At that point Mrs. De Grave had returned to the recreation room. Her eyes darted about. When they landed on her husband, she made a beeline for him.

"Sorry, Mr. Groen, but we have to go upstairs. Come, Bert."

Bert nodded and shuffled after her, leaning on his cane. She is going to make his life hell until she draws her last breath. I doubt she knows that she is a very stale piece of chewing gum.

This afternoon I'm going out for a spin with Geert. It's the first time we'll need our gloves and winter coats. It was warm for November until just recently, but now the red-noses season is here.

Monday, November 23

The cold yesterday seemed to work on Geert's bladder a bit. Half an hour into our ride he suddenly had to pee urgently. We were in the heart of Het Twiske, the nature reserve on the edge of North Amsterdam. It does have some toilet facilities, so we drove in a hurry to the closest one, Geert wiggling from side to side on his motorized wheelchair. On reaching the little hut, Geert hobbled up the path as fast as his aged legs would allow. He yanked at the door, and began cursing and swearing: closed for autumn and winter. As if people won't need to relieve themselves over the next six months.

The need was so acute that Geert disappeared around the corner of the little building. At that moment the park ranger's car came driving up. It stopped next to me, and two gentlemen got out, dressed in forest ranger costumes.

"What's going on here?"

"Good afternoon, gentlemen. Nothing's going on. Just a rather pressing need to go," I said as nonchalantly as I could. One of them promptly went to have a look around the corner of the building. A few moments later Geert, fuming, came back into view, trying to straighten his clothes and to close his flies under his bulky winter coat. The park ranger followed close behind. He took out a little notepad.

"I am citing you for urinating in public."

"Public, public, I'm standing in a deserted park behind a lavatory that's locked!" Geert steamed.

That was clearly of no concern to the custodian. He seemed to be the kind of man who's very fond of the authority his uniform gives him. Luckily his colleague interceded.

"Leave it, Ard. It's fine."

Ard clearly thought the law should be upheld but reluctantly conceded to the other man, apparently his superior.

"Good afternoon, gentlemen."

"The same to you, gentlemen."

And they were gone. I thought it was funny. Geert did not.

"I got my shoes wet too, goddamn it."

"Buck up, Geert, at least we've had a bit of excitement."

Then he too had to chuckle.

Tuesday, November 24

The pork chop Cook served us yesterday had a small splinter of bone in it. It broke one of the last three molars I still possess. I carefully pried the piece of bone and half of a molar out of my mouth.

"What is that?" asked Ria.

"This is a piece of bone, and this is a piece of my molar," I said despondently.

The word went around: Mr. Groen just broke a tooth.

"You should sue the cook!" Mrs. Slothouwer said, seated at a table behind me.

The conversation turned to missing teeth.

"I can still remember what it felt like," said Ria, "when your milk tooth was just hanging on by a thread after you'd been working at it with your tongue for days. It hurt in a nice sort of way. You didn't dare give it that final pull."

Antoine disclosed that he'd once swallowed a tooth by accident.

"I've swallowed five front teeth and two molars," Mr. Dickhout bragged. He likes to turn everything into a competition.

"Anything you can do, I can do better, eh, Dickhout," said Geert.

"Yes, so what?"

"Once the tooth was out, the hole always seemed so huge when you felt it with your tongue," Ria said to bring the conversation back to a safer place. There were vehement nods of agreement.

Yes, yes, never a dull moment here.

* * *

The weather is most depressing: gray, wet, cold, and blustery. I nevertheless make myself go outside every day, either for a little stroll or for a ride. Whenever I find myself hesitating, I glance at a little yellow sticky neatly framed above the dresser. In an untidy scribble it says: "NO WHINING, GROEN, ACTION!!!!"

I found the note in a drawer last week. Once, when I'd canceled an appointment for reasons of constipation, Evert had posted it on my toilet seat. The greatest hazard for the old is laziness. It makes the body grind to a halt. And then you might as well forget about starting over. I rarely regret the things I reluctantly make myself do. Even after struggling against wind and rain, I can tell myself smugly when I get home: I'm glad I did it. That's crucial: reminding yourself beforehand how you'll feel about it afterward.

Wednesday, November 25

"We're a bit old-fashioned here, but that's allowed, since most of us are in our late eighties, and we're still rather fond of Zwarte Piet (Black Pete), even if some people now feel it's racist," Antoine said.

"Zwarte Piet is a smashing fellow. If I were black I'd be bursting with pride about him," Geert declared.

"Age discrimination is really a much more serious problem," Graeme suggested, "because I'd like to see a very young Sinterklaas for a change, accompanied by a couple of doddering, gray-haired Black Petes."

"But wouldn't Sinterklaas then have a black beard?" asked Ria.

"In which case he may have to get frisked before setting out on his ride across the rooftops," Graeme hypothesized.

"Well, with all those suspicious unclaimed packages, it's going to be a shambles anyway. The fear of bombs is taking on hysterical proportions. Soon all packages, whether or not they're gifts, will be outlawed."

This was at an Old But Not Dead Club meeting; the members putting their own unique stamp on society's conundrums. There was a great deal of laughter.

We had one serious item on the agenda: should we try to find a new member to replace Evert, and if so, who?

All agreed that we'd welcome some fresh blood, even if only to save our club from having to be disbanded someday for want of members. But we are going to take our time. At the next meeting, after Sinterklaas (St. Nicholas's Day), each member can propose someone new, but it's not compulsory. Then we'll try out the candidates for a few weeks without telling them they've been nominated, and then we'll put it to a vote. All rather involved, but that's on purpose, because it's a critical choice. Besides, it will keep us occupied. The older you are, the truer the adage that rest leads to rust.

I am thinking of proposing Mr. Okkie for membership.

We also drew lots for Sinterklaas presents. I have to buy a gift for Edward, accompanied, naturally, by a suitable piece of doggerel verse. Or, rather, three. Because this year's rules are: one gift of €10 maximum, and two joke-presents, together worth no more than €5. There's going to be a crush at the discount shop. Leonie is offering a prize for the silliest gift.

Thursday, November 26

Pharmaceutical giant Pfizer is buying out its competitor Allergan for $160 billion. Together they have a turnover of $60 billion dollars a year. The morning paper says so.

"I've got quite a few euros sitting in that lot," said Mrs. De Gans. Most of the residents swallow at least a few pills a day, but De Gans is truly a major consumer. When she comes down for morning coffee, she sets down on the table in front of her two pill dispensers holding the day's supply of medicines. She then proceeds to swallow a whole repast of pills in all colors of the rainbow.

"You must have a bookkeeper to keep track of all that," Ria said admiringly. Oh, no, Mrs. De Gans managed it all by herself.

Wednesday is her biggest day, when she has to swallow seventeen pills. I was sitting next to her as she counted them out.

Actually, the merger of the two pharmaceutical companies is mainly to cut their American tax bill by billions of dollars. Mrs. De Gans hopes that means her pills will cost less.

"Even though it's my insurance that pays for them," she added.

Our Turkish friend Mr. Okkie always has to answer for the actions of the land of his birth. This time the Turks shot down a Russian jet that may or may not have been flying in Turkish airspace.

"Your Erdogan's playing with fire. If Putin gets pissed off, there'll be hell to pay," Mr. Pot snapped at him. Okkie wasn't all that sure what paying hell had to do with it, but he felt he had to respond.

"He isn't *my* Erdogan. He's a bad and dangerous man. He had a palace built for him that has 1,150 rooms, not because he likes having people come and stay, but because he's a megalomaniac." This isn't exactly what Okkie said, since his Dutch isn't perfect, but the message was clear. He sounded calm, but if looks could kill, we'd have been rid of Pot for good.

Friday, November 27

During a brief power outage yesterday afternoon, five inmates suffered falls. The damage wasn't as bad as it might have been: just one fractured wrist and some bruises. When the lights went out many of the residents, instead of calmly staying where they were and waiting for whatever came next, promptly got up, crashing into things in the dark in search of candles they must have lying about in a drawer somewhere. And where had they left those matches? It was lucky they didn't find those, actually, since we'd likely have gone up in flames otherwise. Old people, you see, despite their supposed wisdom, placidity, and experience, tend to panic. Whereas in this case the solution was simple: to shuffle calmly to the door, visible in the dark thanks to the crack of light shining in underneath, and open it to let in the corridor's emergency lighting. In the end most people did open their doors, to ask anxiously what was going on. Nobody had a clue. Ten minutes later the lights came on again; everyone sighed with relief, and the casualties were seen to.

"My immediate thought was that it was a terrorist attack or something," Mrs. Quint told anyone who would listen.

"We have no means of escape, especially if the elevator doesn't work," Mr. Pot said, adding fuel to the fire. "Without an elevator, we're like rats caught in a trap."

Mrs. Quint did not appreciate being likened to a rat. Ria tried explaining that it was a simile, but I don't believe Quint had ever heard of that word.

"Don't you *ever* call me Milly," she said indignantly.

Later came management's official explanation: the cause of the outage was work being done in an electricity substation. A few residents had their dinner brought to their room just to be safe, because they were worried about taking the elevator.

Monday, November 30

I've had a couple of difficult days. Friday afternoon I ambled over to Evert's flat without thinking. I even knocked on his door before realizing that he was dead and buried. I stood there in front of his door and broke down, shuddering without tears. I informed the dining room I would not be down for dinner and went straight up to bed. It was 4 p.m. I must have fallen asleep, because I woke up at 10 p.m. all in a muddle. Then I tossed and turned until the early hours of the morning, when I dozed off again, and overslept. I woke up when Antoine came knocking at my door.

"We missed you at coffee, Henk, and I thought, I'll just go and check on him. You look awful, actually... What's the matter?"

I glanced in the mirror and saw a bedraggled old bloke with a two-day beard. Two skinny legs emerged from a pair of too-baggy, diaper-lined underpants. The shirt in which I'd lain in bed for twenty hours was, like my face, no longer completely unrumpled.

I told Antoine about my little breakdown. It felt good to get my sadness off my chest.

"It isn't unusual, I think, for a great loss to hit you only after some time has passed," said Antoine. "It has to find a spot."

Then he prepared some breakfast for me, and left me alone. Later in the afternoon Leonie stopped by.

"I just came to make sure you weren't thinking of doing anything funny," she said to explain her visit.

I promised not to do anything "funny."

It turns out that Evert meant more to me than I realized. He inadvertently helped me keep up my zest for and belief in life. From now on, whenever I'm down in the dumps, I'll have to make do with his framed yellow sticky, "NO WHINING, GROEN, ACTION!!!" I was glum the rest of the day, and then decided I'd had enough of all the self-pity.

Shower, shave, comb through hair, a spritz of cologne, clean shirt, dapper suit, bowtie, and polished shoes. My appearance downstairs at the Old But Not Dead table didn't set off a round of loud cheers, but close enough.

"At last! Our beloved Mr. Groen is back," said Leonie, beaming.

I believe I acknowledged my friends with a slight bow.

Tuesday, December 1

Just one more thing about our ally Saudi Arabia. Rumor has it that next Friday the Saudis are going to decapitate fifty-five opponents of the regime.

"I don't know if that's setting a very good example for ISIS," Graeme wondered out loud. "It's becoming a bit of a beheaders' society over there, if you ask me."

Mrs. Duits didn't remember which beheaders were our friends and which our enemies.

"You can always tell a terrorist by his beard," Mr. Pot explained. Someone remarked that most young men in the Netherlands have beards nowadays, because beards are in. Which makes it harder to spot the terrorist in our midst. Mrs. Duits suggested the problem could be solved by pressing all non-terrorists to shave their beards.

"Surely it isn't too much to ask, for the good cause? At least then you'll know that every bearded man is a terrorist."

In North Korea mustaches and beards are against the law, Edward informed us, but he had no idea if that had anything to do with terrorism.

And while we were at it, we proceeded to tackle the problem of climate change. We all agreed the climate isn't what it used to be. According to the latest predictions, a thirty-five-degree warming of the earth could make sea levels rise as much as two hundred feet, instead of the sixty-five or hundred feet originally forecast.

"Well, then we'll be needing extra high dikes," said Ria gloomily.

"As tall as a twenty-story building," Graeme calculated.

Antoine told us that once, years ago, he'd walked on the Oosterschelde dam. It had felt reassuringly sturdy. But a year later he'd seen the same dam from an airplane.

"Then it seemed a thin little pencil line against a formidable sea."

Wednesday, December 2

This afternoon the cast comes off. In the meantime I have become quite dexterous with my left hand. I can even pull on my socks one-handed, with the help of my sock-pulling gadget. You just shouldn't be in a hurry. I also mastered typing these entries at an acceptable pace, after several days of cursing, sighing, and practicing. I am very glad nevertheless that I'm being liberated this afternoon. It was growing itchier and more uncomfortably hot every day. Ria lent me a knitting needle that let me scratch myself carefully under the plaster.

The Old But Not Dead Sinterklaas party will be held at Ria and Antoine's, since their flat is the largest and they have the best food. I am struggling with writer's block: the poem for Edward just won't come. Seeing that his speech is virtually unintelligible, I am now considering writing a gibberish poem for him; nothing but meaningless sounds. Except for one real word at the end of every line. Finding rhymes shouldn't be too difficult. For example:

Bze monie da twila Edward
Hul marto zwervilba rill card

Maybe it's too lame, although I know Edward is fond of silly jokes. A major advantage of my poem is that for the first time in years Edward can read his St. Nick verse out loud, and after the initial perplexity, everyone else will be able to understand him.

I'll buy him a coloring book, which is very fashionable at the moment. It's meant to calm you down, although in Edward's case that may be dangerous. If he calms down even more than usual, he'll come to a complete standstill. They have a special coloring book for seniors, according to the brochure, not too childish, but not too complicated either. Just the thing for Edward.

Thursday, December 3

My arm feels so much better without the cast! My skin is even whiter and more wrinkled than before, but how nice it is to have the fresh air on it, and how delightful to scratch unencumbered! The doctor, the nurse, and the lady at the desk all cautioned me to be very careful.

"Good idea. I'll just give up kickboxing for a little while."

No, I did not actually say that.

I did my gift shopping at the discount shop.

1. For the windowsill: a plastic flower in a pot, which sways cheerfully (or irritatingly) from side to side all day long on solar energy.
2. An enormous yellow ducky for the bath, or for the shower.
3. Reading glasses festooned with little reading lights on either side.

All together, less than €8. I can't think how they can manufacture items for that little, even in poor countries. I have solemnly sworn to myself that I will not buy anything known to involve child labor, but you can never be sure. Where there's money to be made, honesty tends to fly out the window.

The coloring book for seniors has also arrived, so roll on, Sinterklaas.

Friday, December 4

When, last week, one of my three remaining molars broke in half, I decided not to do anything about it. The remaining half was far back, and visible only if I yawned without covering my mouth. And since I was strictly raised as a hand-over-the-mouth sort of man, there was no aesthetic reason to go to the dentist. And if there isn't a good reason for it, I don't go, because I've been terrified of the dentist for eighty years.

But now I've been having an annoying toothache for a few days, and after three strips of paracetamol, I fear there's no avoiding it. I made an appointment for Monday. That leaves three days for the toothache to go away of its own accord. In that case I'll cancel the appointment. If I could, I'd ask a dentist to put me under completely. But I don't have the nerve to ask, although apparently one could.

When I was headmaster, I used to dread the school dentist's yearly visit. Hearing the shrill, shrieking sound of the drill make its way from the staff room (which had been cleared for the dentist's use) into my classroom made me break into a sweat. The dental assistant would summon the children one by one. Some returned quickly, with a happy no-cavities smile. But most of the pupils had to submit to the horrifying drill. I felt each and every child's fear vicariously.

Saturday, December 5

I've been thinking more often of late about my time as a primary school headmaster. The memories tend to return on special days, at Sinterklaas, Christmas, or Easter. Pleasant nostalgia.

Before Sinterklaas especially, the whole school buzzed with excitement, the little ones because of their devout belief in Sint, the older kids because they were in on the big secret. I still remember that when I was young and my father told me Saint Nick did not exist, I was convinced that before long he'd summon me again, this time to reveal that God, too, was a total fabrication. But he never did. I had to discover for myself, years later, that opinions about God's existence are, to put it mildly, rather divided, and that the gods themselves don't always agree about it.

As headmaster, in any case, I did believe unconditionally in Sinterklaas, the great friend to children, year in, year out. He was the most important guest of the school year. My heart melted at every child who sang a song for him, did a handstand for him, or even just bashfully waved at him. In those days the fact that Piet was black, and that he thought two plus two equaled five, didn't bother anyone. On the contrary, it was the reason the little ones liked him so very much.

I am almost childishly eager for the Old But Not Dead Club's Sinterklaas party. I think there should be more celebrating, with more enthusiasm. We in the Netherlands, with the possible exception of the carnival in the South, are not ones for wild partying. We tend to think: just act normal, you're peculiar enough as it is.

The Sinterklaas festivities in the recreation lounge usually amount to a CD with Sinterklaas songs and a holiday gingerbread man (*taai-taai*, which means "tough-tough") instead of the usual biscuit with the coffee. And the gingerbread men are usually judged to be stale.

"My teeth can't deal with that," is what Mrs. Smit says of anything that's harder than vanilla pudding.

Sunday, December 6

Last night Sinterklaas and Zwarte Piet honored the Old But Not Dead Club with a visit in the flesh. For an instant I thought Evert had risen from the dead and come back to earth as the old saint. I wasn't that far off, since his son Jan looks very much like him and he was our Sint for the day. He had persuaded Grietje's grandson Stef to be mad enough to play Piet. I have to say this was one of the most unkempt Sints I have ever seen in my life, and the Piet accompanying him also made a rather bedraggled impression, but that did not detract from the surprise. Sint Jan and Piet Stef had dressed themselves at Edward's, who was in on the plot, and then paraded over to Ria and Antoine's flat, tossing ginger nuts at the odd resident as they went. We, unsuspecting, were just on our first glass of wine when there came a loud banging at the door. It was the good saint and his sidekick standing at the door with a big sack filled with presents.

After the unexpected guests were given something tasty to drink, the good bishop started the proceedings with a moving poem in which he thanked all those present for having provided Sinterklaas's dad with some magnificent final years. Sint himself was a bit overcome; a tear rolled into his beard. The people around him, too, had to swallow a tear or two. Piet Stef broke the tension by offering each in turn a large gaudy handkerchief. There was a little something in the sack for each Old But Not Dead member. I received a splendid *Atlas of Amsterdam*.

It was a memorable evening. Nice or silly gifts, funny poems, and five-star refreshments. The prize Leonie had put up for the most unusual present went to a balcony gnome with a casket of rum under its chin crafted by Geert.

I did, however, nearly break my arm again; when I got

home I tripped on my little rug in the bedroom and was sent sprawling. I landed on my bed, luckily. I can imagine the raised eyebrows in the plaster room at the hospital—

"That isn't alcohol I detect on your breath, is it, Mr. Groen?"

Monday, December 7

Just a bit over three weeks to go, and then that's it for this diary. The daily obligation has been a therapeutic exercise: I write, therefore I am. Gymnastics for the mind. For body and mind the same thing is true: *Use it or lose it.* Some professor wrote that once after a long study, but you could easily have worked it out for yourself.

In order to fill the looming emptiness and keep the mind in shape, I have set myself a new challenge: in January I am starting on a novel. The only idea I have so far is that it's about two elderly men. After all, old men are my specialty. They will inevitably resemble Evert and Hendrik somewhat. I'll probably name them Ahrend and Nico, after my two grandfathers. Unavoidable circumstances won't make things easy for Ahrend and Nico, but that only makes life more worth living.

It's growing on me.

Tuesday, December 8

My toothache kept getting worse, so yesterday I went to the dentist. My dentist isn't the type to calmly help you get over your fear of dentistry. He doesn't say much, but starts muttering rather worriedly to himself as soon as you open wide for him.

"Hmm, not a pretty picture. We'll just have to do something about that, won't we?" At least, that's what I understood. Picture the head looming over me rigged out like the riot police, for my dentist dons not only a surgical mask and gloves to peer into my mouth, but also a sort of splashguard over his eyes. As if he's got a dangerous terrorist sitting in his chair instead of a terrified old man. Next he stared at his computer screen for a while and then tried to talk me into a crown costing €1,100, not covered by my insurance. Couldn't he suggest a cheaper option? I asked anxiously.

"Well... I could pull the tooth out, of course, but that's rather an extreme solution."

I found €1,100 rather extreme as well, especially for a molar that was only biding its time back there anyway, so I asked him to go ahead and pull it immediately. I thought it was very brave of me, but alas, it wasn't possible. There was no room in his appointments schedule. I have to go back on Friday. Which gives me another two days of working myself into a panic. I bought some more paracetamol on the way home.

Tonight the club is having dinner out. I made a reservation in a Thai restaurant near here that's known to be good. I wasn't sure if we had already eaten Thai, but then decided that if I didn't remember, it wouldn't make any difference. At least not for me. I don't expect any great outcry from my fellow club members if it turns out that the kitchen of Thailand has already been explored.

Wednesday, December 9

It was delicious, I received plaudits for an excellent choice. The staff were very friendly too. The only thing was, it was a bit embarrassing—the sight of a waiter with very short legs wearing enormously baggy trousers sent us into fits of the giggles. God punished us immediately, for Ria was laughing so hard that she peed in her pants. She immediately confessed it, and then there was the whole business of having to find a pull-on diaper... Anyway, it took a while, and in the meantime the food grew cold. Fortunately it tasted fine, even cold.

We were also very pleased with the bill. We are and always will be Dutch men and women, even when the cost of the dinner was borne by the Old But Not Dead kitty, filled to bursting with the money Evert left us. We did not neglect to raise our glasses to him, naturally.

Yesterday afternoon a Residents' Committee delegation, consisting of Leonie, Graeme, and myself, had a "secret" meeting with the Workplace Council about the director's reorganization plans. At the last meeting Mrs. Lacroix had insisted she wanted to go with us, but Leonie had given her the wrong date.

"I didn't think her painting show needed to be discussed with the Workplace Council," she said drily.

In order to keep it quiet that our Committee is girding up for a fight, Leonie had arranged to meet the chairman and secretary of the Eldercare Sector Workplace Council at the ferry dock café.

We presented the management's plans to them, and

they said that at the very least our director was jumping the gun a bit. The secretary is going to seek legal advice to see whether instituting a partial closure without a go-ahead from the Eldercare Workplace Council is permitted. He thought not. If it does turn out to be against the law, we decided it would be wise to delay revealing what we know for as long as we can. Our tactic will be to make Director Kerkhof seriously underestimate us. If at our next meeting, less than two weeks from now, he brings us a more detailed closure plan, we'll act shocked, but fatalistic.

Just for fun, we also practiced saying, "Well, I suppose you know best," to see which of us was the most convincing.

Thursday, December 10

Mumba is dead. She didn't feel well and then she just keeled over and died. Her mother, Thong Tai, and sister, Yindee, were at her sickbed. Very moving. Mumba is, excuse me, *was*, a toddler elephant at Artis Zoo. We were all quiet for a moment at coffee.

Artis recently announced they will no longer give the animals names, to make it less personal. Isn't that kind of patronizing to the public? Had it already been so, we'd be saying, "Have you heard? Pachyderm 3 is dead."

I have to admit: it does make it feel less sad.

There is a new nature program on TV that's very popular now: *The Hunt*. It involves fatalities and a great deal of spilled blood, for the program is all about hunting. I am very fond of nature, but after watching one and a half episodes of *The Hunt*, I'm out. It's too grisly for me. My sympathies are always with the underdog: the little deer running for its life from a lion, the seal being pursued by the polar bear. When I see that seal dangling from the bear's mouth, I can't exactly rejoice for the bear. Note that the program is broadcast by the Evangelical Network. I don't think a bloodied Bambi fighting for its life enhances the honor and glory of the Lord particularly, but the evangelists seem to take a different view. The whole thing just strengthens my sense of disbelief when it comes to the creation: it's always eat or be eaten, death and decay. Who in his right mind would create such a world?

However, meandering on my mobility scooter through the Twiske nature reserve under a bright winter sun, as I did yesterday, I can't helping thinking to myself: you've done a fantastic job, Creator.

Friday, December 11

This morning I caught myself humming, unconsciously perhaps, a song from Bach:

Come sweet death, come blessed rest
Come lead me to peace
For I am weary of the world

After three bars I realized what the lyrics meant.

Don't you have anything more cheerful in your repertoire, Groen?

Saturday, December 12

Yesterday we had a club meeting to discuss the filling of Evert's spot. There are two candidates: Mr. Okkie and Mrs. Heineman. The latter is a newcomer who came to us from another care home that had to close. Apparently we do still occasionally let in new residents, on an emergency basis at least.

I am a fan of Mr. Okkie, but I have to say that Heineman would be an asset too. She wears an enormous pair of glasses, has huge breasts, and a healthy dose of self-mockery. She joked that her glasses are so large that she's signed them up for a maintenance plan from the window washer. And as far as her prominent bosom goes, she likes to warn, as Evert too used to say: "If equal in all other respects, ladies with big tits go first." But unlike Evert, she means it in the sense of being ceded priority when entering or exiting the elevators or the dining room.

We vote ten days from now. The chosen candidate will be invited to participate in the Old But Not Dead Christmas dinner on a probationary basis.

Statistically speaking, we members of the Old But Not Dead Club may count ourselves lucky, considering the fact that so far this year we have lost just one of our comrades, even if he was an exceptionally great club member. But aren't we all? Yes, we are!

The odds are that we'd have had two members leave us by now, or, in the worst-case scenario, three. Time works inexorably against us. As the years accumulate, the chance of meeting your maker rises exponentially. I would rather not dwell on it, but here I go anyway: In the not-so-distant future, every member of the original Old But Not Dead Club will be dead and gone. Not a happy thought.

I am feeling rather somber these days, no matter how hard I try not to. I have an appointment with the doctor next Monday. I'm going to ask him for some pills to cheer me up a bit, since just telling myself "no whining" doesn't seem to do much good anymore. Yesterday my friends expressed concern about my mood, even though I was doing my very best to be jaunty.

Sunday, December 13

"Christmas markets are very vulnerable to terrorist attacks," said Mr. Pot.

There is some trepidation about our day trip next Wednesday to the Aachen Christmas market. Mr. Pot has decided not to go because of the risk.

"Then you're doing exactly what the terrorists want," Graeme said.

"I don't care," Pot replied.

He wanted his money back, and so he sought me out, since I am the Residents' Committee Treasurer. I had to disappoint him.

"The rules are clear: once you've signed and paid, no refunds. Most of the expenses are already incurred, you see."

I saw the disappointment on his face slowly turn to pure rage.

"The registration fee can be refunded only in case of

death," Leonie added, "but of course I wouldn't want to put any ideas into your head."

"How do you mean?" asked Mr. Pot suspiciously.

"Joking," Leonie said, smiling.

Since he isn't getting his money back, he's going to have another think about whether or not to come along. On second thought, Germany did seem to be quite a safe country, actually.

I then casually reminded him of the evacuation of Germany's soccer stadium just recently.

"Yes, it was either a Code Orange or Code Red, I don't remember which," Graeme added. Which wasn't true, but anything's fair game to keep Pot off the bus.

I am not looking forward to this outing myself. Six hours in the coach for the sake of two hours of wandering about inhaling bratwurst grease. It's lucky that I love bratwurst. *Mit Sauerkraut*, please.

One lady asked the Committee to prohibit beer drinking. She had nothing against beer, mind, but was afraid that if people drank, a single rest stop on the journey home would not be sufficient and we might be late for dinner. Our response was that we don't believe in prohibition.

Monday, December 14

This morning I was supposed to have an appointment with the GP. He was out sick, I was told when I signed in at the desk, but his new colleague in the group practice could see me.

This was a young, not bad-looking woman. (I'm not sure, actually, when you should use "not bad-looking" and when you're supposed to say "good-looking." Is "good-looking" better than "not bad"?) I was already a bit nervous, and having to see an unfamiliar doctor didn't help. I needn't have worried. My own doctor tends to look pensive and worried, and specializes in awkward silences. I don't like awkward silences while I'm in the examination room. It makes me think the doctor is wondering how best to break the bad news to me.

This new doctor was a breath of fresh air. She greeted me brightly, with a twinkle in her eye.

"Hello, Mr. Groen, I am Doctor Steenbergen. How are you?"

I hesitated. Should I say "well" or "middling" or perhaps even "terrible"? Under normal circumstances you say "very well, thank you," even if you're feeling terrible, but in the case of a doctor that isn't very helpful, is it?

"If I were to express it as a number, I'd give it a five," I said after giving it some thought. "And you?"

"Um . . . eight and a half . . . no, just eight." And she went on, "Just a failing five? What can I do for you to make it a passing grade? What seems to be the trouble?"

I immediately felt at ease, and related in uncharacteristic detail all that's been weighing me down of late. She listened calmly, asking the occasional question.

Twenty minutes later I left her office with a prescription for citalopram. I hadn't even taken one pill yet, but already felt quite a bit jauntier.

The doctor had said, "Normally I'd first send you to

the psychiatric consultant, but in this case we'll just cut corners a bit. At your age we're not going to waste any time. I think your request is well justified."

I thanked her profusely. Her only condition was that I return in two weeks to report how I was doing.

I went straight to the pharmacy to pick up the antidepressant and took the first pill when I got home. According to the doctor they only start working after a week. "But," she added, "if you have enough faith in it, you'll feel some improvement in a day."

I started reading the insert, but the long list of possible side effects made me feel even more depressed, so I threw it away. I doubt the intention is to have the leaflet and the pills cancel each other out.

Tuesday, December 15

Yesterday Leonie and I met with Peter Johanson, a lawyer who's an old friend of Antoine's. Friendly bloke, early sixties, with a long career in social law.

"My heart is with the vulnerable and indigent," he explained with a big grin.

"You sound a bit like a missionary," said Leonie.

"More like a man with a mission. If I can throw a spanner into the bureaucratic works somewhere, or foil an arrogant trustee or two, I am a happy man."

It seems we've caught ourselves an old provocateur. I decided his motivation was more than sufficient to take our chances with him. Our lawyer further told us we were his first eldercare matter, and that he would be honored to thwart the closing of our care home, or at least to postpone it considerably.

We told him about Van de Kerkhof's plans. He asked a few incisive questions and then started nodding to himself.

"I can see possibilities. We're going to let that Kerkhof dig his own grave."

A noble ambition.

Johanson is to remain under the radar for the time being. He will, however, immediately begin studying the legal precedents and parent company's regulations. We'll let the Workplace Council deal with all official contacts with management and board. The Council has its own legal counsel.

Tomorrow we're off to Aachen with forty-seven other residents. I have a hip flask of brandy in my bag to help me get through any difficult moments. If, for instance, a singer or songstress manages to capture the driver's microphone.

I mustn't forget the earplugs.

Good news from Paris: the climate is saved. Just in the nick of time too, according to Mrs. Schansleh, because "Once you've whipped the egg, you can't unwhip it." The residents are happy for their children and grandchildren.

Thursday, December 17

It wasn't as bad as I'd expected. Upon boarding, the Old But Not Dead members quickly secured the last two rows for ourselves. It's an old law of nature that the seat you claim at the outset is yours for the remainder of the trip. At the front of the bus there was a scuffle for the first rows. Mr. Pot thought he had the right to claim a front seat, even though it was already taken, because that was where he'd sat the year before.

"That was last year, and this is a different coach," he was told.

Sulking, he had to make do with the fourth row. Pot had decided to come after all, in spite of his fear of a terrorist attack, because otherwise he'd have paid good money for nothing.

"So you'd rather get blown up, then?" Graeme asked in passing.

It was quite a trek: over a hundred and twenty miles there and a hundred and twenty miles back. But the group at the back of the bus was as elated as a class on a school outing, so the time flew by.

You have to love German Christmas markets. The beer tankards were gigantic and the sausages snapped nicely as you bit down on them. There was German Christmas music, played by a live brass band whose members all looked as if they were extremely partial to beer and sausages. The tuba player looked ready to explode at any minute, and a few of the horn players were clearly bound for a glutton's death.

There was also an abundance of Christmas rubbish for sale. I saw a sign meant for hesitant customers: GANZ NICHT TEUER (NOT AT ALL EXPENSIVE). Shopping fever and penny-pinching were engaged in a bitter struggle. First one would win out, then the other.

On the way home quite a lot of alcohol appeared to have been smuggled onto the bus and, with a cup of brandy, beer, or wine in hand, the miles flew by. The problem that had been feared did come to pass: we had to make an extra bathroom stop.

"I'm going to pee in my pants," Mrs. Hoensbroek yelled, "I can't keep it in any longer!"

"I have to go even more," Mr. Dickhout one-upped her.

The driver was forced to stop. A quick rest stop can take forty-five minutes, and so we arrived home late for dinner.

Cook refused to reheat the soup for us.

"I'm not going to be thrown off my schedule."

He still doesn't get it: he's wasting the goodwill he will shortly need when his job is on the line.

Friday, December 18

Sometimes it's almost as if the residents enjoy bragging about the ailments that come with age. Yesterday it was memory's turn.

"My memory has become a black hole; nothing escapes from it anymore," said Mrs. Van Diemen, when at teatime she wasn't able to get any of her table companions' names right. And the solution appeared to be retreating further and further out of reach: "I've already tried watching that memory training program on the telly twice, but I don't notice any difference," said Van Diemen with a sigh.

Mrs. Smit put in her two cents. She'd returned from the

shop downstairs empty-handed on two separate occasions this week.

"I couldn't remember what I was going to buy."

"I should think it was a pack of biscuits," I surmised.

"How did you know, Mr. Groen?" Smit asked, astonished.

I told her that I am sometimes clairvoyant. That provoked wide-eyed stares. To forestall being asked to read their fortunes, I quickly added that I was only joking. Smit could not accept it, after the miracle of the biscuits.

As a matter of fact, I too often find myself on my way somewhere without any notion of what I was going to do. When that happens I'll return to my starting point and have a good look around. Then I'll usually remember: "Ah yes, I was fetching the scissors to open that package."

Saturday, December 19

Yesterday was the great A Prize Every Time Christmas bingo tournament. Half an hour before the start, a great throng was already gathering at the overflowing prize table, as people tried to decide which prizes they would want to win. Even some residents who on normal days no longer leave their rooms had dragged themselves downstairs for the event, since you can't let an opportunity like this slip through your fingers. Four residents at a competing care home had even come to join in. That led to a bit of a brawl, since Mr. Pot insisted they be told to leave.

"Bingo is for our own residents only," Pot insisted loudly. A few supporters nodded in agreement.

"So you think we should close the borders?" asked Ria.

Yes, Pot confirmed wholeheartedly.

The Residents' Committee's decision, however, was that this bingo was open to the public, and everyone could stay.

"We'll accept a whole tsunami of aged strangers if we have to," Leonie clarified.

Some people decided to be clever and order five bingo cards, but you were only allowed to have one card in play. The Committee had not anticipated the consequences of the Prize Every Time concept. The first completed cards started coming in at a measured pace, but as the numbers continued to be called out, many more prize winners began surging forward, in waves of ten or fifteen at a time. The jury, consisting of Graeme, Ria, and myself, then had to draw lots to determine the order in which the contestants could choose their prizes. Some suspicious residents insisted that we check every single card. The cheaters were sent back to their seats. In short: there was a pandemonium of greedy residents, armed with rollators and canes. They were falling all over one another, desperately trying to get their hands on a Christmas candle, a garden gnome, or an almond-roll pastry. Once again it was clear that the veneer of civilization among the elderly is but paper thin. With all the squabbling over the prizes, the hour grew late. When we proposed canceling the second round in view of the time, there was a popular insurrection, wherefore we quickly withdrew the suggestion. Halfway through the second bingo round, Cook came stomping out of the kitchen, where the dinner was getting ruined.

"It can't possibly be more overcooked than usual," Mrs. Heineman ventured to remark. "Just put it in the blender for a lovely potato-cauliflower shake."

Cook almost blew his top, and as far as I'm concerned, Heineman should be offered a place in the Old But Not Dead Club.

Sunday, December 20

With all the terrible things happening in the world, there is fortunately also some good news, for Antoine was proud to report that United Airlines, the world's largest airline, will start serving genuine Oss stroopwafels on all its flights. The Dutch wafer—"heavenly caramel between two crisp waffles"—will be enjoyed high up in the sky by some 138 million international passengers a year. Antoine was beaming. He may be forgiven: he was born in Oss.

Graeme decided that the other major airlines had now lost their competitive edge for good, and suggested we all buy shares in the stroopwafel industry.

Jazz is a bit difficult for beginners, especially improvisational jazz. Yesterday afternoon the entire Old But Not Dead complement went to Bimhuis, Amsterdam's jazz heaven. It brought out every cliché under the sun.

"It *is* nice to watch," said Leonie.

"And rather clever too," Geert thought.

"But you can't exactly clap along," Ria remarked.

Edward thought he had seen the drummer before, at the special needs farm.

In short, Graeme, who had arranged the outing for us, wasn't having a very good day.

"I suppose this kind of jazz may be a bit hard to understand," he had to admit. We consoled him afterward in the café, and a few drinks later he was on top of his game again.

We spent the rest of the evening discussing the decision to send Christmas cards to our worst enemies: Mrs. Slothouwer, Mr. Pot, and Cook. To keep them on their toes.

Monday, December 21

I was born in an age that had neither TV nor cars. There was one person on our street who had a telephone. We were allowed to use his phone to ring the doctor if necessary. I never went on holiday, and no one I knew had ever been in an airplane.

Today, with the exception of one or two stubborn old coots in this home, there isn't anybody who doesn't have a TV, computer, or telephone. You can speak to anyone at any time and any place, and you can travel to the other side of the world in a single day.

My parents owned one Bible and one old encyclopedia. Today, thanks to the computer, every household has access to more information than the greatest library in the world.

People of my generation have seen so much "progress" that we can't keep up. Over the past ten or fifteen years, I have started slowly but inexorably to lose my grasp on the world. I now gaze at it with mild bemusement from a fitting distance.

The young people don't have much of a grasp on what's happening either, but they don't care. They think the world is just the way it is, and they barely notice that everything is constantly changing. I assume that in 2090 teenagers of today will look back on their lives with similar befuddlement.

That's about it from Hendrik the Philosopher.

"I'm reading here that there are all kinds of bugs mixed into our food. Mealworms, buffalo worms, morio larvae, crickets, and grasshoppers. Creatures I've never even heard of," Graeme said at morning tea.

"What kind of food are those creatures mixed into, then?" asked Mrs. Schaap worriedly.

Graeme looked it up in the article.

"They're in pasta, in chocolate, and in sandwich spread, for example."

Mrs. Schaap decided never to eat pasta or chocolates again. Sandwich spread wasn't something she ate anyway.

"I wouldn't be surprised if our cook put them in our Christmas dinner too," said Leonie, "and if they're free-range, that's entirely possible. Free-range maggots, for example."

The people sitting close to her shuddered, aghast.

"Don't worry, just kidding," she said. "And besides, I'm not having dinner here on Christmas Day."

Tuesday, December 22

The election of a new Old But Not Dead member was canceled at the last minute. Just before we were to vote, Ria and Antoine made a suggestion: considering that it is always possible that we'll lose another member, why not be proactive and take on both candidates at once, on a probationary basis?

"It may sound a bit crude, but the harsh reality is that it won't take years for another one of us to die, so we might as well spare ourselves the trouble of choosing between them by accepting both of these excellent candidates," Antoine said solemnly. The logistical problem of squeezing more than eight passengers into the van is to be solved on a case-by-case basis—unless we left the driver home. It's true that six of the members still possess a driving license, but not one of them would dare to ride in a van chauffeured by him or herself now.

We immediately informed Mr. Okkie and Mrs. Heineman of their selection. They were both extremely honored and accepted the offer. Mrs. Heineman's name is Lia. Now we have a Lia and a Ria. Which could lead to some mix-ups, but a good mix-up now and then can't do any harm. Mr. Okkie said it was okay with him if we just called him Okkie.

Yesterday's Residents' Committee meeting with Director Van de Kerkhof was uneventful. Kerkhof took great pains to be noncommittal on the subject of our home's future, and we took great pains to keep our powder dry for the great offensive that's yet to come.

The meeting was over in less than forty-five minutes. Kerkhof seemed to be satisfied, suspecting nothing. We'd like to keep it that way for a little while longer.

Wednesday, December 23

I was mortified. I had just paid for my eggs, Christmas chocs, and fresh parsley at the supermarket checkout, when a gentleman in uniform sporting a big "S" (for Security) pin posted himself officiously in front of my shopping cart. Could he just have a look in my cart? I probably blushed scarlet, and felt myself breaking into a sweat. Of course the gentleman could have a look. Triumphantly he pulled a tube of mayonnaise from beneath my plastic shopping bag and held it up.

"What have we here? Would you please come with me to the office?"

Pitying looks all around me.

I stammered, "Oh, I totally forgot, no, really. It must have slipped under my bag by accident. I'll go pay for it at once."

Would I come with him anyway, please, since it was too late to pay for it now? I tried to make it clear to the store detective that I'd never risk getting arrested for shoplifting a measly seventy-eight-cent tube of mayonnaise, but he was a man of principle, or perhaps he had a boss who forbade his staff to think for themselves. I was marched through a gauntlet of head-shaking customers, or so it felt to me, to a small office somewhere over to the side. There the assistant manager gave me a talking-to as if I were a toddler. I found myself in a humiliating, impotent position, forced to humbly nod yes and amen.

He ended his sermon with, "Normally we report every shoplifting incident, but just this once I won't call the police."

At that point I did manage to recover my dignity a bit, just in time, or I'd have felt like a terrible coward for the longest time.

"I seriously doubt the cops will come running for an old codger's accidental theft of something that's worth seventy-eight cents," I said, "but do by all means call the police, I implore you."

The manager was left nonplussed by this masterful turning of the tables, if I may say so myself. No, fine, I could go now.

"I should like to see you call the police anyway, just for the record."

"No, sir. Just go."

"Then I'll do it myself."

I was gently pushed out the door.

Couldn't I pay for the mayonnaise, at least? I could. I handed him €1 and said, "Keep the change."

At home I was able to relate what happened with my head held high. Geert fell out of his chair laughing. He's thinking of going back to the same market and shoplifting a tube of mayonnaise himself.

Thursday, December 24

Geert was assigned by Ria and Antoine to make a Dutch shrimp cocktail for the Christmas supper, and the recipe called for a pinch of paprika. Leonie, who was designated to be his assistant/supervisor, looked at the jar and did a quick calculation.

She cocked her head. "This jar is twenty-seven years past its date," she told him. Geert wasn't fazed. Yes, that could be right, he said, since that spice rack was a gift for his fortieth wedding anniversary, in 1988.

"No one will notice. It isn't a twenty-seven-year-old liver sausage."

"But the paprika is rock hard, you won't even get it out with a hammer and chisel. Isn't that a good reason to buy a fresh jar?"

Sulking, Geert went to the shops and returned with a big, brand-new spice rack, to show that it wasn't because he was a skinflint that he'd had some spices slightly past their expiry date.

"All my spices will now be good for many years past my own expiration date," he grunted.

Everyone is busy getting ready for the Christmas supper. Antoine is the head chef, Ria is the sommelier, and Leonie the general dogsbody. The preparation of a Christmas spread worthy of the Old But Not Dead demands some creativity now that we can no longer use the kitchen in Evert's sheltered accommodation flat. Where necessary, the home's rules concerning cooking in the rooms get stretched just a bit. With no serious consequences, so far at least. Would-be tattletales probably realize they're looking at serious trouble if they tell on us.

Someone posted a note on the board putting us on notice that there will be a fire drill on Christmas Day. The note soon disappeared and was replaced with an announcement by the management that it was a mistake, and that the fire alarm would not go off at Christmas. The cat, however, had been let out of the bag.

"But what if a fire should break out, what then...?"

Friday, December 25

Christmas is a backdrop against which a solitary pensioner heating up his microwave meal only stands out all the more poignantly. According to the Institute for Social Research, no less than 74.6 percent of all people over eighty-five lived alone in 2014, as compared to 65.8 percent in 2002. If you don't have children who like to have dear old Dad or Mum over for Christmas, you are better off here in the care home. Especially if you're in the Old But Not Dead Club.

As it happens, the latest happiness statistics from the same institute are quite positive. The average Dutchman gives his life a 7.8 "happiness quotient." Not bad. I am trending in that direction myself these days. The pills are doing their work.

It is notable that the average Dutchman thinks that he is doing well, but also thinks that the country itself is doing poorly. This paradox seems to be a typically Dutch phenomenon.

I completed most of my work for the club's Christmas dinner yesterday: with the help of my electric kettle I boiled nine eggs, peeled them, cut them in half, and spooned out the yolks. Ria and Antoine are well aware which tasks I can and cannot be entrusted with. In a little while they'll drop off their exquisite filling for my devilled eggs. I'll pipe it out in pretty rosettes using a pastry tube. I practiced yesterday with instant mashed potatoes, but you couldn't tell it was supposed to be roses. It looked more like a wildflower bouquet.

In a few hours I shall put on my best suit and the new shirt I bought; it has some glittery thread woven through it. A bit daring, but the saleslady thought I could carry it off. And who am I to contradict her?

Saturday, December 26

Inviting the probationary members to our Christmas supper was a great idea. Between the two of them they filled, both literally and figuratively, the empty space left by Evert. Except for the fact that he makes a great deal of noise when he eats, Okkie is definitely an asset. Leonie brought up his loud chewing with some tact:

"Sitting next to you at dinner means there's no need to put on any music, Okkie-boy."

Graeme asked if the sound effects were a cultural thing;

our friendly Turk replied that it's the Greek Orthodox, in fact, who are the noisiest masticators.

"See, now you've learned something about other cultures," he added.

Lia immediately felt at ease with us. She has a merry laugh, which made her ample bosom shake rather dangerously close to the soup.

"Not to worry, Hendrik, I know exactly how and where they're hanging," she said upon seeing my worried expression. Evert would have got on with her famously.

The food was outstanding, but perhaps we're growing a little blasé on that front. Okkie and Lia were in heaven, raving about the delicious dinner, whereas the rest of us took it almost for granted that our star chefs Ria and Antoine would wow us with the most delectable dishes. We wound up singing Christmas carols. Geert and Edward were barred from joining in, but Okkie had a surprisingly good voice, and Lia a lusty alto.

Sunday, December 27

It was the wrong way around, for me. I am the type who likes to save the best for last, and I'd have liked to see the order of our two Christmas dinners reversed. The feast with my friends on Christmas Day was just about perfect, and yesterday's dinner with the other residents was a bit of a let-down in comparison. Whereas, objectively speaking, it was quite adequate. Although one does have to like pork cutlets in a cream sauce, as I do, because that's been on the Boxing Day menu since the year one. Nicely pink inside, and for that reason invariably sent back to the kitchen by several of the diners.

"I don't like raw meat," said Mrs. De Grave, and she made her husband, sitting next to her like a dead little bird, send back his as well. They were sitting directly across from me.

"With his stomach, it's especially important for him not to eat raw meat," Mrs. De Grave explained, "because he'll catch salmonella before you know it."

When, fifteen minutes later, the cutlet came back cooked to extreme well-doneness, Mrs. De Grave complained that it was dry.

With table companions like these, it isn't easy to stay in a good mood. Luckily I was warmly squeezed in between Ria and Lia, two charming ladies who more than made up for the sour couple opposite. Not only did Lia impress me with her engaging, witty conversation, but she also managed to work down great quantities of food. She must have put away at least a pound of Brussels sprouts.

"The sprouts are scrumptious, Henk, give me another spoonful, will you?" She also finished our across-the-table-companions' tiramisus, because the De Graves were worried about the raw eggs.

After two days of Christmas, I am tired of all the eating, drinking, and sitting, and am therefore giving myself a day of abstinence. Which seems to be the fashionable thing to do these days. I'll go out for a couple of strolls, partake of nothing but bread and cheese, restrict my drinking to tea, and read a good book. I've posted a sign on my door: NO VISITORS PLEASE. My legacy from Evert.

Monday, December 28

When it comes to swallowing antidepressants, I am in the company of a million of my compatriots. I never realized there's so much depression in our country.

The pills work quite well in my case. Some weeks ago, whenever I found myself fretting about the insignificance of everything, I would get the blues. Nowadays, when I find myself contemplating how man is less than a grain of sand in the desert, it actually gives me comfort. The greatest human in the world is but a mote of dust in the universe. That applies even to Ronaldo, no matter how high he leaps when he scores. Ronaldo chalks up a goal, and the billions of stars in the sky just keep turning.

"None of it matters, so you might as well enjoy it, Hendrik," I tell myself, and the best thing is: I believe what I'm telling myself once again.

It's true that antidepressants can easily lead to addiction. Once you start taking them, it's hard to give them up. Fortunately the doctor and I agreed that at my age, addiction wasn't such a big problem.

"You'll just kick the habit in the coffin," Okkie postulated when I mentioned it to him.

Tuesday, December 29

"We live in a fireworks-free zone, but the young people refuse to comply."

"So where's the police?"

Someone had seen two officers hanging out at the

fritter stand at the shopping center, and had gone up to them.

"It's all very well standing here calmly having a fritter, meanwhile, just up the street, we're getting blown sky high by the firecrackers, rollator and all."

"You seem quite unscathed, for someone who was just blown up," the fritter vendor remarked. The cops had proceeded to drive past our building a couple of times and had told a few boys to move along.

Old people are by nature rather skittish, but it takes on epidemic proportions on the last days of the year. The fear of being startled guarantees that the slightest bang will make people jump. Most of the residents won't set foot outside between Christmas and New Year's as a result.

I am also rather timorous, but I won't allow myself to be deprived of my daily stroll or scooter ride by a few hooligans. Bring on the heart attack.

Wednesday, December 30

What will people be talking about in 2040 when they look back on the year 2015? The battle against global warming? ISIS terror attacks? The refugees? No, I think, actually, they'll be talking about the Old But Not Dead Club. Quite right too. A bright beacon in dark times. A turning point in the culture and the dawn of senior emancipation. In 2040 the world will have 10,000 Old But Not Dead clubs. The restaurants and museums won't know what to do with us. The travel industry for seniors will make billions. The most fabulous care homes will spring up everywhere to accommodate the tidal wave of ornery old people who don't want to live alone. Respect and deference for gray hair will prevail, as will Canta- and mobility-scooter congestion.

Statues of our gang will be erected in a park in North Amsterdam and draw thousands of elderly visitors every year.

"Look, the one there with the dog, that's Evert. And the ones with the pots and pans on their heads must be Ria and Antoine. There's Geert, Edward, and Graeme, such a good likeness!"

I am standing beside Evert, arm in arm with Eefje. We're beaming.

Thursday, December 31

I was in good spirits for most of 2015, until November, when I fell into a funk. Evert's death affected me greatly, and that made Eefje's loss come back and hit me hard again. I was dragging myself about with a droopy head and an exhausted body. That's when you need true friends to give you a good scolding.

"You're getting to be an old bore, you know that, Hendrik?" Antoine said.

And Leonie goaded me by taking aim at my weak spot—Evert: "Evert would have said he couldn't stand looking at such a sad sack. Either buck up, or fuck off, Hendrik," she said, honoring Evert's memory with her choice of words.

Their wise counsel helped me; that and the doctor's little pills.

I hit rock bottom, but I'm over it now. I am on my way back and enjoying life again with perhaps three-quarters gusto. My mood is a B average, and sometimes even a B+. Tonight, for example, New Year's Eve: Geert has secretly hung a string of firecrackers from Ria and Antoine's balcony, and the champagne is on ice. Graeme has made up a quiz. Okkie is going to teach us a Turkish dance. At midnight we'll hug one another awkwardly and a bit tipsily, but most affectionately.

A new year—how you get through it is up to you, Groen; life doesn't come with training wheels. Get this show on the road. And keep looking on the bright side.

About the Author

Hendrik Groen started his pseudonymous diary on the literary website of *Torpedo* magazine. He says about his first novel: "There's not one sentence that's a lie, but not every word is true." *The Secret Diary of Hendrik Groen* has been translated into over twenty-five languages.

Reading Group Guide

DISCUSSION QUESTIONS

1. Though it stands alone as its own story, *On the Bright Side* picks up the story and characters Groen first introduced us to in his breakout debut, *The Secret Diary of Hendrik Groen, Age 83 ¼*. If you read the first book, how did you feel the characters changed since you last saw them? What did this book teach you that the first did not?

2. At one point Hendrik says, "A research study has shown that eighty-year-olds are happier than they were aged forty. Forty is the low

point on the happiness scale." Do you think that eighty-year-olds are happier? Why might forty be the low point on the happiness scale? What would you consider to be the high point on your personal happiness scale?

3. Hendrik and members of the Old But Not Dead Club frequently have to contend with other people in the old-age care facility who prefer everything to stay the same, frozen in time. How do the Club members resist becoming complacent, and what do you think is the most effective method? What do you do to break out of your own routines?

4. Hendrik mentions how there is so much technological progress that the old folks can't keep up with it all, but at the same time there is still violence in the world just like there always has been. He wonders, "So, on balance, can one really call it progress?" Do you think that there is such a thing as genuine, objective progress? Why or why not? How would you define an ideal of progress in your own world?

5. The Old But Not Dead Club tries to shake things up by going on culinary adventures. If you were put in charge of their next outing, what restaurant would you choose and how do

you think the characters from the book would respond to it?

6. Hendrik writes, "Parallel worlds are everywhere, having hardly anything to do with one another. In our care home we find ourselves somewhere on the very outer edge of it all. Until we tumble off." What are some other parallel worlds? Can these worlds ever cross one another? Discuss, using examples from the book.

7. Some of the members of the Old But Not Dead Club deal with depression. How do the other club members support them? What are some of the techniques they use to pick each other up? Have you ever had to help someone through a tough time? If so, what did you do?

8. Hendrik oftentimes compares the elderly to young children. How are they similar? How are they different? What do you think this says about the process of growing older?

9. Frida stumps Hendrik when she asks what he most likes about himself, until he goes to Evert for help with the answers. What do you like or dislike most about yourself? What makes this a difficult question to answer? Do you think that

you are a more accurate judge of other people or of yourself? Do you see yourself the way others see you?

10. Hendrik and his friends oftentimes complain about their elderly care facility, but at the same time they remain aware of the downsides of independent living at their age. Discuss the benefits and drawbacks of living in an old-age care home. What do you think is the best option, and why?

11. Evert refuses chemotherapy and radiation treatment for his cancer. Were you surprised by his choice? Do you agree with his decision? Why or why not?

12. In the first diary entry Hendrik focuses on statistics about death. The last entry ends with him saying: "A new year—how you get through it is up to you, Groen; life doesn't come with training wheels. Get this show on the road. And keep looking on the bright side." Has Hendrik's mindset changed over the course of the book, and, if so, how? How does he perceive his future? Has this book changed your own thoughts regarding life and aging?

A CONVERSATION WITH THE AUTHOR ABOUT *THE SECRET DIARY OF HENDRIK GROEN*

Where did the idea for *The Secret Diary* come from? What was the hardest part of writing it? The easiest?

On the one hand you have the old people who are shuffling toward the inevitable end—sighing, complaining, and submissive. On the other hand you have senior citizens who manage to complete the last stage with dignity, good cheer, and contentment.

That mix of sadness, humor, strength, and weakness fascinates me, and that's what is at the heart of this book.

You write with tremendous tenderness about your characters, even as you highlight the comedy of their personality quirks and situations. Do you have favorite people or scenes? Why do you think the characters act the way they do?

I am polite and friendly myself, cautiously critical and moderately optimistic. A touch unhappy with myself, because I'd really prefer to be more like my friend Evert: stoic, blunt, and a rebel. Eefje, in her own charming way, possesses the same qualities. The thought of her sometimes makes my heart skip a beat. I am equally fond of the rest of the Old But Not Dead Club. They're not members of the Club for nothing. But I also have a soft spot, tempered with exasperation, for the cantankerous Bakker and the conniving Slothouwer sisters.

The book has become a huge worldwide bestseller. Is that connected to your decision to remain anonymous? What has surprised you the most about the book's reception, or its connection to its audiences?

I think the book's success has to do with two irrefutable realities: First, everyone hopes to have a healthy old age. And second, old age comes with ailments.

Everyone can relate. Even if you don't identify with it yourself, you'll recognize your father or mother, grandpa or grandma.

Hopefully, the fact that I prefer to not be in the spotlight has had only a very minor effect on my book's popularity.

What has moved me most is that many old people have been inspired by my book to not give up on life, but to mine even these last years for all they have to offer. Apparently a number of Old But Not Dead clubs have seen the light. Hendrik is proud as punch about that.

With warm regards,
HENDRIK GROEN